D1426759

# SAVING TIME

*By Jodi Taylor and available from Headline*

## TIME POLICE SERIES

DOING TIME      HARD TIME
SAVING TIME

## THE CHRONICLES OF ST MARY'S SERIES

JUST ONE DAMNED THING AFTER ANOTHER
A SYMPHONY OF ECHOES
A SECOND CHANCE
A TRAIL THROUGH TIME
NO TIME LIKE THE PAST
WHAT COULD POSSIBLY GO WRONG?
LIES, DAMNED LIES, AND HISTORY
AND THE REST IS HISTORY
AN ARGUMENTATION OF HISTORIANS
HOPE FOR THE BEST
PLAN FOR THE WORST
ANOTHER TIME, ANOTHER PLACE

## SHORT-STORY COLLECTIONS

THE LONG AND SHORT OF IT      LONG STORY SHORT

## THE CHRONICLES OF ST MARY'S DIGITAL SHORTS

WHEN A CHILD IS BORN
ROMAN HOLIDAY
CHRISTMAS PRESENT
SHIPS AND STINGS AND WEDDING RINGS
THE VERY FIRST DAMNED THING
THE GREAT ST MARY'S DAY OUT
MY NAME IS MARKHAM
A PERFECT STORM
CHRISTMAS PAST
BATTERSEA BARRICADES
THE STEAM-PUMP JUMP
AND NOW FOR SOMETHING COMPLETELY DIFFERENT
WHEN DID YOU LAST SEE YOUR FATHER?
WHY IS NOTHING EVER SIMPLE?
THE ORDEAL OF THE HAUNTED ROOM

## ELIZABETH CAGE NOVELS

WHITE SILENCE
DARK LIGHT
LONG SHADOWS

## FROGMORTON FARM SERIES

THE NOTHING GIRL      LITTLE DONKEY (digital short)
THE SOMETHING GIRL      JOY TO THE WORLD (digital short)

———————

A BACHELOR ESTABLISHMENT

# JODI TAYLOR

# SAVING TIME

HEADLINE

First published in Great Britain in 2021 by
HEADLINE PUBLISHING GROUP

1

Cataloguing in Publication Data is available from the British Library

Hardback ISBN 978 1 4722 7323 9
Trade paperback ISBN 978 1 4722 7324 6

Radiation Symbol © dkvektor/Shutterstock

Typeset in Times New Roman by CC Book Production

Printed and bound in Great Britain by Clays Ltd, Elcograf S.p.A.

Headline's policy is to use papers that are natural, renewable and recyclable
products and made from wood grown in well-managed forests and other
controlled sources. The logging and manufacturing processes are expected
to conform to the environmental regulations of the country of origin.

HEADLINE PUBLISHING GROUP
An Hachette UK Company
Carmelite House
50 Victoria Embankment
London EC4Y 0DZ

www.headline.co.uk
www.hachette.co.uk

# Roll Call

## TIME POLICE PERSONNEL

Commander Hay — Commander of the Time Police. Beset on all sides. Her face takes a bit of a bashing again.

Captain Farenden — Her adjutant. Tasked with looking on the bright side. No matter what the personal risk.

Major Ellis — Former leader of Team 236 and yet, somehow, unable to shake them off. Like head lice.

Major Callen — Second in charge of the Time Police. Head of the Hunter Division. The jury's still out on him.

Lt Chigozie
Lt Fanboten
Lt Dal — All nice, normal TP officers. Well,
Lt Grayling — normal, anyway. Well, officers, anyway.
Officer Curtis
Officer Rockmeyer

Senior Mech — Very sound on radhaz threat symbols. Which is just as well.

| | |
|---|---|
| The doctor | Amateur matchmaker and quite enjoying himself. Which makes a change. |
| Lt Filbert | Senior security officer. |
| Officer Varma | Member of security team. Brighter than most. |
| Officer North | New briefing officer. Her first briefing session is a sensation. Everyone is eagerly awaiting her second. |

## TEAM 171

**Looking to cause trouble.**

Lt Sawney

Officer Hooke

Officer Maru

Officer Scrape

## TEAM 235

| | |
|---|---|
| Lt Grint | About to embark on the petal-strewn path of romance. This should be interesting. |

Officer Hansen

Officer Kohl (Socko)

Officer Rossi

# TEAM 236 – TEAM WEIRD

**Things are not getting any better.**

Officer Farrell

Officer Lockland

Officer Parrish

Various other officers    Not assigned speaking roles and too numerous to mention, but always rumbling away in the background.

# ST MARY'S PERSONNEL

**The temporal equivalent of Mad Aunty Edna who has to be invited to family occasions because she'll come anyway and is always discovered in the bar singing and showing her knickers for a Guinness**

| | |
|---|---|
| Dr Maxwell | Matthew's mum. |
| Chief Technical Officer Farrell | Matthew's dad. |
| Mikey | Matthew's special girl. |
| Adrian | Matthew's special girl's brother. |
| Dr Bairstow | Director of St Mary's. No relation to Matthew. |
| Mr Evans | One of Matthew's many uncles. |

| | |
|---|---|
| Miss Lingoss | One of Matthew's many aunts. |
| Professor Rapson | Matthew's special girl's supervisor. |
| Mr Swanson | Another of Matthew's uncles. In charge of the Poison Cabinet. Short-sighted. All right – practically blind but no serious incidents so far. |

# Prologue

**Voice communication from Commander Hay, officer commanding Time Police HQ, to Captain Farenden**

**Time:** 0908 UTC
**Date:** REDACTED

*Charlie, what the bloody hell's going on with Team 236? Are they in or out? Are their Form D12s completed yet? How can one small team make such a business of deciding which department to grace with their presence? Put a rocket up someone's backside and get it sorted.*

**Electronic communication from Captain Farenden to Major Ellis, officer i/c Team 236**

**Time:** 0915 UTC
**Date:** REDACTED

*Matthew, has your bunch of shambling misfits completed their training yet? Any idea which unfortunate department(s) will be bearing the brunt of them in future?*

1

**Voice communication to all members of Team 236 from Major Ellis**

**Time:** 0916 UTC
**Date: REDACTED**

*Have you lot sorted yourselves out yet? You qualify in a week's time. Department heads want to know which, if any of you, they can expect to welcome. As does Commander Hay. As do I. Get on it. Now.*

**Voice communication from Major Ellis to Captain Farenden**

**Time:** 1421 UTC
**Date: REDACTED**

*My compliments to Commander Hay. Team 236 are still considering their options.*

**Voice communication from Commander Hay to Captain Farenden across her desk**

**Time:** 1422 UTC
**Date: REDACTED**

*Options? What do they mean, options? My compliments to Major Ellis and tell him to tell his team they're in the Time Police now. Not some fire-trucking holiday camp.*

**Electronic communication from Captain Farenden to Major Ellis**

**Time:** 1423 UTC
**Date: REDACTED**

*For God's sake, Matthew – get your team sorted out. She's reaching for her paper knife again.*


**Electronic communication from Major Ellis to Captain Farenden**

**Time:** 1427 UTC
**Date: REDACTED**

*Just hide the bloody thing, Charlie, and we'll all be fine.*


**Voice communication from Captain Farenden to Major Ellis**

**Time:** 1428 UTC
**Date: REDACTED**

*Get your team's Form D12s on my desk by Friday or I swear I will go off sick and leave you to handle this by yourself.*


**Electronic communication from Major Ellis to Captain Farenden**

**Time:** 1428 UTC
**Date: REDACTED**

*Being shot has not improved your temper much, has it?*

**Electronic communication from Captain Farenden to Major Ellis**

**Time:** 1428 UTC

**Date: REDACTED**

*Shooting your fire-trucking team would go a long way towards improving everyone's temper. Never have I more longed for the good old days when Parrish, Lockland and Farrell would certainly have been blasted into fiery oblivion by the first real Time Police officer whose path they crossed.*


**Electronic communication from Captain Farenden to Major Ellis**

**Time:** 1627 UTC

**Date: REDACTED**

*I haven't heard from you. Did you get my message?*


**Electronic communication from Major Ellis to Captain Farenden**

**Time:** 1628 UTC

**Date: REDACTED**

*Yes. Did you get my hurt silence?*

**Voice communication from Commander Hay to Captain Farenden conveyed through her office intercom**

**Time:** 1650 UTC
**Date: REDACTED**
*What the fire truck is happening with those idiots in 236, Charlie? Give them one week and then shoot the lot of them and we'll start again.*


**Electronic communication from Captain Farenden to Major Ellis**

**Time:** 1650 UTC
**Date: REDACTED**
*Matthew – be warned. She's warming up the firing squad.*


**Electronic communication from Major Ellis to Commander Hay**

**Time:** 1651 UTC
**Date: REDACTED**
**Subject: Team 236 – Trainees Farrell, Lockland and Parrish**
*Ma'am,*

*I have the honour to inform you Team 236 have officially completed their training period and, with effect from next week, will be available for assignment as fully qualified Time Police officers.*

*Form D12s have yet to materialise but are, I am convinced, imminent.*

**Electronic communication from Commander Hay to Major Ellis**

**Time:** 1652 UTC
**Date: REDACTED**

*Don't give me that crap. Find out what they're doing and advise soonest. Don't make me come down there, Major.*


**Automatic Reply from the desk of Major Ellis**

**Time:** 1652 UTC
**Date: REDACTED**

*Major Ellis is not currently available. For urgent matters, contact Captain Farenden, who is providing cover until his return.*

Commander Hay settled herself at her desk, opened up her scratchpad, picked up her coffee and gazed expectantly at her adjutant.

'You're wearing your bad news face, Charlie.'

'A whole shedload for you this morning, ma'am.'

'Oh – you're going to come straight out with it, are you? Normally there's a bit of banter and obfuscation as you slip me the details of our latest debacle and hope I won't notice.'

'Not today, ma'am. I'm not even going to try.'

She sighed. 'Go on, then. Let's have it all over with at once. Rip the plaster off, Charlie, but don't blame me if I scream.'

He sighed. 'Well, in no particular order: Imogen Farnborough's appeal has failed. The date of her execution is yet to be determined, but certainly within the next twenty-eight days.'

'Well, that's no surprise, is it? She was lucky to escape the consequences of her first offence – there was no chance of escaping her second.' She thought for a moment. 'Make a note to ask Ellis to keep an eye on Parrish, will you? He and Farnborough used to know each other well – I'm not sure how he will react.'

'She tried to have him killed, ma'am.'

7

'Very true, but given their former relationship and the possible involvement of his father at Site X, I still think his reactions should be closely monitored. What about our other prisoner – the ghastly Mr Geoffrey?'

'The oil-slick Geoffrey sang like the proverbial cassowary, ma'am. Unfortunately for him, he didn't know as much as he thought he did, and a lot of his supposedly valuable intel turned out to be . . . shall we say, considerably enhanced, and didn't really tell us any more than we knew already. Yes, we picked up a lot of their lower- and mid-level people, but those at the very top appear to have slipped through our net. Geoffrey was promised his death sentence would be commuted, however, so it'll be life for him. I don't suppose it matters because he's not the type to thrive in our prison system. I believe bets are being laid on how long he'll last. A projected lifespan of about six months appears to be the most optimistic estimate.'

'Put me down for seven weeks and two days, Charlie. What's next on your list?'

'The word on the street is that Farnborough's mother, the Right Honourable Patricia, will resign from the government any day now.'

Commander Hay sighed. 'Damn. Go on.'

'Site X is being dismantled. The components manufactured by Parrish Industries are generic and not, according to Parrish Industries' legal eagles, manufactured for a specific client or purpose. Their legal department wishes to point out that Parrish Industries abhors the use to which their product has been put, but they take no responsibility for said use once their product has left the factory. They regret they are unable to assist further with our enquiries.'

She sighed. 'And the worst news?'

Captain Farenden stared out of the window. The air lanes were thick with rush-hour traffic. The Belfast shuttle chugged past on its way to Croydon. He was conscious of a wish that he was on it.

Taking a deep breath, he said, 'Eric Portman, Farnborough's boyfriend – the one who got her into all this – got off. We didn't have enough to hold him. Forty-five people are willing to swear he was with them at the times in question. Including two MPs. Not that their word counts for much. The official explanation is that an imposter has been taking the Portman name in vain.'

Commander Hay's face in no way registered her intense frustration at this news, but to be fair, her face rarely registered any expression at all. In her youth, during a particularly bloody chapter of the Time Wars, there had been an accident. The door had blown off her pod in mid-jump. The results had not been pretty. Lt Marietta Hay had been the only survivor, and when they'd eventually managed to get her out, half of her face was considerably older than the other half. It had been some time before she had been able to accept her survival for the miracle she was continually being told it was.

Taking a deep breath, she said, 'Are Portman's lawyers actually suggesting Imogen Farnborough didn't know who she was dating? They went out for three months, for heaven's sake.'

'His team did an excellent job of discrediting her evidence. They argued that her obvious mental instability rendered it unreliable and referred to the fact that, at her trial, even her own defence team had tried to claim she wasn't fit to plead. That defence failed, as we know, but it did allow the Portmans' legal team to highlight her unreliability and throw massive doubt

9

on her statement. They followed that up with lots of outraged innocence from the Portman family themselves, who made a few minor endowments to worthy causes to show the world what nice people they are, together with a couple of massive donations to those who matter, and that was the end of it. I suspect he's celebrating in a bar at this very moment.'

'Damn and blast, Charlie.'

'Indeed, ma'am.'

Hay pushed her chair back and began to pace. 'We had them. We had their people, their pods, we had Shoreditch, we had Site X, we had what they were doing to those poor sods in the Stone Age. And still the top dogs got away from us. I'd happily return Imogen Farnborough to the wild if we could have got just one of them.'

'Well, looking on the bright side, ma'am, which as your adjutant I am required to do no matter what the personal risk, we have dismantled Site X. No more experimentation on Neanders. Big Pharma has retired back to its lair, muttering. A large and sophisticated Temporal Tourism operation has been shut down before it did any real harm. Fifty-six arrests and five pods impounded. And, with luck, Eric Portman looking over his shoulder every moment of every day for the rest of his life.'

'We lost Nuñez and Klein. We nearly lost Lockland and Parrish, as well. Parrish lost two fingers.'

'Well, as to that, ma'am, yes – Nuñez and Klein were unfortunate but they were buried with full honours, if that makes a difference. And their sacrifice ultimately led us to Site X. Lockland and Parrish survived their ordeal in the snow. Yes, Parrish lost two fingers to frostbite but he now struts the corridors with

10

a dramatic black glove on his left hand, threatening to hire a redhead to cut up his meat for him.'

She blinked. 'Why a redhead?'

'Apparently he already has a blonde and a brunette and requires a redhead to complete the set.'

She sat back down again. 'How is he even still alive?'

'I don't believe losing a few fingers is generally fatal, ma'am.'

'It wasn't his missing fingers I was referring to.'

'Oh. Well, much as it pains me to admit ignorance in the face of my commanding officer, I don't know. I suspect if I tried even half the things he seems to get away with, I'd be floating face down in the Thames by now while the entire female population of London lined the banks and cheered. He just . . . gets away with it, ma'am.'

Hay sighed again.

Captain Farenden tapped his scratchpad. 'Major Callen has requested a slot for his monthly meeting, ma'am.' He waited.

'I want you present, Charlie. Nothing formal. Just tuck yourself away in a corner and take notes. In fact, I don't ever want to find myself alone with him, however briefly. Make sure you're always there.'

'Yes, ma'am.'

He waited but nothing more was forthcoming. 'Moving on, ma'am, I do have one final piece of news you may or may not regard as good.'

'Go on, Charlie, hit me with it.'

'It's taken a while, ma'am. About two months longer than . . .' He stopped, apparently groping for a word.

'Than what?'

'I'm struggling to construct a sentence that doesn't contain the word "normal", ma'am. Ah, I have it. It's only taken about two months longer than more conventional teams, ma'am, but, believe it or not – Team Two-Three-Six graduate tomorrow.'

'Only two months longer? From where I'm sitting it's seemed endless.'

'A fact I hope you won't mention at their formal swearing-in tomorrow afternoon, ma'am.'

'No. Wheel them up here. They can retake the oath. I'll hand them their flashes and give them my famous *Welcome to the Time Police* speech. You hand them details of their Death in Service benefits and we both wish them good luck for the future.'

'And following that, ma'am, I suppose we step back and let them get on with it.'

'Well, there's the mandatory one month's hands-off supervision – I expect Ellis and North will split that between them – and then off they go. Out into the wild blue yonder.'

Farenden grinned. 'It's going to be interesting to watch their progress, ma'am. On a slightly related matter, Officer North has requested an appointment this morning.'

She sighed. 'After what Lt Grint and his team did to her . . .'

'Indeed, ma'am, but you will remember the expected fallout over that unfortunate incident failed to materialise.'

'I believe that has been mainly due to the mature attitude adopted by North herself. There was a great deal of support for her at the time and at one point I feared we'd be blocking the walls with our Time Police dead. That there weren't more casualties was entirely due to her intelligent handling of the situation.'

'Yes, she would have had a spectacular career with us.'

'She still can – if we can persuade her to stay.'

'I've pencilled her in for 1100 hours.'

'Was she clutching her resignation?'

'Not that I was aware, ma'am, but she made the appointment via her com link so it was difficult for me to tell.'

'I'm not going to let her go, Charlie, even if I have to nail her to a desk.'

'An innovative solution to our staffing difficulties, ma'am, and, simultaneously, a warning to the rest of us.'

Hay's hand drifted towards her paper knife.

'I'm so sorry, ma'am – did I say warning? Obviously, I meant inspiration.'

Hay's hand drifted away from her paper knife. 'I thought you did.'

An hour later, Captain Farenden ushered Officer North into Commander Hay's office. The commander, who had spent much of the intervening time marshalling her arguments against Officer North leaving the Time Police, was cheered to see her carrying a file under one arm.

'Good morning, Officer North.'

'Good morning, ma'am. Thank you for seeing me.'

'I believe you had something to discuss.'

'Ma'am, arising out of the unfortunate incident at Versailles when, perhaps, some officers paid less attention to the briefing than they could have done, I've put together a recommendation that all teams be provided with historical context before they embark on a jump. It shouldn't be over-detailed – we're not St Mary's – but it would give a background and perspective for each individual mission that may prevent similar incidents occurring in future.'

She passed over the folder and sat staring out of the window as the commander read it through.

'And this would be provided by you?'

'My opinion is that I would be the best person for the job. I have the background knowledge.'

'You think they would listen to you?'

'Yes. I believe I have hit on an innovative way of gaining and retaining their attention, ma'am. And I do think the more perceptive among them will recognise the value of attending.'

'And the less perceptive?'

'May not be around long enough to regret not listening to the historical background and perspective that might have saved their lives. A striking example of Darwinism in action. However, I hope to make clear the wisdom of attending briefings which have been tailored to their team's individual requirements.'

'What will you do if no one attends?'

'Without actually saying so, ma'am, I shall endeavour to give the impression that anyone failing to take advantage of this useful and possibly life-saving opportunity has slightly fewer brain cells than testicles.'

The words 'Lt Grint' were not spoken.

'So, it is only male officers from whom you expect to encounter difficulties?'

'Frankly, ma'am, yes, but the insult works even better for our few female officers.'

'Is your continuing presence in the Time Police contingent upon my consent and approval?'

14

North hesitated. 'I don't want to leave the Time Police, but now that I'm no longer a Hunter, I have to find another role for myself. I have discussed this with Major Ellis who was very encouraging.'

If Commander Hay considered Major Ellis had his own reasons for North-related encouragement and none of them had anything to do with providing historical perspectives, she did not say so.

'In addition, ma'am, Team Two-Three-Six will soon be qualified . . .' She tailed away.

'I am always very reluctant to lose a good officer.' Commander Hay closed the file. 'Shall we say a trial period of three months? I'll leave it up to you to decide the depth and detail of your briefings and the form they will take. This will be your project, Officer North. At the end of three months, I will be requesting evaluation reports from my senior officers as to the success of your initiative. And from you too.'

North nodded. 'Yes, ma'am.'

'In theory, I think this might work very well. You are aware your former boss – Dr Maxwell – once provided something very similar during her mercifully short secondment here.'

'I am aware, ma'am, and I believe they were quite successful.'

'Well, no one died, which is always my criteria for a successful initiative. Keep me informed, Officer North, and good luck.'

'Thank you, ma'am.'

At that precise moment, Team 236 were assembled in Luke's room, peering at the Graduation Countdown Calendar pinned to the back of his door.

'Ta-dah!' cried Luke, crossing through the last day with a flourish.

'Ta-dah!' cried Jane and Matthew, dutifully watching him cross through the last day with a flourish.

'That's it, people. We've done it. Who'd have thought? A quick handshake with Commander Hay and then Jane sews on our flashes because she's the only girl on the team, and away we go.'

'Happy to,' said Jane, 'and I know exactly to which appendage I shall be attaching them.'

'The flashes are woven on,' said Matthew, in a placatory tone. 'They'll just give us new kit.'

'So, what does Hay give us tomorrow?'

'Sympathy regarding our life choices, presumably,' said Luke, gloomily.

'Ceremonial flashes to signify our new status,' said Matthew.

Jane sighed. 'Shame. I was looking forward to wielding a bodkin.'

Luke shook his head. 'Jane, I have to say, being in the Time Police has certainly brought out the worst in you. You used to be such a sweet little thing. How you've changed.'

'I have,' said Jane complacently. 'You, on the other hand, are as big an arsehole as you've always been.'

Matthew nodded his agreement.

The three of them grinned at each other. Yes, all right, they'd taken the long way round – and some of it had been a little dodgy – but now, here they were, fully qualified Time Police officers. Almost.

'We can bear arms,' said Luke. 'I can't wait.'

'Weapons training first,' said Matthew.

'What – point and press?' said Luke scornfully. 'It's not rocket science. Otherwise, half the people here couldn't do it.'

'Blasters are a little more wayward than you might think,' said Matthew, the only member of the team to have fired one so far. Yes, he'd successfully played his part in fighting off the enemy when TPHQ had come under attack, but there was an ex-flowering tree at the front of the building that would never be the same again. Or its decorative planter. Matthew and his blaster had truly embraced the *scorched earth* policy.

Back out in the corridor they were joined by their former fellow trainees – Team 235.

'All right, mate?' said Kohl, who was known, for reasons that were never disclosed, as Socko.

'Yeah,' said Luke in surprise. 'Why do you ask?'

Socko shuffled. 'Well . . . you know.'

'Ah, got it. You're just being nice to me because of my fingers.'

'Well, of course we are,' said Hansen. 'No one here can stand

17

you, but we feel sorry for you so we're making the effort. The least you can do is reciprocate.'

'Sorry,' said Luke. 'I hadn't realised. Can we organise some sort of hand signal so I know when you're trying to be nice? Otherwise, I'm afraid the world is none the wiser.'

Socko grinned. 'How about we thump you half a dozen times? Would that be enough for you to get the message?'

'Not you, Jane,' said Rossi, hastily. 'We've all seen the legendary Lockland knee in action.' He indicated Matthew and Luke. 'Just these two.'

There was some good-natured shoving. Jane glowed. This was what it was like to be accepted. She was one of them. She could hold her own. She was a Time Police officer. Now all she had to do was make sure she was a good one.

Rossi was talking about the graduation ceremony.

'It's not huge – not like when you smart arses got your medals for bringing down Site X. Just Hay shaking you by the hand, congratulating you on having lived this long, conspicuously not promising you'll still be alive this time next week and handing you your flashes. Have you been allocated your office yet?'

'Same corridor as you but further down,' said Jane.

'Can you see the river?'

Luke nodded. 'We can. If Jane stands on my shoulders and leans eighty-five degrees to the left, then yes, our new office has a fine view of the river.'

Team 236 did indeed have a tiny space to call their own. As Luke said, all right, it wasn't huge, but as long as none of them put on any weight they'd be fine. And it was their very own. Somewhere in which to work, write their reports, take a snooze after lunch and so forth.

And, as qualified officers, they could bear arms. Their first training session was booked for the day after graduation. They would start with the small blasters and then work up to the larger ones. Luke could hardly wait, although Jane couldn't see herself getting much past the little ones. The ones that would happily nestle on her rip-grip patches. Eventually, if they wished – and it was apparent that Luke did – they could graduate to everything up to and including the building-smashers.

There would also be a small pay rise. As Luke said – nothing but good times ahead.

They split up at the end of the corridor. Team 235 went to find their team leader, Lt Grint; Matthew disappeared in the direction of the Time Map and Luke and Jane went to inspect the damaged front of the building, still under repair from the recent attack.

They stood for some time, looking at the craters, the shattered gardens, and the boarded-up windows, and then went down to watch the river flow past.

'You're very quiet, Jane. What are you thinking about?'

'Well, actually – and don't read anything into this – I was thinking how much I enjoyed living further downriver. You know – when we were in your apartment. I think I could get used to being rich.'

'That's a shame. You're not ever likely to be rich in the Time Police.'

'No.' She hesitated a moment and then said, 'Luke – when you wrote out your report – did you mention Parrish Industries at all?'

'I did. How could I not? The Parrish Industries logo was

there in plain sight.' He paused. 'I'm going to go and talk to my father about it. See what he has to say.'

She nodded. 'All right. Can I play devil's advocate here?'

'Why would you need to?'

'Well, I think you need to decide whether you're going as a Time Police officer or Raymond Parrish's son.'

'Obviously I'm both.'

'I'm not sure you can be. Which is the most important to you?'

Luke stared out across the river. The cold wind rippled the water and made him shiver. At least, he assumed it was the cold wind. 'I don't know.'

'Have you thought that by going to see him you could be making things worse?'

'He knows all about our investigation into Site X. He probably knows more than I do, and I was actually there.'

'Then why go to see him?'

'I want to hear his explanation.'

'But we've heard it. Parrish Industries manufactures generic components. They're not responsible for the use to which those components are put.'

'Not good enough, Jane. I want to see his face when he says that.'

'Again – will you go as Officer Parrish or Luke Parrish?'

'It won't be an official visit.'

She turned to face him. 'Do you want me to come too? I don't think you should go alone.'

He smiled down at her. 'That's kind, Jane. Can I let you know?'

'Of course. When are you going?'

'Soon, I hope. I submitted my application for a twenty-four-hour pass this morning.'

His com bleeped. The read-out said *Ellis*.

'What do you bet that's what he wants to talk to me about?'

'Good luck.'

He left her watching the river flow past.


Major Ellis – soon to be the former officer in charge of Team 236 – was in his office.

'Come in, Parrish, sit down. How's the hand?'

Luke flourished his dramatically black-gloved hand. 'I wouldn't have thought I could possibly be any more appealing to the female sex, but apparently I was wrong. I'm fighting them off with one complete and one three-fingered hand.'

'Two fingers and a thumb,' said Ellis, automatically.

'That's what Jane keeps saying, but you have to admit Three-Fingered Luke sounds much better than Two-Fingers-and-a-Thumb Luke.' He stared down at his gloved left hand.

'I'm sure you're right,' said Ellis, 'but with your permission – and even without it – I shall continue to refer to you as Trainee soon-to-be Officer Parrish.'

Luke shrugged. 'I've been called worse. And in this very building, too.'

'Does your injury interfere at all with your ability to do your job?'

'Surprisingly, no. Except for typing, of course, but I usually get Jane to do that for me anyway. You know – because she's a girl.'

Ellis sat back in his chair. 'You're still angry, aren't you?'

Luke shrugged.

'You can dictate your reports. As you've always done. As everyone else does.'

'I'm sorry,' said Luke. 'I thought I'd embrace traditional Time Police culture and disparage women at every opportunity.'

'I so look forward to seeing you attempt that with every female officer here.'

'Why don't we call one in and I'll give it a go?'

'I know you're angry but stop pushing me, Parrish. It's not going to work.'

Luke shrugged again.

Ellis regarded him briefly and then brought up a data stack. 'I've been reading your report on your adventures at Site X. There are one or two areas on which I require clarification.'

'Well,' said Luke, 'I'm guessing that would be the section of my report concerning the organisation apparently responsible for its construction.'

'The components for its construction,' corrected Ellis. 'Not the actual site itself.'

'Don't forget the Shoreditch facility,' interjected Luke. 'Built by the same Parrish Industries.'

'No – again – while the components were manufactured by Parrish Industries, there is no evidence we can find that shows they built either Site X or Shoreditch.'

'But pretty well everything was supplied by them,' said Luke.

Ellis was silent.

'By my dad,' said Luke, in case the significance of this statement was not clear.

'Yes, I know.'

'He's the one who's been . . .' Luke stopped and stared out

of the window. Majors in the Time Police were entitled to considerably bigger office windows than recently qualified officers. The River Thames flowed past, glittering in the cold sunshine, thronged with water taxis for the more well off. Public clippers served lesser mortals. A grimy tug chugged past, towing a long line of barges on their way to pick up their cargo from the Rotherhithe depots.

Luke turned back. He and Ellis regarded each other for a moment and then Ellis, seemingly changing the subject, said, 'I received your request for a twenty-four-hour pass.'

Luke nodded. 'Yeah – I thought I'd enjoy a night on the town before resuming the burden of my Time Police responsibilities again.'

'Ah – absolutely nothing to do with confronting your father over this issue then?'

Luke held his gaze, challengingly. 'I had intended to work that into some part of the proceedings.'

'To hear his explanation, presumably.'

Luke nodded. 'Yes, I managed to get an appointment.'

Ellis reflected briefly on a son who had to make an appointment to see his own father.

'Do you think you'll get any more from him than the statement issued by the company lawyers? That the components are generic and widely distributed. That Parrish Industries are not responsible for their use by third parties, illegal or otherwise.'

Luke shrugged.

'Our best legal brains have been all over this, Parrish. What makes you think you'll get any more from your father than our legal people?'

Luke folded his arms. 'Surely even the Time Police must

admit I'm likely to know Raymond Parrish better than they. Frankly, I've seen him wriggle out of tighter spots than this. If you open the window, you'll probably be able to hear him laughing.'

'Are you advocating moving against your father without concrete proof?'

'Well, it's not as if the Time Police have never done that before. Why not now? Why not hold him until proof is obtained? Or is it one rule for the rich and another for everyone else?'

'Parrish,' said Ellis warningly.

'His company logo plastered all over every surface? Everyone taking their instructions from Mr P? Don't you think it's obvious?'

'My opinion is irrelevant,' said Ellis evenly. 'As is that of everyone in the Time Police except that of Commander Hay and her advisors.'

Luke shrugged once more. Ellis, who knew he was doing it on purpose, swallowed down his irritation and refused to be drawn.

'Parrish, you do remember it was your father's wish you joined the Time Police, don't you?'

'Yes, of course, but perhaps he thought he could turn me to the Dark Side and I could be useful to him.' He paused. Honesty compelled him to say, 'Unlikely though that might seem. Or maybe he thought you'd chuck me out after the first week. And when you didn't, he pretty soon tried to get me back out again, didn't he? Personal visit to Commander Hay?'

'Who offered you the choice to leave.'

'She did and I opted to stay.' Luke held up his glove again. 'Not sure it's the best decision I ever made.'

'I disagree.'

There was another silence.

'Your father has made no attempt to reclaim you since then.'

'We don't actually know that, do we? In fact, I suspect if he approached Hay now, she'd hand me over in a flash.'

Ellis shook his head. 'You underestimate her loyalty to her officers.' His voice hardened slightly. 'And mine.'

'Only because she dislikes me slightly less than she dislikes him.'

'She doesn't dislike you.'

'Oh, come on.'

Ellis grinned suddenly. 'Well, it's true she has occasionally expressed a mild regret she ever clapped eyes on you – usually followed by a desire to inflict a painful and lingering injury on you – but that doesn't mean she dislikes you.'

'She only keeps me here because I'm the son of the man in whom the Time Police are extremely interested.'

'She kept you here long before that.'

'So, am I the very promising soon-to-be Officer Parrish or am I only the son of Raymond Parrish, prime suspect in our current temporal Time-travelling investigation?'

'I'm going to bat that back to you. In what capacity are you visiting your father? Time Police officer? Or his son?'

Luke shrugged yet again. 'Interestingly, Jane asked me that. Twice, in fact. Haven't given it much thought. After all, this is me and we all know I don't do deep thinking. Or even, if you listen to Jane, any thinking at all.'

'Parrish, I once said that if you ever found yourself in any difficulties, you could come and talk to me.'

'I remember.'

'The offer still stands. And it's genuine. Don't reject it just because you're Luke Parrish and can't help being an idiot.'

Luke grinned.

'Are you going alone?'

'Probably. After all, no one ever wants to advertise the family shame, do they?'

'Take someone with you.'

'I'd rather not if it's all the same to you.'

'It isn't. If you want your pass signed, then take someone with you.'

Luke sighed and nodded. 'All right.'

Ellis opened his mouth to say, 'I think you mean "All right, *sir*,"' caught the anticipatory gleam in Luke's eye, swallowed down his irritation and dismissed him.

Following their formal graduation, Team 236 treated themselves to a small celebration that night.

'Now that we're real Time Police officers,' said Jane, glowing with excitement because eating out was still a massive treat for her. Matthew nodded, because after his days as a beaten and starving climbing boy in 18th-century London, any and all food was good. The restaurant was small and cosy and, as Luke pointed out, within easy staggering distance of TPHQ, being situated just around the corner from the Flying Duck pub, a favourite haunt of the Time Police.

'This is nice,' said Luke, looking around as they seated themselves. The prevailing colour scheme was a cheerful red and white. Gingham tablecloths covered the tables and red curtains were drawn to shut out the dank night. Green bottles held candles covered in stalactites of melted wax. The ceiling – a feature for which the restaurant was famous – was made of hundreds of empty – at least Jane hoped they were empty – wine bottles, laid horizontally, label side down.

Luke glanced up as well, probably calculating how long it would have taken him to drink his way through that lot. Matthew also looked up.

'Probably calculating the weight,' said Bolshy Jane. 'That's a lot of bottles.'

'Do you think it's safe?' whispered Wimpy Jane.

'Hell of a way to go if it's not,' said Bolshy Jane. 'What's on the menu tonight, sweetie?'

Jane sighed, convinced the voices in her head were far more likely to kill her than being crushed flat beneath the massive weight of a ceiling of wine bottles.

'*Empty* wine bottles,' said Bolshy Jane, regretfully.

Jane ignored her.

Matthew was, as always, reading the menu from top to bottom. That he could apparently eat four times as much as officers twice his size was a matter of endless speculation and amazement to his colleagues. It was rumoured he had hollow legs.

'What are we eating?' said Luke.

'I'll have the fish,' said Jane.

'So will I,' said Matthew. He raised puppy dog eyes to the waitress. 'Can I have extra chips?'

'Of course,' she said.

'And extra fish?'

She smiled at him. 'Of course you can. Would you like a couple of extra bread rolls, as well? And butter?'

Matthew beamed. 'I would. Thank you very much.'

'You're very welcome.'

They smiled at each other.

'Have you quite finished?' said Luke. He turned to the waitress. 'If there's anything left, I'd like the steak, please.'

Jane waited until the waitress had withdrawn, opened her mouth to query his choice, recognised the gleam in Luke's eye and closed it again.

They sat in silence as two waitresses brought Matthew's supplementary order. Plates of additional rolls and creamy butter were spread across their table. Matthew, who had obviously never heard the phrase, 'Don't fill up on the bread,' immediately got stuck in, munching happily until their actual order arrived.

Under the sympathetic eye of every woman in the place, Luke ostentatiously struggled to cut his steak with a spoon, sighing loudly and exuding pathetic helplessness at every move. Matthew ignored him, concentrating on his food as always and barely raising his eyes from his plate. It was Jane, unable to bear the sight of a perfectly able-bodied man wrestling with a steak and a dessert spoon, who finally snapped.

'*Use the fork, Luke.*'

Matthew snorted wine.

'Good one, sweetie,' cried Bolshy Jane.

Luke laid down his spoon. 'Oh, come on, Jane, how long have you been waiting to say that?'

She grinned at him. 'Almost since the moment your fingers dropped off.'

'Was it worth the wait?'

Jane looked at Matthew, still wiping himself down. 'Oh yes.'

Matthew took himself off to deal with his inadvertent wine

ingestion. Luke picked up his glass, looked around and said quietly, 'Jane, you're not in contact with Birgitte, are you?'

She looked up, surprised. 'Since we saw her in Glasgow? No. Why?'

'Only I've been trying to get hold of her and there's no reply.'

'Give it a day or so.'

'It's been over a week.'

'Perhaps she's gone on holiday.'

'I've talked to the Design Centre where she works. She hasn't been in to work and she's made no application for time off.'

'Have you tried her wife?'

'Also no response. Birgitte never mentioned going away, did she?'

'Not to me, no. Luke . . .'

'I know, Jane, but it's a little bit worrying, don't you think? I find Birgitte after all these years, she tells us what she knows about a possible attempt to kidnap me as a child, we promise to keep in touch and then she drops off the face of the earth. Too much of a coincidence, I think.'

'What are you going to do?'

'Come right out with it when I see Dad. I'm the one with the questions – I suspect he's the one with the answers. Now – enough of Dad and gloom. Here's Matthew back again. Shall we have another bottle of wine and see if we can get him to do that again?'

Jane rose early the next morning, full of enthusiasm and optimism. She was a fully qualified Time Police officer. Who would ever have thought? She donned her uniform, arranged her sleeves to show off her new flashes and admired herself in the mirror. Her long-coveted flashes gleamed white on her upper arms while underneath her name badge, a small green and purple ribbon declared she was the proud holder of an award for meritorious service. It would be accurate to say there was a very small swagger to her step and her ponytail swung cheekily behind her. In only a little over the training period allotted to more normal teams and against all the odds, Team Weird had gone from zero to hero. Conscious of an unfamiliar but very enjoyable glow of satisfaction, she strode along the corridor towards the lift.

She was unaware of it at the time, but another team watched her go. The silence was not friendly. Team 171 was comprised of very traditional officers.

'Would you look at that,' said Hooke, turning from the notice board where they'd been studying the duty rosters. 'I've done nearly ten years in this fucking shithole. Ten sodding years I've worked my bloody arse off and never so much as a sniff of a commendation, far less an award. And a bloody girl, too. She's been here ten minutes and look at her – swaggering about as if she owned the place. Makes you want to spit.'

His mate shrugged. 'That's what happens when you get a bloody woman in charge. This place is going to the dogs.'

'Or bitches,' said Hooke, cleverly. Everyone laughed.

Their team leader, Lt Sawney, was staring after Jane. 'Fancy a bit of fun, boys?'

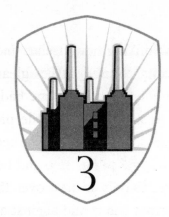

3

A day later, just after their first weapons training session – during which no one from Team Weird had inadvertently burned down a part of TPHQ – Lt Grint hailed Officer Lockland.

'Lockland – I need a non-man.'

Jane blinked, feeling her face turn the familiar scarlet. 'What, now, sir?'

'Immediately, yes.'

There was no way Officer Parrish was going to let this go. 'Shouldn't you at least buy her dinner first?'

'Eh?'

Lockland intervened hastily. 'Never mind. How can I help you, sir?'

'Team One-Seven-One. They're in BeeBOC – same as me – and they're looking for a female officer. They're taking down a group of lowlifes and they need someone to make initial contact. Later today, probably. Lt Sawney asked me to check whether you'd be interested. They've cleared it with Major Ellis, apparently, and he has no objections.'

'They asked for *me*?' said Jane in amazement.

'Yes.'

'Why?'

'Just what I was thinking,' said Luke. 'Why?'

She wheeled on him. 'Shut up, Parrish.' She turned back to Grint. 'I'll do it, sir.'

'Report to them asap. They're in their office. Second floor, east corridor.'

'Thank you, sir.'

Jane set off immediately in a very agreeable flutter of excitement. Not only had she survived long enough to qualify, but another team was actually asking her to join them for a special assignment. Who could ever have imagined such a thing? Certainly not Jane herself. What a slap in the face for all those who thought she'd never make a proper officer. If Time Police officers could float, Jane would have floated all the way to Team 171's office.

Luke watched her hurry away and frowned.

'What?' said Matthew.

'I don't know. Did any of that strike you as odd?'

Matthew shrugged. 'She doesn't look like a Time Police officer. None of us do. Which is probably why they want her.'

'True. But why would she . . . ?'

'She just wants to fit in,' said Matthew. 'She's desperate for acceptance and she'll do anything to get it.'

'Yes, but Sawney. He's nearly as low a life form as those he's trying to take down.'

'Ellis wouldn't have agreed if he thought she couldn't handle it.'

'Again, true. Look, are you doing anything this afternoon?'

'No.'

'I've got a visit with my dad lined up but Ellis says I can't go unless I take someone with me. I wondered – since you're not busy – do you want to come?'

'Yeah, sure. What do you want me to do?'

'Not a thing. Just stand around, look as if you haven't a clue what's going on, and say nothing. You know – playing to your strengths.'

'Yes, I think I can manage all that easily enough.'

'In an hour then?'

Matthew peered at him from underneath his still very non-regulation hairstyle. 'You sure you want to do this?'

'Why wouldn't I?'

'It's up to you, of course, but I can't help feeling there will be consequences. One way or another.'

'With luck, yes. See you in an hour.'

Jane found the right office quickly enough. Team 171 were already assembled and waiting. Their team leader, Lt Sawney, gave her a friendly greeting.

'Come in, Lockland. Grab a seat. Anywhere will do. Quick introductions. That's Scrape on your left, Hooke and Maru on your right. Boys, this is Lockland. She'll be joining us for this one.'

They looked at her and nodded. No one smiled. Jane refused to be intimidated.

Sawney coughed for attention. 'Right, let's get started. Lockland, this briefing is mainly for your benefit. We had ours yesterday and the first thing we decided was that we needed someone like you to be our initial contact person. You up for that?'

Jane nodded.

'OK, then. This is an interesting one. Right up BeeBOC's alley.'

BeeBOC was the Big Business and Organised Crime department – the biggest department within the Time Police. Time
travel can be extremely lucrative – especially if done illegally –
and there were always people and organisations out there
willing to take the risk in order to benefit from the rewards.
The department was always busy. Team 236 had aspirations
in this area. After the Hunter division, BeeBOC was generally
reckoned the department to be in and Jane was conscious that if
she did well then it would go a long way towards opening some
doors for them. They would be regarded as proper Time Police
officers. People might even stop calling them Team Weird. And
Team 171 had actually asked for her. She still couldn't quite
believe it. Oblivious to the nudges and grins, she took out her
trusty notebook.

Sawney activated a data stack. 'Believe it or not, someone
out there is claiming they can sell Time.' He paused for comment.

'What?' said Jane, dumbfounded.

'Yes. Basically, they're targeting old rich people. A chance
to buy themselves more Time. Recapture their youth and such-
like.'

Jane blinked. 'How? Are they actually claiming they could
take their customers back in Time and then they – the customers – would be correspondingly younger?'

She could hardly believe there were still people who didn't
know how dangerous that was. For a start, the customer was
already alive ten or twenty years ago. There would be two
of them in the same Time. Although not for very long, she
reflected, because the universe has a very nasty way of dealing
with two versions of the same person in the same Time. The

results were unbelievably messy and unbelievably painful. Something the Time Police were always telling people and then complaining bitterly because no one ever believed them. During their training, Team 236 had sat through three separate modules on the perils of that happening.

And secondly, everyone has their own internal clock and these don't change. It doesn't matter how many times someone jumps up and down the Timeline, they themselves will still continue to age normally. If Jane was eighty years old and jumped back ten years then she'd still be eighty.

'Relax, Lockland. It's just a con,' said Sawney. 'They're not saying they can prolong your life, they're not offering a centenarian an extra ten years – because who wants extra Time at that age? They're offering to give you more Time when it counts.'

Jane frowned. 'Are they saying they're selling people more Time between, say, thirty and forty years of age?'

'Well done, Lockland, that's it. Yes, they're claiming they can sell you not only extra Time, but quality Time as well. I don't imagine many people would jump at the chance of being ninety again, but thirty, on the other hand . . .'

'But . . . how could that work?' asked Jane, scribbling in her notebook. 'It's impossible, surely.'

'It doesn't work. It's a clever con. Although no one discovers that until after they've parted with a ton of untraceable cash.'

'Yes,' said Hooke. 'And they don't make the mistake of underselling themselves. The bigger the con, the bigger the price, I always say. According to the sales pitch, you can buy an additional two years, five years, or ten years – whatever you can afford. They don't do more than ten years, because, they say, friends and family would notice the difference and become suspicious, thus rather cleverly giving themselves some dubious credibility. "It doesn't matter how much money you offer," they say virtuously, "you can't have more than ten years. Sorry.'"

Sawney continued. 'The poor dumb cluck of a punter – or victim, I suppose we should call them – then goes off and mortgages their life to get the money together, convinced that a benevolent and principled organisation is looking after their best interests. People genuinely think they're buying extra Time. Postponing the inevitable. And to get that, they will pay sums of money that would make our ears drop off if we poor underpaid sods in the Time Police could even imagine amounts that big.'

'But . . . how?'

'They claim they've developed a drug that resets a person's body clock.'

Jane grappled with this thought. 'Impossible, but it sounds plausible.'

'Especially to people who want to believe – yes.'

'How on earth do they go about supposedly resetting someone's body clock?'

'Good question, Lockland. We're not sure, but we think there's an injection – in a suitably "medical" environment, obviously. Remember, their victims are paying a fortune so no expense is spared in the set-up.'

'And what's in this injection?'

'We think probably a combination of some sort of mild but fast-acting anti-depressant and something that renders you very open to suggestion. Both substances are probably hugely illegal but that's nothing to do with us. The point is the punter wakes up feeling great. Everyone staggers back in well-simulated shock at the supposed improvement. Huge congratulations all around. Does the punter want to take a look? Well, of course they do. A subtly doctored mirror is produced. Shouts of "Wow, look at you – you look amazing." And away goes the victim, considerably poorer and definitely not any younger. The so-called extra Time lasts only as long as it takes for the euphoria to wear off.'

'At what point do they usually discover they've been duped?'

'Shortly before the point they decide prosecution is not worth the public humiliation of being seen to be so easily conned. Many of them are rich and prominent people who can't afford for the public to find out that yes, they really are that stupid.'

'Bloody idiots,' said Maru.

'Yes. Don't take offence at this, Lockland, but this is where you come in.'

Everyone laughed. Including Jane.

'The hard work has all been done on this one. We know more or less how the con is pulled – now we want someone to go and persuade them to commit themselves. In other words, we want you to pose as a gullible punter.'

'Um . . .' said Jane, tentatively.

'Problem?'

'Well, surely I'm not old enough to be a credible customer, don't you think?'

'We rather thought you could be making enquiries on behalf of a family member. A much loved and very rich family member. A grandparent, perhaps.'

'I do have a grandmother,' said Jane, a picture of her extremely unlovable grandparent making an unwelcome appearance in her thoughts.

'Well, there you are then. Dream up some sort of cover story about wanting to buy Granny some extra Time. We'll use our info to get you an appointment. You persuade them to incriminate themselves – and as soon as we've got what we need, we'll kick the doors down and arrest everyone in sight. With luck, we should be able to wrap this up in a single night.'

He waited while Jane finished scribbling and then continued. 'We've had this bunch under obbo for about a fortnight now and as far as we can establish, an initial contact is made in a public place and the punter invited to a private meeting. We're a bit vague about what happens next, which is where you come in, Lockland. Get us as much info as you can. What happens next, where it happens – names, places, dates, if you can get them. We'll be listening in, and as soon as you've got what we need, we'll be in through the door and take them down.'

'So, I'll be going in on my own,' said Jane.

'Yes. They're a bunch of amateur con artists and we reckon they'll be falling over themselves to give each other up, but we need you to make the initial contact and then get us as much intel as possible. No insult intended, Lockland, but you really don't look like one of us, so we don't reckon you'll have any problem at all.'

Jane nodded, still scribbling in her notebook and oblivious to the glances over her head.

'Where and when do I meet them?'

'I'll let you know later today.'

'What happens if they discover who I am?'

'We'll never be very far away, Lockland. We'll be in like a flash if anything looks like going wrong. Won't we, boys?'

Jane took herself back to the Team 236 office, only to find it empty. Shrugging her shoulders, she sat down to review her notes. The mission seemed straightforward enough.

'Are you sure about this?' enquired Bolshy Jane, irritating as ever.

Jane sighed. Regular medicals had failed to pick up on what she suspected was undiagnosed schizophrenia.

'You should listen to her,' said Wimpy Jane, equally irritating, but in a completely different sort of way.

Jane ignored her as well.

'Only you've never worked with this team before,' said Bolshy Jane.

'She's right,' said Wimpy Jane. 'They're a bit of an unknown quantity and I didn't much like the look of that Sawney bloke. Or any of them, really.'

'Shut up, the pair of you.'

'Just saying,' said Bolshy Jane. 'A few basic precautions might not be a bad idea. You know what they say – hope for the best but plan for the worst.'

'They asked for me,' said Jane, defensively. 'They actually asked me to join their team for this one. What could possibly go wrong?'

Both Bolshy and Wimpy Jane remained annoyingly silent.

Jane lunched alone. Matthew and Luke had gone out. They'd been very cagey about where. She wondered if Luke was

39

hauling Matthew off to some fleshpot somewhere. Well, she'd undoubtedly hear about it when they got back.

Lt Sawney found her as she was leaving the dining room. 'Lockland – we're going this afternoon.'

'So soon? Where?'

He shunted her into nearby Briefing Room 4. The rest of the team awaited them.

'Walthamstow. Do you know the William Morris Gallery?'

She shook her head. 'No.'

'Doesn't matter. There's a bit of a garden at the front. Meet them there. Wear something red.'

'How will I know them?'

'You won't. They'll know you. Because you'll be wearing something red. We've set you up as Carol Jessup with a failing but very rich granny who will remember you in her will if you can pull this off.'

'Although obviously I'm concerned for my granny,' said Jane.

'If you want to be, yes. Just make sure you get us enough to arrest them. Something for us to work with.'

'What about a wire? Will I wear one?'

'No, if they've any sense they'll search you at some point.'

'Oh.'

'Problem?'

'No, but how will you . . . ?'

'You can carry an ordinary com – something from any high street shop that could be carried by a normal member of the public.'

'Won't they pick that up?'

'We hope they do. Everyone's got at least one these days

and we think they'd find it more suspicious if you're *not* carrying something. They'll examine it, discover it's perfectly normal and then neutralise it in some way. Having done their due diligence, with luck they'll feel perfectly safe and tell you everything we need to know.'

'But how will you know . . . ?'

'We'll be outside with a listening stick.'

A listening stick was simply a long-range aerial, but since it was generally reckoned this term was beyond the technical abilities of most officers, it was usually known as a listening stick.

Sawney continued. 'They pick up everything. Let the illegals do whatever they want to your com – we'll still be able to hear everything going on.'

'OK,' said Jane, hoping she sounded more confident than she felt. 'What about back-up?'

Sawney nodded vigorously. 'At least one of us will be with you at all times. You won't see us so don't look for us. I know this isn't your first undercover job so you know the rules. Just get into the role and relax. Remember. Carol Jessup. Rich granny. You'll do anything – you'll pay anything. You get the info. We've got your back.'

'Is there a codeword? For if things go wrong.'

'Of course. "Corkscrew". But you won't need it. Off you go and make yourself look pretty.'

Startled, Jane stared at him for a moment, surprised to find there was a vast difference between Luke Parrish saying that sort of thing and Lt Sawney saying that sort of thing.

'Joke, Lockland.'

He disappeared along with his silent team.

'Bit of an arsehole,' said Bolshy Jane.

'Really?' said Wimpy Jane. 'Actually, I thought he was quite a big arsehole.'

'She's right,' said Bolshy Jane. 'I think you need to watch your back.'

'So do I,' said Jane, and went off to visit the security department.

An hour later, Jane slipped quietly out of TPHQ.

In an effort to look considerably wealthier than she actually was, she was wearing one of the outfits she'd acquired during the Site X assignment.

Never having had smart clothes before, Jane had fallen prey to the lure of online shopping using someone else's line of credit. Telling herself that a stylish appearance was essential to the success of their undercover mission, she'd started small. A scarf. A top. A bag. Then there'd been the dress. Then the other dress. In case she spilled something on the first one. Then the suit. And the shoes. Then the other shoes. Then the really well-cut trousers she could wear anywhere. Then the jacket to go with them. And so on. She'd been horrified at the total but Luke, whose credit she was plundering, hadn't even bothered to look. The whole experience had been simultaneously terrifying and enjoyable.

Astonishingly, once the mission was over with, she'd been allowed to keep them all. Actually, no one had ever mentioned all the nice things she'd accumulated on that mission. Including Jane herself. She did occasionally endure a crisis of conscience, wondering whether she should declare her newly extended and very smart wardrobe and offer to return it. Bolshy Jane had had some pithy things to say to her on that subject and Jane hadn't raised it again.

There was no one to see her go. Luke and Matthew had still not returned. She suspected Luke had gone off to see his father. And if so, had he taken Matthew with him? She hoped so. She'd had only a very brief glimpse of Parrish senior but, to her, he had appeared quite terrifying.

Walking up to Barricade Bridge, she picked up the down-river public clipper. She had a long journey ahead of her but the day was sunny, the air crisp, and the river sparkled around her. The Limehouse Cut being under repair and renovation, she disembarked at Blackfriars and headed north down a maze of tiny streets. St Paul's rose spectacularly from behind a clutter of buildings. Around her, people shopped and chatted in the autumn sunshine. This mission promised to be considerably more pleasant than dying in the snow at Site X.

She picked up the Regent's Canal and bought herself a ticket to the Hertford Union. The canal was busy – as it always was – but from there she was able to hop on to the River Lee Navigation and head north again, enjoying a coffee on the way. Finally, she alighted at the Tottenham Lock. Although it was now late afternoon, the sun continued to shine. A perfect, lovely, crisp autumn day, she decided.

A short walk brought her to the William Morris Gallery. Unsure how to proceed, she paused outside and looked around. There was no one in sight. Was she supposed to go inside after all? They hadn't said so. They'd said to wait in the garden.

She sighed. The temperature was dropping and people were beginning to leave the gallery and head for home. She was suddenly aware of feeling uncomfortably isolated. Sawney had said not to look for them and so she didn't, but what should she do? Stand here like a lemon? Walk about? Sit down and wait to be contacted?

She couldn't help comparing Team 171's briefings unfavourably with those of Major Ellis. It was quite possible that if they'd had Sawney as their team leader then none of Team 236 would ever have qualified.

'Actually, it's quite possible that if you'd had Sawney as your team leader none of you would even have survived,' said Bolshy Jane.

Jane found herself unable to comment. Spying a bench, she sat down, carefully adjusting her red scarf for maximum visibility.

A chilly wind sprang up. The sun sank behind neighbouring buildings. Jane shivered and tried not to think about how cold the return trip would be. She must be sure to get an inside seat.

'Surely you'll go back in the pod with the others,' said Bolshy Jane.

'Of course,' said Jane, uncertainly, suddenly realising that hadn't been mentioned.

She sat for nearly an hour. Surely that was long enough for anyone, however suspicious, to be reassured she was alone. She certainly felt alone. She could see no sign of her back-up anywhere, which meant that either Team 171 were very good at being undercover – or they weren't there at all. She hadn't got the impression they were that good. On the other hand, they had said she wouldn't see them.

'And you're not seeing them, are you?' said Bolshy Jane, darkly.

Late afternoon had turned to early evening and darkness fell. Surely she wouldn't be expected to sit here all night. Sooner or later an attendant or security guard was bound to ask her to move on. She shifted on her bench, using the movement to take a surreptitious look about her. There was no one in sight. Anywhere. Was it . . . was it actually possible that Sawney and his team were playing some sort of stupid joke? That they'd set her up? Sent her here to sit in the cold for nothing? Were they laying bets on how long she'd wait before finally realising she'd been had?

She should go back to TPHQ. The mission had failed. Jane was just reaching for her bag when a young man and woman walked slowly past. Reaching the end of the path, they turned and retraced their steps.

'Hello, are you Carol?'

Jane nodded.

'Nice to meet you, Carol. Please come with us. It's not far.'

Jane stood up, her limbs stiff with cold. 'Where are we going?' she asked, and it was only as she did so that she suddenly remembered she hadn't switched on her recorder. And the suspects were just about to give her the address. She twitched her scarf so that it came loose and blew off, landing a few feet away.

With a smile, the man picked it up for her.

'Oh . . . thank you . . .'

Jane fumbled with her bag and under cover of stuffing the scarf into an inside pocket, activated her recorder. She was tempted to ask their destination again. Surely a genuine punter would want to know that. No one in their right mind goes off in the dark with two strangers.

'Um, sorry,' she said, stopping. 'I don't think I can do this if I don't know where I'm going.'

'Of course not,' said the woman. 'So sorry. We're just in

a bit of a hurry to get out of this wind. I'm Layla and this is Horst and we're not going very far. We live in a flat a couple of streets away. Horst and I are just the meeters and greeters. We're here to link you up with the right people, so you can talk through the details, agree the price and a time and date, and then we'll escort you back to pick up your transport. Did you come via the Hertford Union or the Limehouse Cut?'

'Hertford Union,' said Jane, recognising a gentle probe when she saw one, but outwardly willing, for the sake of the mission, to be lulled. And lured.

They walked up and down several almost identical avenues. Gates opened into tiny front gardens. Most windows stared blindly out into the street, their curtains already drawn. Their inhabitants were, no doubt, snug and warm inside, and, unlike Jane, not on their way to a sinister rendezvous to meet with a bunch of criminals and comprehensively break the law. By now it was too dark to make out the street signs but Jane was certain she saw the same tree go by at least twice. She tried to relax. All this was as to be expected. They wouldn't take a direct route to wherever it was they were going.

She could hear footsteps on the pavement but only theirs. She gave herself a little shake. Of course Sawney and his crew were close by. At least one of them would be watching her at this very moment.

She flashed a look up at the man – Horst – on her right, and Layla on her left and opened her mouth to ask how much further. It was unnecessary.

'Here we are,' said Layla cheerfully, pushing open a front gate.

Jane had an impression of a small, square front garden with

red and black tiles leading to a recessed front door. This was a garden flat. Another door painted in a different colour presumably led to the one upstairs.

Horst pushed open the front door. Jane's fears were slightly allayed. This was no sinister criminal hideout. The hall was brightly lit. Coats hung on hooks. Shoes were scattered around in the way that shoes always manage somehow, no matter how neatly they've been stowed away. There was a faint smell of vanilla. Jane told herself that very few criminal dens smelled of vanilla.

'Let me take your coat,' said Horst.

'Brr,' said Layla. 'It's only when you get inside you realise how chilly the evenings are these days. Let's go into the kitchen and get warm. I expect you'd like a drink, Carol.'

'Oh, yes, please,' said Jane, remembering she was Carol. 'That would be very nice.'

'Come through.'

Under the guise of tidying her hair in a mirror, Jane took careful note of the layout. A long, narrow corridor stretched before her. The half-open door on her left seemed to lead to the sitting room, with windows to the front. Then the kitchen. Then the bathroom. Two closed doors at the end were almost certainly bedrooms which would overlook the tiny back garden.

Far from being some kind of sinister drug manufactory, with a haze of toxic fumes and dubious stains, the kitchen was warm and cosy. A fashionably vintage look with shabby units and worktops.

The Time Police have procedures for going into a situation blind. Firstly, note your exits. The one I came in through,

47

thought Jane. And the back door is on the left-hand wall. One window over the sink. Blind not drawn. All accessible.

Secondly, since she was unarmed, she should check for potential weapons she could use in the event of an emergency. OK – there was a set of good knives on the wall. A substantial-looking wok lay within easy reach. A spray bottle of kitchen cleaner had been left on the draining board. A wine rack with six full bottles stood on the worktop and if she wanted an empty bottle then there was the recycling box in the corner. Jane nodded to herself. She could fight a war with that lot.

Layla and Horst invited her to sit down at the kitchen table. Jane unobtrusively laid her bag on the chair next to her where it sat mostly concealed by the patterned tablecloth. She smiled at her hosts and made a business of rubbing her hands together.

'There's coffee,' said Layla, 'or I can do a mean hot chocolate.'

Well, that was reassuring. Not many criminal masterminds made hot chocolate for their victims. This was almost *too* comforting and cosy. There was even a small ginger cat curled up by the radiator, completely ignoring everything going on around him. At least Jane assumed it was a him. She was sure she'd read somewhere that all gingers were toms and all tortoiseshells were female. Something to do with genetics, she thought.

'Sweetie – stop daydreaming,' said Bolshy Jane.

'Oh, yes, a hot chocolate would be very nice, thank you.'

Layla busied herself with some patterned mugs, and Horst began. 'So, Carol, what can we do for you?'

'Um, well,' said Jane, sticking to the truth because it was easier to remember, 'I received a message to be at the William Morris Gallery and someone would meet me there.'

'Why was that, Carol?'

'I'm sorry?'

'Why would you want to meet someone today?'

'Well, um, my gran's not very well.'

Their faces registered immediate concern. 'Oh, I'm so sorry to hear that,' said Layla, setting a steaming drink in front of Jane. 'My granny died last year and I miss her so much.'

Liar, thought Jane, and immediately felt much better. However, she nodded in sympathy and silence fell.

'You were saying about a message,' prompted Horst. They clearly weren't going to do anything to incriminate themselves.

'Well,' Jane said, looking around the kitchen. 'No one's listening to this, are they?'

Both Horst and Layla assured her they were not. 'Although,' said Horst, opening the kitchen drawer and pulling out an implement, 'shall we put everyone's mind at rest?'

He waved some kind of wand at her.

'Yes,' thought Jane. 'If you think that tuppeny-halfpenny little thing is going to pick up my big rufty-tufty Time Police gizmo, you're very much mistaken.'

The wand bleeped. They'd found her high street com device.

'Here we go,' thought Jane.

4

Since the visit to Raymond Parrish was unofficial, Matthew and Luke changed into civilian clothes. Although in Matthew's case, that didn't necessarily mean plain clothes.

'Good God,' said Luke, surveying Matthew's superhero T-shirt, baggy jeans, orange puffa jacket and light-up trainers with the built-in sound system. 'Oh, I've got it. You lied about your age to join the Time Police. You're really only eight years old, aren't you? That's why you're so small and skinny. Why didn't I guess that?'

Matthew surveyed Luke's simple but expensive jacket and trousers. 'I'm surprised you're not going in uniform.'

'I would if I could,' muttered Luke. 'But an arrest in civilian clothes is just as valid. I checked.'

Matthew stopped walking. 'You're expecting to arrest your dad?'

Luke shrugged. 'He's Mr P. The bloke in charge of Site X. The one everyone takes their instructions from. I don't under-stand why no one else can see that.'

'The evidence is all circumstantial. Do you think Hay wouldn't have him behind bars if she had even the tiniest proof?'

'She would if he was anyone other than Raymond Parrish.'

Matthew turned to him. 'So how is this going to work, exactly? You place one of the richest and most powerful men in the world under arrest. We march him out of his own building, and not one of his employees raises a finger to stop us? Do we bring him back by public clipper? Have you thought this through at all?'

Luke sighed. 'To answer your original question, I'm not expecting to arrest my dad, no. Although it would be interesting, wouldn't it? Theoretically, we would have the authority.'

'We?'

'Well, yes. I'm hoping he'll be so blinded by the stylishness of your get-up today that he'll just quietly surrender out of shock.'

'While his security people just stand back and not shoot us in any way as we try to exit the building with our controversial prisoner.'

'I assume you get this unhelpful attitude from your parents.'

'Well, obviously.' Matthew stuffed his hands in his pockets. 'Whose parents would I get it from?'

'Jesus, you're weird. And badly dressed. And don't get me started on your hair.'

'Do you want my help or not?'

Luke sighed. 'Yes.'

'Then shall we go? Or do you want to stand around and complain about half a dozen other things?'

'Any chance of you changing that T-shirt?'

'Absolutely none. Come on.'

They passed through the atrium and into the outside world, taking the public clipper from Barricade Bridge to Westminster. The day, while sunny, was chilly and the top deck almost deserted. Matthew would have been quite happy to make the journey in silence. Small talk was a curse other people had to endure. Not so Luke Parrish. He turned to Matthew. 'So – how's life with a wanted illegal?'

Matthew bristled immediately. 'She's not a wanted illegal.'

'Not at this minute, no, but she was. And will be again, I'm certain. You don't foresee a possible conflict of interests in the future? Because I think that's inevitable, don't you?'

Matthew said nothing, watching the north bank slide by.

'You must have *some* plans for the future. I mean, none of us is going to be in the Time Police forever, are we?'

Matthew folded his arms, managing to look even more than usually stubborn. And defiant. And defensive. 'I'm going to marry her one day.'

'Not while you're in the Time Police, you're not. No married officers, remember.' He turned to look at Matthew. 'You're not thinking of leaving, are you?'

'No, of course not. Well, one day perhaps. It occurred to me when Hay suspended me. One day the three of us will all go our separate ways.'

Luke was amused. 'If you live that long. You're proposing a relationship with a known illegal. And you a member of the Time Police. And yes, she's under amnesty at the moment but, well . . . she is one of the Meiklejohns, isn't she? Can't see that amnesty lasting long. And what would you do? Where would you go? Where would you live?'

Matthew shrugged. 'Haven't really thought about it. Gallivant up and down the Timeline, I expect. Easily outwitting my ex-Time Police colleagues. Having adventures. Causing trouble. Enjoying ourselves.'

'Bloody hell,' said Luke. 'On the other hand, you are

descended from lunatics. Are your grandparents perhaps in some kind of padded room somewhere?'

Matthew grinned. 'Dunno. Mum says my grandad died before I was born. And my grandmother.'

'What about your dad's parents?'

'I don't know if they've been born yet.'

Silence fell and then Luke said, 'I don't know, Matthew – no one ever derails a conversation quite like you.'

They finished their journey in silence.


Raymond Parrish lived in one of the poshest of London's posh areas. Luke and Matthew strolled through St James's Park then turned into St James's Square, which was built around a large central garden containing, among other things, a statue of William III on horseback.

'He's got one hoof raised,' said Matthew, pointing. 'Which means the king died while on the job. No – not that sort of job. And his horse's back leg is resting on a molehill – which was what caused the horse's fatal tumble. At Hampton Court, I think. Jacobites everywhere still toast the little gentleman in the black velvet waistcoat.'

Luke stopped and stared at him. Matthew wondered if, now they were so close to their destination, Luke was actually putting off the moment of arrival.

'Matthew, how do you know these things?'

Matthew blinked at him. 'How do you not?'

They stared at each other and then at their surroundings. The buildings around the square were magnificent. Most were either exclusive private clubs or expensive offices, including those of Parrish Industries, in front of which they now stood.

Matthew regarded it with awe. The tall, stone-fronted house had a flight of wide, shallow steps leading up to the front doors. The highly polished brass plate informed him he was standing outside the international headquarters of Parrish Industries.

'Your dad lives *here*?'

'Penthouse apartment,' said Luke, briefly.

Matthew paused on the bottom step. 'Look, is it easier for you if I don't come in? I'm happy to wait in the garden over the road – it looks really nice in there. Your dad might not talk freely if I'm present.'

'I don't think you being here will make a great deal of difference to him, but it will to me.'

'In that case,' said Matthew, accepting the inevitable, 'lead on.'

The heavy wooden doors stood open, giving an entirely erroneous impression of welcome.

The inner glass doors opened automatically as they approached. Two men and two women sat behind a smart wooden counter.

'Luke Parrish,' announced Luke. 'To see Raymond Parrish. I have an appointment. This is Matthew Farrell – another member of the Time Police.' Everyone looked at Matthew. Luke sighed. 'He's a member of the plain-clothes section.'

Everyone still looked at Matthew, who grinned and pulled out his official ID.

The security officer remained unimpressed.

'Thank you, sir. If you could look up, please.'

Matthew scowled at the camera and then back at the security officer. Whose face didn't change. 'Thank you, Officer Farrell. If you'll take a seat, Mr Parrish, I'll let Ms Steel know you're here.'

They seated themselves. Matthew looked around him.

54

What he could see of the ground floor was semi open plan but had retained many original features. The high ceilings and tall windows made the space light and airy. Autumn sunshine pooled in bright patches on the expensively gleaming wooden floors. About ten to fifteen people bustled about – busy but not noisy – and about the same number stood in groups discussing something or other, or sat quietly on long sofas, documents spread in front of them.

They were not kept waiting for long. Matthew looked up to see a tall, slender woman coming down the stairs, her dark skin contrasting with her short silver hair. Matthew had a strong suspicion this was the sinister Ms Steel.

'Mr Parrish.'

Luke stood up. 'Ms Steel. You've changed your hair.'

'I have indeed. How are you?'

'Very well, thank you.'

'Would you like to come with me, please?'

'Where are we today?' enquired Luke, affably. 'In his office or up in the penthouse? I suppose that all depends on whether he's just fitting me into his busy day at short notice or whether he's actually remembered I am a member of his family.'

Ms Steel was unperturbed. 'I believe Mr Parrish is in the penthouse.'

'Ah – note to self – remember I'm his son. Do you think I should do one for him, too?'

Behind Ms Steel, Matthew shook his head warningly.

Ms Steel showed no sign of taking offence. 'He's on an international conference call at the moment. He won't be long – he knows you're here.'

They entered a lift where Ms Steel used her card to take them to the penthouse floor and exited to a broad space, carpeted and quiet, containing a comfortable waiting area, a desk and a receptionist who looked up. 'Good afternoon. Mr Parrish will be with you very shortly. Can I get either of you anything?'

'No,' said Luke. He strode to the window and studied the view.

Ms Steel broke the silence. 'How is Officer Lockland? I hope she has now completely recovered from her injuries at Site X.'

'She's very well, thank you,' said Matthew, reluctantly entering the conversation since Luke showed no signs of responding. His statement was true because at that moment Jane was heading towards the William Morris Gallery flaunting her red scarf and waiting to be approached by a couple of minor criminals.

Contrary to Luke's expectations, his father kept them waiting only moments. Matthew couldn't help feeling a long wait would have been a good thing. Luke might have calmed down a little. Alternatively, of course, a long wait might have enraged him even further. Matthew sighed. Luke was very enraged these days. On the other hand, he had a lot to be enraged about.

The receptionist consulted his screen and informed them that Mr Parrish had finished his call.

'Thank you, John. This way, please.' Ms Steel led them through a set of double doors on the left.

'Mr Luke Parrish for you, sir.'

5

Team 236 might only have qualified very recently – Lt Grint had made a series of very unkind comments concerning training wheels – but Jane knew better than to panic. Well, actually, she did panic, because that was what a normal person who wasn't an officer in the Time Police would have done.

'What's that?' she said, staring at the bleeping wand and panicking.

'I was about to ask you the same thing,' said Horst. Despite his ominous words, he still managed to look pleasant and friendly. Jane wondered if he'd been born that way. As a meeter and greeter he was perfect. Non-threatening and friendly, but big enough to be intimidating should he need to be. And, at the moment, he was hovering between the two. Jane was unsure how to read him.

Horst and Layla, however, weren't important. Jane assumed they were just a front – barely connected to the scammers Jane was looking to expose. They might even be a couple of actors hired for the evening. This might or might not be their flat. That might not even be their cat. Perhaps even he had been hired. Most likely they were being paid a small sum to be the shield from behind which the real people would emerge if – when – Jane checked out. Then Horst and Layla would disappear and everyone would get down to the real business.

Jane dragged her eyes away from the wand and tried to gaze innocently at the pair sitting across from her. Yes, the gizmo had bleeped, but no one had yet crossed the line between the legal and the not so legal. Was the mission over before it had even really begun? What would Sawney and the others say when she reported her failure? How humiliating would that be? No. She was a member of the Time Police. Time Police officers did not lose their nerve.

Without a word, Horst and Layla stood up. Layla picked up the cat who uttered a mew of protest at this outrage. Still without a word, they left the kitchen. Jane watched as they walked down the hall and slammed the front door behind them.

'Are you absolutely certain about all this?' said Bolshy Jane, making yet another unwelcome appearance.

'Of course,' said Jane, with much more confidence than she felt. 'Why not?'

'Well . . .' said Bolshy Jane, and left it at that.

'And where's the other one? She's usually the one whimpering in the background.'

'Gone for a bit of a lie-down,' said Bolshy Jane. 'She's convinced this will all end in tears and just for once, I'm inclined to agree.'

'Rubbish,' said Jane, stoutly, suddenly concerned that professional humiliation might not be the worst of her problems. She looked around the suddenly not nearly so bright and welcoming room. Had they left simply because the wand had bleeped? What was she expected to do now?

'I think something's gone wrong,' she remarked, carefully. Her com remained silent.

'Hello – is there anyone there?' The remark could apply to either her back-up or the people for whom Horst and Layla worked and she felt quite proud of the ambiguity.

No one replied. So much for ambiguity.

She tried again. 'Is anyone there?'

Still no response.

Jane began to have a very bad feeling about this. Had she been rumbled? Had they all been rumbled? Had Sawney and his team already been taken out? Was she on her own in this enclosed space?

'For God's sake, you idiot,' said Bolshy Jane. 'Get out of here.'

Jane scraped her chair back across the floor and at exactly the same moment the front door opened and three men entered the house. Three very big men, Jane couldn't help noticing.

She stood up in not entirely simulated agitation.

'Who – who are you?'

They said nothing, merely walked single file down the hall towards the kitchen.

'Oh my God,' said Jane, still in character. 'You're the Time Police, aren't you? I'm sorry. I haven't done anything wrong. Honestly. I was just having a hot drink.' She gestured to the half-drunk hot chocolate as if hoping it would add verisimilitude to her story. 'I have to go. My gran's not well.'

The men stood just inside the kitchen door. Still no one said anything and Jane ran out of things to gabble. What should she do now? The best thing was to continue as if her back-up were still in place. Communicate this situation as clearly as she was able. 'Look, I don't know who the three of you are, but you're frightening me now.'

Still no sign of Team 171. She was on her own. Jane backed against the sink. The Time Police have a procedure for this sort of thing. Plan A is to get the hell out of there. Plan B is to protect your rear – the corner of a room is good – yell for help and just hang on until it gets there.

Jane had not yet given up on her mission. Looming ominously was probably perfectly normal behaviour for an illegal organisation doing something illegal in an illegal manner.

'Girl, you're kidding yourself,' said Bolshy Jane.

'Yes, please initiate the codeword,' begged Wimpy Jane, making a special reappearance. Actual Jane noted, without surprise, that even the voices in her head were ganging up on her tonight.

'Stay back, all of you,' she said sharply to the three men. 'Or I shall be forced to call the police.'

One of them said, 'Search her.'

'Oh dear,' thought Jane and closed her eyes. She had, however, foreseen this eventuality and guarded against it with underwear so sensible it was almost inaccessible without a PIN number, together with a tightly fitting leotard over that. Though looking at the size of the two men bearing down on her, she had a feeling this might prove insufficient.

She assumed the tallest one was the boss. He had given the order. Another one was a little on the hefty side – all right, he was fat. He seized her by the arms and held her firmly. His body felt soft, hot and unpleasant. The third was also tall but very thin. Fatty and Skinny.

Skinny searched her thoroughly. His hands were all over her, some of them in areas even Jane herself didn't access that often. She braced herself but either these men were extremely professional or, more likely, no one found Jane particularly attractive, because neither of them availed themselves of the opportunity to cop a feel. Jane was unsure how she felt about that.

'What's this?' said the boss, as Skinny pulled Jane's high street com device – and hopefully, the reason for the bleeping wand – from her pocket and handed it over.

'That's mine,' she said. 'No one told me not to bring a com. Everyone has them. It's nothing.'

Fatty ran a wand over it.

'No signal, boss.'

Jane told herself this was all going well. The com unit was just a blind. Things would settle down and they'd start incriminating themselves any second now. She tried very hard to imagine Team 171 crouched somewhere, glued to their listening equipment and poised to remove her at the first sign of real trouble.

'I told you that,' she said virtuously. 'Now let me go. I've changed my mind about all this.'

'Not so fast,' said Skinny.

They pushed Jane on to a chair. Skinny stood by the door, Fatty by the sink, and the boss at the table, opposite her.

Her bag, unnoticed so far, but glowing like a beacon in her imagination, lay on the chair next to her, tucked under the table and obscured from view. She could only hope it was recording away for dear life. If she herself could get something out of these men, then the evening might not be a complete write-off.

The boss clasped his hands in front of him. 'Well now, Carol. Tell us why you're here.'

61

'I was brought here,' she said, answering his question literally, to give herself time to think.

'Why?'

'Two people met me and brought me here.'

'Again – why? And stop wasting my time.'

'I'm buying Time,' said Jane softly. And truthfully.

The man laughed. 'And how does that happen?'

'I don't know,' said Jane, seriously. 'I was hoping to find out.'

He looked her up and down. 'You've barely left school. What would you want with extra time?'

'I don't,' said Jane. 'I actually think it's a stupid idea. It's for my gran.'

'You want to buy time for your old granny?'

'No,' said Jane. 'I don't. I don't want to do this at all. It's against the law and I'll go to prison if anyone finds out.'

'But you're here.'

'She made me come.'

'How?' he said mockingly. 'How did an old, frail woman manage to do that?' Obviously, no one had ever made him do anything he didn't want to do in his entire life. Jane, on the other hand . . .

Jane cast her mind back over the years. At least there was no need to lie for this bit. She swallowed. 'When I was smaller, she would punish me if I didn't do as I was told. Sometimes even *when* I did as I was told. It depended how she was feeling at the time. She had her specific ways. You get into the habit of obedience because the alternative hurts so much. After a while, just the threat of pain is enough. By the time you realise what's happening, it's too late.'

She looked down at the tablecloth, concentrating on carefully smoothing out the creases. 'And then, of course, there's the constant humiliation, hurt and general unkindness. And just when you feel you can't take it any longer, she offers a little light at the end of the tunnel. Apparently, when she's dead everything will be mine . . . except I'm pretty sure it won't be. That will be her final petty punishment . . .'

'But you can't afford to take that risk.'

She looked at him in surprise that he would seem to understand. 'No.'

'And you're going to give her what she wants.'

She clasped her hands in front of her and looked at him. 'Eventually.'

He looked right back. 'No . . . I don't think I believe your little story.'

'Every word of it is true,' said Jane, indignantly. Because it was.

He was mocking her again. 'Prove it.'

Being very careful not to disturb her bag on the chair beside her, Jane pushed back her own chair, kicked off one shoe and peeled off her sock. He craned his head to look.

For a moment there was silence and then he said, 'Nasty.'

'The other foot's worse.'

'And no one ever noticed?'

'An unfortunate childhood accident is, I believe, the official version.'

'So, we give you . . .' He paused.

Jane spoke firmly and clearly for the benefit of Team 171's listening stick. 'You agree to give me what I want – extra Time for my grandmother – for which I will agree to give you a very large sum of money. When I have secured the deal, I shall go home and inform my grandmother that if she wants to proceed, then things will change for the better. For me, of course.'

She replaced her sock and groped for her shoe.

The boss nodded. 'Hand over the money.'

Jane shook her head. 'You know I haven't got it on me at the moment. Any more than you have what I want on you. Besides, we haven't agreed a price. Have we?'

There was a cold silence. Everyone looked at Jane.

'So,' she said, aware of Time ticking on. 'Where do we go from here?'

'You'll be contacted.'

'No – I mean how will this actually work? Physically, I'm not sure I can get my grandmother here. She's too sick to move very far. Would you come to our house? Will I need to provide any medical facilities?'

He nodded at Jane's com, still lying on the table. 'Is that thing still off?'

The fat man ran his wand over Jane's com device again. 'Yes.'

'Sure?'

'Certain.'

'Even so . . .'

Fatty took a bowl from a shelf and filled it with water. Picking up Jane's com, he dropped it into the bowl. The small plop sounded very loud in the silence of the kitchen.

Jane surreptitiously wiped her hands on her jeans, still unsure whether she had enough to nail them. 'My back-up is out there somewhere,' she told herself. 'They'll pull me out when – if – things get hairy.'

64

As if he could read her mind, the boss spoke. 'Anyone outside?'

Fatty consulted his electronics again. 'Not that I can see.'

'They're not there,' said Wimpy Jane. 'They've been discovered. They're probably dead and you're on your own.'

'Or they were never there in the first place,' said Bolshy Jane. 'Either way you're still on your own.'

The boss leaned forwards, lowering his voice. 'You pay cash. On receipt, you'll be given an address. A small, private, but very temporary medical facility. Trust us – we'll make sure your granny doesn't have far to travel. She won't be allowed to eat or drink anything for an hour beforehand or an hour afterwards. Understand? The procedure takes about twenty minutes and is invariably free of complications. The patient is usually a little woozy afterwards. Recovery time can take longer than the actual procedure, but that's usually to do with the age of the patient and is nothing to worry about. You can be with her during the recovery period but not during the actual procedure itself. When she's recovered, you can take her home. A warning – half an hour after you leave, we're gone – the facility is gone – everything is gone. We never see each other again. That's it.'

Jane was conscious of disappointment. No names, dates or addresses so far. Very little for the team to work with.

'She wants ten years,' she said as firmly as she could.

'And she will get them if she can pay for them.'

'Who do I pay?'

'The person who asks for the money.'

'What happens when the ten years is all used up?'

'That,' said the man with a grin, 'can sometimes be a bit

of a shock. We strongly recommend a top-up long before that point is reached.'

Clever, thought Jane. Implying they'll still be in business ten years from now.

There was another pause. Jane channelled her grandmother. The real one. 'This top-up – is there a discount for an existing customer?'

'That's not my area,' said the boss, getting to his feet. 'You'll have to renegotiate when the time comes.'

'With whom?'

'The person who contacts you.'

It was like talking to a brick wall. To probe any further might be risky. Of course they weren't going to give her any details in advance of receiving the cash. They probably hadn't even set up the temporary medical facility yet. Sawney would have to find another approach.

'He should have known this wouldn't work,' said Bolshy Jane.

'And the cost?' she said.

The boss pulled out a small card, wrote something and showed it to her.

'Wow,' said Jane, with perfectly genuine astonishment.

He shrugged. 'If you can't pay it, then someone else will. Write down your contact details on the card.'

Jane wrote down the email address Sawney had given her and pushed the card back. 'Well,' she said, 'all that seems acceptable. I'll wait for someone to contact me regarding date, location and payment, shall I? Um . . . how will that happen?'

She waited hopefully for something – anything – concrete, but the boss only shrugged, gesturing for her to rise. Jane hesitated fractionally because now there was the problem of her bag. Should she leave it where it was? Safe and undiscovered. If she drew attention to it, they would almost certainly search it and she was only *almost* confident they wouldn't find the concealed recorder. And if Sawney and his team were outside and ready to apprehend the illegals as soon as they left the flat, then one of the team could retrieve it for her. Better to leave it where it was, she decided.

Now they were all on their feet and ready to leave. Twenty seconds more and she'd be out of here. She'd meet up with the team and they'd discuss how to proceed. It was perfectly possible, she thought, that the illegals would still contact her with the incriminating details Sawney needed.

'Check the coast is clear,' said the boss and Skinny slipped out into the hall. Fatty was packing his equipment away. Jane began to move around the table. The leader indicated she should precede him through the door and as he turned, he bumped against the kitchen chair. Jane's bag fell to the floor, bursting open on impact. The contents spilled across the floor.

In full view of everyone.

6

Sometime earlier, outside in the back garden, Sawney and Scrape were standing motionless under the deep shadow of an old apple tree. Sawney was wearing headphones.

Scrape eased his position. 'She's been in there a long time. Do we know what's going on, sir?'

Sawney shrugged. 'Nothing important yet.'

'It's very quiet, sir.'

'Quiet is good. Stop worrying.'

'What do we do if it all kicks off?'

'If it all kicks off then we give it a minute or two – just long enough for girlie to learn a lesson she won't forget in a hurry – and then we go in and save the day. We're the heroes and there's another one of them in tears and out of the service before the end of the week. Neat, eh?'

Hooke's voice sounded in his ear. 'The two original contacts are leaving. The ones from the gallery.'

'Pick them up.'

'Can't, sir. Three more illegals approaching. We'll blow our cover.'

'In that case, let them go. They're not important. It's the other three we want. Hold your positions until I tell you to move.'

'Copy that. Three illegals entering now.'

Sawney tilted his head, listening.

They waited in silence as events played out.

Back in the kitchen, Jane bent, not too swiftly, to pick up her bag, but the boss got there first. Scooping up the bag and the contents, he turned them over in his hands. 'What's this?'

For one moment, she considered denying all knowledge of it. She could tell them it was Layla's, perhaps. But if they looked inside, they'd find her tickets.

'My bag,' said Jane, 'I nearly forgot it. Thank you.'

She held out her hand.

He stared hard at her for a moment. 'Hold on.'

Fire truck.

Very slowly, one item at a time, he began to lay the contents of Jane's bag on the tabletop. The red scarf, a handkerchief and a make-up bag containing a few virtually unused cosmetics. Two pens. A purse with a small amount of money. Just enough to get a prudent girl home in the event of an emergency. No plastic, obviously. Absolutely nothing that could identify her in any way. And the tickets. One for the Thames clipper. One for the Hertford Union Canal. One for the River Lee Navigation. Jane felt her stomach turn over. She'd caught the clipper at the Barricade Bridge stop. Battersea. If he examined the ticket – which he was doing – would he make the connection? Battersea and the Time Police were one and the same in most people's eyes. In the same way that Westminster was the government. And Wimbledon was tennis.

The boss looked at the tickets. He looked at Jane. He looked back at the tickets. He tossed two on the table and kept the one from the public clipper.

'That will teach you to be frugal,' said Bolshy Jane. 'You should have bought single tickets. You won't do that again, will you?'

No, thought Jane. I very probably won't.

He upended the bag but nothing else fell out. He ran his hand around the lining but found nothing. Well, he wouldn't because the com unit was built into the ornate clasp at the top. Jane flushed and did her best not to look at it.

'You set out from Battersea,' he said, suspicion in every word.

'No,' said Jane, abandoning honesty with enthusiasm. 'I set out from home. I boarded the Thames clipper at Battersea.'

'Where's home?'

'Why do you want to know?' demanded Jane, feeling that suspicion was legitimate. He very determinedly hadn't told her anything of substance – he could hardly complain if she did the same. She backed away from him. Unfortunately, this took her further from the way out of the flat but she felt it added realism to her cover. 'Oh my God, you are the Time Police! I haven't done anything wrong. No money has changed hands. I want my solicitor.'

'Shut up,' he said, apparently thinking deeply. 'Why Battersea?'

Jane blinked. Anything to gain a little time. 'What?'

'Why did you board the clipper at Battersea if you don't live there?'

Jane forced herself to remain calm. Her heart was racing, her palms clammy. 'I had some things to do first. I made some calls, visited a few shops, and then I walked to the nearest stop. Which just happened to be at Battersea. By Barricade Bridge.'

'So, you don't live anywhere near Battersea?'

'Good heavens, no,' said Jane, without thinking. 'Miles away.'

'And yet your ticket is a return to Battersea.'

For one sickening moment Jane could think of nothing to say. Nothing at all. Instead of springing into action, the best her brain could do was dwell on the fact that had Matthew and Luke been her back-up, they would have been kicking the front door down by now.

The boss grabbed her arm and dragged her across the kitchen. 'We'll all go out the back way. Together.'

'No,' said Jane, not in any way having to struggle to sound panicky. 'I'm not going anywhere with you.'

Fatty peered out of the window into the dark, squinting left and right. 'In case you haven't noticed – Jimmy hasn't come back.'

There was a nasty silence. Both men looked at Jane and the boss tightened his grip.

She struggled quite feebly. 'Where are you taking me? Where are we going? You're hurting me. Let me go.'

Fatty was ramming the last of his kit into a bag as fast as he could go. What would they do with her? Jane pictured herself lying on this lovely stripped pine floor in a spreading pool of her own dark red blood.

'Pull yourself together,' snapped Bolshy Jane. 'This is a kitchen and there are more lethal implements in here than the armoury at TPHQ. Plan your next moves.'

Jane still had one arm free. What was within snatching

distance? The spray cleaner. Grab with right hand, pivot and spray. With luck it would catch the boss full in the face. He would stagger backwards which would put her next to the wok. Forehand swing with that, depending on whether he still had hold of her. Fatty would be less mobile so she'd deal with him second. Or, if he'd had the sense to get out of her way, she'd be straight out of the door, yelling for help as she went. Yes, better. And she'd grab the bag on her way. She had a plan. Everything would be fine.

As if he knew what she was thinking, the boss ground his fingers into her flesh. 'Fucking Time Police bitch.'

Jane didn't waste her breath denying it. She was already reaching for the kitchen spray. At the same time, she shrieked, 'Corkscrew. Corkscrew. Corkscrew.'

'What?' said Fatty, looking up. 'What's she talking about?'

'It's the bloody codeword,' shouted his colleague.

Jane whirled and aimed the spray at his eyes. An impressive example of resourceful thinking and physical coordination. Sadly, the spray was empty and the trigger closed on air. No pressure. No spray. It must have been rinsed and left out for recycling.

What is the point of saving the fire-trucking planet if I'm not around to enjoy it? thought Jane. She flung the spray bottle at the boss man's face and tried for the wok. Seemingly aware of her intentions, he yanked her away. The wok eluded her outstretched fingers.

But there was a toaster. One of those big chrome affairs with attachments that could probably pick up signals from Jupiter. Jane grabbed at it with her free hand and hurled it at the window.

No sooner had it left her hand than she realised it was still plugged in at the wall. There was a moment's confusion as everyone ducked the boomeranging toaster.

Jane spotted a rolling pin – a decorative marble affair on a stand. It would, no doubt, make a first-rate weapon but an even better missile. In what she liked to think was one smooth movement, she seized it and flung it at the window. It was considerably heavier than she expected, and for one nasty moment she thought it would fall short, but it didn't, impacting the window with a crash. The glass crumbled rather than shattered.

'Stupid SmartGlass,' said Bolshy Jane.

Actual Jane had a tiny moment of opportunity to shout into the night. 'Corkscrew. Cork—' before she was snatched away from the window. 'Get the front door. She'll have back-up. We'll use her to bargain our way out. They won't shoot if we've got her.'

'No,' panted Jane, her duty clear. Team 171 were out there somewhere. She had to believe that. No Time Police officer would abandon another. She should do everything she could to delay the illegals until Sawney and his team could get in here to make the arrests. Remembering her training, she kicked out at his shin. Sadly, she was in civilian shoes and it hurt, but it must have hurt him as well.

The boss backhanded her hard, causing Jane to fly across the kitchen and bounce off Fatty, who seized her.

Fire truck.

The two men closed in.

In the garden, the noise of breaking glass had sounded loud in the still night air.

Team 171 heard Jane's voice. 'Corkscrew. Cork—'

'Shit,' said Scrape. 'They've rumbled her, sir. We should go.' He flicked down his visor.

'Let's give it a moment, shall we, lad?' said Sawney, not moving. 'Make sure the lesson's well and truly learned. Besides, we don't want to screw things up by going too soon. They might still have useful intel to give us.'

Scrape slowly raised his visor again. 'But, sir . . .'

Maru's voice sounded in their ears. 'She's called it, sir. Are we going in?'

Sawney grinned. 'No. Let her discover it's not all knitting and flowers in the Time Police. She'll be all right for another minute.'

Jane was not all right. Punches rained down upon her. She fell hard against the table. There was a sudden stabbing pain in her ribs. One of the men seized her hair and banged her face into the tabletop. And again. She felt her nose bend. Blood was running into her eyes. She couldn't see. Someone punched her in the kidneys. The pain was excruciating. Her legs wouldn't hold her. She fell to the floor and tried to roll away. One of them grabbed her legs and tugged. Her head hit the table leg and the world went away for a moment or two.

They were trying to drag her out. To use her as a hostage. To get away . . . She should resist . . .

She had forgotten the codeword. 'Help . . . Sawney . . .' Her lips wouldn't move properly. Sawney's team wouldn't be able to hear her . . .

She hung on to a table leg as they kicked at her repeatedly.

'Remember your training,' shouted Bolshy Jane. 'Remember.'

And she did remember. Things to do when lying on the floor having the shit kicked out of you.

'Firstly – don't. But if you can't avoid it, then grab a foot or leg.' She could hear the instructor's voice – which, for some reason, sounded very much like Bolshy Jane. 'Because then suddenly the advantage is with you. The assailant is standing on one leg. Vulnerable. Because you've got their foot.'

There was a foot. Right here and now there was a foot. Jane lunged for it, ignored the stabbing pain in her ribs because her life could be at stake here and ribs always healed eventually, grabbed something with both arms, pulled and twisted. It worked. There was a crash and down he came. And, because everyone is due a little luck sooner or later, he brought the wok down with him. And several other things as well – a fruit bowl and a spice rack – but mostly the wok. And it had a long handle. And because it was expensive, it was heavy.

You don't swing wildly because that gives your opponent time to wrest the weapon back and use it on you instead – so she didn't. She didn't aim for his face either – too far away and her vision was blurred. Too risky.

A wok to the groin, however, wasn't risky at all.

'Making a bit of a habit of this, sweetie,' said Bolshy Jane, cheerfully, as kitchen implement impacted illegal genitals. He gave a kind of choking grunt and curled up like a woodlouse.

Jane shouted for help again. Surely if Team 171 was outside the house, they must have heard the commotion by now. And what about the people in the flat upstairs? Where was everyone? Why was she doing this all by herself?

Behind her she heard Fatty struggling with the door into the hall. Well, that was fine with her. One less to deal with. Only he couldn't get the door open because both Jane and his colleague were enacting the role of draught excluders. Jane rolled away, found a chair, used it to pull herself to her feet, then hurled it as hard as she could at the recumbent figure still on the floor. Like the wok, it was a good quality chair. It hit him squarely on the head and shoulders and he fell back, dazed.

In some kind of blind panic, Fatty was still clawing at the door. Fortunately, he seemed more concerned with escape than dealing with Jane. She wheeled round. Don't stop. Don't lose momentum. Don't give them time to remember there were two of them and only one of her. Keep attacking. Use whatever she could find. Knives. There were knives. Find one before they did. Were they armed? Why had she agreed to this mission? In fact, why had she even got out of bed this morning?

The man on the floor was lying quite still. Even better, he was bleeding heavily from a nasty chair-related gash over his ear. Fatty abandoned the door into the hall and headed for the back door, which would do him no good at all because it was locked.

In his haste, Fatty trod in his colleague's blood, slipped, squealed and smacked hard on to the floor.

Jane seized her wok again and this time she did swing. She had once been privileged to watch Officer North attack a man using only a metal tray. It was an image that had stayed with her for a long time. She greatly admired North – a competent and respected officer who obviously knew her way around a tray. Jane, alternately exhilarated and terrified, swung again. She had to keep him on the ground. He mustn't be allowed to get up. He yelped and yelped again, waving his arms in a vain attempt to ward her off. More by good luck than good judgement, Jane's first wallop had been across the bridge of his nose. His eyes were already swelling badly, obscuring his vision and evening the odds a little.

76

On the other hand, he was a fat man. Not many of her body blows were doing him much harm. And the boss was beginning to stir. She saw him struggle to push himself up on to his knees.

The handle came spinning off the wok. Fire truck. It hadn't been designed for this sort of treatment. Now it was just a bowl and a short stick. Jane flung the stick away, and stared wildly around for another weapon.

Chopping board. She swung it sideways and it caught the leader across the back of his head. He yelled in shock but stayed up on his knees. Jane raised it high above her head and slammed it down with as much force as she could muster.

Never had she wanted her trusty baton more. Or her sonic. She'd come into this unarmed. She'd never do that again. Even a can of hairspray would have come in useful.

Fatty was wheezing badly – hitting the floor so hard hadn't done him any good at all – and trying to pull himself up on to his feet again. Fire-trucking hell. If it wasn't one, it was the other. She was fighting on two fronts. Why couldn't they both stay down?

Wine rack.

Jane seized a green bottle – contents unknown but hopefully expensive – raised it two-handed, and brought it down on Fatty's head. Wine and glass flew everywhere. He went down like a tree.

The boss, however, was reaching out to the table to pull himself to his feet. Edging backwards, Jane kicked something wooden across the floor. The spice rack. Bending, she was about to defend herself with the whole thing, but a jar of chilli powder caught her eye.

Mistake. She should not have taken her eyes off him. He lunged for her. His bloody fingers closed on her leg. Jane shrieked, kicked out, grabbed for the jar, ripped off the lid, closed her eyes, held her breath and threw the whole lot in what she hoped was his face. Judging by the screams, it would appear she had been at least partly successful. He fell on to his side, hands clawing at his eyes, feet kicking. Chest heaving, Jane stepped back out of range and took stock of the situation.

Blood and wine had pooled on the floor. Glass from the window covered the sink and draining board. More glass scrunched on the floor under her feet. A broken wok lay off to one side. At some point the fruit bowl had upended. Someone had trodden on a satsuma. Hot red powder covered a large area and the sharp smell made her nostrils twitch. There were bloody handprints all over the table and worktops.

Now that she had time to think about it, she hurt all over. Really all over. Her face felt enormous. She could barely see. Her ribs stabbed hot pain with every breath and she was pretty sure she'd broken a finger. It wasn't supposed to dangle like that. She leaned against the table and took a few deep breaths, wiping her powdery hands on her jeans.

'You need to get a move on,' said Bolshy Jane, urgently. 'They'll begin to stir again in a minute and you're in no fit state to do this all over.'

'Good point,' said Jane, picking up her bag and slinging it over her shoulder.

She pulled open the kitchen door. It cracked painfully into the side of the former leader's head which probably counted as Time Police brutality. Jane found she didn't care. Cautiously stepping over the writhing, whimpering body, she squeezed through the gap and out into the hall.

Her coat still hung where she had left it. There were half a dozen zip-ties in an inner pocket. She found them and hobbled back into the kitchen, incidentally cracking the fallen man's head again. She rolled him on to his front and tried to pull his hands away from his eyes but he wasn't having any of that so she zipped his legs instead.

Fatty put up no sort of resistance at all as she zipped him too.

Having secured her prisoners, she hauled herself painfully to her feet again.

'Unknown man number one – by the authority vested in me as an officer of the Time Police – I arrest you for . . . the illegal selling of Time – an offence under an Act whose name and date I can't remember for the moment – and for assaulting a Time Police officer in the execution of her duties – an offence under every Act. And that goes for you as well, unnamed man number two. Both of you – you're nicked.'

The front door seemed a very long way off but she got there eventually. She reached painfully for her coat, opened the door, stepped out into the cold night and stopped dead in surprise.

Maru and Hooke were standing there. Right there. In the front garden. Not even six feet away. Just standing there. And there was Skinny. Zapped and zipped. Lying at their feet.

They'd been here the whole time. They'd been here the whole fire-trucking time. They'd heard her struggle. They'd heard her shout and not one of the buggers had come to her aid.

Still buoyed up with adrenalin, Jane snarled, 'Corkscrew, you bastards.'

Maru and Hooke stared at her, then Hooke opened his com. 'We've got them, sir.'

'You mean I got them,' said Jane. 'They're in the kitchen. I've already arrested them. It's my collar. Watch out for the glass.'

And then she went to sit on a nearby wall. Just for a minute.

7

It would be fair to say that, so far, today had not been the best day of Jane's life. And it was about to get worse.

Since they'd expected to be transporting prisoners, Lt Sawney and his team had travelled by pod. Not for them the tranquil peace of the London Waterways System. Jane and the illegals were loaded aboard and then it was everyone back to TPHQ.

Sawney was off the moment they touched down in the Pod Bay.

'Right, get these fire truckers checked into security first. Then off to MedCen with them. Don't want them claiming they gave their statements while too injured to know what they were doing. I want your reports as soon as possible. Good collar, boys. Well done.'

He strode off. Hooke and Maru pushed their three prisoners out of the pod. Scrape lingered for a moment, saying, 'Are you all right?' to Jane.

Jane, very conscious of her black eyes and the massive lump on her forehead where she'd impacted the table leg, nodded once but said nothing. There was nothing to say.

'Lockland, I . . .'

Scrape floundered in the face of her silent hostility, gave it up and trotted off after his teammates.

Left by herself, Jane limped out of the pod and stood, vaguely wondering what to do next.

A passing mech stopped and stared, saying incredulously, 'Lockland?'

It seemed too much trouble to answer.

'Where are your teammates?'

'Gone.'

'MedCen for you, I think. This way.'

He walked beside her as she limped across the Pod Bay floor. There was something she should be doing. Yes – the recording. Her version of events. The true version – not the Team 171 version which, she was certain, would be very different to her own. She held out her bag.

'Can you hand that into security for me, please. Give it to Varma. I think it's got everything they'll need.'

He took it without looking. 'Yeah, sure.'

The mech opened the doors for her and the world suddenly smelled of disinfectant. Gratefully, she hobbled through.

Thirty minutes later Jane was all patched up.

'Well,' said the doctor, clearing away the bloodstained wipes and dressings. 'You'll live.' He seemed even more than normally depressed about it.

Jane nodded.

'One hell of a fight you've been in, Lockland.'

'You should see the other guys,' said Jane, wearily.

'I did. They brought them in just before you. Did you do all that? Including the chilli?'

Jane nodded.

'Good move,' the doctor said, concentrating on what he was doing. 'I don't want to worry you, but word is that Sawney and his team are claiming the collar. Worse, they're saying you lost it out there, botched the mission and they had to go in and rescue you.' He still didn't look at her. 'But you probably didn't hear that from me.'

It was as if someone had lit the fuse a long time ago and only now was the bomb going off, but go off it did. Jane was conscious of white-hot fire running through her veins. This was it. This was the end and she really didn't care. As long as she could take down those bastards from 171, she'd be happy.

She slid off the couch.

'No, no, no, no, no, no,' said the doctor calmly, not moving. 'Where do you think you're going?'

'To kill them all,' said Jane between swollen lips, not taking her eyes off the exit.

'Understandable but rash.' He regarded her for a moment and then crossed to a cupboard on the wall and removed a hypo. 'Turn your head.'

'Why?' said Jane, determined never to trust anyone in the Time Police ever again and starting now.

'Because you won't get six feet down the corridor without a shot of this. It'll buy you thirty to forty minutes. Don't waste them.'

The hypo hissed.

Jane blinked, her pupils suddenly the size of dinner plates. 'Wow.'

'They're in the bar. Small celebration. You didn't hear that from me, either.'

'Oh. OK.'

'I have to tidy this cupboard now,' he said, turning his back on her.

'High as a kite but not stupid,' said Jane, and slipped out of the cubicle.

There are several bars scattered around TPHQ. The first, commonly known as the Pig's Bar, is for those who can't be bothered to make the effort, and is usually populated by body-fluid-covered officers who are, for one reason or another, in more need of a drink than a shower. A certain informality of dress is acceptable. Except pyjamas. Commander Hay had made her views on officers who drank in their pyjamas very clear.

The most popular – and the largest – is on the second floor. A reasonable standard of dress is expected and compared with the Pig's Bar, the usual atmosphere is quiet and restrained.

The third bar, rather better appointed than the other two, is situated on the top floor and usually frequented by senior officers – the general feeling being that they're better off up there, out of the way and doing no harm to anyone.

Jane limped into the Pig's Bar – Team 171's natural habitat, she guessed, but they weren't there. In fact, the place was nearly deserted. Sighing, she set out for the lift. Despite the pretty massive dose of painkillers, every step sent pain shooting through her ribs and the ache in her bruised kidney was making her feel sick.

The second-floor bar was a big room, designed to accommodate a large number of people. The right-hand corner was occupied by the bar itself – an L-shaped affair. The rest of the room was full of tables and chairs. In general, if you wanted to stand up and drink then you went downstairs. Here you sat down because, Time Police thinking went, it was more difficult to instigate rowdy behaviour when seated. This thinking was sometimes correct but mostly not.

The room had recently been redecorated in the standard Time Police colour scheme – vibrant shades of beige and grey. Various prints of famous London landmarks hung on the walls. The Tower, Barricade Bridge, the Gherkin, the Folded Napkin, the London Eye, the Startled Hamster and others. Against all the odds their colour schemes were also predominantly beige and grey. The only spots of colour were the labels on the bottles behind the bar. And any moment now, a blood-splattered Jane, of course.

Her fury carried her, limping and leaning heavily to the right, along the corridor. Every step hurt – from the soles of her feet to the top of her head – but she wasn't going to stop now. She moved slowly and jerkily in through the double doors, where she was forced to pause for a moment. Not only to lean on a chair and get her breath back, but to decide what to do next. She really hadn't planned ahead at all. It would have been useful to have formulated some sort of strategy during the time it had taken her to limp here, but she'd been too angry, too suddenly fed up, too betrayed, and in too much pain to think coherently. Now, here she was.

As were Team 171. Somewhere.

She couldn't find them initially. She stood just inside the doorway scanning the room. She saw Lt Grint and his team at the bar, North over by one of the windows, and plenty of other people she knew, but she couldn't find . . . Yes, she could. There they were. Not that far away. Sitting at a table by the wall. She couldn't have missed them. Or they her.

No one could miss her. All conversation slowly died away. Jane could see her own reflection in the mirror behind the bar and even she had to admit she didn't look good. An enormous egg had half closed her right eye which, at this moment, was a promising shade of plum. Another bruise highlighted her cheekbone. By this time tomorrow they'd have met and her face would be one enormous bruise the size of Africa. Her lips were swollen and split in two places. Her hands were still red and raw and her knuckles bruised. Her jeans and top were stiff with dried blood. More blood matted her hair and was smeared across her face. It wasn't her blood but no one here knew that – and she was still leaning at an angle of about twenty degrees because for some reason that hurt less than standing upright.

'All in all,' said Bolshy Jane, staring at the apparition in the mirror behind the bar, 'you've looked better.'

Team 171 were sitting around a small table. There were a good many empty glasses on it. Sawney and Hooke sat on one side with Maru opposite and Scrape on the end. He looked up to see Jane. His eyes widened and then he nudged his neighbour.

That Sawney was surprised to see her was obvious but almost immediately he recovered himself. Making an *I've got this* gesture to his team, he looked past her. 'Where are the other two weirdos? Have they left you all on your own?'

'Well, you'd know about that, wouldn't you? Tosser.'

His eyes narrowed. 'You don't speak to me like that, Lockland. Remember who you are.'

'I called,' said Jane, ignoring this. 'I called and called and you and your useless bloody team hid in the garden.'

Sawney flushed. 'You take that back.'

'You hid in the garden while I was beaten to a pulp in the

kitchen. And then, when it was safe, when I'd done all the hard work, then you went in and pretended to arrest two already unconscious men.'

He laughed. 'What? You're not claiming you made the arrest, are you?'

'Why not? That's exactly what I did.'

Sawney put down his pint with a bang. 'Look, girlie, I'm being very patient, but you can't just barge in here flinging accusations around. I wasn't going to say anything, but the truth is, you just couldn't hack the mission – which everyone can see from the state of you – and we had to jump in and rescue you. I was trying to spare your blushes, Lockland, but actually, you were a bit of a dead loss. I'm not angry with you as such – I'm angry with myself for expecting more from you. But let's face it – you're rubbish. And the rest of your team. A girl, a weirdo and a playboy. Eh, boys?' He looked around the bar as if expecting approbation.

More anger surged through Jane, straight to her mouth and bypassing her brain completely. 'That's a girl, a weirdo and a playboy who have more commendations and awards than you or any of your team of losers, Sawney. A little free advice – if you want to carve a career in the Time Police, then don't hide in the garden when it's all going down in the kitchen.'

Sawney leaped to his feet.

Jane trembled but stood her ground. She didn't think he'd hit her – not in public, anyway – but there were plenty in here who shared his opinion. They probably wouldn't join in but they wouldn't jump in to save her either. With hindsight, it might have been wise to wait for Luke and Matthew to return from wherever they'd taken themselves off to, although she couldn't help feeling their presence might not have been that helpful. Luke, in particular, could be a bit of a double-edged weapon sometimes.

Behind Jane, unseen, North put down her drink and opened her com. Casually, she turned away, keeping her voice low. And standing quietly at the bar, Lt Grint, talking football with his team, also turned around for a better view.

Having surged to his feet, Sawney appeared unclear as to what to do next. He seemed surprised that no one was cheering him on. Even his team remained seated. And Scrape had somehow managed to widen the distance between himself and his teammates even further.

'Listen, Lockland, the higher-ups have made things easy for you because you're a girl. They wanted more girls in the force, so it doesn't matter how useless you are – you're in. I don't happen to agree with that policy. If you want to be an officer, then you should expect to be treated the same as the rest of us.'

'You mean abandoning your colleagues to be beaten up and then claiming their collars afterwards is a regular Time Police officer thing?'

'Our collar, Lockland. You were crying in the garden, remember?'

'No – I don't remember, because that's not how it went down. I went in there. I got the evidence. I got beaten up. I called for help. I arrested the illegals. You waited in the garden until it was all over.'

Behind her, Officer Varma appeared in the doorway, scanning the room. North got up to join her and the two stood talking quietly, heads together.

'Look,' said Sawney. 'There's Varma over there. Why don't

you ask her who brought in the illegals? Who filled out the paperwork? Who did all the real work while you were getting over yourself? Eh? Varma – tell her I'm right.'

Varma came forwards to stand beside Jane, who wasn't sure this was necessarily a good thing. Officer Varma was an experienced security officer. Jane should know – she'd once been interrogated on suspicion of murder and she knew, first-hand, how effective Varma could be. Had Varma listened to the recording? Surely she must have. But suppose the mech hadn't handed the bag over. Suppose he hadn't realised the significance of it. Suppose he thought it was just an ordinary handbag. Suppose he agreed with Sawney?

'No, he wouldn't,' said Bolshy Jane. 'Not every officer is Sawney. Think of Ellis.'

'Lt Sawney is correct,' said Varma. 'Team 171 brought in the illegals.'

'Thank you,' said Sawney. 'Thought for a moment this might be a case of all the girls hanging together. Glad to see you're not putting the sisterhood first, Varma.'

'Thank you, sir,' said Varma, brightly. 'May I suggest, for the sake of clarity, you tell us all the story as you told it to me? For example, did they take much subduing?'

'Well, yeah. That kitchen was a mess, I can tell you that.'

'I can imagine, sir. Must have been a hell of a punch-up.'

'It was.'

'And yet your hands are clean.'

Everyone looked at Sawney's hands – and then at Jane's bruised and swollen knuckles and taped fingers. There was a fractional pause and then Sawney shrugged. 'Zapped them,' he said dismissively. 'Big time. They didn't go quietly.'

'Ah, yes, of course, sir. That would account for it.' She began to turn away as if to leave. Sawney sat back down again. He was just reaching for his pint when Varma apparently remembered something. 'Oh – just one last thing, sir. I can't seem to find the record of you handing in your sonics for recharging.'

'Well, no, we haven't got around to it yet.'

'Really? And yet you *were* in security earlier. Sir, I must advise you that's in direct contravention of regulations. Your sonics must be nearly empty. Suppose you get called out again this evening? Never mind. Shall we do it now?'

'Good idea,' said North quietly, stepping up. 'I too am curious to see these discharged weapons.'

'Well, you can just piss off, the pair of you.' Sawney sat back, looking pleased with himself. The matter was obviously closed.

Grint lumbered over. 'You going to tell me to piss off, as well?'

'No – obviously – but . . .'

Varma opened her com.

'Lt Filbert, sir. Have we yet downloaded Lockland's recordings? . . . Really? . . . Respectfully, sir, are you sure? . . . Well, that's interesting.'

She switched off her com and turned to Sawney, whose face was a blank.

'What recording? Lockland wasn't wired.'

'No,' said Varma, 'but her bag was.'

There was a frozen moment as Sawney took in the implications. He changed tack. 'Look,' he said, 'I don't know what they told you down there in security, but it's not true. I can see why you girls want to be counted as regular officers – and good for you – but face it – I mean, look at Lockland here. One mission and she's half dead.'

90

'Well, she wouldn't be,' said North, 'if you hadn't waited until she'd overcome the illegals and arrested them all by herself before daring to venture through the door.' Her tone dripped contempt.

Sawney ignored her. 'She's a liar as well.'

'As well as what?' said Jane, beginning to feel she was being elbowed out of her own confrontation.

Varma tilted her head as if listening. 'Thank you, sir. I'll put it on the common link.'

Jane's desperate voice filled the room. 'Corkscrew. Corkscrew. Corkscrew.'

Followed by the sounds of a struggle. Breaking crockery. Overturning furniture. The impact of blows. The boomeranging toaster. Jane's cries of pain. And then . . . faintly . . . 'Help . . . Sawney . . .' And then the clang of the wok. Panting. Cursing. The wok again. And the chopping board. Finally, the pepper and the screaming. A silence. And then Jane's breathless voice again. 'Unknown man number one . . .' They listened to Jane working her way through the arrest procedure, concluding with, 'Both of you – you're nicked.'

'Well,' said Varma, closing her com. 'That seems clear enough, I think, Lt Sawney. You and your team failed to come to the aid of an officer in distress.'

The room was deathly silent. Four officers had failed to respond to another officer's call for help. There was no greater sin. People began to get to their feet.

North spoke. 'I'd like to take this opportunity to make it clear to Lt Sawney that I will never, unless expressly ordered to do so by a senior officer, work with him and his team again. Everyone else is, of course, free to make up their own minds.'

91

Varma had been watching Scrape, whose body language was speaking volumes. 'Something to say, officer?'

There was complete silence in the bar.

Sawney twisted in his seat. 'Scrape, keep your mouth shut and wait for me in my office.'

'No, let him speak,' said Grint, looming over everyone like a slightly more rugged Ben Nevis. 'Out with it, lad.'

Scrape swallowed. His voice was very quiet. No one was under any illusions as to what he was doing. He was breaking ranks. Speaking out against his teammates. 'He . . . *we* wanted to give the illegals every opportunity to incriminate themselves. So we waited. Perhaps a little too long.'

'I shouted,' shouted Jane, nearly beside herself with chemically assisted fury. 'You heard me. I threw the fire-trucking rolling pin thing through the sodding window. I shouted "corkscrew" until I was nearly bloody unconscious and you bunch of stinking arse-wipe cowards just abandoned me. I called for help and you didn't even bother to fire-trucking reply. Not even a "Hang on, Lockland – we're on our way". You stood outside and listened to me being kicked nearly unconscious because you're a bunch of dickless, pickle-tickling, lying cockwombles with all the personal appeal of amoebic dysentery and not a decent set of balls between you, and you abandoned a fellow officer for no better reason than you're frightened of women.'

Sawney surged forwards, his face purple, his fist raised.

For a big man, Grint could move very quickly. Jane swore afterwards she felt his slipstream. Sawney had second thoughts.

Varma looked at Scrape. Her voice was gentle. 'I understand this is difficult for you . . .' she looked at the other team members, 'but is it true?'

92

'No,' said Hooke.

Maru hesitated, looked at Sawney, and then shook his head. Which could have meant anything.

'Yes,' said Scrape, loudly and defiantly.

'Scrape, you're off my team.'

'And proud to be so,' said Scrape. Leaving his drink behind, he stood up and took two symbolic steps to one side, disassociating himself from Sawney and his team.

Sawney wheeled about and strode from the bar. Hooke followed him and after a moment, so did Maru. Scrape stood alone, staring down at the floor, contemplating the end of his career in the Time Police.

North nudged Grint.

'What?' he said, irritably.

She turned so her back was to the rest of the interested room and said quietly, 'You owe me a solid, remember?'

Grint groaned.

'He's a good lad.'

Grint groaned again.

North grinned, patted his shoulder and went back to her table.

Varma looked at Jane. 'I'll get the records amended. Your collar.'

'Thank you,' said Jane, feeling the ground suddenly shift beneath her feet as her legs gave way.

Grint instinctively grabbed her and then stood helplessly, unsure what to do next.

Full of drug-induced bravado, she grinned at him and informed him he was a nebula. 'That's one better than a star, sir.'

Excitement over, everyone else sat back down again and carried on drinking.

8

Jane opened her eyes to find herself back in MedCen.

'Oh,' she said, quite surprised by this. On the other hand, it had been one of those days.

'All right?' said the doctor.

'Yes,' said Jane, wondering why her entire body felt as limp as a plate of overcooked spaghetti. She looked down at herself – now gowned and covered with a light blanket.

'Take it easy for twenty-four hours. Doctor's orders.'

'OK,' said Jane, very willing to do just that.

'You have a visitor. He just wants to see how you are. Are you feeling up to it?'

'Yes,' said Jane, modestly pulling up her blanket.

She was expecting it to be Luke, or Matthew, or even Ellis, but her visitor was Lt Grint.

'Oh,' said Jane and blushed scarlet.

The same confusion was reflected in Grint's own face. 'I . . . um . . .' He seemed unable to get any further.

All his attention ostensibly on his scratchpad, the doctor grinned to himself.

Finally finding the courage to look directly at her, Grint found himself distracted. 'Jane, what happened to your feet?'

If Jane had blushed before, she was nearly incandescent now. 'Um . . .'

The doctor reached out and discreetly pulled the blanket down to cover her feet.

With some thought of changing the subject, Jane said, 'Thank you for bringing me back to MedCen.'

'Um . . .' Grint fell silent and stared at the floor.

So that hadn't worked. She tried again. 'Um . . . What can I do for you, sir?'

Still staring at his scratchpad, the doctor shook his head in disbelief.

'I . . . um . . . well . . . Would you like . . . um . . . do you fancy going out one evening . . . you know . . . dinner . . . per-haps . . . or something. Next week sometime.'

Now it was Jane's turn. 'Um . . .'

The doctor rolled his eyes.

'Not if you don't want to,' said Grint, quickly.

Jane rather had the impression he'd be quite relieved if she said she didn't want to, but the last remnants of what she liked to think of as her courage drug were still stamping their way around her system, kicking inoffensive corpuscles out of the way, and she heard herself say, 'Um . . . yes . . . all right.'

'Oh . . . right . . . good. I'll be going then.'

'Yes,' she said. 'Good.'

He left. The doctor stood aside to let him out.

Jane frowned. 'What just happened?'

'Well,' said the doctor, tucking his scratchpad away. 'I think you just pulled.'

There was no response. He looked up. Jane was asleep.

Grint was outside and seemingly anxious. 'She seemed a bit out of it, doc. Will she remember in the morning?'

The doctor looked at him. 'Probably. If you remind her.'

'Oh.'

'Nicely.'

'Well, yes. Of course.' He paused. 'How?'

'Write her a note. Or send her a small gift.'

'Right.'

The doctor considered the officer standing in front of him. This was Grint, after all. 'Flowers. *Not* the latest edition of *Bombs and Blasters*. Not even the edition with the WMD pull-out for readers to keep.'

'Oh. OK.'

Lt Grint departed, a frown furrowing his brow.

The doctor regarded the battered and deeply sleeping Jane. 'I'm really not paid enough for this job.'

After some thought, Grint decided to go with flowers. And a note to accompany them. Which caused him no little difficulty.

> *To: Officer Lockland J*
> *From: Lt Grint G*
> *Subject:* ~~*Future Social Dinner*~~ *Unspecified*
>
> *Para 1*
> ~~*I am writing to I would like Further to*~~ *I hope you are well. I hope you like the flowers.*
> *Para 2*
> *I am writing to remind you about* ~~*our date our dinner*~~

*when you said you would go out* ~~possibly perhaps going~~ ~~out with me on a date~~ *which you said you would do but might not remember. But if you don't, it doesn't matter.* ~~Although I would like it.~~

*I respectfully remain,*
*Lt Grint G*

He stared at this for some time. There was forty-five minutes of his life he was never going to get back again. He stared at it some more and then got up to find Officer North, on the grounds that much of this was her fault anyway.

North read the note through once. Then again. Then looked at Grint's big, shiny face. 'No, it's very good. Short and to the point. I think with one or two tiny adjustments, it would be perfect.'

He held out his pen and she made one or two tiny adjustments.

*Dear Jane,*
*I hope these flowers help you to feel better. I was a little concerned about you last night. I'm not sure if you remember, but you agreed to go out with me one evening next week. If you have changed your mind, then I shall quite understand, although I would be very disappointed. I thought we could try that Italian place next to the Flying Duck. How does next Thursday at eight sound? Just flash a yes or no to my scratchpad.*
*Get well soon.*

Grint read it through and nodded. 'Thanks.'

'You're welcome.


There were repercussions to Jane's adventures, of course. Lt Sawney, who had booked himself in for a session in the gym the next afternoon, unexpectedly found himself next to Major Ellis, who appeared to have turned up just on the off-chance of finding a sparring partner.

'Oh good,' said Ellis, with a smile that fooled no one. 'I was worried I wouldn't be able to find a partner at such short notice.'

Sawney's eyes flickered from side to side.

Around them, all activity ceased.

'Actually,' said Sawney, with a smile as false as Ellis's, 'I'm partnered with Hooke.'

'No, you're not,' said North, materialising at Hooke's shoulder. He jumped. She smiled at him in a manner that was in no way reassuring. 'If Officer Hooke would like to have a go at me – I'm not doing anything for thirty seconds.'

Hooke wasn't bright but he wasn't stupid. He looked away.

Ellis tossed Sawney a pair of gloves. 'Put those on.'

'No,' said Sawney.

Ellis dropped his on the mat. 'You prefer to fight without them? Fine by me.'

Three well-placed blows later, Sawney was on his back and Ellis was blowing on his knuckles.

'Ice,' said North, helpfully.

'In a minute,' he said, and turned to Hooke.

Who was no longer there.

*     *     *

Nothing happened at TPHQ of which Commander Hay was not, in one way or another, aware.

'Well, Charlie, has justice been done?'

'I think so, ma'am. Officer Lockland is recovering well. Lt Sawney appears to have walked into something unfortunate but his nose has been successfully reset.' He hesitated. 'I have to inform you though that the word on the street is that no one will work with Team One-Seven-One. We have a choice of either disbanding and reassigning them – if we can find anyone to take them – or dismissing them from the service.'

'I can happily live without Sawney. If he wants to resign then don't put any obstacles in his way. As enlisted men, Hooke, Scrape and Maru will need to buy themselves out. Think of a figure, Charlie, and then halve it. They abandoned a fellow officer. I don't particularly want to keep any of them.'

'Scrape spoke out, ma'am. In public. That took some balls.'

'Very well, if Scrape wants to stay . . . if anyone will take him . . .'

'Actually, ma'am . . .'

She sighed. 'I knew it. What devilish plot have you hatched now, Charlie?'

'You're too kind, ma'am, but on this occasion, I didn't have to do a thing. Lt Grint has indicated a willingness to take Scrape.'

She eyed him shrewdly. 'Does Lt Grint *know* he is willing to take Scrape?'

'I believe Officer North has informed him of it, ma'am.'

'You see, Charlie, all our little staffing difficulties resolve themselves eventually.'

'And Maru has applied to rejoin Logistics. Whence he originally came.'

'Good God – is this a happy ending?'

'Well, not for everyone, ma'am. But for us – well above standard.'

9

Returning to TPHQ at the end of his twenty-four-hour pass, Luke was furious. Furious at what had been done to Jane. Furious he'd missed the confrontation in the bar. Particularly furious he'd missed Jane call Sawney's team a bunch of dickless, pickle-tickling, lying cockwombles, which, he maintained, was probably a once in a lifetime event. Furious he'd missed Ellis knocking Sawney into the middle of next week with only three blows. Furious that Sawney was now beyond his reach. Furious he'd missed it all. And it wasn't as if he hadn't been furious when he left his father, reflected Matthew. In fact, he'd been furious when he set out from TPHQ. At this exact moment, Luke Parrish was a tightly wound ball of seething ferocity.

'We can't even have a go at Sawney,' he said, kicking the already battered furniture in their office, 'because Ellis got there first – although good for him. Who'd have thought Goody Two Shoes Ellis could do so much damage with just three punches. Bloody Hooke can't be found anywhere. Maru's hiding in Logistics – and it wouldn't be wise for me even to poke my head round the door at the moment because I'm not flavour of the month with some of the female staff there, although I can't think why – and Scrape's been drafted into Grint's team.'

Matthew regarded him with misgivings. Luke's visit to his parent, made while Jane had been out with Sawney's team, had not gone well. Not well at all.

Ms Steel had announced them. 'Mr Luke Parrish for you, sir.'

'That's Officer Parrish,' said Luke. 'Accompanied by Officer Farrell.'

Standing slightly behind Luke, Matthew looked about him. He was unsure what he'd expected to see but his imagination hadn't even come close. He stood in a large corner room with tall windows in two walls. A SmartDesk stood across the corner, with two comfortable visitor chairs set opposite.

The view from all the windows was of expensive roof gardens at various levels, elegant garden furniture and surprisingly tall trees. In some parts of London, there was more greenery at rooftop level than on the ground.

Two long sofas ran parallel to one wall with a gleaming coffee table between them. On the corresponding wall opposite stood a modern briefing table with six chairs placed down either side. Typical of Raymond Parrish, there was none of this touchy-feely, democratic, all-inclusive, round-table nonsense. An imposing chair set at the head of the table was an obvious indication as to where Parrish senior's backside expected to come to rest. There was no art, but three large and six small screens decorated one wall. All were blank at the moment. A discreet door led to what Matthew could only assume were the Parrish private quarters.

The prevailing colours were a rich, dark brown, cool grey-green and warm honey. In short, it was a very pleasant room.

Matthew, accustomed to the battered interiors of St Mary's and then the sterile environment of TPHQ, had never seen anything quite like this and stared around. Luke, who had been in this room many times and had no happy memories of it – didn't. The familiar faint smell of his father's aftershave took him right back to his childhood – as possibly it was meant to do.

Raymond Parrish rose to his feet. 'Luke – how are you?'

He made no attempt to shake hands. For a start, the desk was too wide to reach across. Neither did he walk around it to greet his son. Matthew found that interesting. His own father, never a demonstrative person, was always quietly welcoming. A hand on his shoulder or a warm smile. The two Parrishes stood at opposite ends of the room.

'Fine, thanks,' said Luke. 'You?'

'Very well, thank you.'

'This is Officer Farrell – a colleague.'

'I'm very pleased to meet you, Officer Farrell. Can I offer anyone any refreshments?'

Matthew shook his head. That he was refusing food and drink was an indication of just how overawed he was feeling at this moment. However, Luke had asked him to come and so here he would remain. He looked around for a discreet seat and found a chair in a corner by the discreet door. Out of the line of fire, or so he hoped.

'Would you like me to leave, Mr Parrish?' asked Ms Steel, her eyes on her scratchpad, neatly solving the problem of which particular Mr Parrish she should be addressing.

'Yes, please,' said Luke.

Matthew recognised a bid for control when he saw it.

Luke crossed the room and held the door open for her, smiling as she passed him on her way out. 'It is always good to see you, Ms Steel.'

'It is always good to see the Parrish charm in action, Mr Parrish.'

Luke closed the door firmly behind her and moved straight into the attack. 'Well, Dad, I see you've moved into illegal Temporal Tourism. How's that working out for you?'

Not a muscle moved in Raymond Parrish's face. 'My understanding is that until your arrival on the scene, Luke – and that of your colleagues, of course – Temporal Tourism was proceeding very profitably. I trust both you and er . . . Officer Lockland are now completely recovered.'

Luke ignored this. 'You don't deny it?'

'I deny many things on an hourly basis, Luke. You will have to be more specific.'

'That you were involved in illegal Temporal Tourism.' He remembered the things he'd seen from the observation lounge at Site X. 'And worse.'

'I deny that I myself was involved. It would appear that some of our products, however, cannot make the same claim.'

'You supplied the components for Site X.'

'The company supplied some of them, yes.'

'And you didn't know? Come on, Dad – nothing happens anywhere in the world that you don't know about.'

'I fear you are overestimating my abilities.'

'I'm not underestimating your communications network.'

There was a pause. 'Shall we sit down over here? Less confrontational, I feel.'

Raymond Parrish moved out from behind his desk, gesturing to the sofas on the other side of the room. Luke remained where he was, fighting the all too familiar sensation of losing control of the situation to his father. That his carefully constructed

104

arguments would begin to dissolve even before he had the opportunity to make them. Because his father was right. His father was always right.

No, he was not. Not on this occasion. Luke gritted his teeth. He was a Time Police officer. He should have made this an official visit – except Ellis would never have allowed that. Or Hay. He was here unofficially – as his father's son – with all the disadvantages that entailed.

On the other hand, he was his father's son.

Luke smiled politely. 'Thank you.' He took a seat directly opposite his father and they faced each other. 'Off you go, then.'

Raymond Parrish looked puzzled. 'I'm sorry?'

'Off you go. Twist the conversation. Don't answer my questions. Or only address those for which you have a compelling answer. Or answer completely different questions than those asked. Or indicate, subtly, that this is all a waste of your valuable time. Or throw the whole thing back at me and make it my fault. You forget, Dad, I've been on the receiving end of your tactics for years, so off you go. Give it your best shot. Then, when you've worked your way through your usual routine, then perhaps you'll answer my questions properly.'

'Luke, why are you always so quick to believe the worst of me?'

Luke shrugged. 'It must be a family trait. Something else I've inherited from you.'

'I have already addressed this issue. My people were under instructions to cooperate fully with Time Police enquiries and they did. Nothing was concealed. Full access was granted to all our records, and the conclusion was that although some Parrish Industries' products had certainly been used for an improper

105

purpose, there was no evidence that we had ever known of or were responsible for the unlawful use to which they had been put. Commander Hay and I spoke at length. Several times. I held nothing back.'

'Ah,' said Luke, softly. 'The frank, open stare – the sincere voice – now I know you're lying.'

There was a silence.

Luke said abruptly, 'I went to see Birgitte.'

Not a flicker crossed Raymond Parrish's highly trained face. 'Birgitte von Essendorf? And how is she?'

'Very well. Very successful.'

'I am pleased to hear that. She has always struck me as being a talented and resourceful woman.'

'Has?' said Luke, swiftly. 'You've seen her recently?'

There wasn't even a fraction of a pause from Raymond Parrish. 'No.'

Both Parrishes were watching each other like cats.

'I expect,' said Raymond Parrish, 'that you had a lot to talk about.'

'We did indeed. Mostly – as it always is – about you.'

Raymond Parrish smiled. 'A worthy subject.'

'An interesting subject, certainly. We talked about that night.'

'Which night would that be?'

'The one when people came into our house and you sacked her and packed me off to boarding school. The one I'm sure you will remember if you give it just a little thought.'

'I don't have to. Of course I remember that night.'

'I would be interested to hear what really happened. Of course, I won't get that – I'll get *your* version of what really happened, which probably won't bear any relationship to the truth.'

Raymond Parrish regarded his son steadily and then appeared to come to a decision. 'Very well.' He turned to Matthew, still sitting quietly and wondering what to do should the Parrishes – senior and junior – come to blows.

'Officer Farrell, I do beg your pardon – these are typical Parrish bad manners. We are renowned for them. I imagine if you've known my son for any length of time, then you'll be very familiar with the arrogance with which we treat our fellow men. And women, of course. I'm afraid things are about to get very personal, and possibly a little ugly, and to save you any embarrassment, you might want to wait outside. John will look after you.'

Matthew looked at Luke. 'Whatever you want me to do.'

'That's very trusting of you,' said Raymond Parrish, smiling.

Matthew looked at him. 'I'm a Time Police officer. My loyalty is always to my colleagues. No matter what.'

Luke smiled. 'He's protection.'

'My dear boy, do you imagine I'm likely to gun you down?'

'Not mine – yours.'

Another, different sort of silence settled on the room.

Matthew looked at Parrish senior. 'Yes, I really am. What was going on at Site X wasn't pretty and he and Jane nearly died there. Luke holds you at least partly responsible. And in case you were wondering, yes, he is looking for trouble.'

Raymond Parrish sighed. 'Very well – perhaps it is time.' He brushed imaginary dust from his immaculate jacket and then said abruptly, 'You remember your mother?'

Only a Parrish could ask that question, thought Matthew, overlooking, for the moment, the fact that he had once forgotten his.

'A little,' said Luke. 'Tall – at least she seemed so to me. Thin. Unhappy. Married to you.'

'Yes,' said Raymond Parrish slowly. 'You remember her name, of course.'

'Of course I do,' said Luke, surprised and not a little annoyed. 'Alessandra Polli.'

'Polli was her mother's maiden name, Luke. Your mother's full name was Alessandra Polli Portman.'

It wasn't often that Luke Parrish could think of nothing to say. Difficult social situations, unhappy girlfriends, creditors, people he couldn't be bothered with – most of these could be eased through with a generous application of Luke Parrish charm, possibly followed by a small donation to the bank account of their choice.

It was very apparent he could think of nothing to say now. Matthew watched his lips form one half word after another until, finally, he found his voice.

'Are you telling me I'm related to that git Eric Portman?'

'Only through your mother's side of the family.'

'*Eric Portman?*'

'Your indignation is understandable but I think there might be slightly more important issues to explore at the moment.'

'Such as why I'm only just hearing this now?'

'It is not an edifying story.'

'If our family is involved, then it wouldn't be.'

'You never knew my father, did you?'

Luke shook his head.

'Well, whenever you are dwelling on my particular shortcomings as a parent, you can console yourself with the thought that things could have been worse. Considerably worse.'

Raymond Parrish paused and looked thoughtful, then rose to his feet and opened the door. For one moment Matthew thought he was about to leave the room completely. Leave Luke and his questions unanswered. What would Luke do then?

'John, do you think you could organise us some coffee, please? Thank you.' He closed the door and sat back down again.

'As you know, Luke, your grandfather founded the firm. From nothing, as he was very fond of telling me. He started small and took on talented people. People he could trust. Acquired this and that – most of it through legitimate means – always building the company. Taking it to new heights. He built it all. There is no doubt he was instrumental in making Parrish Industries what it is today. Yes, I built on his achievement – as I hoped one day that you would build on mine – but without his strong foundations, I would not be where I am today.

'Portman Technology – as it was then – was very much a world leader in many areas at the time, and your grandfather was particularly keen to attach himself to their coat-tails. His reasoning was that, yes, Parrish Industries employed gifted people who had brilliant ideas, but Portman's had the financial clout to back them up.'

'A merger?' enquired Luke, interested despite himself. 'But they hate us – and it's mutual.'

'It hasn't always been so, but no, not a merger. I think my father envisaged Portman and Parrish – equal partners. They, however, wanted a takeover – Portman style – and the removal of the Parrish name completely.'

'Ah.'

'As you can imagine, that wasn't what your grandfather said.

He pointed out – quite eloquently, I thought – that actually the Portmans needed the Parrishes far more than the other way around. Good ideas, he said, would always attract financial interest, whereas without a continual influx of new methods and innovations, a company would, inevitably, fail. Believe me, he was very persuasive.'

The door opened and John entered, bearing a tray.

'Thank you, John. We'll serve ourselves.'

There was a brief moment while cups were filled – by Raymond Parrish himself. Matthew took his back to his corner and waited.

'My father proposed a different sort of merger. The marriage of a female from the house of Portman to a male member of the house of Parrish. I think everyone panicked because he himself was a widower, but it turned out he meant me. And Alexander Portman's granddaughter – Alessandra.'

'And you agreed to this?'

Raymond Parrish stirred his coffee. 'I had no great love in my life. Parrish Industries took most of my waking moments. I had met Alessandra on several highly chaperoned occasions – she was quite lovely. I could find no reason to object. And she was a Portman. I indicated I had no objections and the marriage took place. You were born a year afterwards. It should have been a happy event. My father was delighted – another boy to carry on the line. The Portmans already had several boys born to that generation, so you were less significant to them, but they were pleased, nevertheless.' He stirred his coffee reflectively. 'Although, with hindsight, pleased is the wrong word. "Relieved" might be more accurate.'

Luke hadn't moved. Eventually, he broke his father's gaze,

twisted his cup in the saucer and said, 'Why were they relieved?'

'A successful birth, obviously.'

'Why would it not be? Presumably you could afford the very best care.'

Raymond Parrish hesitated for a moment and then continued. 'A short while before your birth, it had become apparent that Alessandra had some problems. A troubled personality had been successfully concealed from the rest of the world – including my father and me. This had been managed, more or less effectively, with . . . medication . . . but she had, over the years, and completely unknown to everyone outside her family, become almost entirely dependent not only upon them, but upon certain derivatives.'

'You mean,' said Luke, 'living with you drove her to drug addiction.'

His father's voice did not change. 'I mean, Luke, that before our marriage, long-standing problems had been concealed from me by a careful combination of drugs and ensuring Alessa and I were never alone together for too long. A family member was always close by. If I noticed at the time, I thought her family were simply ensuring she was adequately chaperoned. And as I said, she was very beautiful, and in her happier moments, quite enchanting. I was . . . what is the expression used today? . . . yes, smitten.' He put down his cup with a very steady hand. 'Very smitten.

'Unfortunately, her pregnancy meant that she discontinued her meds. I was unaware of this. At that point, I wasn't even aware she had needed them in the first place.

'She was very unwell after your birth. She found it difficult to relate to you. I did my best to protect you. She wasn't violent – I don't think she would ever have deliberately hurt you – but she was very capable of taking you somewhere and forgetting where she had left you. Once it was in a street some three miles away. You were soaking wet but otherwise unharmed.

'Think what you will, Luke, but . . . well. I shielded her as best I could. During her calmer moments, we discussed living together as a family. The Portmans wanted her back. And you as well, Luke. Alessa herself wanted to live with me.'

'And you,' said Luke. 'What did you want?'

Raymond Parrish stared at his hands. 'I wanted my Alessa back.' He cleared his throat. 'With my help, she voluntarily placed herself in a special unit. My father was furious that she would do such a thing – nothing must ever be allowed to dent our perfect family façade – and the Portmans considered my actions as reneging on our deal.

'My father died shortly afterwards and the Portmans insisted on removing Alessa from the care that, I was convinced, was doing her some good. The regime was strict, but not brutal. They imposed firm boundaries which, I think, she found re-assuring and supportive. She accepted both her treatment and her medication, and, in time, I think, would have found a way to live with it. But the stigma was too much – despite my protestations, the Portmans removed her to their own pri-vate establishment. I couldn't argue. They were certainly rich enough to afford the very best for her.

'Matters were complicated by my refusal to divorce her. I suspected the Portmans would attempt to annexe large portions of Parrish Industries – and you – as part of her divorce settle-ment and that could not be allowed to happen.

'Eventually . . . I don't know whether the Portmans put her up to it or whether it was her own idea, but she tried to gain custody of you. My legal people told me she didn't have a chance in hell – not that I would have surrendered you anyway. I had engaged all the appropriate staff – nursemaids, nannies, au pairs – or whatever they call themselves – security guards, the lot. We didn't live here then – we had the house in Bloomsbury, if you remember.

'And then, of course – that night. Alessa had employed some people to get you back. By the greatest good luck, my conference finished early that day and I came straight home, so I was actually in the house when it happened. Whether your mother had been officially backed by the Portmans, I don't know. I suspect not. Any attempt they made would have been much more efficiently carried out, I think. No doubt Ms von Essendorf will have furnished you with all the details she knows – which, for her own protection, isn't much.'

Luke was as white as snow, staring at his father in disbelief.

Matthew, recognising that this was very much how Luke had looked on his medical evac from Site X, got to his feet and stood between them, temporarily removing Luke from his father's sight. 'I think you should stop now.'

Raymond Parrish sighed heavily. 'Yes.'

He got up, touched a panel on the wall, and pulled out a decanter. 'Luke, my boy . . .' He poured him a glass. 'Drink this.'

Luke said hoarsely, 'You can't stop. I have to know everything.'

'There's not much more to tell. I placed you in a school. It wasn't, perhaps, the most nurturing environment in the world, but it was very, very secure. You were safe there.'

'But not happy,' whispered Luke, not looking at him.

'But you were safe.'

'It is possible to be both.'

Raymond Parrish waved that aside. 'That, however, was not the only issue arising out of my unfortunate marriage.' He sat back, observing his son.

With infinite precision, Luke lined up his coffee cup, his glass, and the teaspoon. His hand was not very steady. 'You have been watching me, haven't you?'

'Yes.'

'All these years. Watching and waiting.'

'Yes.'

'And the conclusion that you have come to?'

'I won't deny, Luke, that over the years, you have frequently displayed a certain . . . unsteadiness of purpose that has caused me some concern. You can't deny it. Drink . . . drugs . . . women . . . fast cars . . . long periods of boredom interspersed with life-risking activities. No ambitions, no goals – just a seemingly unending desire to get through life as pleasurably and pointlessly as possible. Yes, there have been times when I wondered whether you had inherited . . .'

He broke off.

'My mother's instability,' said Luke flatly. 'Yes, I can well understand your concern. These years must have been a nightmare for you. Thank heavens you were unselfish enough to keep all this to yourself. It would have been a bit of a tragedy if I'd mistaken your misgivings over my mental state for callous indifference, wouldn't it? Oh – wait.'

He tossed back whatever was in the glass. A little colour returned to his cheeks. 'Well,' he said mockingly. 'Didn't that distract us nicely from the real business of the day – your involvement in Site X. Which has suddenly become much less important. As, no doubt, you intended. Thank you again for yet another lesson from the master.' Raymond Parrish's face hardened. For a moment both father and son looked very like each other.

'Other than the innocent provision of various component parts, Site X was nothing to do with me. Believe or don't believe . . .' He shrugged.

'I don't think I do believe.'

Raymond Parrish shrugged again. 'Then I have nothing more to say.'

'That's it? That's all you've got? Nothing more to say?'

'I've told you a lot more than I wanted to and probably a lot more than I should. I shall leave you to make up your own mind. As I said, I wish you weren't always so quick to believe the worst of me, but if that's the decision you have made . . .'

'It is.'

'Yes, it's always easier to hang on to the security of old prejudices than address frightening new perspectives, isn't it?'

Luke stood up and said formally, 'Thank you for seeing me.'

Raymond Parrish inclined his head. 'How is your hand?'

Luke didn't look at it. 'Almost completely healed. Hardly any loss of function at all.'

'I am very pleased to hear that.'

'Well – goodbye.'

'Goodbye, Luke.'

'We'll see ourselves out.' He pulled open the door and went out without a backward glance.

Raymond Parrish turned to Matthew. 'Officer Farrell.'

116

'Yes, sir.'

'Keep an eye on him, please.'

'I intend to, sir.'

'Thank you. John will see you both out.'

Matthew closed the door behind him.

After his visitors had departed, Raymond Parrish remained seated for quite some time, apparently deep in thought. Eventually he crossed to his desk and opened his com. 'Lucinda?'

'Yes, sir?'

'Could you come in, please?'

Ms Steel entered.

'Is she here?'

'Yes, sir.' She paused. 'You didn't mention . . . ?'

'No, I am not yet ready to give up all my secrets. Ask her to step in, please?'

He was standing by his desk when the door opened and a woman entered, moving quietly but with great assurance. She was of medium height with dark red hair. Seating herself in the visitor's chair that gave her the best view of the door, she waited.

Raymond Parrish stared out of the window. 'Your last employment ended prematurely.'

'It did indeed,' said Lady Amelia Smallhope. 'We were very lucky to escape undetected when the Time Police shut down Site X.'

'That was an unfortunate occurrence.'

'Agreed.'

'Our plans have been considerably derailed.'

'They have.'

'Thank you for saving my son and his colleague.'

'I do feel we might have slightly overstepped our remit, but we assumed Mr Parrish junior's well-being would temporarily assume top priority. And that of his colleague, of course.'

'You assumed correctly and you will find an appropriate remuneration has already been made. However, there is no doubt that the dismantling of Site X has caused us a problem.'

'It is always our duty to overcome the obstacles placed in our path by the unworthy,' stated Lady Amelia. 'As dear Papa always said. Although he was usually referring to the blood-sucking ghouls from HMRC – known affectionately across the country as "those blood-sucking ghouls from HMRC". Followed by detailed and imaginative, but sadly illegal, plans for removing the entire organisation at a stroke.'

Raymond Parrish smiled slightly. 'Had the earl ever required my assistance in that worthy objective, he would only have had to ask.' He thought for a moment and then said, 'I understand you were actually present at Site X when the Time Police arrived. Did you happen to catch sight of . . . ?'

'Yes. We stayed well clear and made no attempt to contact him.'

'Wise. He walks a dangerous line.'

'In a slightly unrelated matter . . .' said Lady Amelia.

'Yes – the purpose of your visit this morning.'

'You will receive Pennyroyal's full report in due course, the gist of which is that the recent attempt on the life of Birgitte von Essendorf was unsuccessful.'

Raymond Parrish went very still. 'You will kindly ensure that does not happen again.'

Lady Amelia continued. 'Steps have already been taken.'

'Discreet steps, I hope. I don't want this coming back to me.'

'Pennyroyal is always discreet. And effective, of course.'

'And yet – a failed attempt?'

'As you said – that will not happen again.'

He nodded. 'Then you have your instructions.'

Matthew, meanwhile, had followed Luke back out into the street. They paused on the pavement. Dusk had fallen while they were inside and lights had gone on all around the square. A chill wind stirred Matthew's hair – still somewhat longer than regulations allowed. He stared up and down the street, genuinely unsure how to proceed next. He wished Jane were here.

Almost as if he could read his thoughts, Luke turned back to him and said brightly, 'I wonder how Jane's getting on? I wouldn't be surprised if she's arrested the entire gang by now and is halfway to yet another commendation. What do you think?'

'Yes,' said Matthew. 'Luke . . .'

Luke rattled on regardless. 'She might even be back at TPHQ already.'

'Probably,' said Matthew, more concerned than ever. 'Luke . . .'

'We should probably be getting back, but do you fancy a drink first?'

Matthew did not consider this to be a good idea at all. 'Not really. Luke . . .'

'Oh, don't worry about the cost. My treat. I haven't said anything and neither did Ms Steel, but for some reason she never shut down my bank account so I still have access.'

'Luke, I don't think . . .'

'Oh, come on. We don't have to be back until tomorrow afternoon. Let's have an exciting evening, shall we?'

'Not a good idea, Luke. Have a drink when we get back, maybe?'

Luke stared at him. 'Are you worried I might be toppling off the rails again? You could be right. Mustn't go showing instability of character in case the old man has me locked away like my mum.'

'I don't think that was quite . . .'

'It's not that late. We could have a meal first, if you like. Eating always makes drinking more respectable. I know a nice little place not too far from here. But I can always go by myself. Drinking alone isn't always a sign of mental instability, is it?'

'Luke . . .'

'What do you reckon? Public clipper or shall I fork out for a water taxi?'

'All right,' said Matthew, making a sudden decision. 'Let's go on somewhere. I know a good place – it's not close by, but the walk will do you good.'

'Where are we going?'

Matthew pointed. 'East.'

Forty minutes later they had arrived.

Luke looked at the narrow lane hemmed in by tall buildings. 'Where the hell are we?'

Matthew pointed to a street sign high up on a building to his right. 'Grit Lane.'

'Why are we here?'

Matthew was looking around. 'It didn't look like this when I lived here. It was a blind alley then. The sun never shone.

Everything was always cold and wet – especially when you don't have any shoes. It stank to high heaven. Raw sewage, rotting food, mouldy straw. It was ankle-deep in summer and frozen hard in winter.'

'A vivid word picture, but why are we here?'

Again, Matthew ignored the question. 'There were tenements all down both sides. Hundreds of people lived in them. Three or four families to one room. The one over there didn't have a roof. The walls were black with soot. The Scropes lived in the ground-floor rooms just over there. Their boys – us – we lived in an old wooden hut just where that trendy wine bar is now. I say hut, but mostly it was a collection of wood thrown together any old how and where old Scrope used to keep his cart at night. It let in the wind, rain, rats, everything. There were three of us. We didn't have much of anything. No one fed us much because climbing boys should be kept small and skinny. No one ever spoke to us because a kick was all the instruction we ever needed. Little Joseph got lost in the chimneys once. We could hear him crying. There was Scrope cursing him and the master of the house shouting at us because the noise was upsetting his wife. He refused to pay us afterwards. Scrope was livid. Joseph was too scared to come out. They had to smoke him out in the end. When we got back, old Ma Scrope grabbed him. We could hear her beating him. He couldn't work for a week afterwards. Even Scrope had to let him off.'

Luke put his hands in his pockets and rocked back on his heels. 'What's your point? Are you trying to tell me my life hasn't been that bad?'

'Yes.'

'You're going to tell me that my dad did his best to keep me safe in the only way he knew how.'

'Yes.'

'You don't know what it was like. What he was like.'

'No.'

'You're saying it was nothing compared with your life.'

Matthew sighed. 'I was rescued. Right out of the blue. One day a group of people swept into our yard. There was a bloke who turned out to be my dad and a team of Time Police officers. I heard words. And shouting. Then my dad kicked the door in and swept me up in his arms—'

He stopped, abruptly.

'Yes?' said Luke. 'And?'

'I was being saved. I was being taken away from the worst life you could imagine, and I bit him. I kicked and struggled. I fought him every inch of the way back to the pod. I didn't want to go.'

'Again – your point?'

'My point is that we always prefer the familiar. No matter how bad it is. I didn't want to leave the only world I knew. I don't know where I thought I was being taken – if I'd thought about it rationally, I'd have realised it couldn't possibly be any worse than the world I was leaving – but I still clung to the world I'd known. Because it was all I had.'

'What are you saying?'

'I'm saying it's the same for you. Your dad was bang on. He said it's always easier to cling to old prejudices than face frightening new perspectives, and he was right. Just saying.'

Apparently having exhausted his word count for the day, Matthew stood looking about him, his eyes very bright. Luke guessed whatever he was seeing and hearing, it wasn't people passing back and forth, greeting each other, pulling out chairs and having a quiet drink after work.

'Do you want to drink here? I mean, will it bother you?'

'Where better?' said Matthew.

'Exorcise a few ghosts? Both of us?'

'Why not?'

'Are you going to answer everything with a question?'

'Would you like me to stop?'

Luke pulled out a chair at one of the outdoor tables, activated the heater and summoned a waiter. Matthew sat down, wondering if the crisis was temporarily averted or whether, by introducing alcohol into the mix, he might not have made things considerably worse. On the other hand, Luke was going to drink, come what may. Better he drank with Matthew, who could at least see him safely home.

Neither he nor Jane were famed for their social skills but he reckoned of them both, Jane would probably be the best one to deal with this. He'd have a word with her as soon as they got back. In the meantime . . .

It was only when he had managed to steer Luke back to TPHQ, very much later, that they discovered Jane had had an eventful evening of her own.

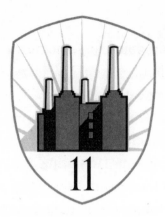

11

Jane was discharged from MedCen two days after the Waltham-stow mission. Matthew turned up to help her get her stuff together while Luke had his final examination, prior to being cleared for full duty.

'Did you really call One-Seven-One a bunch of cock-wombles?'

'I don't know,' said Jane, checking she'd emptied her locker. 'I don't remember very much. It doesn't seem likely, does it? I don't even know what it means.'

Matthew grinned at her. 'Well, not to argue with a sick person, but apparently you do.'

'Oh dear,' said Jane.

Bolshy Jane just laughed.

'Nice flowers,' said Matthew, as she carefully wrapped the wet stems in toilet paper, adding jokingly, 'Do you have an admirer?'

Jane turned her usual shade of sunset.

Matthew pounced. 'You *do* have an admirer. Well done, you. Who is it?'

She kept her back to him.

He grinned. 'Anyone I know? Jane, you might as well tell me because once Luke gets to hear of it, your life will be a misery.'

'Well, Luke's not going to get to hear of it, is he?'

'He is if I tell him.'

Jane turned a tragic eye upon him. The other was still a rich purply bloodshot colour. 'You wouldn't.'

Matthew grinned again.

She sighed. 'It's Grint. He's asked me out for a meal.'

Matthew gaped for a moment and then pointed in the direction he vaguely assumed Grint to be at that particular moment. 'Not . . . ?'

'Yes.'

'Wow. Are you going?'

'Of course not.'

'Why not?'

'Well, I . . . um . . .'

Matthew looked at her shrewdly. 'Jane, have you ever actually had a date before?'

Even more scarlet-faced, Jane shook her head.

'Well, I can understand you not wanting to break your duck with Grint, but he's harmless enough.'

'He calls me a non-man.'

'Only because he likes you. Look at all the grief he took over that business with Mrs Chubb and her fridge. The man blew a hole in the social services ceiling for *you*, Jane.'

This gave Jane something else to worry about. 'Do you think he'll bring his blaster on a date?'

'Of course not,' said Matthew, making a mental note to have a word with someone. North, perhaps. 'Not on a first date, anyway. Trust me, you should go. You'll probably have a very nice time.'

She looked around to check there was no one in sight and lowered her voice. 'But I won't know what to do.'

'That's all right – neither will he. In fact, he'll be the one person in the world who knows even less about dating than you do.' He eyed Jane for a moment and then said very casually, 'A pity he looks so rough.'

Jane found herself quite indignant on her potential date's behalf. 'No, he doesn't. He's not bad-looking. In a blunt-object sort of way.'

'Luke won't like it,' said Matthew, stirring the pot even harder.

'What's it got to do with him? Although you're right – he won't.'

'Hmm,' said Matthew. He stared thoughtfully at Jane for a moment and then said, 'Well, I'm sure you'll have a lovely time. I'll go and see if Luke's finished.'

He wandered away, stationing himself where he was certain to encounter Luke returning from his examination.

'Have you heard?' he said, meeting him at the drinks dispenser. 'Jane's got a date.'

Luke very nearly dropped the coffee he was drinking. 'What? No! A real date?'

'Yes.'

'Well, good for her. Who's the lucky chap?' He paused. 'It is a chap, isn't it?'

Matthew nodded, his eyes bright with mischief in a way that, had he been his mother, would have aroused deep suspicion in her boss, her husband, her colleagues – even people she hadn't met yet.

'Do we know who?'

Matthew took a step backwards in preparation. 'Grint.'

Luke gaped. 'Grint?'

'Yes.'

'*Grint?*'

'Yes.'

'Our Grint?'

'Is there another?'

'Jane?'

'Yes.'

'And Grint?'

'Yes. Have you always experienced difficulties when attempting to assimilate new ideas?'

'Jane is going on a date with Grint?'

'Ah – still not moved on from that. Yes.'

'Why?'

'I expect he asked her.'

'Well, I'm betting she didn't ask him.'

'You never know with Jane.'

'But . . . they can't. She can't . . .'

Matthew regarded him with interest. 'Why not?'

Luke's brow darkened. 'He probably wants to take advantage of her.'

Matthew frowned. 'Are you sure? I mean . . . it's Grint . . .'

Discarding his coffee, Luke strode to Jane's cubicle where she was still waiting to be discharged.

'What's all this crap about you and Grint?'

A grinning Matthew oozed silently out of sight.

Jane blinked in surprise. 'What?'

'Jane, are you out of your mind?'

'No,' she said, defensively.

'You can't possibly consider going out with Grint.'

Much to her surprise, Jane said, 'Yes, I can.'

'Do you know what sort of evening he has planned?'

'Well, I don't think he's going to drag me off to his love nest. It's Grint, for heaven's sake.'

'You don't know that.'

'Yes, I do – he's quite distinctive, you know. And huge. I couldn't possibly mistake him for someone else.'

'No, I mean about the love nest – although I'm betting you wouldn't know a love nest if you found yourself in one.'

'Matthew said . . .'

'Matthew's another one who wouldn't know a love nest.'

'Are you actually trying to tell me I can't go?'

Luke considered for a moment, then drew himself up, a younger Raymond Parrish. 'Yes. Yes, Jane. I am.'

'Well, you can just fire truck off, Parrish – I'm going and if he wants to whirl me off to twenty love nests, then I'm all for it.'

Luke turned on his heel and strode off, nearly colliding with the doctor who had come to discharge Jane.

'Why are you still here, Parrish?'

'I'm not,' he said shortly, pushing his way through the doors.

Around the corner, Matthew grinned again, shoved his hands in his pockets and walked off, whistling.

Lt Grint was not whistling. He was hunched over his scratchpad. Things were proving considerably more difficult than he had anticipated. He had stared at the blank screen for so long that his scratchpad had given up on him and switched itself off.

He scowled fiercely. This should not be so complicated. He had organised entire missions with fewer difficulties than this.

Now there was a thought. The Time Police have procedures for organising everything. There had to be something somewhere. He pulled up the Mission Planning data stack. This was more like it. He had only to follow the instructions.

1. Define the Mission Objective.
2. Identify Possible Threats.
3. Identify Available Resources.
4. Determine Courses of Action/Tactics.
5. Plan for Contingencies and Adjust 4 Accordingly.

He got stuck in.

Point 1. Define the mission objective.

Well, that was easy. Go out for a meal. He typed it in and sat back. Good start.

Point 2. Identify possible threats.

Well – none – obviously. This was a civilian situation. Ambushes, anti-personnel devices, blaster fire, radioactivity, loss of limbs, pod malfunction, death – he was unlikely to encounter any of those. He went to move on and then thought for a moment. Just because this was a civilian situation didn't mean there wouldn't be threats at every turn. Civilian threats – mockery, failure, humiliation, Luke Parrish, bad weather, bad choice of venue, poor food, nothing to talk about, spilling food down his front . . .

A trifle daunted at the number and complexity of these civilian threats, he sat back to think. All right. There was nothing he could do about Luke Parrish. Except shoot him, perhaps. If he was very lucky, an opportunity might occur and he knew any number of people who would swear it had been an accident.

Bad weather was easily dealt with. Umbrella. No – two umbrellas. One each. Grint was aware he took up too much room to share an umbrella successfully. No, as you were – Jane would probably bring her own.

Nor was poor choice of venue a problem. They were going to the same place Team 236 had had their graduation celebration and everyone said how good the food was there.

Grint slowly began to feel he was getting the hang of this. Spilling food down his front was easily handled by avoiding social-death foods like spaghetti bolognaise – the eating of which he always avoided in public.

OK – this was going well.

Point 3. Identify available resources.

After considerable thought, Grint reluctantly decided he should go unarmed. As in, he'd leave his weapons behind. He was well aware that an officer of his size and experience constituted a weapon in himself. Should he ever decide to holiday in a foreign country, it was very possible said foreign country would designate him an invasion force.

Point 4. Determine courses of action/tactics.

Well, rendezvous with Jane successfully, achieve their destination, execute the mission objective and return safely to base. Grint saw no reason why a civilian mission should differ from a non-civilian mission. He ended his list with *No Fatalities* and solemnly underlined it. Or injuries, either. Even Grint was aware that injuring one's partner on the very first date could prove problematic in the securing of a second date. He frowned. The possibilities of a second date were deep waters into which he was not yet ready to venture.

Point 4, however, took care of Point 5. No further adjustments were required. He moved on to list the personnel and equipment required to achieve a successful outcome.

Equipment – he'd covered that with the umbrellas. Money – yes, obviously. Smart outfit – that was easy – he had one. Like many Time Police officers, Grint was uneasy out of uniform. His jacket, shirt and trousers were all black. A colour he was comfortable with. He made a note to check whether anything needed laundering.

OK – venue, food, what to wear – all covered. What else? The answer came from nowhere. Conversation. He would be expected to converse. With Jane. What on earth did women talk about? Books? Yes. He definitely remembered overhearing North discussing a book with someone once. Some research might prove useful. Painstakingly he brought up the library catalogue, clicked on fiction, frowned and made a few careful notes.

Sighing, he eased his back. He seemed to have been at this for hours. He glanced at the clock. He *had* been at this for hours and he still wasn't anywhere near finished. At this point, Lt Grint seriously contemplated volunteering for duty on the night in question and sending a brief message to Jane regretting he was unable to take her out after all.

Gritting his teeth, he moved on. He was a Time Police officer – so was Jane. Theoretically they should have plenty to talk about. Theoretically.

He moved on to list the personnel required. That was easy. Just him and Jane.

He rubbed his eyes. How much longer, for heaven's sake? He had the uneasy feeling that in similar circumstances, Luke Parrish would just fling on the nearest jacket, check he had enough money and sally forth with the female officer of his choice, whereas he, Grint, had spent most of the evening anticipating a whole raft of unfamiliar civilian social protocols and was exhausted. Ignoring the regulations prohibiting personnel from drinking in their rooms – along with all the rest of his fellow officers, it should be said – Grint helped himself to a much-needed beer from the mini chiller under the bed and began to draw up a timetable.

1955 hours – arrive downstairs to rendezvous with Jane.

2000 – Jane arrives.

2002–2005 – greetings.

2006–2012 – make way to venue. Hold on – Jane wasn't yet back to full duties. She would walk more slowly than usual. Grint amended this to 2015. He made another careful note on his action list to reserve a table for that time.

2015 – arrive at venue. Order preliminary drink. Scan menu. Order food. Light conversation. Grint printed out his list of things to talk about and tucked it safely away.

2130 – approximately – finish meal.

2145–2150 – finish drinks. Pay bill. Leave venue.

2200 – return to TPHQ and . . . Grint paused. Vast canyons opened beneath his feet. Return to TPHQ and engage in . . . farewell remarks.

2205 – return to room.

Grint nodded in satisfaction. Sorted.

12

Jane was putting on another possibly illegally obtained item of clothing – her only smart coat. Black, obviously, with a high, soft collar that would keep her warm.

'Do you want me to come with you?' asked Luke, standing in the open doorway to her room.

She turned from the mirror. 'What? Why?'

'Well, you know . . .'

'No, I don't.'

'I just thought you might . . . you know.'

'Again, no, I don't. And if I did want anyone, why would it be you?'

'Who better?'

'Nearly anyone, I would have thought.'

'Where are you meeting him?'

'I'm not telling you that.'

'What time?'

'I'm not telling you that, either.'

'Where are you going?'

'I'm definitely not telling you that. Could you step aside, please.'

'Jane, I don't know what's got into you. You'd never have behaved like this six months ago.'

'Six months ago, I'd never have told you to fire truck off, Parrish, but I'm telling you now.'

He raised his hands in surrender. 'All right, all right, don't zap me. That's a point. Have you got your sonic with you?'

'Why would I need a sonic?'

'You know, just in case.'

'What the hell sort of dates do you go on?'

Luke grinned.

'You're disgusting. I'm going now.'

And off she went.


A washed and burnished Lt Grint had arrived nearly ten minutes early and had spent the greater part of that time pacing the atrium, oblivious to the grins and nudges of his on-duty colleagues.

At exactly 1955 hours, the lift doors opened, and with some relief, he saw Jane walking towards him. The same relief was felt by Jane when the lift doors opened and she saw Lt Grint standing exactly where he should be.

Grint smiled. 'Hello . . .' He stopped, unsure how to proceed. What did he call her? *Lockland* seemed . . . wrong. *Jane* seemed . . . not quite right. He dealt with the problem by not calling her anything at all.

'Hello,' said Jane, prey to exactly the same indecision. *Sir* seemed too formal. *Lieutenant* seemed . . . not quite right. *Gordon* was . . . unthinkable. She decided she wouldn't call him anything at all.

'Shall we go?' he said and she nodded. They walked slowly

along the embankment towards the Flying Duck public house which, rumour had it, had been there longer than TPHQ itself.

The evening was quite chilly. Jane was well wrapped up in her smart coat and pashmina. Grint remembered his list of things to say and the order in which to say them. 'You look very nice.'

'Thank you,' said Jane, wondering how on earth to reciprocate. Grint out of his uniform looked very similar to Grint in his uniform.

They turned left, away from the river. The restaurant was a little further down the road, just opposite Battersea Park.

'I've been here before,' said Jane, to break the silence. 'We had a team meal here after we qualified.'

'Yes,' said Grint.

With mounting panic, Jane realised her repertoire of small talk was now completely exhausted and they hadn't even sat down yet.

The restaurant was warm inside. Delicious smells wafted their way. The red and white gingham tablecloths reminded Jane a little of the kitchen in Walthamstow, but other than that, everything was quiet and comfortable.

Their waiter was very young. A student, possibly. Grint glowered at the wastrel.

Until this moment, Jane hadn't given much thought to her personal appearance. Or rather, she'd lingered over her choice of attire and been careful with her hair, but she had entirely forgotten her face. Her bruises were at the yellow and brown stage. Not nearly as spectacular as the purple and red of last week, but certainly eye-catching. All conversation in the restaurant ceased. Everyone looked at Jane and then, as if on a string, all eyes swivelled to Grint. Their waiter, about to show them to their table, paused.

'I have a table booked,' said Grint, seemingly unaware.

All eyes swivelled back to Jane.

'Oh,' said Jane, suddenly comprehending and touching her face. 'No. No, it wasn't him.'

Realisation hit Grint harder than an unexpected tax bill. He swelled with indignation – not a particularly reassuring sight to those at the nearer tables.

Their waiter ushered them to a quiet table in the corner, mostly obscured from public view. Only half the tables were occupied at this early hour. Jane was almost certain this hadn't been their original table, but it was now. Still, at least they weren't next to the toilets.

The waiter hovered, awaiting their drinks order. Jane was still fairly unaccustomed to wine in the evening – or indeed at any hour – but she hoped a glass would help her get through what promised to be an even more awkward than anticipated evening. I shouldn't have come, she thought, smiling timidly at the unsmiling Grint across the table.

Grint also was in unfamiliar territory. He was aware of the existence of wine – girls drank it. He himself was a beer man, but Jane, obviously more sophisticated than he had given her credit for, was drinking wine, therefore, so should he. Perhaps a nice glass or two would help him get through the evening.

He took surreptitious stock of his surroundings. Main entrance to his right – about twenty feet away. Two empty tables between him and any hostiles erupting through the door. Toilet door to his left. Unisex by the looks of it. He'd check it for windows and other methods of clandestine entry at the first opportunity. Kitchen door also to his left – full of civilians with knives. Stay alert. Approximately ten people in the room, excluding staff. Average age around forty. No one appeared to be armed. Two waitresses. One waiter. Average age twelve. Students, all of them. In the event of any trouble, take them out first.

Having performed his risk assessment, he became aware of the silence. More conversation was obviously called for. Comment positively on the surroundings. 'This is very nice,' he said, looking around.

Jane nodded. 'Have you been here before?'

'No, this is my first visit. I hear good reports, though.'

More silence fell. Grint was conscious of unease. This was not going well. Under cover of the table, he surreptitiously consulted his list and selected a subject more or less at random. Without looking up, and much more loudly than he had intended, he demanded, 'Do you like kittens?'

The waiter, who had chosen that moment to lean across Jane to fill her water glass, was rather startled to be included in this bizarre couple's conversation and was slightly thrown. 'Oh. Er. Yes,' he said. 'Do you?'

Jane concentrated hard on the checked tablecloth. Grint stared across the room. The waiter withdrew, advised his two colleagues to keep an eye on Table Three and began to gird himself for a return trip with the menus.

'I . . . um . . . sorry . . . I made a list of things to talk about,' mumbled Grint. 'And a timetable.'

'What an excellent idea,' said Jane swiftly, forgetting her own embarrassment in her efforts to ease his. 'I wish I'd thought to do the same. I do like to plan ahead, don't you? Um, if that's what you were doing under the table, then you can take it out. I really don't mind.'

The waiter, arriving for the tail end of this exchange and considerably intrigued as to what they could possibly be talking about, presented the menus as slowly as he could manage.

Grint rummaged subterraneanly for a few moments, eventually producing a much-crumpled piece of paper.

The waiter sighed slightly, a disappointed man.

'So,' said Jane, sipping her wine for courage and comfort. 'What's next on the list?'

'Books,' said Grint, very aware he wouldn't be doing the heavy lifting with this one. Unless Jane was also a subscriber to *Bombs and Blasters*, of course. He cleared his throat. 'What are you reading at the moment?'

'Well, at the moment I'm reading *Wuthering Heights*. For about the twentieth time,' said Jane, slightly conscious of letting the side down and considering it unlikely Grint was familiar with Emily Brontë's classic work.

It was to be an evening of surprises. For both of them.

Grint frowned. 'Is that the one where everyone lives in the kitchen and shouts at each other across the moors?'

'That's it, yes. Have you read it too?'

Even the waiter looked impressed.

'Did it at school,' Grint said quickly, before anyone could begin to suspect him of unnecessary literacy. 'Everyone hates everyone else, right? I don't know why they didn't just call it a day and come in out of the rain.'

'I never thought of that,' said Jane, fascinated by this fresh insight.

'And,' he said, warming to his theme, 'I'd have caved in

Heathcliff's head with a saucepan, chucked his body in a bog and claimed he'd gone off on his travels again, wouldn't you?'

'Well, I hadn't actually considered it until this moment, but now you come to mention it – what a good idea.'

Grint nodded. 'Would have been a shorter book, too.' It was obvious this would have been a powerful point in the book's favour.

The waiter considered coughing gently to indicate he was awaiting their order and decided against it.

Jane was thoughtful. 'Wouldn't the bog have preserved his body, though? It does, you know. They're always finding pre-historic people in bogs. And it could have floated to the surface at any time. I don't think a bog is necessarily the best place to hide the person you've just murdered.'

'What about setting fire to it?' suggested Grint. 'I'll have the steak, please. Rare.'

'I don't think it would ever have stopped raining long enough for them to get a good fire going. Quicklime, perhaps? Um . . . tuna for me, please.'

The waiter nodded. 'Actually, in some circumstances, quick-lime can actually *preserve* the body.'

They looked at him.

'Reading chemistry at uni.' He gestured around. 'Student loans. You'd be better off with lye. If you can heat it, a lye solution can liquify a body in about three hours. Job done.'

'Useful,' said Grint, tucking this titbit away for future ref-erence.

The waiter departed. 'What a nice boy,' said Jane.

Grint, who hadn't noticed, nodded.

'Well,' said Jane. 'Now that we've gruesomely murdered one

of the most romantic heroes of his age – and learned something in the process – what's next on your list?'

Grint smoothed the paper. 'Pets.'

'Never had one,' said Jane sadly. 'You?'

'I had a cat when I was a kid,' said Grint. 'My mum was frightened of dogs.'

'Oh,' said Jane, suddenly realising she had learned two things about Grint in one sentence. Three, if you included the fact he'd actually had a mother. 'What was his name?'

'Clawed,' said Grint and spelled it out for her in case she hadn't got the joke.

'Clever,' said Jane. 'And did he? Claw, I mean.'

'She. And yes. She was a big fat lazy thing. She'd sleep on my face at night and I'd have nightmares and wake up thinking I was suffocating.'

'O . . . K,' said Jane.

Grint was conscious of some alarm. They seemed to have covered pets in just half a minute. His list wasn't going to last long at this rate. Fortunately, Jane had more to say on the subject.

'I wish I'd had a pet when I was young. The nearest I ever had was a taxidermied seagull. It used to terrify me.'

'Um . . .' said Grint. 'Surely it was . . . you know . . . dead. Wasn't it?'

'Oh yes,' said Jane, quickly. 'I know that now, but it was in a glass case and every time I passed it, I was convinced it was watching me, and my gran used to say if I wasn't good then she'd send it into my bedroom at night to bite me while I slept. Sometimes I would get up in the middle of the night and stand on the stairs. Just to check it was still there. In its case, I mean.' She laughed, nervously. 'It always was.'

140

'Right,' said Grint, who had always felt that the rules and regs pertaining to the shooting of civilians – whether such actions were necessary or not – were a considerable hindrance to him in the conscientious execution of his duties.

'But – that's how I came to join the Time Police. I dropped it. The seagull, I mean. And its head came off.'

'Yes?' said Grint cautiously, not seeing the connection.

'Oh, I was so scared that I ran away to join the Time Police.'

He was still thinking that one over when Jane enquired what was next on the list.

'Fashion,' he said, gloomily.

Their food arrived. Jane picked up her napkin and grinned at him. 'Off you go, then.'

He surveyed her outfit. 'Er . . . I see black is very fashionable this year.'

Emboldened by the arrival of her excellent food, Jane decided he could probably handle a little gentle mockery. 'Nice try, but black is fashionable every year.' She gestured at his own clothes. Both of them had stuck to a colour they were comfortable with.

'Well, it doesn't show the dirt,' he said, looking down at himself.

'Or tomato sauce. That's why I went for the tuna.'

Grint panicked. 'You don't like pasta? Do you want to go somewhere else? Only someone said this place is very good.'

About to lay Grint's steak in front of him, the waiter paused, looking from one to the other.

Jane made haste to reassure everyone. 'Oh, it is. It's just – well, promise you won't laugh.'

Grint, never famed for spontaneous merriment, solemnly promised he wouldn't laugh.

'Well, I'm just such a messy eater. Especially spaghetti. The sauce goes everywhere. You should be grateful. You could be going back to HQ covered from head to foot in tomato sauce. That's why I'm having the fish.'

Grint beamed at her. 'That's why I'm having the steak. For exactly the same reason.'

The waiter heaved an audible sigh of relief, plonked down Grint's steak and, unable to think of a reason to remain, departed.

Jane nodded. 'Very wise – you can't go wrong with steak.'

There was a pause. Grint wracked his brains. 'So how are you feeling now . . . ?' He baulked again at referring to her by name, rank or gender. Still best not to call her anything at all. 'Are you almost recovered?'

'Yes, thank you. My bruises have nearly faded. I'm still a little stiff and I can't walk very quickly – as you saw on the way here – but I'm back to full duties next week.'

There was another pause.

'This is very nice,' said Jane, looking around. 'Do you come here often?' And could have kicked herself.

Grint shook his head. 'Don't go out much.'

The words *and never with a date* hung in the air.

'I mean,' he continued, cutting into his steak, 'I'm usually busy. You know – there's a lot on these days – and if I want a bit of company I go to the bar or . . . you know.'

Jane watched him eat, seemingly completely unaware those few sentences had revealed a whole sad world of solitary loneliness.

'Well, this is very pleasant,' she said. 'I'm so glad you

asked me. And I'm really looking forward to seeing the dessert menu. I mean, the food at TPHQ is fine, but they don't really do desserts, do they? Not properly, I mean.'

'I suspect,' said Grint, 'that most Time Police officers find the thought of anything with whipped cream to be slightly effeminate.'

Jane laughed.

Grint, who'd never made a female laugh before – not for the right reasons, anyway – looked up in surprise. She smiled at him. He smiled back.

The rest of the meal went quite well. Their waiter was attentive and in a moment of giddy recklessness by all parties, more wine was poured. They even ordered dessert.

'With lots of cream,' said Jane, firmly.

And then coffee. Their meal was over.

The waiter appeared with the bill and hesitated between them.

'Thank you,' said Grint.

Jane opened her mouth to say she'd pay for herself. The waiter, standing strategically behind Grint's chair, caught her eye and shook his head slightly.

'Well,' said Jane. 'That was the nicest meal I've had for a long time. Thank you very much. I'll leave the tip, if you like. I think our waiter deserves a good one because now we know how to dispose of a body quickly and cleanly, and you never know when that sort of knowledge will come in useful.'

A moment later and they were outside in the cold night air. They walked slowly back along the river, mostly in silence but not awkwardly so.

'Actually . . .' said Jane, stopping by a bench. 'I'm feeling a little . . .'

'Yes, of course,' he said. 'Sorry. You should have said.'

'Only for a minute,' she said, sitting down. 'And the lights are so pretty.'

And they were. Stretching away into the distance, every tree in the avenue along the embankment was festooned with golden lights. As if the river were imprisoned between giant golden chains.

'A couple of years ago,' said Grint, 'before you joined up, the lights were all blue. It was quite a sight.'

'I can't imagine anything more beautiful than this. Everything is smothered in gold. I wonder what it looks like from the air.'

'I've seen it,' said Grint. 'The river is like a black path. A ribbon of darkness threading its way through a golden city.' He stopped, embarrassed. 'Well, that's what I thought, anyway.'

'Lucky you to have seen it.' She shivered. 'It's chilly in the evenings now. Winter is on its way.'

Grint was vaguely aware that here was an opportunity to move a little closer to Jane and put his arm around her. It occurred to him he'd once led a hugely outnumbered charge against a group of armed illegals hiding out in the Carpathians with more confidence than he was feeling at the moment. He bottled it. 'We should be moving. You don't want to catch cold.'

Jane nodded and they resumed their slow stroll.

'Um,' said Grint, aware of yet another social problem looming. 'I was wondering. When we get back – do you want to go in separately?'

Jane stopped in surprise. 'Why would I want to do that? Do you?'

'No.'

'OK then.' Daringly she held out her arm to him.

He stared as if he'd never seen an arm before and then took it. They walked very slowly back along the bank, occasionally pointing out a river police launch racing past or a party boat, bright with lights and music. It was very possible that neither were in much of a rush to return home.

The outside of TPHQ looked as if a small war had been fought there. Which, actually, it had. Much of the front of the building was still boarded up and the area pitted with craters. Giant scorch marks decorated everything. A few sad stumps of former trees were all that was left of Commander Hay's pleasure gardens.

'They're starting on the repairs next week,' said Grint. 'Too embarrassing to have people know how vulnerable we were.'

Only one of the front doors was still unlocked – for the benefit of those suffering an out-of-hours temporal crisis, pre-sumably – and they made their way inside. Considering the atrium was usually almost deserted at this time of night, Jane was astonished at the number of officers who had found a reason to be around that evening. Normally only a few guards would be on duty, wandering slowly around, peering at screens and complaining about how quiet everything was.

Tonight, for some reason, there were officers everywhere. Talking in groups, studying notice boards, admiring the remains of the indoor gardens and not venturing too close to the koi carp. They couldn't all be on duty, surely. Many of them were in civilian clothes. It was all very puzzling.

Everyone looked up as they entered. All talk ceased. People grinned at them. Grint glared. It made very little difference.

He and Jane crossed the atrium together, their footsteps very loud in the silence, and presented themselves to the nearest officer who opened his mouth to comment. Over Jane's head, Grint stared stonily at him and somehow the remark the officer had been about to make – something witty that he'd spent all evening waiting to say – dwindled into the perfectly innocuous, 'What's the weather doing out there?'

'Chilly,' said Grint, holding his eye, and if Jane wanted to assume he was talking about the weather, then that was fine by him.

The officer checked over their IDs and they took the left-hand lift to Jane's floor. Grint's room was on the one above hers.

Their ordeal was not yet over.

The lift doors opened to reveal Luke Parrish inspecting a notice board as if he'd never seen it before. Which was perfectly possible.

Grint scowled. 'What's he doing here?'

'Well,' said Jane in her clearest voice – who would have thought school elocution lessons would ever have made themselves useful? 'I think Officer Parrish is attempting, very unsuccessfully, to replicate the actions of a conscientious and likeable member of the Time Police.'

Luke turned around and executed an admirably realistic start of surprise. 'Good heavens. Back already? Does this mean the whole thing was a massive catastrophe?'

'*Au contraire*,' said Jane – her school's French lessons – ditto. 'A very pleasant evening.' She turned to Grint and held out her hand. 'Thank you for a lovely meal.'

He took it very carefully as if concerned he might inadvertently wrench off a couple of her fingers. 'Did you . . . um . . . enjoy . . . ?'

Jane turned every known shade of scarlet. 'I did. Did you . . . um . . . ?'

He nodded.

Luke made no attempt to tactfully disappear.

'If we do this again,' said Jane, incandescent at the thought of being so publicly promiscuous, 'you must allow me to treat *you.*'

Grint found his words. 'That would be very nice. Goodnight . . . er . . .'

'Goodnight . . . um . . .'

Luke watched the lift doors close behind Lt Grint and then turned eagerly to Jane. 'So, Jane – how did it really go? Tell the truth, now.'

'Oh, it was great. I had a lovely time. Good food, good wine, good conversation . . .'

'Good conversation? What on earth did you talk about?'

'Well, I think the most useful thing I took away from the evening – and given who I'm talking to – was how to dispose of a body successfully in less than three hours.'

'What?'

'And literature.'

Luke's face registered complete and utter disbelief. 'Lit . . .'

'Yes, you know – those things you can read? Books?'

'What sort of books?'

'The classics, mostly. It was good. He had some interesting insights.'

'Jane, you idiot. You picked up the wrong bloke. You were supposed to go out with Grint.'

'Fire truck off, Parrish.'

He was saved from premature extinction by the appearance

147

of Matthew, rounding the corner, his hands in his pockets, whistling. Catching sight of Jane, he executed a lamentably unrealistic start of surprise and grinned at her.

Jane scowled impartially at the pair of them, stomped down the corridor and slammed the door into her room.

Matthew stopped in front of Luke and said nothing in his own particular way, merely switching his grin to full beam.

Luke scowled ferociously.

Holding Luke's gaze, Matthew wandered off down the corridor and back to his own room. Like the Cheshire cat, his grin was the very last thing to disappear.

Grint and Jane's date was the hot topic of the day. Speculation as to how things had gone was rife and imaginative, permeating every level of the Time Police. Even Commander Hay and Captain Farenden were not immune.

'So,' said Hay, sitting back in her chair and sipping her coffee the next morning. 'Grint and Lockland?'

'Astonishingly, ma'am – yes.'

'Do we know how it went?'

'Well, I do, ma'am.'

There was a pause.

'Are you going to make your commanding officer beg?'

'My duty is, as always, to clear away all obstacles and smooth the path of my commanding officer's working day.'

'Then don't just sit there, Charlie, smooth.'

'My sources inform me Lt Grint and Officer Lockland walked to the Italian restaurant round the corner. The one next to the Flying Duck. He had the steak – she had the fish. There was a certain amount of initial blushing and awkwardness, but contrary to expectations, they managed to converse pleasantly throughout the meal. After their meal – for which Lt Grint paid – they took a short walk along the embankment. Returning to TPHQ, they parted on Officer Lockland's floor and a tentative second date was mooted.'

Commander Hay regarded her adjutant with unbridled admiration. 'Outstanding intel, Charlie, even for you.'

'I accept your praise with becoming modesty, ma'am.'

'So, basically, no one died.'

'Er . . . no, ma'am.'

'At no point did Lt Grint discharge his weapon?'

'No, but I don't believe he had found it necessary to arm himself for the occasion.'

'A successful evening, then?'

Captain Farenden blinked.

'What, Charlie?'

'Well, nothing, ma'am. It's just that I couldn't help reflecting that your criteria for a successful romantic rendezvous seems to be that no weapons were discharged and no one died.'

'Anything wrong with that?'

'Absolutely not, ma'am.'

13

'Major Callen is here, ma'am,' announced Captain Farenden over her intercom the next morning. 'For your monthly meeting.'

Commander Hay looked up from the file she was reading. 'Ask him to come in, please.'

'No need,' said a voice at the door. 'I am already in.'

They regarded each other in silence for a moment. Major Callen stood waiting, several files under his arm and wearing what an unkind person would definitely describe as a mocking smile. His greying blond hair was cut short, his cold blue eyes creased at the corners and he was known throughout the entire organisation as a good officer but a bit of a sarky bugger. Other than that, no one knew much about him. He kept himself to himself.

Hay pulled the first of her files towards her. 'Sit down, Major. Shall we begin?'

He looked over his shoulder. 'Actually, I was waiting for your chaperone to join us. And here he is. Good morning, Captain.'

Captain Farenden ignored this remark, seated himself at the foot of the briefing table and pulled out his scratchpad.

Callen raised his eyebrows.

Hay shrugged. 'Most of my meetings are minuted, Major.'

'Nice bit of alliteration.'

'Do you have something to say about being recorded, Major?'

He smiled. 'So much, Commander, but since I suspect no second in command has ever had less access to his commanding officer than I do, I shan't waste this rare opportunity for face-to-face communication.'

'You find this situation amusing?'

'Far from it, but I am becoming reconciled to your hostility.'

'Any hostility is in your own mind, Major.'

'Commander, two of my people were murdered, and not only did you fail to inform me of that fact, but you also failed to mention you had seen fit to replace them without any consultation with me. I am not convinced these are the actions of a commanding officer who has complete confidence in her second in command.'

'And I'm not convinced your first loyalties are to the Time Police.'

'Since I have no idea how to convince you otherwise, I shan't even try.' He glanced over at Captain Farenden. 'Are you ready? Shall we begin?' He looked across the table to Hay. 'Actually, I have only one item of any real interest – the rest is routine stuff you can safely ignore until our next monthly meeting.'

'I don't think so. A full report, please, Major.'

'As you wish, Commander.' He passed over a file. 'Here are my department's deployments as at close of play yesterday. Unless, of course, you know differently, which is very possible. I've highlighted any changes, but as you can see, very little has altered since our last meeting.

'My budget figures . . .' he passed over a data stick, 'show a small overspend on equipment, but figures for the remaining year should be lower than average, meaning we will probably reach the end of this financial period slightly under budget.

'Two of my officers are currently in MedCen. Faulkner broke his arm in a training session and Keeley is having his appendix removed.' He glanced at his watch. 'As we speak.'

He closed his folder. 'That's it. Makes you wonder how people manage to make their meetings last all morning, doesn't it? Really, you know, I could just flash all this to your scratchpad and we need never meet at all.'

She ignored this. 'My best wishes to Faulkner and Keeley for speedy recoveries. What was the interesting item to which you referred earlier?'

'Ah, yes. I'm not sure what you'll make of this. Or whether there is anything to be made . . . I had five teams out last week – pursuing various unrelated illegals in various Times – and three of them came back reporting the illegals were already dead when they caught up with them.'

Hay frowned. 'Murdered by their own people?'

'Two of them were thought to be operating on their own so probably not. You're not asking the right question, Commander.'

'The correct question being?'

'How did they die?'

'Murdered, you said.'

'No, I said they were dead when my people caught up with them. Of the same cause.' He leaned forwards. 'They'd all had their right arms blown off.'

'All three of them?'

152

'Yes. Three identical wounds.'

'But separate incidents?'

'Yes. All unconnected, as far as we can see.'

'But obviously connected in some way we can't see.'

'Not yet.'

'Were the bodies brought back?'

'Yes. MedCen are examining them now. Would you care to indulge in a little playful speculation, Commander, or shall I just retreat to my lair until the time of our next meeting?'

She ignored this as well.

'Charlie, what's the time?'

Captain Farenden consulted his watch. 'Ten past ten, ma'am.'

'Major?'

'Well done, Commander – you got it more quickly than I did.'

'You're left-handed, Major.'

'Yes, but I wear my watch on my left wrist, just like everyone else.'

Captain Farenden frowned. 'But it was their right arms, ma'am. What has that to do with watches?'

She smiled thinly. 'Let's not deprive the major of his moment of glory.'

'Thank you, Commander – I will admit job satisfaction is seldom and insufficient these days so I must seize every opportunity to brighten my working day. Bracelets, Captain. My unfounded suspicion is that someone out there is producing a portable Time-travelling device that can be worn as a bracelet or cuff.'

'I'm assuming they do work at least once since these illegals were all found at different points in the Timeline.'

'They were, Commander. I had considered the possibility they are single-use devices. They get the . . . shall we say, victims, safely to their chosen destination, but they don't get them back again. Thus conveniently eliminating any possible future inconveniences.'

'An interesting thought. I feel sure you are waiting for me to instruct you to put all available people on this so that you can complacently inform me you've been all over it for the past week.'

Callen got to his feet. 'How well you think you know me, Marietta. Captain.'

He nodded to Farenden and left the room.

Commander Hay sighed. 'Why must he always make himself so unpleasant?'

They say the onlooker sees most of the game. Captain Farenden, from his position as onlooker, had a very good idea what motivated Major Callen, but kept his face very carefully blank. 'No idea, ma'am.'

Meanwhile, Team Weird were striding along the corridor on their way to their new office.

'Can anyone hear rattling?' enquired Matthew, innocently.

Luke sighed. 'I told you. We're qualified officers. We can go fully armed.'

'We can, but most don't,' said Matthew. 'You look like a weapon enthusiast's Christmas tree. Isn't all that a bit heavy? And how do you sit down?'

'I could discharge something all over you,' said Luke, shortly. 'That would lighten the load.'

Matthew fanned the air. 'I can hardly breathe for testosterone.'

There was a short scuffle.

Jane sighed. Boys and their toys. 'Here we are.'

They filed inside, bright, excited and all ready to receive their first proper assignment as a qualified team. Office still seemed rather a grand name for this tiny room but it was large enough for a data table and four chairs – because the usual Time Police team consisted of four individuals.

'We need posters,' said Luke, looking around at the bare walls. 'I'll have a big red sportscar with an attractive woman sprawled across it. Matthew can have the Time Map specs and Jane can have a kitten.'

'Books,' said Jane, looking around at the bare walls. 'We need to scrounge a bookcase from somewhere.'

'And shelves for mugs and things,' said Matthew, looking around at the bare walls. 'And our own supplies of coffee and sugar. And biscuits. And chocolate. All our favourite snacks, anyway.'

'Right, that's the interior design sorted,' said Luke. 'What's next?'

'Actually, I think we're supposed to put up the fire regs and evacuation instructions, team rotas, pod availability schedules, standing orders and all sorts of other stuff,' said Jane.

'And we will,' said Luke soothingly. 'If there's enough room after we've put up our own stuff.'

Their scratchpads bleeped simultaneously.

There was a moment's paralysed excitement and then . . .

'We've got one,' shouted Luke.

'Our first proper mission,' said Jane, her face alight. 'What is it? You tell us, Luke. What have we got?'

'Bloody hell,' said Luke, tapping at his scratchpad.

'What? What?'

Luke looked up, an expression of horror on his face. 'Henry Plimpton. Again.'

'Well,' said Matthew. 'I suppose that's quite appropriate, really.'

Henry Plimpton had been their first ever trainee assignment. As Ellis had said afterwards when they'd all got their breath back, the most impressive thing about that mission had been the number and variety of mistakes Team 236 had managed to commit during what had been a very simple assignment.

Team 236 were, however, very fond of Henry in a strange sort of way. And yes, all right, the mission hadn't gone completely according to plan, but they'd got there in the end, and, as Luke had said after a couple of stiff drinks and a thorough shower to remove any lingering traces of the 20th century, you never forgot your first, did you?

Unlikely as it seemed, Henry Plimpton – short, plump, mild-mannered, 20th-century Henry Plimpton – had indulged in a spot of illegal Time travel for the purpose of cheating the public lottery. Team Weird had tracked him down – not much tracking required because he was sitting quietly at home at the time – and despite their ineptitude, they had managed to overcome his wife, his children, his dogs, his neighbours and eventually the man himself.

'Although not,' said Luke significantly, 'until after an epic chase through some of the grimier aspects of the 20th century.' Of which there had been many – edge-to-edge dog poo, feral children, a world slowly drowning in plastic, policemen buried under the road, appalling taste in music – and they'd only been there a few hours.

But, typically Team Weird, they'd got there in the end, by which time they'd become quite friendly with the family – scones and cake had helped – and eventually Henry, after a short visit to TPHQ to give his statement, had been allowed to return to the bosom of his ever-noisy family. Which, as Luke had said, was punishment enough for offences far greater than Henry's.

This unexpectedly generous action on the part of the Time Police had been justified by Henry's willingness to cooperate, together with the understanding that he would be strictly monitored in future – something which hadn't seemed to bother him in the slightest. Three such monitoring visits had taken place – carried out by other teams who probably hadn't had very much to do at that time, and a member of security. However, now that Team Weird was qualified, it seemed likely that monitoring him would fall permanently to them in future. Jane was quietly pleased nothing horrible had happened to *la famille Plimpton*, but Luke was appalled.

'Again?' he demanded. 'Is this some sort of punishment? Did we not suffer enough the first time? I hate the whole 20th century. It's dirty, disease-ridden, dreary, dismal, depressing and any other words you can think of beginning with d. Bloody Time Police – we've confounded everyone by surviving our training. Then we confounded them again by actually being awarded medals and commendations and things, and this is their revenge. They're trying to kill us by using the 20th century as their murder weapon. This is the end of Team Weird. We'll never survive a second time.'

He collapsed face down on to the table.

'Dramatic,' said Matthew, admiringly.

'Another word beginning with d,' said Jane, nodding.

'And dickhead,' said Matthew.

'I think you mean delightful,' said Luke, sitting up.

Other words to describe their forthcoming mission would also include devastation, destruction, disaster and death, but that was all to come.

They went armed, of course. They certainly weren't expecting any trouble from Henry – indeed, Matthew was rather hoping for tea, cake and scones again; Henry and his family did not stint themselves when it came to mid-afternoon snacks – but Team 236 was fully qualified now and Luke was determined to bear arms at every conceivable opportunity. Even, rumour had it, to go to the bathroom.

Team 236 assembled outside their pod.

Pods are the method by which the Time Police travel up and down the Timeline, righting wrongs and generally being the good guys. Not that they were bothered about being the good guys. Unlike St Mary's Institute for Historical Research – whose pods were carefully designed to blend discreetly into the background – the Time Police didn't do discreet. Or even background. These were sinister boxes of varying sizes whose main purpose was to add shock and awe to whatever catastrophe was occurring at the time. Remedying the situation was generally felt to be of secondary importance. The main thing was that everyone now knew the Time Police had arrived and things would deteriorate accordingly.

The interior consisted of a console, a row of chairs bolted to the floor and a couple of lockers. Again, unlike the St Mary's pods, there was no bathroom because, the Time Police said, they weren't girls. Well, yes, all right, some of them were but mostly they weren't. Presumably officers relieved themselves against rocks, trees, or around the back of the pod. A small shovel was provided for those special occasions.

Again, because they weren't St Mary's, the insides were bleak and cheerless – a bit like the Time Police themselves, said Luke Parrish – and usually smelled pleasantly of woodland pine.

It was nice to be back with her own team, thought Jane, seating herself at the console and busying herself with the familiar start-up procedures – power levels, coordinates, equipment status and so on. She began to work her way across the board, taking comfort in the familiar routine.

Matthew busied himself stowing their gear and Luke, as usual, stood in the middle of the pod and told them both what to do.

'All set,' reported Jane, eventually. 'Greens across the board. Ready whenever you say.'

'Let's go.'

'Pod – commence jump procedures.'

The AI responded pleasantly. 'Jump procedures commenced.'

The world flickered.

'Well,' said Jane brightly, as she began to shut things down. 'Here we are again.'

Luke groaned. 'I can already feel the plague rats gathering.'

'No, you can't,' said Jane. 'Stop being such a baby.'

'I am an officer of the Time Police,' said Luke with dignity. 'I am not a baby.'

'In that case you can interrogate the AI.'

'I am the team leader,' he said with even more dignity. 'I do not interact with AIs.'

'Well, someone has to,' she said. 'And protocol says it's the team leader.'

'Don't see why,' muttered Luke. 'It's not as if it ever says anything useful.'

On this occasion, however, he was wrong.

Jane shook her head and addressed the AI. 'Pod . . .'

She got no further.

'Warning.'

'What?' said Jane, startled.

'Warning.'

'What?' said Luke.

There was the very faintest hint of impatience in the AI's measured tone. 'Warning.'

'What does that even mean?' said Luke.

'I am endeavouring to convey a warning.'

'We're still inside the pod, you moron. About what are you endeavouring to convey a warning?'

'The parameters of that query are too broad to compute. Please review your query and rephrase.'

'What is the nature of your warning?'

'An event has occurred.'

'What sort of event?'

'I am endeavouring to ascertain. My sensors are relaying contradictory data. An event has occurred. Comparisons of present readings against the readings from your original jump reveal many discrepancies.'

'What sort of discrepancies?'

'The data is overwhelming me and I am unable to supply specifics at this time. My recommendation is to wait while I assimilate the data.'

'Forget it,' said Luke. 'I'm not hanging around here a second longer than is necessary.'

'In that case, my recommendation is to proceed with caution.'

'Yes,' said Luke sarcastically, 'because we always plunge blindly out of the door without checking conditions first.'

'I can supply details of air composition . . .'

'Shut up.'

'. . . levels of contamination and . . .'

'Shut up.'

'. . . pollution, together with . . .'

'Is there *any* way of shutting you up?'

'An appropriate adjustment to my power levels would . . .'

'Shut up. Just shut up. Don't say another word. I mean it.'

Unusually, the AI, famed for having the last word, especially where Officer Parrish was concerned, remained silent.

Luke turned to the console. 'Jane – what have you got?'

'We've landed close to our original site. Activating the cameras now.'

She operated the controls and a nearby screen flickered into life.

As before, they were in a large public space, surrounded on three sides by garages with heavily graffitied up-and-over doors, three or four of which had now buckled beyond any future use. Old pieces of shredded plastic, caught for eternity in the branches of a dying tree, still fluttered in a light breeze. The tree was slightly more dead than on their last visit.

In one corner, the rusted old wreck of a car that had perched precariously on crumbling bricks now appeared to have fallen off. It lay, skewed to one side, abandoned. Weeds grew even higher between the cracks in the oil-stained concrete. The same air of weary defeat hung over the space.

They regarded the screen in silence until Jane said, 'We could send out a drone.'

'I'd love to, Jane. In fact, I'd like to send a drone to carry out the entire assignment, but we're required to have eyes on Henry so we'd better get cracking. The sooner we start, the sooner we can leave. Has anything particularly dire happened that would justify our idiot AI's forebodings?'

'No earthquakes, rains of blood, toxic clouds or acid rain,' reported Jane, scanning her read-outs. 'No nuclear fallout, no raging fires. A few odd readings but otherwise everything seems OK.'

'Unusual for the 20th century,' said Luke. 'Perhaps that's what's confusing the AI. Come on – Time's a-wasting.'

He marched to the door.

'I still think the drone should do a bit of a recce first,' said Jane.

'What for?'

'Well, one does not simply walk into Mordor,' said Matthew.

'Don't see why not,' said Luke, opening the door.

'Good job he wasn't part of the Fellowship,' muttered Matthew to Jane as they prepared to follow him out. 'The book would only have been three pages long.'

Luke turned. 'No recce required because this time we know what we're doing. Sonics and string within easy reach, people. No sense in making it easy for the 20th century to kill us. We don't know what we're going to find so I'll go first. Matthew – you all right to bring up the rear?'

Matthew nodded.

'OK, people – let's go and cause some trouble for someone else this time, shall we?'

They exited the pod.

As before, the first thing that hit them was the smell. Burned rubber. Burned wood. And burned dust. This time, everything was covered in a thick layer of dust. Jane could taste it at the back of her throat.

'Bit weird,' said Luke, scratching a line in the fine powder with his boot and peering down at it.

'Just like us,' said Jane. 'Right – Number Seventeen Beaver Avenue, everyone.' She consulted her trusty notebook and pointed. 'That way.'

They set off. As a unit this time. Together, compact, alert. Very nearly proper Time Police officers.

'Something's different,' said Luke, halting as they reached the main road.

'No cars,' said Jane suddenly. 'There's no traffic. Listen.'

They listened. Silence. No cars. No thumping music. No shouting children. No barking dogs.

'Something's happened,' said Luke. 'Stay sharp, everyone.'

'Here's Beaver Avenue,' said Jane as they rounded a corner.

And stopped dead.

Beaver Avenue was gone.

There are two definitions of the word 'devastated'.

Devastated: great destruction or damage.

Devastated: severe and overwhelming shock.

Both applied equally here.

Beaver Avenue was gone. Completely gone. All that remained was a wide, irregular crater full of and surrounded by endless mounds of broken bricks, roof tiles, charred wooden trusses and twisted metal things that might once have been cars. Standing vertically forlorn, one or two jagged tree trunks emerged from the rubble. An almost miraculously intact lamp post was all that remained. Beaver Avenue had been devastated.

Team Weird stood open-mouthed in stunned disbelief. They were devastated.

They stared around them. The only sound was an untidy festoon of black and yellow scene-of-crime tape flapping in the wind. Solid red and white security barriers blocked the entrance to the former Beaver Avenue. One or two had blown down and lay awkwardly on their side. That this had happened a while ago was very apparent. There were no ambulances, no rescue teams digging through the rubble, no TV crews, no overhead helicopters. Just almost an entire street reduced to silent, deserted rubble. Jane was reminded of the news shots of faraway war zones.

Luke pulled out his scratchpad. 'Pod – what happened here?'

'You have indicated a desire to remain unbriefed on this incident.'

'No, I haven't.'

'Yes, you have.' It spoke in Luke's voice, '"Shut up. Just shut up. Don't say another word. I mean it." End quote.'

Matthew and Jane were very careful not to look at each other.

'I don't sound like that.'

'The rendering is ninety-three per cent accurate.'

'Yes, well, never mind that now. What's happened?'

'There has been an explosion.'

'You think?'

'Information is scarce.'

'So, what can you tell us?' said Luke, impatiently.

'Very little. More information can be obtained by consulting the archives at TPHQ.'

Luke sighed. The AI threw him a bone.

'As previously stated, I can provide readings on air quality.'

'What?'

'Percentage and composition of dust and so forth.'

Luke coughed artificially. 'Yes – it's dusty.'

'A fact of which I endeavoured to apprise you on our landing.'

'What do you have on the explosion?'

'Massive but localised.'

'Targeted?'

'That is likely.'

They went back to surveying the scene before them. The implications . . .

'We're too late,' said Matthew hoarsely. 'It's taken out the whole family.'

'It's taken out the whole street,' said Jane, in disbelief.

'They must have come back for him,' said Luke. 'To make sure he didn't talk.'

Jane dragged her eyes away. 'Who's they?'

'The people who originally sent him his Time-travelling device? I don't know.' He looked around again. 'They didn't mess about, did they?'

'Unless . . .' said Matthew, thoughtfully. 'Unless Henry took himself out.'

Luke turned to him. 'What do you mean?'

'Well, he was always tinkering, wasn't he?' said Matthew. 'Perhaps it was an accident. He tried to build himself a pod. Or somehow he acquired another one and it blew up.'

Jane pulled out her recorder and began to pan around. Matthew followed suit.

Luke stood silently. Henry's family had been loud and quarrelsome, yes, but not deserving of death.

'I think we should gather as much info as we can,' he said. 'Before we go back to TPHQ. Let's see if we can find out exactly what happened here. Look for witnesses.'

Matthew nodded. 'Over there.'

The former Beaver Avenue had been a short cul-de-sac with three pairs of houses on each side which curved slightly to the left. On the opposite side of the road, at the very end of the street, one house remained standing. Well, leaning. A flapping tarpaulin covered most of the roof but it looked as if it was still occupied. A tea towel and two shirts hung from a makeshift washing line and a bicycle was propped against the gate.

'Come on,' said Luke. 'Watch for trip hazards, people.'

They walked wide around the cordoned-off area, picking their way across what had once been an open grassy space. Two black plastic bins on wheels had somehow escaped the blast and lay at a crazy angle.

'A breeding pair, perhaps,' said Luke. 'I never really grasped the 20th-century habit of surrounding themselves with rubbish.'

Jane couldn't help remembering the last time they'd been here. There had been people all over the place, hanging out of windows and shouting down to others as they passed by. Children who should almost certainly have been in school were playing football in the street. And there had been thumping music everywhere, because it was a well-known fact that the worse the music, the louder it should be played. As if the perpetrators were compelled to compensate for their abysmal taste by inflicting it on as much of the world as possible.

Team 236 approached the battered house from the front. All the windows were missing and two massive wooden buttresses were keeping it on its feet. Matthew carefully moved the bike and Luke went to open the gate, which came off in his hand.

'Bugger,' he said, trying to prop it back into place again. It wouldn't go and eventually he had to lean it against the remains of an overgrown hedge. It wasn't as if it had been serving any useful purpose, anyway.

They walked up the short path to the front door. Jane knocked very gently, just in case that was the final straw and the house fell down.

Nobody answered.

'They've probably been evacuated,' said Matthew, still watching their rear, although for what he wasn't quite sure. 'This house can't be safe, surely.'

'Course it's bloody safe,' said an indignant voice. An old man had appeared from around the corner of the house. 'No point knocking there. Door don't work no more.' He stared at them for a moment before adding, 'Oh – it's you again. You from the council?'

'Er . . . no,' said Jane, before Luke could antagonise their only possible witness. 'We've . . . um . . . come to hear your side of the story.'

'You from the paper?'

They gathered from his expression that being 'from the paper' would not be a Good Thing.

'From the office of the prime minister,' said Luke, grandly.

That didn't work at all. The old man spat. 'Bloke's an idiot.'

'He's preparing a report for the . . .' Jane ran her mind back through the list of sovereigns she'd learned at school, 'Queen . . .'

'God bless her.'

'Indeed. Her Majesty is concerned that the cause of the . . . incident is ascertained as quickly as possible.'

'And then I'll get my compo?'

Team Weird eyed each other.

'Compo?' ventured Jane.

'Compensation. For my bloody house. Look at the state of it.'

Obediently, they looked at it, but gently, in case their combined stares proved too much for it to withstand.

Jane certainly didn't want to raise hopes that might later be cruelly dashed, so she leaned forwards and said confidentially, 'It won't do any harm.'

'Ah. Gotcha. You'd better come in.'

The old man led them along a cracked concrete path and around the side of the house. They pushed aside the dispirited washing, eased themselves past the inevitable plastic bins on wheels and entered through the back door.

The kitchen was probably the biggest room in the house. Which was just as well since it was obvious the old man had taken up residence in it. A sleeping bag on a foam pad lay along one wall. An old Belfast sink with a wooden draining board occupied the space under the window, both of them spotlessly clean. The worktops had a scrubbed look about them and the floor covering, although faded and with a small hole whose edges had been carefully taped down, was also very clean.

The third wall contained a door that had, presumably, once led to the rest of the house – when there had been a rest of the house – and a table and chairs occupied the fourth wall.

A jam jar stood on the windowsill with a small handful of garden flowers pushed into it. Jane felt a lump in her throat.

A small dog regarded them from his basket then yawned and decided they weren't worth the effort.

By unspoken consent, Matthew and Luke left the interview to Jane. She took out her trusty notebook and laid it on the table in front of her. The old man eyed it so anxiously she decided to leave it closed.

'Well, now, Mr . . . ?'

'Fernley.'

'Mr Fernley. I have to say, we were surprised to find you still here.'

The old man started to fill a kettle.

'Oh God,' muttered Bolshy Jane. 'We're going to have to drink tea again.'

Mr Fernley cackled. 'If bloody Hitler couldn't shift me, then that lot of numpties at the town hall won't, neither.'

He ignited his little camping gas stove with a roar and the already nervous Team Weird very nearly jumped out of their skins. This was a house living on borrowed Time.

They've still got gas, thought Jane, eyeing the cylinder. Maybe this was just an unfortunate accident, after all. She smiled. 'Can you tell us what happened, Mr Fernley?'

'Arnold Andrew Fernley,' he said, obviously having told this story many times before. 'Born here in Lower Spurting in 1928. Lived in this house nearly all my life. As I said on my compo form. Family home.'

He paused and took a deep breath. 'It were about . . . oh . . . four or five months ago now. Last April. I were in here, not me front room, which is probly what saved me. I went down for me paper, then me and Jasper came in for a quick cuppa and – bang. And a bloody big bang it were, too. Big white flash. I heard me winders go. Glass everywhere. I heard me roof go, too – tiles crashing into the garden. Ruined me rhubarb. There was this rumbling. Went on forever, it did. Then lots of screaming. Jasper bolted under the table . . .' he pointed to the table, just in case they hadn't recognised what they were sitting around, 'and I followed on quick as I could. For a minute there, I thought Hitler were back.'

'You knew it was an explosion?'

'Oh, yeah. Took me right back to 1941, it did. When the Germans was after the aircraft factory in Whittington and kept

170

missing it. Don't know how they managed that. Bloody big place it were. Housing estate now.'

Jaws working, he reflected on this sorry state of affairs.

'The explosion,' reminded Jane, gently.

'I tried to get out but there were glass everywhere and I couldn't get me door open. Electric gone, of course. Water everywhere acos me pipe had cracked. Poor old Jasper here'd damn near crapped himself. We just sat under the table together till the rescue people turned up.'

'Do they know what caused it?'

'Not exactly. They know *where* it happened though. Either Number Fifteen or Number Seventeen. Semi-detached pair, but it were one of them.'

'Number Seventeen?' said Jane, pretending to consult her notebook. 'That's the Plimpton house. Did any of the family survive?'

Mr Fernley shook his head. 'Nah. None of them. Not anyone on either side of those two houses. Nor opposite. Took the full force, they did. Nothing left. And not much of the others. They had to pull them down in the end.'

'You survived though, Mr Fernley.'

'I did. Couple of big trees in next door's garden took the brunt of it. Lost most of me roof but otherwise we're all fine here.'

'Are the council fixing it?' asked Jane.

'Are they buggery. They want me out and I ain't going. You tell them that.'

'I certainly will,' said Jane, stoutly. 'That's scandalous.'

'That's exactly right,' he said, nodding vigorously. 'Scandalous is what it is.'

'And so sad about the Plimptons,' said Jane. 'Such a nice family.'

Luke turned astonished eyes on her and she ignored him.

'*He* were all right,' said Fernley. 'And *she* weren't too bad. Kids were a bit of a dead loss, although they might have grown out of that, of course.' He sighed. 'We'll never know now, will we? Bloody dogs were a pest though. Ran wild everywhere. Except in my garden. My Jasper soon sorted them out.'

Jasper grinned evilly and yawned again, stretching his little legs out in front of him.

'Anything else you can tell us, Mr Fernley?'

He shrugged. 'Not a lot. It were just an ordinary day. Me and Jasper went down the shop for the paper and some ciggies.'

'Did you walk past the Plimpton house?'

'It's on the way so I had to. Except not that day – I couldn't walk past the house because some bastard lorry was pulled up outside. On the pavement, so I had to walk around it in the road. So no – I didn't walk past the house as such.'

'What sort of lorry was it, Mr Fernley?'

He shrugged. 'Dunno. Not one of them big ones on the motorways – smaller. A Luton, I think. For local deliveries.'

'Do you know what they were delivering?'

He shook his head. 'The back were open but it were empty.'

'Did you see the driver?'

'I told all this to the police.'

'Indeed you did, Mr Fernley. They've written a note at the bottom of their report to say how observant you were.'

'National Service,' he said, incomprehensibly. 'They taught us proper then.'

'Yes, indeed,' said Jane, all at sea. 'And it shows. About the driver?'

He shook his head. 'I heard her talking. Couldn't see nothing over the hedge.'

'Who was she talking to?'

'Her. The missis. Them dogs were barking up a storm so don't ask me what they were saying.'

Luke intervened. 'Were all four Plimptons in the house at the time of the explosion?'

'Must have been.'

'Did they find the bodies?'

Fernley fixed Luke with an incredulous stare. 'Have you seen out there?'

'I think we were hoping to learn that some of them weren't in at the time,' said Jane, hastily.

'Well, I know *she* were in. And I know he were as well acos I saw him come home from work about thirty minutes before it happened. And them kids were in acos I could hear the music, so yeah, I reckon they were all home. And it were teatime, too, so they would be.'

An ear-splitting whistle pervaded the kitchen and all members of Team 236 nearly jumped out of their skins. Again.

'Ah,' said Mr Fernley with satisfaction. 'You can't beat a singing kettle.'

He got up and began to do ritualistic things with the kettle and spoonfuls of tea, finally pouring bright orange liquid into four mugs. Jane, looking around the kitchen and recognising the signs of one who didn't have a lot in this life, thanked him warmly and, as he turned away to replace the tea cosy, made signs to Luke that he was to drink it. Or else. Matthew was already stirring in the standard two large sugars required to make the liquid even remotely drinkable.

'Anyway,' continued Mr Fernley, pouring out a dishful of tea for Jasper and adding milk he would probably have done better to keep for himself, 'the police did them test things – you know – like on CSI – not that there were much left to test, but there were three in the house and one in the garden so they reckoned it were them.' He sighed. 'Close as they could get, anyway.'

Jasper lapped loudly and messily.

Team 236 sipped their dreadful tea in silence. It all fitted. Once again, the unfortunate Henry Plimpton had taken delivery of something he shouldn't have. The scene was easily imagined. Henry in his shed with the parcel. His wife in the kitchen, organising another gargantuan meal. The two kids upstairs doing those things 20th-century teenagers did. The two dogs in the garden, probably. The TV on – the sound turned up to be heard over the thumping music upstairs. Henry goes to open whatever it was and – boom. No more Henry. No more family. No more house. No more Beaver Avenue, either. Had it been a deliberate attack? Or had Henry simply been clumsy in his tinkering and blown himself up, the delivery a mere coincidence?

'How many casualties altogether?' enquired Matthew, replacing his empty mug.

'Six dead, eleven injured. One died the next day. Mrs Chatterjee. She were nice. I liked her.' Mr Fernley sighed. 'For a month – six weeks – you couldn't move around here. They thought it was a terrorist attack perhaps, then a gas main, then an unexploded bomb from the war, then foreign spies, then aliens from outer space – you name it, they blamed it. They don't know, though. And now they want me out so they can clear the site, rebuild and forget it.'

'Well, you'll get a nice new home, Mr Fernley.'

'No, I bloody won't. They'll build bloody great four-bedroom monstrosities with two garages – executive accommodation,' he spat the words, 'and I'll be shunted off to one of them boxes in Rushford. Sheltered my arse. Stuck up in the air. No garden. And poor old Jasper'll be taking the short walk to the vets acos they don't allow pets. No, I ain't going.' A glint of evil humour appeared. 'They'll have to dynamite me out of here.'

'That's the spirit,' said Jane, approvingly.

Luke had swallowed as much of the orange fluid as he felt was socially acceptable. 'Well, thank you very much, Mr Fernley, you've been very helpful.' He paused a moment. 'Have you had the press round here?'

'I certainly have,' he said. 'Bunch of nosey arseholes. Not one of them more than twelve years old. You tell them to piss off and they're back again half an hour later.'

'Well,' said Luke, 'you might want to think about telling them your story. How you've lived here for donkey's years. How you and Jasper fought for your lives under this very kitchen table. How even Hitler couldn't drive you out and now the council wants to rip you from your home against your will. And how they want to kill Jasper just so they can make a lot of money. Get the public on your side.'

Mr Fernley stood for a moment, his jaws working – a sign of intense thought, Jane realised. 'Ah,' he said. 'I might. You led me right before, so yeah, I might just do that.'

'We'll be off then,' said Jane, before Luke could derail municipal plans for Lower Spurting any further.

Mr Fernley saw them out of the back door. A massive and hitherto unnoticed crack ran its jagged way from the lintel up the wall and into the eaves. You could have put your hand in it – should you wish to do such a thing. Luke paled slightly. 'Don't hang around, Mr Fernley. You cut that deal as soon as you can.'

Fernley nodded and banged the door closed behind them. Automatically, Team 236 ducked. Dust and small stones clattered around their heads.

'Do you think they'll be all right?' asked Jane, anxiously.

'Well, if the house doesn't come down around his and Jasper's ears then yes, I expect so,' said Luke. 'Let's get back to the pod, shall we?'

15

Their return trek back to the pod was eerily quiet.

'I suspect we're in some kind of restricted zone,' said Luke. 'We should leave before the authorities send someone to investigate us.'

The pod was exactly where they'd left it and Jane closed the door with relief.

'They're eliminating witnesses,' she said, as Matthew handed around the coffee.

'Anything to take away the taste of that tea,' said Luke, accepting his with rare gratitude. 'Trust me, the tea tax is the best thing that ever happened to this country. Is my tongue orange?'

'Yes,' said Matthew. 'I'd get that checked out if I were you. Looks serious.'

'Somehow,' said Jane, pulling out her notebook and scribbling away, 'someone found out that Henry was . . .'

'. . . assisting us with our enquiries,' said Luke, helpfully, 'and they decided to take him out.'

'Yes,' said Jane, with a shiver, 'but a whole street, Luke. Talk about overkill. It's monstrous. Such a . . . a chilling disregard for innocent people. Surely it would have been easy enough just to have shot Henry on his way to or from work. There was no need to murder so many people.'

'Sending a message, perhaps.'

'To whom? Henry's dead – and his whole family with him.'

'Not to him, dummy – to us.'

'And to anyone else who might possibly have been considering assisting us with our enquiries and who has now, almost certainly, had second thoughts,' said Matthew.

'There's someone very ruthless out there,' said Jane, and then could have bitten off her tongue. She'd made the remark in all innocence. She shot a look at Luke, who was frowning into his mug. Perhaps he hadn't heard her.

'We should be getting back,' she said, turning to face the console. 'Download our images. Write our reports.'

Luke put down his mug. 'No – can we hang on a moment? There are some things to talk about and I don't want to talk about them at TPHQ.'

Jane and Matthew looked at him.

'Does no one think it's strange that I visit my father – I challenge him on one or two issues – and this happens?'

'Are you saying,' said Jane, breaking the long silence because it was obvious Matthew wasn't going to, 'you think your father did this? Your dad actually blew up a street?'

'I'll admit when you put it like that it sounds . . .'

'Wrong,' cried Jane.

'Unlikely,' amended Luke. 'But if you include the physical evidence of a Parrish Industries presence at Site X, everyone taking their instructions from Mr P, my visit to his office to discuss his possible involvement – the common denominator for all that is Raymond Parrish, my father.'

Both Matthew and Jane stared at him.

'You said it yourself, Jane. Someone is eliminating witnesses. I know we're not officially involved in the Site X investigation – Hay and Callen are handling that – but I start poking around and suddenly our only lead, poor old Henry, is a loose end to be got rid of. It all makes perfect sense.'

'It would make perfect sense for whoever was in charge, but that person may not necessarily be your dad, Luke. There's no evidence Henry worked for him.'

'I know there's no hard evidence, Jane, and I'd be inclined to believe you except . . . Look, let's suppose that Henry *was* working for my dad. Suddenly the Time Police are uncomfortably close. Site X is discovered. That's all right – he has legal people who can handle that, but wait – there's another problem out there. A loose end who has foolishly brought himself to the attention of the Time Police.'

Jane put down her mug. 'That doesn't make sense, Luke. Henry wasn't a criminal mastermind. He was only in it for personal gain. All he wanted was a winning lottery ticket and a new life.'

'If you could just accept that Henry *did* work for my father, then all this makes perfect sense, Jane. I'm convinced Henry is the link between Site X and my dad. Henry worked for him in some minor capacity, but off-site, so to speak.' Luke began to speak faster as he developed his theory. 'He's nicely concealed in the 20th century and no one even knows he exists. And then he gets greedy. He saw a means of escape from a pretty shitty life. He had a pod – courtesy of my dad – and he thought he'd use it to cheat the lottery. No one would ever know. Henry would give his family a shedload of cash to ease his conscience and quietly disappear.'

They thought about this.

'It's possible, I suppose,' said Matthew, reluctantly. 'But it's hardly a discreet method of disposal, is it? Taking out a whole street, I mean. As Jane said – why not just shoot him? Or run him over as he crossed the road? Or poison him with tea? Or vanish him somewhere with a pod. Or . . . ?'

'Yes, all right,' said Luke, impatiently. 'But if his employer is trying to make a point to us, the Time Police, and anyone else who's thinking of assisting us with our enquiries – what better way?'

'But Henry has already told us everything he knew.'

'Perhaps he hasn't. Perhaps he had something else to say. I don't mean he was deliberately concealing anything from us – I mean he didn't realise it was so important. And he had to be eliminated before – either accidentally or otherwise – he said something that would blow the whole thing wide open. Whatever the whole thing is.'

They looked at each other.

'Actually,' said Jane. 'That does seem likely. Although,' she added quickly as Luke opened his mouth to speak, 'that still doesn't mean it was your dad.'

'Oh, come on,' said Luke, even more impatiently. 'What are the odds of two sets of murderous illegals out there? Henry worked for Mastermind A and Site X was founded by Master-mind B?'

'I could accept that,' said Matthew. 'More easily than I'm convinced either mastermind is Mr Parrish.'

Luke and Matthew glared at each other.

'All right,' said Jane, hastily. 'Just for one moment – never mind *who* ordered it – *how* was it done? Think about it. All the Site X staff were rounded up. And everyone at Shoreditch as well. There's no one left.'

'Actually,' said Luke, slowly. 'No, they weren't. Think about it. Who did we miss?'

'Well, the person in charge, obviously.'

'Other than him. Come on, Jane. Who else do we know was there? And they just melted away, didn't they?'

Jane suddenly had it. 'Luke – the pilots. Smallhope and . . . Pennyroyal.'

'Who?' said Matthew, spilling his coffee.

'The people who piloted the pod. Didn't you get a sight of our final reports?'

'No,' said Matthew slowly. 'I didn't. Restricted.'

Luke continued. 'You saw them both, Jane. When they were pretending to be those tour guides. Smallhope looked OK but I wouldn't have trusted Pennyroyal one single inch. Would you?'

She stared at him. 'You think Pennyroyal did this? Caused the explosion?'

'Why not?'

'He didn't,' said Matthew with certainty.

'How do you know? You weren't even there. Luke – is it possible that Pennyroyal is Mr P?'

'He's not,' said Matthew with even more certainty.

'You can't possibly know that,' said Luke. 'You've never even met either of them.'

'Yes, I have. I know them. Both of them. They work for the Time Police.'

181

It is doubtful whether a silence anywhere has ever been more absolute. Or lengthy.

Eventually, Luke said, 'Smallhope and Pennyroyal work for the Time Police?'

'Unofficially, yes. They're bounty hunters. Sorry – recovery agents.'

There was more silence along very similar lines to the previous silence.

'Of course,' said Jane suddenly, sitting up with a jerk.

'What?'

'The snowsuits.'

Matthew looked mystified.

'At Site X. When the repulsive Mr Geoffrey had us thrown out into the snow – someone had hidden our snowsuits just where we would find them.'

Luke grinned. 'We didn't find them, Jane – you fell over them.'

'Not the point I'm trying to make. Who put them there? How did our snowsuits get from the locker room to outside the facility? Just where and when we would need them?'

Luke shrugged. 'I don't know. At the time I was just grateful.'

'As was I, but when you think about it – which I hadn't until now – it must have been Smallhope and Pennyroyal. It couldn't have been anyone else.'

'Why not?'

'Because they work for the Time Police,' said Matthew patiently. 'I keep telling you.'

'Spies,' said Luke.

'Bounty hunters,' said Jane, doubtfully.

'Again – recovery agents,' said Matthew.

Jane frowned. 'I find it hard to reconcile whoever bombed Beaver Avenue out of existence with the two people who left our snowsuits for us to find. They saved our lives. We wouldn't have lasted ten minutes otherwise.'

'Did the Time Police know about Site X before you got there?' asked Matthew.

'No,' said Luke with certainty. 'They didn't.'

Jane was still trying to work it out. 'So however Smallhope and Pennyroyal knew about it, it wasn't through the Time Police. And how were they able to insinuate themselves into the organisation in such key positions? It doesn't make sense.'

'It does,' said Luke, slowly, 'if they work for someone else as well.'

'Such as?' said Jane, suspecting she already knew the answer.

'Well, they might do some work for the Time Police, Jane. In fact, I'm sure Matthew's right and they do – but they might also be freelancers. In which case, there's nothing to stop them working for someone else at the same time, is there?'

'Such as?' said Jane again, this time definitely knowing the answer.

Luke took a breath. 'It's obvious. They work for my dad as well. Or mainly for him. They probably recognised me immediately and knew I was Time Police. They might have known Imogen Farnborough was also at Site X, or they might have just guessed it would all go tits up somehow.' He looked at Jane. 'I know I said you saved my life, Jane – and you did – but it's possible that I saved yours, too. If it had been only you, then they probably wouldn't have bothered with the snowsuits. They saved us only because they knew keeping me – us – alive would probably earn them a substantial bonus.'

There was more silence in the pod as both Matthew and Jane grappled with this very likely scenario.

'A good point,' said Jane, watching Luke's face. 'But not the only explanation.'

Luke struck the arm of his chair in exasperation. 'Jane . . .'

'No, Luke. Think about it for a moment. Smallhope and Pennyroyal were at Site X. With us. So, who organised the attack on TPHQ? It couldn't have been them. They just wouldn't have had the opportunity.'

Luke opened his mouth but Jane was still speaking.

'And a similar argument applies to your dad. How did he know we were at Site X? You yourself saw that Geoffrey had no idea we were Time Police, so why – and how – could he have tipped off your dad? In fact, the only people who knew the prisoners were being transferred from Shoreditch back to TPHQ were . . .'

She stopped.

'The Time Police themselves,' said Matthew quietly.

They looked at each other. No one seemed willing to pursue that train of thought. Deep waters loomed. Treacherous, deep waters.

'Should we say anything?' said Jane timidly.

Matthew shook his head. 'I can't imagine that Hay and Ellis haven't already considered this.'

'And yet they haven't done anything about it,' said Luke.

'They might be privy to info we don't have and the last thing we need is to stir up trouble unnecessarily,' said Jane. 'Aren't we in enough trouble?'

'Are we in trouble again?' enquired Matthew.

'It's us,' said Luke, gloomily. 'Of course we're in trouble

again. We just don't know it yet. Not a word of this to anyone. Not even Ellis. Or North.'

'God, no,' said Jane. 'Come on. Let's get back.'

Back in their grandly named office, Team 236 sat down to write their reports.

'What are you saying in yours?' enquired Jane, peering at Luke's data stack.

'Keeping it strictly factual,' said Luke. 'No wild speculation. Just what we saw and our witness interview.'

Ellis appeared in the doorway. 'How did it go? How's Henry?'

'Dead as a doornail,' said Luke, grimly. 'Along with his family and a significant proportion of the population of Beaver Avenue.'

Ellis stared disbelievingly for a moment and then stepped into the tiny office and closed the door behind him.

'What happened?'

'To precis the reports we're still writing,' said Luke, 'a surviving witness claims a delivery was made to the Plimpton house earlier in the day. Henry was seen to arrive home from work. Thirty minutes later, he, his house, everyone else's house – indeed almost the whole of Beaver Avenue – was just a big hole in the ground. The entire street's gone, except for one house at the very end, and I don't think that's long for this world.'

'This is ... unbelievable,' said Ellis. 'I ...' He stopped, thinking through the implications.

'Yes,' said Luke, grimly. 'A bit of a game changer, don't you think?'

'I certainly do. As a courtesy, would you let me see your reports before you send them off to Hay, please.'

'Of course, sir,' said Jane.

If they thought that was the purpose of Ellis's visit, they were wrong.

'Now then,' he said, briskly. 'The real reason why I'm here.'

His former team regarded him suspiciously.

'As I'm certain you will remember, Officer North is announcing her historical perspective briefing initiative in ten minutes and you will want to be there to support her.'

'Will we?' said Luke. 'Only I rather had plans and . . .'

'I distinctly remember you saying you wouldn't miss it for anything, Officer Parrish, even if you don't. Shall we go?'

Arriving at Briefing Room 1, they were requested to leave their weapons at the door.

'Why?' demanded Luke, for whom the novelty of striding dramatically around the building, fully armed and ready for anything, had still not yet worn off.

'The nature of the briefing calls for everyone to attend unarmed.'

'Exciting,' said Matthew as Luke reluctantly deposited his weapon.

'I certainly hope so,' said Ellis.

Any unspoken fears Ellis might have had about North's briefing being poorly attended were not realised. Briefing Room 1 was packed. Standing room only. Team 236 stood at the back alongside Major Ellis. A buzz of anticipation ran around the room.

The briefing began punctually because, for North, there was no other way of doing things.

'Good afternoon, everyone. Thank you for coming. The purpose of this briefing is to inform you that, with immediate effect, a new initiative is to be launched. From now on, and as an important part of all Time Police pre-mission briefings, an historical perspective is to be provided, thus ensuring teams are fully aware of *all* circumstances likely to be encountered during their upcoming missions. I should inform you these sessions are not optional and attendance is compulsory.'

The room groaned.

'Why?' enquired a voice from the crowd. 'We've done this before and it's a waste of fire-trucking time.'

'Bloody history,' said someone else. 'I bloody hate it.'

'Just shoot the buggers and go home,' said someone else.

'All very valid arguments,' said North, smoothly, 'which I intend to completely ignore.'

The room groaned again.

Lt Grayling stood up, hands on hips and prepared to argue. 'I don't see the bloody point. It's Time, not stupid history, that's the important thing here.'

Possibly only Major Ellis recognised the gleam in Officer North's eyes at having been granted such a perfect opportunity.

'Really?' she said. 'Well, let's say you're standing on a street corner, improbably minding your own business and doing no one any harm, and you see a young man brandishing a gun. What is your first move?'

'Like someone said – shoot the bugger and go home,' said Grayling promptly, nodding his head at the shouts of laughter around him.

'Like this?' North opened a drawer in the lectern, pulled out a small handgun and shot Lt Grayling in the chest.

The gunshot reverberated around the room. For a few seconds, no one moved. Shock was written across every face including – it has to be said – that of Major Ellis. For the briefest of seconds, the room was full of frozen statues.

Like the tiny-brained dinosaurs of old, it seemed to take Lt Grayling a few moments to decide whether he was dead or not. The realisation that he was, in fact, still alive, did not improve his temper any. 'What the fire truck . . . ?'

Grayling's team scrambled to their feet and were shot at in their turn. The smell of old-fashioned cordite made Jane's nose twitch. The room was in uproar. Officers instinctively reached for the weapons they realised too late they'd left at the door. Someone hit the alarm which, for some reason, a prudent briefing officer had disconnected earlier.

A number of people might have stormed the podium except Officer North appeared to have forgotten to lay down her weapon and surrender.

'Percussion caps,' she said, tossing the gun on the desk and waiting calmly for the uproar to die down.

'That's my girl,' murmured Ellis, leaning against the wall with his arms folded.

'What?' said Luke.

'Nothing.'

Lt Grayling blinked, took a deep breath and patted himself down. 'What the fire truck was that? I damn near shat myself. What the fire truck do you think you're playing at?' His deep unhappiness with the current situation had obviously not been appeased by the joy of finding himself still alive.

'In case you missed it, Lieutenant, I've just shot you, and since you appear to be relatively unimportant in the scheme of things, I'll probably get away with it. *You*, on the other hand, by killing the unknown young man we were discussing earlier, have just shot the person responsible for the assassination of Archduke Ferdinand in Sarajevo.'

North gestured to the other members of his team, still unbelievingly inspecting themselves and each other for non-existent bullet holes. 'Thanks to you, World War One does not now take place. Neither – because the seeds of the second were almost certainly sown in the first – does World War Two. Congratulations, Lieutenant – with one simple, thoughtless action, you have, single-handedly, changed the lives of nearly everyone in the world, disrupted the entire 20th century, and massively changed the course of history. Over twenty million people who should be dead are now alive. Which means that many of you . . .' she gestured around the room, 'do not now exist – not in your current incarnation, anyway. Many of you are now probably female. Congratulations on the upgrade.

'However, because of one careless action – the shooting of the assassin, Gavrilo Princip, by Lt Grayling here, for no better reason than he saw a gun *and drew the wrong conclusion* – paradoxes now abound. The Time Police are completely overwhelmed. Billions die. The Timeline implodes and all life ceases to exist. All thanks to an inadequately briefed member of the Time Police. If there was any history left, then, for all the wrong reasons, Lt Grayling and his team would certainly be going down in it. *Because they went in inadequately briefed.*

'Turning to the rest of you . . .' she turned to the rest of the room, who were still standing or sitting in attitudes of frozen disbelief and shock, 'the more intelligent among you will, by now, have realised the advantages of taking part in this new initiative. Attendance is not voluntary in any way so don't make me come looking for you. My first briefing – covering the next three days' scheduled missions – is at 1500 hours tomorrow in Briefing Room 3. Make sure you sign up in good time. It is unlikely that anyone else will be shot but I make no promises. Be there or be the cause of the end of Time itself – up to you.'

Picking up her files – and the gun – North strode out of the door, leaving stunned and disbelieving officers behind her.

Officer North was unsurprised to receive a message from Commander Hay requesting her, Officer North's, presence at her immediate convenience. North returned the gun to a grinning Varma and set off for Hay's office.

'Officer North.'

'Ma'am.'

'From the number and nature of the complaints I've received, I gather you gave your preliminary briefing today.'

'That's right, ma'am. About half an hour ago.' Her scratchpad bleeped. She ignored it.

'I don't think I need to ask how it went.'

'No, ma'am.' Her scratchpad bleeped again.

'Would you like to answer that, Officer North?'

'No, it's fine, ma'am.'

'Is gunfire likely to feature prominently in any future briefings? Will you perhaps be attacking officers with a rocket launcher?'

'That rather depends on how quickly they grasp my points, ma'am.'

Her scratchpad bleeped yet again.

'Please answer that, Officer North.'

North pulled out her scratchpad, glanced at the screen and raised her eyebrows.

'What is it?'

'Requests to attend tomorrow's briefing, ma'am. Seventeen so far. No – eighteen.'

'You do know they only want to see if you'll shoot someone again, don't you?'

'To ensure maximum attendance and the complete attention of her audience, a committed and competent briefing officer has many weapons in her armoury, ma'am.'

'Not literally, I hope. I have to congratulate you on going one better than the perfidious Dr Maxwell. During her time here, and to the best of my knowledge, she never actually shot anyone just to make a point.'

North found it impossible not to look smug. 'No, ma'am.'

'Well, good luck to you. As Captain Farenden will testify, I myself frequently fantasise about shooting vast numbers of Time Police officers on a regular basis. I find it very therapeutic.'

'Everyone should have a hobby, ma'am.'

'Thank you, Officer North. Keep me apprised.'

'Thank you, ma'am.'

16

Captain Farenden waited for Officer North to leave, checked the message one more time, sighed, got up and limped into Commander Hay's office.

She looked up. 'Yes, Charlie?'

'The date of Imogen Farnborough's execution has been set, ma'am.'

Commander Hay said nothing.

'Will you be attending, ma'am?'

It was Commander Hay's custom to attend all executions. She could not have told anyone why a sense of responsibility compelled her to do so.

'I will, yes. Major Callen has also expressed a wish to be present.'

'What about Major Ellis, ma'am? And, as victims of her actions, Lockland and Parrish are also entitled to be there.'

'Inform Major Ellis of the time and date but tell him the decision as to whether he passes that info on to his former team is up to him.'

'Yes, ma'am.'

Major Ellis did indeed think very long and hard about

whether to inform his team before eventually coming to the conclusion that the choice should be theirs.

Officer Lockland declined. Quite vehemently. Ellis was unsurprised.

Officer Parrish accepted. Which *was* surprising. Ellis drew him to one side. 'Parrish, why would you want to put yourself through this?'

'I'm responsible,' said Luke, tightly. 'I told her to cooperate with us and that piece of good advice led her to her death.'

'If she hadn't cooperated and if she had been anyone other than an MP's daughter, then she would have been executed for that first offence. It would still have happened, Luke. Just sooner rather than later.'

'Even so . . .'

'Even so nothing. This is not on you. Imogen Farnborough made her choices. She could have walked away from the entire organisation when she came out of prison. She could have taken a completely different path and she chose not to. She could have got you and Lockland – and herself – safely out of Site X simply by going along with your cover story but she chose not to. Her choices, Luke, and none of the consequences are your fault.'

Luke nodded but said nothing. A circumstance so unusual as to arouse Ellis's misgivings.

'Other than that, how are you?'

'Well, I'm not as easily duped as the Time Police and I'm still convinced my dad's up to his neck in this Site X business. Henry and his family have been bombed out of existence. I didn't like them, but they didn't deserve that. A friend of mine has disappeared in mysterious circumstances. Jane was deliberately abandoned in the middle of an assignment and that she wasn't badly injured is down to her and not the arseholes who were supposed to be her back-up. And Imogen Farnborough, of whom I do still have some happy memories, is about to be institutionally murdered. Oh, and my hand still aches occasionally. Nothing major there, I think you'll agree – Major.'

Ellis ignored this. If he charged Parrish for every insubordination neither of them would ever do anything else.

'To take your points in order – your father has been cleared of involvement with Site X. Why are you so angry? Did you want him to be guilty? The Plimpton affair is not closed. If you want to be involved in further investigations, then say so. If your friend's absence is causing you concern, then approach the civil authorities. Lockland sorted herself out. Your indignation is understandable but she considers the matter closed and so should you. Team 171 has been disbanded and Sawney and Hooke have left the force. Imogen Farnborough was granted an easy life with many opportunities and failed to avail herself of any of them – unlike you, Luke. And if your hand is giving you trouble, then go back to MedCen. I don't think you're special enough to have contracted something with which they, with all their vast experience, would be unable to deal.'

Luke stared at his feet for a while then said, 'The Plimpton investigation isn't closed?'

'No, it is not. We might not have much to go on but that doesn't mean the investigation is over. Far from it. There's a lot there that needs looking into, don't you think?'

'Is this you tactfully telling me to keep away from the Site X investigation?'

'Yes. It was rather well done, don't you think?'

'Not really.'

'Well, you grasped my point easily enough. I was worried I'd made it slightly too difficult for you.'

'Did you really slap Sawney around in the gym?'

'I am an officer in the Time Police – I don't slap. Three well-placed, well-executed blows did the trick.'

'I'll think about what you said about Birgitte.'

'Your friend who's disappeared?'

'Yes.'

'Just a word of advice – make some discreet enquiries before starting a fuss. There might be a perfectly innocuous explanation.'

'Her wife has gone too.'

'Holiday? Retreat? Business trip? Could be anything.'

'I know.'

'Lots for you to be getting on with, then.'

'Yes.'

'Start with the hand.'

Ellis left and a few minutes later his place was taken by Jane, who had also received her official notification.

'Luke, don't go to the execution.'

'I have to. Imogen deserves one friendly face.'

'She won't be able to see you. She won't even know you're there.'

He shook his head. 'I'll know I'm there.'


Traditionally, Time Police executions are always set for noon. In case of any last-minute delays or reprieves was the official explanation. Legend had it that an official had once rocked up mid-morning, flourishing a pardon, only to find things had kicked off at dawn because other people had a busy day ahead of them and had made an early start. From that day onwards, all executions had been scheduled for twelve noon.

'Here are your docs,' said Ellis to Luke. 'Everything you need. You can change your mind at any time – right up until you're in the execution shed. Once they lock the door, no one leaves until it's all over. Understood?'

Luke nodded.

'Report to me on your return.'

'That won't be necessary.'

'Report to me on your return.'

Luke sighed. 'All right.'

'The correct response is, "Yes, sir." I'll overlook it on this occasion but you need to rethink your attitude, Parrish.'

'I shall do it while the firing squad is lining up.'

'Report to me on your return, Parrish.'


Matthew's plans for that particular day involved engrossing himself in the Time Map. It was rumoured the Map Master and her team had put together something ingenious for him to get his teeth into that would, as always, enable him to forget everything going on around him.

Jane's day was to involve Lt Grint. Which had been his idea. It would be hard to say which of them had been most surprised by his unexpected offer to take her out to Kew Gardens. A nice day, he'd said, staring at his feet. Just walking around the gardens.

He hadn't expected to enjoy himself but no one was more astonished than he when he found looking at the flowers and the autumn trees with Jane to be not anything like as bad as he had anticipated.

Jane was very quiet for most of the morning which was no problem for him, and, when twelve noon struck, he made sure they were sitting under a tree, well away from everyone else and where he wished, very much, for the courage to hold her hand.

It was early evening when Grint and Jane returned to TPHQ.

As they entered the lift, he said, 'Will you be all right if I leave you now? I'm on duty at 2100 hours.'

Jane was immediately stricken with guilt. 'You're on nights? Shouldn't you have got your head down sometime today?'

'No,' said Grint, simply.

Jane stared at her feet. 'Well, thank you for ... for doing what you did today. I'm sorry I wasn't better company.'

He held the lift door open for her. 'I'll see you tomorrow, then.'

The first person she saw was Matthew emerging from an exhausting session in the Map Room. 'Hey, have you seen Luke?'

He shook his head. 'I've stayed out of the way in the Map Room all day. I don't even know if he's back yet.'

Jane went to look for Luke.

He wasn't in the Pig's Bar – which surprised her. People often sat there, drinking themselves stupid until their friends – or given this was the Time Police and large numbers of them had no friends – their colleagues came to take them away. He wasn't in the second-floor bar, either. She checked the gym, just on the very faint chance he might be taking out his anger and guilt in a safe and controlled environment. Of course he wasn't. That really only left his room. If he wasn't there, then he was still out of the building and she would have no idea where to look.

Conscious of a feeling of unease, Jane quickened her pace. By the time she got to their corridor she was practically running. She tapped on his door. A typically timid Jane knock, and when she received no reply, untypically, she turned the handle and walked straight in.

He was standing looking out of the window. It was dark out there. It was dark in here as well because he'd obviously overridden the automatic lighting.

'Luke?'

'Go away, Jane.'

His voice was hoarse.

'No,' said Jane. She cleared a space on his bed, which was cluttered with clothes, his helmet, holos and a towel, and sat down.

Wearily, he said, 'Jane – not now.'

Jane remembered her own feelings as the clock had struck twelve noon and said, 'Yes, now,' with unusual firmness.

'No, I mean it. I really want to be by myself for a while.'

Jane had very little social experience. She had no clear idea what to say. Presumably you didn't ask 'How did it go?' after an execution, so she continued to sit in silence.

'Jane – I'm hanging by my fingertips here. I'm either going to punch someone or burst into tears, and I don't want to do either of those things to you, so please go away.'

'No,' said Jane simply, channelling Lt Grint.

'You don't understand.'

'Of course I understand,' she said angrily. 'I was there. With you. I helped you through the snow. I found us shelter. I was with you every step, every second of the way, so don't tell me I don't understand. And definitely don't tell me to push off.'

Luke was silent for so long she thought he'd either become reconciled to her presence or had forgotten she was there. Jane was very accustomed to people forgetting she was there.

Eventually he stirred. Without turning around, he said, 'Three years ago – almost to the day – Imogen was trying out for the Olympic skiing team. I went with her for one of the trials. She came bursting into my room afterwards. She wore a red snowsuit. Her cheeks were exactly the same colour. Her hair was all over the place. She was so excited. So full of life. Everything stretched ahead of her. We were – both of us – on top of the world. After it was over, we didn't come out of my room for nearly two days. Who would have thought – three years later – almost to the day – she'd be dead. Because of me.'

'Luke . . .'

'She didn't get a place on the team, but I've never forgotten that time we had together.'

'Luke . . .'

'Her mother was there, you know.'

It took her a moment to realise he'd changed the subject and that the Rt Hon Mrs Farnborough had not, in fact, celebrated Imogen's Olympic opportunity with them.

'Where?'

'In the execution shed. There's a grim little factory unit in Droitwich the general public knows nothing about. God knows what goes on there because I certainly don't. Want to know,

I mean. That's where I was. And Hay. And Callen, for some reason.'

'You went through with it? You were there? You actually saw it happen?'

'Yes. How else did you think an execution is witnessed?'

'I don't know. I didn't want to think about it.'

'They can't see you but you can see them. Behind some sort of transparent shield, of course.'

'Luke . . .'

'The chair's the only thing you can see. Everything else is dark. They brought her in. She was walking like a zombie. I think they must have drugged her. Whether out of compassion – which doesn't seem likely – or to ensure she didn't give any trouble, I don't know. I hope they'd drugged her. I really hope to God she had no idea what was happening to her. At some point they'd cut her hair. Not very well. She'd have hated it.' He paused. 'There were tears on her cheeks.'

Jane swallowed. 'Do you think she knew you were there?'

'I don't think she knew anyone was there. It was over with very quickly. From door to chair about four seconds. There were three of them. One for each arm and one for the hood. They snapped on her restraints. Three seconds. Four at the most. Then the hood. They stepped back. Out of the light. Don't know where they went. That was another three seconds. She had a little white target pinned to her . . . to her . . . pinned over her heart. Someone, somewhere, must have given the order. You don't see the firing squad at all. They're out of sight in the dark. You can't hear anything. I didn't even know the order had been given. She jerked once. And that was it. They drew the curtains just as the officer went in for the coup de grâce. Twenty seconds from start to finish. If that. Twenty seconds to snuff out a life, Jane. Twenty seconds that will be with me for a lifetime.'

'Luke . . .'

'I think you and Matthew should stay well away from me. Orduroy Tannhauser, Imogen Farnborough, possibly even Birgitte – for how many deaths can one person be responsible?'

'Luke, you're not responsible for the bad choices made by other people.'

He shook his head. 'Please go. I don't want to cry in front of you.'

Jane gritted her teeth. 'No, I won't go. I'm your friend and your teammate.'

'Jane . . .'

She began to cry. 'I was with you, Luke. In the snow. Don't shut me out now.'

He turned to look at her. She couldn't see his face. He was just a black shape against the window.

'Luke, come here a moment. Please.'

He came to sit beside her.

She wiped her nose on her sleeve, half expecting him to say, 'Not your most appealing habit, sweetie,' but he didn't. 'Have you still heard nothing from Birgitte?'

'What? No. Nor from her wife, either. They've just disappeared. Just after we visited them. Jane, it can't be a coincidence. Especially after what my dad said about what happened that night. And then Henry and his family. Yes, I know we can't tie my dad to Site X, but you have to admit someone's doing a very good job of shutting down every possible avenue of enquiry. People are disappearing, Jane. And now, on top of all that – Imogen.'

It crossed Jane's mind that now – at this very moment – Luke was bearing an almost impossible burden. Greatly daring, she put her arms around him and he rested his head on her shoulder. They sat together in the dark room. Her tears ran down into his hair and his tears ran down into her T-shirt.

They sat for what seemed like a very long time. Jane's arms went to sleep.

Someone knocked on the door and they both jumped a mile. The knock came again. Jane rubbed her eyes. 'Is it all right to put the light on?'

'Yeah,' said Luke, turning his face away.

Matthew stood at the door, armed with a giant flask of what she assumed was coffee, and enough sandwiches for the entire Time Police force.

He stared at Jane. 'Why is your T-shirt wet?'

'I suspect Luke blew his nose on me when I wasn't looking.'

'Eww. Gross. Why did you blow your nose on Jane's T-shirt?'

Luke had himself back under control again.

'Because yours wasn't available. Is all that for me?'

'No,' said Matthew. 'Mostly it's for Jane and me. But you can have one.'

They divided the sandwiches between them. Matthew found two mostly clean mugs and one definitely not clean one which they gave to Luke, and poured the coffee.

'This tastes funny,' said Luke, peering at his through the steam. 'What have you done to it?'

'Well, actually, it's not exactly coffee.'

'What? You bastard. Tell me it's not tea.'

'There's coffee in it somewhere but mostly it's brandy.'

'Oh my God,' said Luke, his eyes brightening.

'Oh my God,' said Jane in a completely different tone of voice, staring at her half-empty mug.

Wimpy Jane was horrified but Bolshy Jane was laughing. 'Lie down, for heaven's sake, sweetie – it'll lessen the impact when you pass out.'

Jane passed Luke her mug. 'Here.'

'Cheers.' He sipped the alleged coffee.

Despite her best efforts and worn out by the day, Jane fell asleep almost immediately, a half-eaten sandwich still clutched in one hand. Matthew made himself comfortable on the floor. Luke tossed him a pillow and then curled up beside Jane and tried to think about anything other than Imogen.

He should buy Jane a little present. She was a good friend. And she was right – she'd saved him when they were struggling in the snow. And she'd had precious few presents in her life. Flowers, perhaps. Then he thought again. Jane liked books. Real books. The sort where you had to hold them and turn the pages yourself. She liked reading more than anything – he'd heard her say so. He'd buy her a subscription to one of those posh book clubs. Because books were so expensive these days. Beyond Jane's reach, he suspected. They sent you a book a month. He stirred slightly. Only one? He'd make it two. Two books a month should be enough even for a freak – sorry – bookworm – like Jane.

He lay in the darkness listening to Jane and Matthew's gentle breathing and remembering Imogen Farnborough and her red snowsuit.

Until the brandy kicked in.

17

Commander Hay also had her own task to perform. Not surprisingly, Mrs Farnborough had disappeared immediately after her daughter's execution. Discreet enquiries confirmed she had not been seen in public since.

Sighing, Hay brushed aside the mildly expressed objections of her adjutant concerning the security implications of the commander of the Time Police travelling alone and set out for Mile End.

The Right Honourable Mrs Farnborough lived in a house that, tiny though it was, had probably cost the equivalent of the annual budget of a small country. Or possibly, given the spectacular way London property prices were behaving after their decades-long slump – two small countries.

Mrs Farnborough herself opened the front door. The two women regarded each other for a very long time. Too long. Commander Hay, who knew she had taken a risk by coming here, was about to turn away when, silently, Mrs Farnborough stepped aside. Commander Hay entered and was led through the house to a small courtyard garden situated at the rear. The tiny space was a sheltered suntrap, stuffed to bursting point with plants now beginning to go over, a tiny tinkling fountain, and just enough room for a small table and two chairs.

Looking up, Hay could see even more sophisticated than usual anti-drone technology mounted on the roof.

Mrs Farnborough's face was professionally blank. 'How can I help you, Commander?'

'I came to see how you are. Should you, at any point, wish me to leave, then please just tell me. So – how are you?'

Mrs Farnborough sighed. 'I was not . . . unprepared.'

'Even so . . .'

'Yes. Even so.'

They were both silent for a while and then Mrs Farnborough said, 'I notice you are out of uniform, Commander. May I offer you a glass of wine?'

Commander Hay hesitated and then said, 'Thank you – that would be pleasant.'

She was interested to see Mrs Farnborough herself disappear into the house, to emerge a few moments later with a bottle and two glasses. 'You are alone at the moment?'

'I am alone at all times, but no, there is no one else in the house today.'

They sipped in silence until, eventually, and without looking at her, Mrs Farnborough said, 'What can I do for you, Commander?'

'I told you. I came to see how you are.'

'And I asked you what you wanted.'

Commander Hay set down her glass. 'You once asked me for a favour and I did what I could. I suspect neither of us were happy with subsequent events but it's too late for regret now. I've come to ask a favour of you. I'd like you to reconsider your intention to resign. If you are resigning because of Imogen, I can assure you there is no need for you to do so.'

'My daughter died yesterday. My husband has gone. I have no other children. I find I lack the will to continue. Let others shoulder the burden. I no longer care.'

'I do understand. More than you might imagine. We all carry our own burdens.'

Mrs Farnborough raised a sceptical eyebrow.

Commander Hay hesitated for one moment and then said, 'My face frightens small children. And grown men too, now I come to think of it. I do my job because it's all that's left to me. Without it I would have been lost.'

'And you think that applies to me as well?'

'I would, as always, council against making any important decisions in the aftermath of a tragedy such as you suffered yesterday. I have occasionally had to dissuade seriously traumatised officers from taking a course of action I suspect they might later come to regret.'

'And you think I might come to regret stepping out of the limelight? That I am making the wrong decision?'

'I am saying no such thing. I am not saying do not resign. I am saying do not resign *now*.'

There was more silence in the garden. Mrs Farnborough put down her glass. 'Since you yourself have raised the subject – what did happen to your face?'

'No one is quite sure. I remember very little of the incident. It was during the Time Wars, at the beginning of my career in the Time Police. I was leading a team in Mesopotamia. Religious fanatics were attempting to change the outcome of some Biblical battle. We were ambushed. We fought our way back to the pod.

206

When we arrived, the pod itself was under attack. There were explosions everywhere. We were in the desert. Our pod was the only cover available. I ordered everyone to make a break for it. I remember an enormous explosion as I crossed the threshold. It blew me into the pod. Someone shouted for an emergency evacuation. I was on the floor. Semi-conscious. People were shouting. There was another enormous explosion. The pod . . . heaved . . . I think is a good word. At the same moment the door blew off. The temperature plummeted. Everything went dark. I heard screaming. Cut off suddenly. Everyone died at the same time. I was crushed under the weight of my colleagues but their bodies protected me. To some extent. My face was either burning hot or freezing cold – I was never able to tell. It took them a long time to get me out. The bodies . . . had . . . fused together. I was buried under a welded mass of flesh. People I'd known very well. People I'd led as team leader. I was alive because they had died horribly. I was the only survivor. For a very long time I wished I wasn't.'

'Didn't you want to leave the Time Police?'

'Much more than that. I wanted to run to the ends of the earth. I never wanted to see anyone ever again. I certainly didn't want anyone seeing me. I was very young when it happened. It felt like the end of my world. For a long time, I couldn't look at myself – or anyone else. I certainly couldn't bear anyone looking at me. Fortunately – if that's the word I want – it took me a long time to heal. There was no chance of going anywhere for months, so I was able to work my way through most of the mental trauma while still under Time Police care.'

Hay smiled sourly. 'It wasn't all bad. I used to find it quite useful for intimidating people. I even used to have competitions with myself to see if I could make people wet themselves. Great fun.' She shot a look at Mrs Farnborough. 'Not that I do that any longer, of course.'

'Of course not,' said Mrs Farnborough, topping up their glasses.

Commander Hay picked up her wine and took a sip. 'I can't remember the last time I sat in a garden, drinking wine.'

Recognising a deliberate attempt to change the subject, Mrs Farnborough gestured. 'My sanctuary. Everyone should have a garden.'

'Alas,' said Commander Hay, drily. 'We recently had a spot of bother and our gardens are at the bottom of the Thames.'

'Yes, I heard about that.'

There was silence for a while. The fountain tinkled on and then Mrs Farnborough gestured at their surroundings. 'For people such as us, I suspect gardens are few and far between. If you would like – this one could always be open to you. Although you'll probably need to bring your own wine.'

Hay nodded. 'Thank you. That's a very tempting offer. It's not, however, the whole point of my visit today. There is another reason I would like you to reconsider your resignation.'

'Which is?'

'It is happening again.'

'What is happening again?'

'I suspect that future historians – should any survive – although in my experience it's easier to kill a cockroach than an historian – that future historians will describe this as the second time we lost control of the Timeline.'

She now had Mrs Farnborough's full attention. 'You cannot be serious.'

'But I am. Consider this. We now know big business – very big business – is reopening its interests in Temporal Tourism. Coincidentally – or not – there are moves afoot to restrict or even revoke the legislation preventing this and at the same time to reduce the powers of the Time Police. There's a lot of money to be made in this area so I think we can both see the direction in which this will be heading.'

Without waiting for a response, she swept on. 'Big business is always looking for ways to profit from the past. Not just harvesting treasures, but actually enslaving indigenous races and using them for their own purposes. I have seen people in cages. Babies torn from their mothers and subjected to experimental surgery. People have been hunted for money and sport. They were seen as a free and unlimited resource, there for the exploiting. To be controlled through fear, pain and starvation. To be used as a subject base for experimentation because they're exempt from any legislation protecting their rights or welfare.'

She gave Mrs Farnborough a moment to consider this and then forged on. 'And as if that's not bad enough, how long do you think it will be before someone is offering to *nudge* the course of history down a different but more profitable path? For an appropriate remuneration, of course. How long before someone goes to these people and offers them money to ensure Julius Caesar is *not* assassinated? Or to ensure that Hitler *does* die at Wolf's Lair? Or that Jesus doesn't die on the cross? Or that Jesus *does* die on the cross? Or that Jesus isn't actually crucified. Or even that Jesus died as a baby? Think of it – an icy cold night, a rough stable on the outskirts of a small village, everyone huddled inside, fast asleep – easy target. All of history changed forever.'

Mrs Farnborough remained silent. Shadows began to gather in the corners of the little garden.

Commander Hay hadn't finished. 'Or, consider this. How useful would it be to be able to snatch up inconvenient people and drop them in another century? A safe and bloodless way of eliminating inconvenient spouses, lovers, business rivals, rich aunts, political leaders, or even people who looked at you wrong on the way to work this morning.

'Or – and this is something we grapple with on a regular basis – people who commit a series of crimes so heinous that they are forced to relocate in another Time to escape retribution. This is happening now. The law closes in on them but by then it's too late. They've gone – having bought themselves a safe haven in another century. It costs a very great deal of money, but we both know anything is possible for the very rich.

'And I haven't even started on the damage being done to the fabric of Time itself. We all remember what happened when Time travel was available to all.' Unconsciously, she touched her face. 'They meant no harm but the majority of the damage was accidentally caused by individual tourists. Now imagine legal Temporal Tourism on a commercial scale. Time is nowhere near as robust as it once was. The possibilities do not bear thinking about.'

She became aware her voice was rising and smiled slightly.

'My apologies. You and I both know there are moves afoot to restrict the powers of the Time Police. To tie our hands. I fear we may not prove adequate to any threat that might arise in the near future. I need allies in the government. Highly placed allies. Allies who have the ear of the PM.'

'Are you asking me this because of Imogen?' said Mrs

Farnborough, causing Commander Hay to remember her reputation for blunt speaking.

'No. Forgive me – this is despite Imogen, rather than because of her.' She paused and then said more quietly, 'I understand why you may not feel you can support the Time Police. I wouldn't blame you if you said no, but I do ask you, from my heart, at least to reconsider your decision.'

Mrs Farnborough frowned. 'The PM . . . I've already spoken to her. It's to be announced on Monday . . . After I've had time to put everything in order. Leave things tidy . . .'

'Speak to her again. Please. I am certain she will be overjoyed to hear you have changed your mind.'

'Well, it is true that if I remain in place, her back will not be quite so vulnerable.'

'There you are, then.'

'It's just . . . at this moment . . . I'm not sure I would be able . . . I would not *feel* able to face . . .' She tailed away, unable to articulate her overwhelming grief and loss.

'I understand. Completely. And it is your decision. But it would do my heart good to know that somewhere in the corridors of power I had at least one ally. There are powerful forces ranging against us.'

'Forgive me . . . what you say about the Time Police is . . . concerning. How bad *are* things?'

'They aren't bad at all. But peacetime manning levels are considerably lower than in wartime. Should an emergency arise – a long-term threat – we might experience some difficulties in providing a sustained response.'

'You're building a power base.'

'I am indeed. Ideally, I would like to nip all this in the bud.

I most especially would like to be certain that the government will not decide to reduce expenditure at exactly the moment they should be increasing it.'

'You think that might happen?'

'There are multi-nationals out there that are more powerful and better financed than some nations. And, as we both know, money talks. In fact, it shouts. Money is mightier than the sword. Money opens doors, buys support, makes difficulties disappear overnight. Money buys everything – including governments. If I were feeling cynical, I would say especially governments.'

Dusk fell in the garden. Cold shadows gathered. The garden lights came on, carefully placed to highlight a feature here, a striking plant there. The overhead heater warmed the air around them. Neither woman noticed. Mrs Farnborough said nothing, staring into the middle distance at something only she could see. And then she sighed. 'I had hoped to step back for a while. To step out of the bloodstained arena that is politics. To do something to repair my spirit. Restore my soul.'

'I understand completely, Patricia. There's a whole world out there – a bright, sunlit world of families, friends, music, art, gardens, wine, travel, literature . . . all the things the sacrifices of people like us enable others to enjoy. I'm sorry if you thought you were about to emerge into that sunlight. I'm asking you to step back into the shadows. Back into the bloodstained arena.'

More silence. Commander Hay sipped her wine, leaned back and closed her eyes. Somewhere in the distance, a child shouted and a dog barked. Here, apart from the fountain, was only silence and stillness.

Eventually Mrs Farnborough stirred and sighed. 'What do you need?'

Hay put down her glass. 'Initially – speak to the PM. Please. Withdraw your resignation. For the time being, at least.'

She got up to go and Mrs Farnborough rose with her. 'Are the barbarians actually at the gates?'

'Not at this very moment, but soon, perhaps. The world was caught unprepared last time. I am determined that shall not happen again.'

'Then you too should take a moment to enjoy a glass of wine in a garden. Things are not yet so difficult that one hour, every now and then, will make any difference.'

Commander Hay smiled and sat down. 'I don't suppose it will.'

'Let me top up your glass. Have you read that thing by Wells on the causes and effects of the Time Wars?'

'I have,' said Commander Hay with feeling.

'Ah. Enough said, perhaps.'

'Bloody historians. I hate them.'

At the exact moment Commander Hay was enjoying a moment of peace in a quiet garden, Ms Steel was frowning at her employer.

'Imogen Farnborough was executed yesterday. And before you say anything, Raymond, Luke is not a bad boy. He's not weak, he's not unbalanced, and he's not his mother. He's a young man who is making his own way in the world – sometimes not very successfully – and a friend of his has died in horrific circumstances for which he feels at least partly responsible.

'You threw him into the Time Police for exactly that reason – to teach him to take responsibility for his own actions. You have, as always, got exactly what you wanted but, in this instance, it is your son who has paid the price. It might be nice if you felt it incumbent upon you to put aside your preoccupations with Site X for a few hours and enquire after his welfare. And my resignation can be on your desk in seconds should you feel I have overstepped my boundaries.'

Raymond Parrish was genuinely shocked. 'Good God, Lucinda, I can't possibly afford to sack you. You are the holder of all my secrets. No – when the time comes, I shall have to have you assassinated.'

'Not tonight, if you please, I am joining friends at the Royal Ballet.'

'Sometime next week, perhaps. Pencil it into my diary.'

'Yes, sir.'

'And tell – ask – Luke if he would like to call on me.'

She frowned again.

'Or whether I should call on him, of course.'

'Yes, sir.'

## 18

Captain Farenden was working quietly at his desk when the storm cloud broke.

'Captain!'

Captain Farenden regarded his intercom with misgivings before saying cautiously, 'Yes, ma'am?'

'Ask – no, *tell* – Major Callen I want to see him immediately.'

'Er . . . yes, ma'am.'

'And I know I said I never wanted to be alone with him, Charlie, but I think this morning I do.'

'Er . . . yes, ma'am.'

Major Callen arrived only minutes later.

She looked up as he entered. 'That was quick, Major.'

'You actually asked to see me, Commander. A bit of a first for both of us. As you can imagine, I hastened here with all speed.'

She flung a file across her desk in his direction. 'You're designating all female staff with a "w" after their names? Why?'

He sat back in his chair. 'I need to be able to recognise male/female officers at a glance. If I want a pretty, petite female officer to masquerade as a nightclub hostess or a businesswoman who

215

charges by the hour, I don't want to inadvertently select a male officer who looks as if he's been hewn from a rock face and possesses the complexion of a pepperoni pizza.'

'There are only twenty officers in your department at the moment, Major. Don't tell me you aren't familiar with their gender.'

'Well, obviously, I don't intend to do it with just *my* teams. I always feel it's important to apply the same criteria impartially across the organisation, don't you? You know . . . inclusivity.'

'Why the fire truck are you so determined to wind me up at every opportunity?'

'Camouflage.'

'What?'

'I'm sorry?'

'Your last sentence made no sense.'

'My apologies, Commander. Consider it unsaid.'

'I am not inclined to do that. What is?'

'Pardon?'

'What is being camouflaged?'

'I do not believe I am under any obligation to tell you that. Even a TPO has the right to privacy.'

'I asked you a question.'

'And I said I'm not telling you. With respect, Commander, you cannot compel me to do so.'

'Get out. Get the fire truck out of my office. Now.'

Major Callen walked unhurriedly from the room, carefully closing the door behind him and saying to Captain Farenden, 'I wouldn't go in there for a while if I were you.'

Captain Farenden stood up hastily, propelling his chair across the floor.

Callen laughed and headed for the door. 'By the way, Captain, I was in and out so quickly this morning that I didn't have the opportunity to inform the commander I'm chasing a new line of enquiry following our discussions the other day. I shall report back as soon as I have something tangible.' He grinned at her closed door. 'But not today, I think.'

'Listen, I've been thinking,' said Luke, as Team 236 met for breakfast the next day. 'But I don't want to say anything here. Let's take our toast to our office and have a conference.'

He set off before they could argue.

'Eating in here is not allowed,' said Jane, primly, as they laid two enormous plates of toast on their table. This was true. The Time Police's quite reasonable argument being that since they provided a perfectly good dining room as part of the barely adequate facilities to be enjoyed by their officers, eating elsewhere was unnecessary. And it attracted mice.

'We had mice at St Mary's,' said Matthew, pulling the nearest plate of toast towards him. His appetite was well known to be bigger than he was. Officers marvelled openly at the amount of food he could put away and still remain the smallest, skinniest officer in the building. Excluding Lockland, of course, but only just.

He continued to talk and eat. 'Loads of them. Little brown scuttery things. They were everywhere. You could hear them having late-night parties behind the walls. They ate everything. Food, cardboard, paper, electrical cables, the lot. We reckoned some of them were carnivorous.'

He grabbed another slice.

217

'Nothing you have at St Mary's surprises me,' said Luke, biting into his own toast.

'But they have a cat,' said Jane to Matthew. 'I've seen him.'

'Well, sadly, Vortigern proved himself quite useless in that area so St Mary's was forced to become more creative.'

Luke looked up. 'I hardly dare ask.'

'A snake.'

Jane nearly dropped her toast. 'What? What did people say? Didn't anyone object?'

'Well, I expect loads of people would have if they'd known but they didn't so they didn't.'

'What sort of snake?' enquired Luke, with interest.

Matthew shrugged and took another slice. 'A big one.'

'Did it work?'

'No. The professor released the snake, which shot off, and we never saw it again.' He smiled and bit into his toast, his eyes very bright.

Jane gaped at him. 'What happened?'

'Nothing. We forgot about it. Which turned out to be a bit of a mistake.'

'Why?'

'Someone, somehow, acquired a fifteen-foot-long snakeskin which they left carefully draped over the banisters. It was quite spectacular. People screamed, fainted, ran away, locked themselves in the toilet and so on, and after Uncle Markham pointed out that that was the *old* skin – imagine how big the bugger must be by now – the professor and his team knocked up a couple more flamethrowers. Just to be on the safe side.'

Jane stared at him, her toast forgotten. 'Then what happened?'

'Well, they – we – accidentally burned down the second-floor airing cupboard because someone said snakes liked warm, dark places, and then Uncle Peterson said to pack it in for God's sake before the whole building went up in flames, and he sent for the pest control people, who sent for the local zoo, who arrived with a TV crew because they were making a documentary about the zoo at the time. We were all on TV. For very nearly the right reasons.'

'Did it work?'

'Dunno. Suppose so.'

'You mean you'd left by then?'

'No – they just never found the snake. Either dead or alive. No one did.'

'You mean it's still there?' said Jane, aghast, trying not to think of the several occasions she'd visited St Mary's with Matthew. When cold, reptilian eyes could have been watching her every move. Just waiting . . .

'Must be,' said Matthew, starting on the second plate. 'I imagine it's lying somewhere in a dark, forgotten place, easily thirty feet long by now, coil upon coil upon coil, as thick as a man's waist, jaws that could swallow a car . . . watching and waiting . . .'

Luke and Jane could only stare at him.

Biting into the last piece of toast, Matthew regarded them innocently, his strange eyes glowing beneath his mop of dark hair.

'Just one question,' said Luke.

'Mm . . . ?' said Matthew, muffled by his toast.

'Who acquired the snakeskin?'

'Sadly, no one ever found out.'

Jane scowled at him. 'Just as well, don't you think?'

Matthew chewed, swallowed and grinned.

'You are not normal,' said Luke, at last. 'I know we never talk about it and everyone pretends you are so as not to hurt your feelings, but you're really, seriously, not normal.'

Matthew shrugged. 'No more mice at St Mary's, though.'

'Enough,' said Jane, firmly.

'Aw,' said Bolshy Jane. 'I wanted to hear more about the thirty-foot-long reticulated python lurking in the dark bowels of St Mary's all ready to swallow the unwary. We could get one for TPHQ. They swallow you head first, don't they?'

Jane did her best to ignore the pictures in her mind. 'Luke, what have you been thinking about?'

Luke blinked. 'What? Oh – yes. We should go back.'

She blinked. 'Back where?'

'To Beaver Avenue. To before the delivery that killed Henry and his family. Records can get us the exact time, date, location . . .'

'We don't usually do things like that,' said Matthew, uneasily. 'The chances of changing some small but vital piece of history means we could be up to our knees in paradoxes before we've barely left the pod.'

'True, but we would just observe.'

'Observe the rubble?'

'No, we go back to before the explosion – check out the delivery driver, the van, and so on.'

They thought about this.

'We'd need a strict timetable,' said Jane, thinking it through, step by step. 'We'd have to be absolutely certain about where we should be and when. And then we'd need to present it to . . .' She stopped. Major Ellis was no longer their leader.

'We'll show it to Ellis,' said Luke. 'He can be our trial run.'

'I can't see him being very enthusiastic,' said Jane. 'It's all too easy to change something inadvertently and then the explosion won't occur and then we're in all sorts of trouble. They'll never allow us to do it.'

'Look, we're sitting here eating illegal toast,' said Luke. 'I think that establishes us as badass rule-breakers, don't you? Let's draw up a mission plan. Get cracking, everyone.'

To their great astonishment, their request was accepted.

'I've been considering something similar, myself,' said Ellis. 'However, there will be strict conditions with which you will comply without question. Observation only. Direct interaction with any contemporaries is forbidden. You will speak to no one. Remember the Plimptons have already met you so you will stay out of sight at all times.'

'We thought civilian clothes, sir,' said Jane.

'Good idea. You will not go armed. I don't want anyone accidentally blowing something up before its appointed time. Sonics and string to defend yourselves and even then, only as a last resort.'

They nodded. Even Luke.

'At what time will you arrive? What's your timetable?'

'We're aiming for 1700 hours, sir.'

Ellis considered the data stack in front of him. 'According to this, the delivery van arrives at approximately 1728. As far as we know, Henry usually arrives home at around 1820. Records show the explosion occurs at around 1847 hours.' He flattened the stack. 'You will spend no more than an hour and a half on site, which should be more than enough time. I say again, there will be no interaction of any kind with anyone. You will be in your pod and jumping away by 1830 at the very latest. My final word. Grumble and you're grounded.'

They nodded.

'Of course we will,' murmured Luke.

Ellis shot him a sharp glance but said nothing.

They assembled in the Pod Bay outside one of the smaller pods. All were wearing civilian clothes. Luke wore a simple, and therefore very expensive, jacket and trousers. Jane had dressed in a white T-shirt, black jeans and a khaki body warmer. It was Matthew, however, who had fully embraced the principles of plain clothes, wearing an old but favourite Iron Man T-shirt. Ripped jeans were back in fashion but Matthew's looked as if they had been through a cheese grater rather than a fashion house, and the ensemble was completed with his favourite light-up trainers. With his scruffy hair and short stature, he looked like an even more than usually disreputable student. He and the words Time Police officer were not even on the same continent.

Grinning mechs stood around as Matthew attempted to explain his purpose to a suspicious Senior Mech, which was that Team 236 was going undercover, rather than attempting to undermine society in general and the Time Police in particular. They might have been there still if Major Ellis had not appeared on the scene and exercised major appeasement skills.

Luke ran an eye over his team. 'Right – on board, everyone.'

Jane was very, very careful laying in the coordinates, taking her time, making sure she did everything right. Matthew stood at her shoulder, watching her every move. There had been a time when Luke's impatient sighs would have flustered her but those days were gone. Ignoring him, she concentrated on her task, step by step.

'Good for you, sweetie,' said Bolshy Jane. 'Fetch him one with your chair if he dares to sigh again.'

Eventually the coordinates were done.

'Finally,' said Luke, sarcastically.

Just for that . . . thought Jane. 'Matthew, can you verify my figures for me, please. One more time. Just to be on the safe side.'

Matthew leaned over the console and once again painstakingly ran through Jane's calculations.

'Your conscientiousness is commendable,' said Luke, shifting his weight impatiently, 'but can we go?'

'In a minute,' said Matthew, his attention still on the readouts.

'You're just winding me up,' said Luke. 'For heaven's sake, let's go.'

'This is much more fun,' said Matthew. 'Shall we run through it again, Jane?'

Luke raised his arms in exasperation. 'Pod – jump. For God's sake – jump.'

The AI responded pleasantly. 'Your instructions are unclear. Incorrect protocol.'

Jane turned. 'Luke – just sit still and leave the difficult stuff to us, will you?'

'Well, get a fire-trucking move on. Any moment now we'll have the mechs banging on the door demanding to know why we're still here.'

Jane grinned. 'Pod – commence jump procedures.'

'Jump procedures commenced.'

The world flickered.

They landed exactly where they'd been before. Jane was interested to see the old car had not yet been blown off its bricks.

'Everyone got everything?' enquired Luke. 'Sonics? String?'

'We're not expecting any trouble, are we?' enquired Jane, shutting things down on the console.

'This is us,' said Luke. 'And there's a massive explosion scheduled in around an hour and three quarter's time – so yes, I'm expecting trouble.'

They exited the pod and found their way back to Beaver Avenue for the third time. This time the day was bright and sunny and there were people everywhere. Shopping, talking, dodging the traffic, shouting to make themselves heard.

'Normal 20th-century activity,' said Luke. 'Watch what you're standing in, everyone.'

Cars whizzed past at some speed, occasionally grounding themselves on strange humps in the road, inconveniently positioned just where they would prove a hazard to speeding traffic. There was a smell of exhaust fumes, burning rubber, cigarettes and curry. Litter lined the gutters, often blocking the drains, and the curse of the late 20th and 21st centuries – plastic bags – fluttered in garden hedges and trees or blew colourfully and cheerfully into unreachable places, there to remain until the end of Time.

They were just beginning to make their way towards the not much longer for this world Beaver Avenue when a sudden shrieking klaxon blasted the air with the sort of rhythm that made listeners want to beat their own brains out. Already nervous, Team 236 leaped a mile into the air.

'What is that?' cried Jane, staring around.

'Car alarm,' said Matthew briefly. 'It's the vehicle over there. The silver one with the flashing headlights.'

Jane stared at it. 'What's it alarmed about?'

'Someone's trying to steal it,' said Luke, glancing round. 'It's a security device. The first car I ever owned had one. Theoretically it goes off if someone tampers with your car and then everyone rushes to repel the thief and save the day.'

They waited. There was no rushing and definitely no day-saving.

Jane frowned. 'That doesn't seem to be happening.'

'No.'

'In fact, no one's taking any notice.'

'No.'

'Then why did people bother?'

'How should I know? It's just something people did back then. Install car alarms, I mean. If there's such a thing as a book on quaint, late 20th-century customs and rituals, then the explanation is probably in there.'

'Perhaps the noise frightens off evil spirits and propitiates the gods,' said Matthew, straight-faced.

'Pisses off the neighbours, more like,' said Luke, raising his voice as they approached the screaming, flashing car.

'How long do these things go on for?' shouted Jane over the din.

Luke shrugged. 'Until the battery goes flat. In which case the car's not going anywhere, anyway.'

'Perhaps that's how they're supposed to work,' said Jane. 'Draining the power so the car can't be stolen.'

'Could be,' said Luke. 'Who knows? It is the 20th century, after all. They've only just learned to walk upright.'

A trio of youths shambled past. Two of them, anyway. The one at the back appeared to have an issue with Luke's last sentence. 'You what?'

Matters hung in the balance for a moment but before Luke could open his mouth to make things even worse, Jane and Matthew had bundled him around the corner.

'I don't know why we bring you,' said Jane, crossly.

'Neither do I,' said Luke. 'Happy to wait in the pod if you like.'

Matthew glanced at his watch. 'We should be getting a move on.'

Luke sighed. 'Right, Jane – you're the designated time-keeper. Call it every five minutes or so. We do not want to be in this area at 1847.'

They made their way slowly down Beaver Avenue, making sure to stay on the opposite side of the road. Jane had worried that lingering outside Number Seventeen might be regarded as suspicious but there were small groups of people everywhere. Gossiping, returning home with shopping, walking slowly down the avenue – and up the avenue too. People stood at their garden gates watching the world go by on a sunny afternoon. For once in their lives, Team Weird weren't in the slightest bit conspicuous.

In fact, as Matthew pointed out, he was fitting in perfectly, and if anything, it was the overdressed Luke who stood out from their environment.

'1706,' reported Jane, before Luke could think of a response.

'Stacks of time,' he said. 'We'll stroll casually up and down until 1720, at which point, we'll position ourselves to await the delivery van. When it does arrive, Jane and I will get as close as we can, see if we can ascertain what's actually being delivered, and what happens to the delivery subsequently. Matthew, you stay back and record everything. When you've finished, nip round the back and see if you can find out whether the package stays in the house or gets taken into Henry's shed. Be aware of Jane's time checks. We all meet back here and then leg it back to the pod before Beaver Avenue disappears in a puff of smoke. Everyone got it?'

Matthew and Jane both nodded.

'All right then, here we go. Oh – hang on a minute. Bit of local colour.' He rummaged in his pockets, pulling out a packet of cigarettes and a rather nice lighter. Striking a pose, he lit the cigarette.

Jane stepped back and flapped her hands, uttering, 'Luke, are you actually *smoking*?' in much the same tones as a particularly zealous Christian might demand, '*Are you actually sacrificing newborn infants to the great god Baal?*'

'Yeah,' said Luke, wreathed in clouds of toxic blue smoke. 'What do you think?'

'I think it smells awful.'

'You don't think it makes me look cool?'

'Oh, oh, oh,' said Matthew, putting up his hand and bouncing on his heels, 'I know the answer to this one, miss. Can I tell him? Pleeeeeeeeeease.'

'You know, I really preferred it when you never said more than three words a week,' said Luke. He sighed. 'What did I ever do that condemned me to work with the two least cool people in the entire universe?' He looked at his cigarette, pulled a face, dropped it on the pavement and ground it out with his shoe. 'Come on.'

'Are you . . . are you just going to leave it there?' said Jane, staring at the abandoned cigarette butt.

'Jane – firstly, I'm not touching this pavement. Secondly – this entire area is due to be blown sky-high in about ninety minutes. I don't imagine one single dog-end will make very much difference.'

His words brought it home to them. That this area was due to be blown sky-high in less than an hour and a half. Some of these people, their children, their pets, would cease to exist. Along with *all* of their cars, their houses and their entire lives.

Jane stopped, distressed.

'No,' said Luke, taking her arm, but gently.

'But . . .'

'No. You know we can't.'

'I do know, but . . .'

'There's nothing we can do, Jane,' said Matthew. 'Or should do. It has to happen because it's already happened.'

Jane nodded and squared her shoulders. 'Come on, then. Let's get this done.'

'Time check?'

'1712.'

Luke gestured ahead. 'Up this side of the street, cross over at the top and down the other. We want to end up directly outside Henry's house.'

Their plan went without a hitch. Well – almost without a hitch.

They paused at the top of Beaver Avenue to get their bearings. Adapting himself to his surroundings, Luke leaned negligently against someone's gate.

'Oi,' said a familiar voice. 'Get off my gate.'

Mr Fernley stood in his front garden in his shirtsleeves. Tongue lolling in the heat, Jasper sat alongside him. It would have been hard to say who was eyeing them the most malevolently. Mr Fernley was carrying a pair of garden shears. Jane looked at the overgrown hedge bordering his front garden. It would take him hours of work to get that trimmed. If he was out here when the explosion occurred, then neither he nor Jasper would survive.

'Sorry,' said Luke, stepping away from the gate which, without his support, sagged even further.

Mr Fernley was not best pleased. 'Now look what you've done.'

'Sorry,' said Luke again.

Jane stood frozen.

'Let it go,' said Bolshy Jane.

'But he'll die if he stays where he is.'

'Well, he doesn't die, does he, so stop panicking.'

'But he's talking to us and we shouldn't be here. Suppose that delays him with whatever he's doing and he's still here when the whole street explodes.'

'This is why you were forbidden to speak to anyone,' said Bolshy Jane.

'I have to put it right.'

'Nice thought, sweetie, but there's a very good chance you'll just make it worse.'

'Be quiet, you.' Jane stepped closer to the gate. 'It's very hot today,' she said to Mr Fernley. 'I expect you're gasping for a cup of co . . . tea. *While you read the afternoon paper.*'

Mr Fernley regarded his shears without enthusiasm. 'Ah. Could do, I suppose.' His jaws began to work.

'Enough,' said Bolshy Jane. 'Walk away right now.'

The same thought had obviously occurred to both Luke and Matthew. Unusually united, they both nudged her away from Mr Fernley's house and back down the street.

'He'll be fine,' soothed Luke as they carefully crossed the road to the Plimptons' side. 'We know he survives even if others don't.'

They paused alongside a car for whom the word 'roadworthy' was just a faint and far-off dream.

'Right, look casual, everyone,' said Luke. 'We've just stopped for a bit of a chat, OK?'

Everyone was immediately struck dumb.

'What shall we talk about?' enquired Jane.

Luke sighed. 'Well, I don't think we have long enough to discuss your strange and unusual love life – mine is much the same as it always is – which leaves Matthew . . .'

Matthew said nothing.

'Who's saying nothing so we're back to you again, Jane. Where's your life going?' persisted Luke. 'After the Time Police, I mean.'

'What?' said Jane.

'Well, none of us are going to be in the Time Police forever, are we?'

'Aren't we?' said Jane, who had never, until that moment, even considered life after the Time Police. In fact, according to many officers, there *was* no life after the Time Police. If she did leave – where would she go? What would she do? She could feel the panic rising. Matthew would certainly return to St Mary's. Luke was rich and could do as he pleased, but what about her? What would she do without them? Where would she go? Returning to her grandmother was unthinkable.

'Van,' said Matthew suddenly as a vehicle appeared at the bottom of the road. He pulled out his recorder.

'Right,' said Luke. 'Let's not screw this one up. Everyone know what to do?' He glanced up the road. 'And Mr Fernley and Jasper are on their way to the shop. Don't get in their way.'

Matthew remained where he was, recording the van's slow approach, intending to close in for the details later.

Jane and Luke strolled slowly down the road, making sure they were directly outside the Plimpton house as the van drew up. In fact, so perfectly placed were they that Luke had to step aside as the van mounted the pavement to park.

'Are they supposed to do that?' whispered Jane. 'Are we standing on the wrong bit? I thought pavements were for people, not parking.'

'I think it was a bit of a free-for-all in these degenerate times,' whispered Luke. 'Shush.'

'Afternoon,' said the driver, a young woman, leaping down from her vehicle.

'Afternoon,' said Jane, before Luke could offer any sort of commentary on the standards of 20th-century parking.

The driver trotted to the rear, pulled up the shutter and removed a cardboard box.

About eighteen inches square, thought Jane. And quite heavy by the way she's handling it.

Matthew had moved to the back of the vehicle and was still discreetly recording. The driver consulted her docket, opened the gate and strode up the path, whistling, to thump on the door. A familiar fusillade of dog barks filled the afternoon. Mr Fernley and Jasper crossed to the other side of the road.

Initially there was no response. 'Is she out?' said Jane. 'This could be a stroke of luck. The driver might leave it on the step and we'll get the chance of a good look at it.'

'Unlikely in this neighbourhood,' said Luke. 'It'll be half-inched in no time.'

'It'll be what?'

'Half-inched. Pinched. I'm seamlessly blending into— here we go.'

The front door opened and there stood Mrs Plimpton, start-lingly familiar. Still enormous, still heavily made-up – although her previously long auburn hair was now a light golden frizz around her face. Like an electrified sunflower.

As if by magic, other members of the family began to appear. Kylie, the daughter, hung out of an upstairs window to see who was at the door. Behind her loomed her brother Dwayne's enor-mous head, now shaven completely. Two small dogs leaped up and down behind Mrs Plimpton as if they were on a trampoline, barking hysterically.

That's the whole family, thought Jane sadly. Her faint hope that at least one of them might not have been at home when the bomb went off curled up and died.

Mrs Plimpton shouted something over the din. The driver shouted back again and flourished her docket. Mrs Plimpton signed. The driver handed over the box, returned back down the path, ignored both Luke and Jane this time round, and jumped into her van. The engine started with a roar and a cough of blue smoke. She reversed and drove away. The cloud slowly dissipated to reveal Matthew, still recording away.

'I'm going to nip round the back,' he said, stowing away his recorder. 'See if she puts it in the shed. Back in a minute.' Leaving Luke and Jane to watch for Henry's return from work, he trotted away.

The familiar alleyway was still there. Of course it was – why wouldn't it be? The path ran parallel with the backs of the houses on this side of Beaver Avenue. Matthew made sure to watch where he put his feet because, as before, the alleyway was cluttered with piles of rubbish, sagging cardboard boxes spilling their contents across the path, abandoned fridges and what seemed like hundreds of the ubiquitous plastic wheelie bins. Possibly in an effort to bring a little colour into people's lives, the council had provided black ones, blue ones, green ones . . . and plastic boxes, too. Grey ones, orange ones . . . and most of them scattered all higgledy-piggledy along the alleyway. What on earth did the inhabitants do with them all? Most of them seemed to be acting as a collection point for whatever the residents of Beaver Avenue felt like hurling over their garden walls at the time. Progress was actually quite slow as Matthew alternately eased himself between them or danced sideways to avoid treading in something unspeakable.

Carefully counting the houses, he arrived at the back of the Plimpton residence and called up his team leader.

'I'm around the back. No one in sight. I'm going over the wall to see what I can see.'

Jane spoke in his ear. 'Time's getting on, Matthew. It's 1748. Quick look round and then pull out.'

'Stacks of time,' said Luke. 'Just don't get caught.'

'Copy that.'

The back gate appeared to be locked. Ah – now he knew

what the bins were for. Arranging a brown box in front of a blue bin, which in turn was pushed in front of a black one, he had a multi-coloured staircase. He cast a swift look up and down the alleyway but no one was in sight.

Climbing up the bins was easier said than done. They were sturdy enough but had a tendency to wobble precariously on the uneven ground. Eventually, cautiously, he was able to peer over the wall.

Mrs Plimpton was in the kitchen, and judging by the noise, hurling saucepans at the wall for some reason. A radio played loudly, merging seamlessly with the music upstairs. He wouldn't have to worry about her hearing him. The back door was shut and he couldn't see the dogs anywhere but they weren't in the garden which was good enough for him.

The garden comprised mostly knee-high coarse grass with a cracked concrete path running to the wooden structure in the back right-hand corner. It was no more than ten feet away but, unfortunately, with no cover between it and him.

He was very conscious of time ticking on. Choosing a moment when he judged Mrs Plimpton's back to be turned, Matthew swung himself over the wall, dropped quietly into the garden and moved swiftly towards the shed.

'1756,' said Jane in his ear.

'Still plenty of time,' said Luke. 'Just don't let them see you.'

Matthew concealed himself behind the wooden structure. Cautiously he peered around the corner. No Mrs Plimpton stood in the kitchen staring at him through the window. No Plimpton offspring were at the upstairs windows. He couldn't count on that happy state of affairs lasting forever, though. He should get a move on.

Opening his com, he said, 'Luke, Jane, the garden's empty. I can check out what's inside the shed. Back in a minute.'

'Watch yourself,' warned Luke.

'I will, don't worry.'

The garden shed was larger than he remembered. And in much better condition than before. Henry had obviously taken the opportunity to remodel. He'd been lucky. There wasn't usually much left to remodel after a visit from a clean-up crew. They must have been in a mellow mood that day.

Strangely, for a shed, the really well-made door was completely flush with the jamb. There was no handle. No keyhole. No keypad. Nor any visible hinges. Matthew ran his hands over the surface, stared at it for as long as he dared and then eased himself back around the corner, out of sight. An idea was forming in his head. Because if he didn't know better . . .

He cast another anxious glance at the window. Surely Mrs Plimpton could reappear at any moment – or decide to let the dogs out or something. He made a decision. There was nothing to lose, after all. Apart from feeling a complete plonker, of course, but no one would ever know. Poking his head round the corner again, he said firmly, 'Door.'

Nothing happened. Well, of course it didn't. What did he expect? And yes, he did feel a complete plonker. One more try.

'Open.'

He still didn't expect anything to happen but he was wrong. The door opened. Right in front of his disbelieving eyes, the door clicked and swung open a few inches. Enticing him inside.

Oscillating wildly between triumph and terror, he opened his com again, whispering, 'Luke – the garden shed. It's a pod. Henry's built himself another pod.'

'What? What are you talking about?'

Matthew strove for clarity. 'He's not building a pod in the shed – the whole shed is a pod. I've got the door open and I'm going in to investigate.'

'Matthew . . .'

'Can't hang around – I'm very exposed here.'

He eased his skinny body through the door, leaving it as he found it – very slightly ajar – and looked around.

There was no doubt. The interior was dark but this was a pod. Some attempt seemed to have been made to disguise it. True, there was no maelstrom of garden implements, plant pots, plastic hoses, bicycles, barbecues, bits of washing line, rolls of chicken wire, cans of WD40, unwanted furniture, lawnmowers or lethal garden chemicals, but someone had arranged their handyman's tools to hang neatly around the walls, each clearly labelled. Typical of Henry, he thought. A place for everything and everything in its place. Anyone catching a glimpse of the interior would easily be able to imagine Henry working away quietly, humming to himself, temporarily removed from the noise and chaos of his household.

Matthew looked around. This was a very basic pod. The light hadn't come on automatically as the door opened. There were no seats or lockers – no comforts of any kind. Instead, crates and boxes were stacked neatly around what looked like authentically wooden walls. A wooden pod – was that even possible? He doubted it. There must be some kind of a hidden framework to give it strength. There was no sleeping module, no toilet facilities, and worryingly, no decontamination lamp. And no means of recharging that he could see.

He frowned. What did that tell him? If the pod couldn't

be charged here, then how? This was obviously not its permanent home. And there were no biometrics so it must be a common-use pod that could be entered by anyone simply by saying, 'Open.' Interesting. Very interesting.

There was a kind of console but it was only a very simple affair, disguised as a glorified workbench. And he could see there was no electricity here. No – there couldn't be. Plugging his shed into the national grid would be bound to cause suspicions. Pods use a lot of power. Someone would have noticed the abnormal surges. That was why the light hadn't come on as he entered. What little he could see was solely from the daylight filtering through the slightly open door. There must be . . . He looked under the console. Yes. Batteries. Hefty batteries. How much charge would they carry? Enough for more than one trip. There was no point in jumping somewhere if you didn't have enough power to get back again, was there?

Hugely curious – either a Farrell family failing or a Farrell family feature, depending on which parent was speaking at the time – and forgetting his circumstances entirely, he bent over the console. As far as he could see, the controls were minimal. How were the coordinates programmed in? His fingers traced a path. No chronometer but . . . he looked up. Flicking aside an old towel revealed a very small screen angled across the corner between two walls. Only one camera. No external sensors. So . . . you banged in your coordinates here . . . hit the go button here . . . and presumably closed your eyes and prayed the pod got you there without actually exploding.

He straightened, suddenly. Exploding. Was it possible that the delivery they'd witnessed was only a coincidence? Was it actually this pod that had caused the explosion? Given the levels of devastation, that was perfectly possible. On the fortunately very rare occasions when a pod blew up, the damage tended to be severe and widespread. No, hold on. There was no trace of a radiation signature. It couldn't have been the pod. And at this moment it appeared to be completely inert. The correct expression was *dark*.

He was just wondering whether any previous coordinates would still be in the system – a study of this pod's recent movements might prove extremely useful – when he heard the back door open and Mrs Plimpton's extremely carrying voice ordering the dogs out into the garden. Fire-truckity fire truck. Now what? He had a nasty suspicion they'd be through the open door and into the pod like a flash. To be closely followed by Mrs Plimpton attempting to chivvy them straight back out again.

Very gently, he pulled the door to. Still no light came on. He was standing in complete darkness. He held his breath and waited. Was Mrs Plimpton bringing the delivered box to her husband's shed? Could she get in? And what would he do if she could? Sonic her to the ground, take a quick look around, step over her unconscious body, climb back over the wall and run for it was his only plan.

Fortunately, none of that came to pass. The minutes ticked by. Nothing terrible happened. It would appear she had just been letting the dogs out after all. Which was all very well but completely screwed up Matthew's get-away plans. He would exit the pod only to be enveloped in enthusiastic dogs. Shortly to be followed by the probably much less enthusiastic Mrs Plimpton. And then by her offspring. Sonic them *all* to the ground, step over them, climb back over the wall and run for it was still his number one plan. Strangely, for some reason, he felt more reluctant to sonic the dogs than the Plimptons.

How long had he been standing here?

He held up his watch. 1805. Shit. Time certainly flew when you were trapped inside a strange pod in an environment that would possibly blow up in . . . his heart jolted in shock and then started up again. He had less than half an hour before they had to leave – but that was still plenty of time. Or so he told himself.

He opened his com. 'Luke. Jane. Can you hear me?'

There was no response. He hadn't thought there would be. This pod wasn't sophisticated enough to enable him to contact the outside world. Or for the outside world to contact him. Perhaps if he could get the camera to work . . .

No. Too risky. He shouldn't touch anything. It might be something *he* did that actually caused the explosion.

He looked at his watch again. 1806. Henry didn't get back until 1820. Plenty of time to have a good look around. He'd give it until 1818 at the very latest and then make a run for it – dogs or not. Out of the door. Across the garden and . . .

Shit. How was he to get back over the wall? Matthew Farrell was the second shortest person in the Time Police – Jane held the honour of the actual shortest. All the bins were on the other side of the wall and the gate was locked.

Never mind. Cross that bridge – or climb that wall – later. Luke could always pull him back over.

First thing was to find the control for the light. There must be one. Henry couldn't work in the dark. Matthew groped for the console and gently ran his hands across it. This felt like something . . .

239

Mentally crossing his fingers that it wasn't the self-destruct mechanism so beloved of sci-fi writers everywhere, he flicked the switch.

The light wasn't bright but it felt so after being in total darkness. He pulled out his recorder. There were thirteen crates and boxes, all of different sizes, all neatly stacked – he suspected the fussy hand of Henry Plimpton – and ranged by size. Biggest at the bottom, smallest on the top. The one closest to him was very small. He inspected it carefully. There was no Parrish Industries logo which was something to tell Luke. In fact, there were no markings of any kind on any of the crates in the pod. Not even any address labels, which was interesting. This one was just a normal cardboard box, about eighteen inches square and sealed with duct tape. He pulled out his knife, carefully slit the tape, and gently pulled back the flaps.

And really, really wished he hadn't.

**19**

Luke and Jane, meanwhile, were watching for Henry Plimpton's arrival home from work. As part of his social camouflage, Luke was again holding a cigarette. In deference to Jane, it remained unlit.

'What does Henry actually do?' enquired Luke.

Jane pulled out her trusty notebook. While she did occasionally use her Time Police scratchpad, her notebook would always be first choice.

'According to his statement, he has a part-time job in the post room at the local council.'

'Thus leaving himself plenty of time for extracurricular temporal activity,' muttered Luke.

'Not since we arrested him,' said Jane, flicking a page. 'He's down as cooperative and clean. A model citizen.'

Luke snorted.

'It's a shame,' said Jane, stuffing her notebook away. 'He helped us as much as he was able. He answered our questions. He submitted to routine checks. He didn't reoffend and now this happens to him.'

'I suspect this happens to him *precisely* because he helped us as much as he was able, Jane. There are messages being sent in all directions today.'

'Speaking of which,' said Jane, but Matthew spoke before she could finish the sentence.

'I'm around the back. No one in sight. I'm going over the wall to see what I can see.'

Jane spoke in his ear. 'Time's getting on, Matthew. It's 1748. Quick look round and then pull out.'

'Stacks of time,' said Luke. 'Just don't get caught.'

'Copy that.'

They stood watching life on Beaver Avenue for a while, including Mr Fernley and Jasper making the return trip. Jane took half a step in their direction before she could stop herself.

'It's a hot day,' said Luke, reassuringly. 'They'll be making themselves another cup of orange ditchwater before going back outside to do the hedge. They'll be fine, Jane.'

'Yes, you're right. And we meet him after the blast, so yes, they'll survive and . . .'

Matthew interrupted her.

'Luke, Jane, the garden's empty. I can check out what's inside the shed. Back in a minute.'

'Watch yourself,' said Luke.

'I will, don't worry.'

Luke pretended to puff on his cigarette. 'I was going to ask,' he said. 'How's it going with Grint?'

'Not sure,' said Jane. 'You know he took me out on the day . . . on the day Imogen . . .'

Luke nodded.

'Well, I haven't really seen him since then and I don't like to . . . I mean, suppose he's decided he doesn't . . . I mean, I'm not sure what he . . .' She stared at the ground, ending with, 'I don't know.'

'Oh, dear God.'

'It's all very well for you . . .'

'No, it's not. There's barely a woman in TPHQ still speaking to me, you know.'

'Well, whose fault is that?'

'Theirs. Obviously.'

'I'm not sure that's quite how they see it.'

'Look, Jane, ask him out.'

Jane was quite horrified. 'I couldn't do that.'

'Why not?'

'He might think . . .'

'It's Grint. He doesn't think.'

'That's very unkind.'

'Listen – and this is good advice, so do listen – find something you think he might like to do and drop him a note saying you were thinking of going to . . . whatever . . . an exhibition of the world's biggest verrucae or something . . .'

'What?' said Bolshy Jane.

'What?' said Wimpy Jane.

'*What?*' said Actual Jane.

'. . . and ask him if he'd like to come with you. If he says yes, all well and good. If he says no, then simply assume you're too hot for him to handle and move on. I reckon Rossi would be up for it if his team leader hadn't got there first. Not forgetting Scrape, of course. In fact, Jane, face it – you're pretty much the Team 235 pin-up girl.'

Jane opened her mouth and then closed it again. This was rather a lot to think about. The possibility of her – Jane – initiating some sort of romantic date – and the knowledge that Marco Rossi might possibly . . . or even Scrape. She was tempted to rubbish this thinking but dating was the one area in which Luke Parrish did tend to be a bit of an expert. She tucked it all away to think about later.

'On the other hand, of course,' continued Luke, always his own worst enemy, 'there aren't that many women in the Time Police so I suppose even you . . .'

'Kill him,' said Bolshy Jane. 'Now. No messing. Leave his body here. Massive explosion imminent. No witnesses. No evidence. Don't just stand there.'

'You all right?' said Luke, peering at her. 'Only every now and then you get this funny expression. Like you've gone inside your head.'

'Hush. I'm listening to the voices in my head telling me to kill you,' said Jane. 'They're making a very compelling case.'

'Well, that's not worrying at all.' He opened his com. 'Matthew – just a quick query. Do you hear voices in your head telling you what to do?'

'All the time,' said Matthew. 'Although to be fair, it's usually you.'

A somewhat grumpy silence fell. They could hear sounds from Matthew. And then, 'Luke – the garden shed. It's a pod. Henry's built himself another pod.'

'What? What are you talking about?'

'He's not building a pod in the shed – the whole shed is a pod. I've got the door open and I'm going in to investigate.'

'Matthew . . .'

'Can't hang around – I'm very exposed here.'

They waited anxiously.

'1800,' said Jane.

No response from Matthew.

'I'm not sure he can hear us if he's inside,' said Luke. 'This is making me nervous. Matthew, report.'

Silence.

'He probably can't get a signal,' said Jane, endeavouring to overcome her own misgivings. 'I wouldn't worry too much. No one knows more about pods than Matthew. He was brought up with them, remember.'

They strolled further along the road. And then back again. Just for the look of it, although, as far as Luke could tell, no one was watching them. Or even paying them any attention at all.

'Not one of them knows they only have minutes left,' said Jane, softly.

Luke nodded. 'Do you think this is what it's like to be St Mary's? Pitching up somewhere knowing that in ten minutes, an hour, a day, whatever, everyone they can see is going to be deader than a dodo. And they do that day after day after day. No wonder they're all so bloody odd.'

Jane nodded. It would account for a lot.

'Shit,' said Luke suddenly, staring over her shoulder.

'What?'

'Henry's coming.'

They both moved behind a parked car. Jane looked at her watch and was surprised to find the time was 1814. 'He's early.'

'No, he arrives home at 1820. He's got a few minutes yet.'

Henry Plimpton was exactly as they remembered him. Tiny, tubby, balding, with podgy cheeks and mild brown eyes behind his spectacles. He was wearing a shabby suit, a little baggy at the knees, carrying a briefcase and with his newspaper tucked under one arm.

He'll never get to read it, thought Jane, sadly.

There were fewer people on the street now. Probably everyone was going in for their evening meals.

Henry walked slowly up the road, apparently enjoying what was going to be a lovely evening. Although not for the people of Beaver Avenue.

'Time check,' said Jane. '1818.'

She tilted her head, listening, but there was nothing from Matthew.

Someone called a greeting, to which Henry paused to respond politely. He exchanged a few words and then approached his own house. They watched him switch his briefcase to his other hand and open the gate. The time was 1820 exactly.

And nothing from Matthew.

Luke frowned and opened his com. 'Matthew, where are you?'

Silence.

Luke shifted his weight impatiently. 'Matthew, report.'

Nothing.

Henry walked slowly to his front door, fumbling for his key.

'Matthew – Henry's arrived. Get out of there.'

The door opened as he went to insert his key. Mrs Plimpton smiled at her husband, who greeted her with an affectionate kiss. Jane's heart turned over. That would be their last ever kiss.

Luke was speaking urgently – discretion abandoned. 'Matthew – they're both at the front door. The coast is clear. Make a run for it.'

No response.

Jane tugged at his sleeve. 'Luke – it's 1822. We must go.'

Luke was shouting now. 'Matthew – never mind who sees you. It's too late for that. Just get out of there now.'

Still no reply.

The front door closed behind Henry Plimpton. Beaver Avenue had twenty-five minutes left in this world.

'Come on,' said Luke. 'Let's get round the back – see what's gone wrong.'

They set off at a run. Discretion was no longer important.

'Luke, Matthew said the shed was a pod.'

'Yes,' said Luke, grimly. 'I suspect our Henry's been a naughty boy again. I wonder who could possibly have sent him the wherewithal to build that?'

'I don't know – neither do you – and we don't have time to discuss it.'

'We've still got nearly twenty minutes. Matthew. Respond. Now.'

Nothing.

'Fire-trucking fire truck, Matthew. Answer me. Come in. Come in.'

Now they were running flat out, both of them shouting breathlessly into their coms. Things were not looking good.

Things weren't looking that good for Matthew, either.

He was unable to say for how long he stood staring at the contents of the cardboard box. His heart sank with recognition.

Some time ago, when he'd been living at St Mary's with his parents, there had been a period when he, his father, Mikey, Adrian and Professor Penrose had had to leave St Mary's for their own good.

'We'll be going on the run,' had said Adrian with relish.

'Hunted like dogs,' had said Mikey, bright-eyed with excitement.

'Hunted *with* dogs, perhaps,' had said Adrian. 'How cool will that be?'

'We'll be enjoying many opportunities for extracurricular educational activities,' had said Professor Penrose.

'You'll all be making my life a waking nightmare,' had said Chief Farrell.

Most of that had come true. Except for the dogs bit. Matthew had been slightly disappointed they had not been hunted to distinction.

'*Ex*tinction, dear boy,' had said Professor Penrose. 'Extra vocabulary session tomorrow, I think.'

As Adrian had described it, they'd jumped into a pod – Tea Bag 2 – and crashed around the Timeline in search of adventure and profit.

As Chief Farrell had described it, they'd embarked on a systematic search for a new remote site.

As the professor had described it, Matthew had benefitted from a wonderful opportunity to take advantage of the many educational prospects offered.

Mikey, however, and with enthusiastic assistance from Adrian, had embarked upon the preliminary stages of designing a mobile Time-travelling device. Something that could be attached to the wearer's arm. Jolly useful, she'd said, because you wouldn't have to worry about getting back to the pod and safety. Just press the appropriate control and – bang. The wearer could jump away from whatever crisis was occurring at the time. 'And live to jump another day, Chief,' she'd beamed.

Chief Farrell had smiled, nodded, burned her notes and everything else he could lay his hands on and that had been the end of that.

Until now . . .

Matthew was looking down at around a dozen metallic cuffs whose design was not completely unfamiliar. He had a horrible feeling that Mikey might not have abandoned her creations quite as willingly as everyone had thought, after all. But how on earth had they ended up here? And why?

His first instinct was to slam the box shut and get out of there. The whole area was about to be totally destroyed. No one need ever know what he'd seen. The explosion would remove all evidence of Mikey's invention. He could say nothing, do nothing, and no one need ever know. Yes, that's what he'd do. Replacing the box, he edged open the door.

He'd left it too late. He could hear Mrs Plimpton's voice ringing from the kitchen. 'Ten minutes, Henry, and then your tea will be on the table.'

He heard Henry Plimpton say, 'Yes, dear. I shan't be a moment. I just want to get something from my shed.'

'Ten minutes only,' said Mrs Plimpton warningly. Henry obviously had form when it came to getting something from his shed.

'Yes, dear. Ten minutes.'

His voice was closer. Shit. He was coming in.

At the same moment, Luke sounded in his ear. 'Matthew, come in.'

Matthew opened his mouth to respond but there was no time. He tapped his ear. The traditional response of one who can't talk just at the moment.

Very, very carefully, he closed the door and switched off the light. The interior of the pod was now completely dark. Backing away from the console he collided with one of the stacks of boxes, grabbing blindly at them as the top one nearly fell.

This would have to do. It was the only possible hiding place. As quietly as he could, he eased the boxes away from the wall. They weren't heavy and because of that they weren't particularly stable, either. The top one swayed dangerously again.

Matthew slipped between the boxes and the wall, steadied the top box, crouched, and gave thanks he was little.

A second later the door opened. Daylight flooded into the pod. Matthew shrank back silently against the wall.

He heard someone enter. Henry, presumably. The door closed and a second later, the light went on. There were a few indistinguishable noises. Matthew had no idea what Henry was doing, and he wasn't going to look. Ten minutes, Mrs Plimpton had said. Why couldn't Henry just go and have his tea? Spend the final few minutes he didn't know he had in the bosom of his family.

He checked his watch again. 1837. According to their instructions, Jane and Luke should be gone by now. Ellis was going to go ballistic. Only nine minutes remaining. Matthew had a horrible feeling that even if he sonicked Henry here and now, somehow got over the wall and ran for dear life, he still wouldn't have time to get back to the pod. Would Jane and Luke still be here or would they have gone without him?

Henry was moving closer. Matthew held his breath. Had his hiding place somehow been discovered? He tightened his grip on his sonic and tried not to panic. It was only Henry Plimpton, after all.

And then – a knock on the door. Matthew's first reaction was one of huge relief. This could only be Jane and Luke, come to get him out. He was saved.

His watch read 1840.

The door creaked open. 'Ah,' Henry said. 'Just a minute. I'll bring it out to you.'

There were sounds of rummaging. What was going on? Who was there? Had they come to pick something up? Or drop something off? It wasn't Jane or Luke, that much was certain. He dared not look. He could hear something being shifted under the console. Henry grunted as he heaved at something particularly heavy. Then the sounds of everything being put back. Matthew cursed Henry's habitual tidiness.

Finally, after what seemed like centuries, Henry said, 'Ah, here it—'

And then there was the sound of a gunshot.

Matthew stood, frozen with shock. Henry hadn't died in the explosion. He'd been shot. Why? Had Luke been right all along? Had Raymond Parrish actually sent someone to exterminate Henry? And then blown up Beaver Avenue to destroy all the evidence? And then thought to look at his watch. 1843.

The shed door was still open because he could hear Mrs Plimpton's voice from the garden. 'Henry? Henry? Oh my God. Are you all right? Henry?'

The door slammed tight shut, cutting her off. There were the familiar sounds of a pod powering up.

Matthew swiftly considered his options. He could step out, sonic whoever had shot Henry Plimpton, and . . .

Yes. And what then? It was too late to run.

1845.

251

No. The best option was to remain where he was. Whoever was in this pod with him had a gun and no problems using it. He'd shot Henry in cold blood – he'd have no difficulty doing the same to Matthew. Even though the pod was about to jump to an unknown destination, it was certainly safer to remain hidden and go with it than remain here. Beaver Avenue had only moments left.

The pod began to vibrate. This was going to be rough. Insulated inside their well-made pods, neither St Mary's nor the Time Police had any real idea of how rough Time travel could be. Matthew still had memories of several illegal trips in Mikey's illegal teapot. The bone-jarring landings. Fighting back the nausea. This would be no better. Where's your cheese when you really need it?

There should be a rule, he decided. All illegal Time travellers should carry copious amounts of cheese. It's the only thing that fights off the feeling that you, the illegal Time traveller, have somehow died *en route*. No one knows why cheese has this remarkable effect. Mikey always said it was the calcium – that illegal Time travellers needed strong bones and teeth. Given their frequently rough landings, there might well be something in that particular theory. Her brother Adrian always maintained it was the salt and that you'd get the same effect with a packet of crisps. There had been considerable sibling contention.

A violent tremor interrupted these musings. Matthew's stomach flew south for the winter. The pod was either about to jump or to explode.

There was a blinding flash.

Luke and Jane, meanwhile, were racing down Beaver Avenue

to get to the alleyway behind the houses. No longer caring whether they attracted attention or not, they called continually, 'Matthew. Where are you? Respond. Get back to the pod.'

Simultaneously, they both screeched to a halt.

'Did you hear that?' said Luke, tilting his head.

'I think so,' said Jane, her hand to her ear. 'It sounded like an ear tap. I was running and panting though.'

'Matthew, can you hear me?'

They were back to silence again.

'Imagination,' said Luke. 'Or wishful thinking, perhaps.' He stood, lost in thought, staring at his feet.

'1840,' said Jane, panting. 'What do we do?'

Their deadline for safe evacuation had passed. And even if – when – they found Matthew, they still had to get back to the pod. They weren't going to make it.

They had stopped on the corner. It was decision time. Turn right to get back to the pod. Turn left to go down the alleyway after Matthew. Luke hesitated, glancing to the right.

'Luke, we should go and look for him.' Jane was adamant. 'He might have fallen and hurt himself. He might be unconscious.'

'No,' said Luke, slowly. 'No. Back to the pod, Jane.'

Jane looked at her watch. 1842. 'We can't leave him here. This place isn't going to exist in five minutes.'

'Exactly.'

Jane's voice was laced with panic. 'Luke . . .'

'Jane, I'm not losing anyone else. I'm particularly not losing you.'

'I won't leave Matthew.'

'I'm the team leader. You'll do as I tell you. Back to the pod. Right now.'

253

Jane could feel her legs trembling. This could not be happening. They were Team Weird. They always survived somehow. They were famed for it.

'Our instructions were to evacuate,' said Luke. 'Matthew might be waiting for us back at the pod.'

1843.

'You know he's not. He's in trouble somewhere and we . . .' He seized her arm. She struggled. 'Luke – how can you do this?'

'For God's sake, Jane, do you think I *want* to leave him?'

'Then don't.'

He began to drag her away.

She struggled, shouting, 'Matthew . . . Matthew . . . can you hear me?'

'Jane, there's nothing we can do. Except die with him if we don't get back to the pod in time. It's my call and I'm making it. You can hate me later but right now you move.'

'We can't . . .' She broke off. They both spun around. 'Luke, was that a gunshot?'

'Unimportant, Jane. Move.'

'Matthew might be hurt. He might even be dead.'

'And so are we if we don't get out of here.'

He set off, pulling her with him.

Jane ran alongside, calling all the time, 'Matthew – answer.' She looked at her watch. 1844.

'Luke, we're not going to make it.'

'Doesn't matter. If Ellis finds out we've cut it this fine, we're dead anyway.'

'He was Matthew's mentor. When he was a boy.'

'I know.'

They raced into the garage area. Past the wheelless car still up on the bricks – although not for very much longer. Past the dying tree with its plastic bag flapping eternally in the breeze.

1847.

'Shit,' shouted Luke. 'Door.'

Just for once there was no argument from the AI. The door opened. Luke pushed Jane in ahead of him and threw himself in on top of her.

Mr Fernley had been exactly right. It was a bloody great bang. And there was a blinding white light. The pod literally bounced. For a moment, Jane had the idea she was upside down. And then she hit something with a crash. As did Luke. Things fell around them. Luke could hear debris hitting the pod on all sides. Something hard and heavy landed on the roof with a bang. Dust billowed in through the still open door.

Luke sat up, coughed and called for the door. There were red lights everywhere. Warnings buzzed and bleeped. Jane was still on the floor bleeding from a cut over her eye. She must have bounced off the console when he pushed her inside. Something else for her to complain about later.

He coughed again. 'Pod – emergency – get us home.'

Again, the AI did exactly as it was told. 'Emergency protocol initiated.'

The world shattered . . .


Team 236's pod cracked into existence in the Pod Bay, hit the floor with a crash, slithered a few feet, tipped, righted itself and finally came to a halt against the wall.

Not a second later, the Pod Bay was full of flashing lights and screeching alarms. All non-essential personnel got out as fast as they could go. With a series of thuds that made the building shudder, the blast doors came down. Throughout TPHQ, personnel lined up for immediate evacuation. Shouting officers cleared the panicking public out of the atrium.

Major Ellis was lunching with Officer North as the alarms went off. Seized by a sudden premonition he could not have explained even if he'd had time to, he broke off in mid-sentence and ran from the room. North followed close behind him.

Back in the Pod Bay . . .

Having ascertained there was no danger of imminent explosion, the Senior Mech was issuing instructions to his team to get the crew out, shouting to make himself heard over the clamour of the alarms.

The door opened to reveal the inside of the pod thick with swirling dust.

The Senior Mech's first thought was that given the amount of rubble littering the floor, it was a miracle the pod had jumped at all. The AI's safety protocols had obviously overridden those of the pod. Red lights flashed everywhere. Wires hung from the ceiling, spitting sparks. Jane lay on the floor, her eyes not quite focused.

Someone shouted for a medtec. A medical team was already pushing through the doors from MedCen.

The Senior Mech took one swift look at the console, satisfied himself that nothing explosive was about to occur and began to shut things down.

Luke, his face white with dust and shock, was helped out of the door. He made it only so far and then his legs gave way and he collapsed to the floor. Jane followed.

The Senior Mech stuck his head out of the door. 'Where's the other one?'

Jane was crying. Great tears tracked through the dust and dirt on her face, mingling with the blood.

Luke stared blankly at the doctor, who shook him gently. 'Answer him. Where's your teammate. Where's Farrell? Do we need to send someone back for him? What happened?'

Ellis and North arrived. Both took in the situation at a glance.

Ellis said something. No one ever remembered what it was. He turned away to stare at a wall.

The doctor put his hand on Luke's shoulder, and gripped it gently, saying, 'Look at me, lad. Where's young Farrell?'

Luke found he couldn't look at anyone. He shook his head.

It was Jane who somehow found the words.

'Matthew didn't make it.'

## 20

The Time Police were not an organisation greatly in touch with their feelings but the news that the little weirdo was dead was met with a surprising amount of shock and sadness. Even from those who'd barely known him. The general consensus was that Matthew Farrell hadn't actually been that bad, all things considered.

Some officers remembered he'd grown up with them, gone to school just down the road, sat his exams, asked awkward questions, broken the Time Map – just like a normal kid, even though no one had ever actually used the word *normal* to describe him.

Jane and Luke were both deeply shocked and being treated in MedCen. The Map Master took an hour off and disappeared. Grint and his team raised a glass to Officer Farrell in the bar. Captain Farenden produced his emergency bottle – the one hidden in a secret location in his office and kept only for the direst catastrophes – and poured a small measure each for Ellis and North, both of whom were too distressed to speak. They sat, side by side, in his office, while he kept the world at bay. Commander Hay stared out of her window for nearly ten minutes, speaking to no one.

Eventually she sighed, got up, and went out to Farenden's office. There were formalities ... procedures ... The first, of course, was to notify the next of kin.

'I'll speak to his parents myself,' she said to Ellis.

'Actually, ma'am, if you don't mind, I think I should do it,' said Ellis hoarsely.

'I'd like to go as well,' said North immediately.

Hay shook her head. 'I don't want it to be seen as a lack of respect if I don't go myself.'

Ellis shook his head. There had been some legendary encounters between Matthew's employer and Matthew's mother. Now was not the time for another one.

'No, I don't think they'll see it that way, ma'am.'

'Then please convey my condolences. Such a tragic waste of a young life. And if his parents wish to visit TPHQ – to speak to his friends about him – please assure them they'll be made very welcome. They will, of course, wish to attend his memorial service.'

Ellis nodded. 'Lt Grint has volunteered to jump back to see if he and his team can retrieve the body. I've talked to Parrish and Lockland and from what they've told me, I think it will be a fruitless search but ...'

'But it has to be done. Yes, despatch Team 235 by all means. Make sure they keep themselves under the radar. How are Parrish and Lockland?'

'Lockland is still in shock but I think we all know she's considerably tougher than she looks. Parrish is causing me some concern. First Imogen Farnborough and now this. I should tell you, ma'am, his was the decision to evacuate without Officer Farrell.'

259

'It was the right decision. Anything other would have resulted in both their deaths as well.'

'Agreed, ma'am, but I think he sees it as yet another death for which he is responsible.'

'Keep an eye on him. Keep an eye on both of them. When you come back from St Mary's, we'll discuss what to do with them.'

'Yes, ma'am.'

She tilted her head to one side. 'And you, Matthew, how are you?'

Ellis knew better than to lie. Besides, how he felt must be written all over his face. 'Devastated, ma'am.'

'I can imagine. You were very close at one time. Don't feel you are obliged to visit Matthew's parents. I am perfectly willing to assume that duty.'

'No, ma'am, but thank you.'

'Very well. Come and see me when you get back.'

'Yes, ma'am.'

The Time Police have a procedure for this sort of thing. Both Ellis and North changed into their formal uniforms with full rank and insignia and met in the Pod Bay. The damaged pod had already been returned to its rightful position. Diagnostic equipment was plugged in and a number of mechs were swarming all over it. A sombre Senior Mech wordlessly escorted Ellis and North to their pod, checked over the console and, equally wordlessly, left them. The door closed behind him.

Ellis took his seat. 'When you're ready, Officer North.'

'Yes, sir.'

The world flickered.

*　　*　　*

260

They landed in their usual place on the South Lawn.

'Ready?' said Ellis to North, who was taking a moment to make sure her hat was straight.

She checked her tie, smoothed her sleeve, straightened her shoulders and nodded.

They marched down the ramp to meet Mr Evans, who was on an intercept course but with his blaster in a neutral position to indicate he wasn't about to shoot them dead until they gave him cause.

He stopped short as he saw their formal uniforms, looking from North to Ellis and then back to North again. Briefly, he closed his eyes. 'Oh, shit.'

Ellis nodded. 'I'm sorry.'

'I'll take you in through the front. No offence, but I don't want anyone seeing you before Max and Chief Farrell.'

'Good thought,' said Ellis.

They followed on behind him as Evans opened his com to inform Mrs Partridge they had a serious situation.

They entered St Mary's through the front doors. Ellis removed his hat and clamped it under his arm. They walked straight through the Hall and up the stairs, catching no one's eye.

Dr Bairstow was waiting for them. He stood up as they entered his office.

Ellis and North stood to attention. Ellis cleared his throat. 'Sir, it is my sad duty to inform you that Officer Farrell was killed in action earlier today. Commander Hay sends her deepest regrets and condolences, as, I might add, does everyone else in the Time Police.'

Dr Bairstow exhaled. 'Please, sit down, both of you. Max

and Leon are on their way, so shall we wait until their arrival? It will be easier for you not to have to tell this sad news all over again.'

They waited in silence.

After a shorter pause than Ellis would have liked, Max's unmistakeable voice was heard in Mrs Partridge's office. 'What's up?'

The door opened and Max and Leon stood on the threshold.

North and Ellis rose to their feet.

Max turned deadly white and laid her hand on Leon's arm. He covered it with his own hand.

'No,' she said, faintly. 'No, no, no.'

'Please come and sit down,' said Dr Bairstow, very gently. 'Both of you.'

Leon guided Max to a seat and somewhat blindly found one for himself.

Ellis said again, 'I'm so sorry, but it is my duty to inform you . . .'

Max interrupted. 'Is he dead?'

'Yes.'

'Are you sure?'

'Yes.'

'Where's the body? If there's no body . . .'

'There was an explosion. A very big explosion . . . I . . . There is no body. I'm sorry.'

She said angrily, 'Where's Hay?'

'Ready and waiting to jump to this location should you feel her presence will help in any way. She has asked me to express her deepest condolences. I – I wanted to come and see you myself. As did Officer North.'

North nodded. 'I'm so sorry, Max.'

There was another long silence, broken by Leon. 'Luke and Jane – are they alive?'

'Yes. They were further away from the epicentre. They're battered, a little bloody and very distressed, of course.'

Leon nodded slowly. 'Can we talk to them? To find out exactly what happened?'

'Of course. When they have recovered a little.'

'Jane must be devastated.'

'She is, but I think Luke is hardest hit.' Ellis swallowed. 'We can discuss this in more detail later.'

Silence fell. Leon was gripping Max's hand. They both seemed . . . lost. Diminished somehow. It crossed Ellis's mind that neither of them might ever recover from this. He thought it one of the most painful sights he had ever seen.

Dr Bairstow spoke. 'Are there any practical details with which I can assist you, Major?'

Ellis pulled himself together. 'I don't think so, sir. Not at this moment. But in the future, almost certainly.'

'Mikey,' said Max, suddenly, lifting her head. 'She won't know. She should be told.'

Leon nodded and then looked around as if he had forgotten where he was going and what to do when he got there.

'I'll do it,' said Max. She looked at Ellis. 'If you don't mind.'

'No.'

She touched Leon's arm. 'I'll come straight back and then we'll go and find somewhere quiet. If you like.'

He nodded.

She put her hand on his shoulder. 'I won't be long. I promise.'

She looked over at Dr Bairstow and made a slight gesture.

The one that says to keep an eye on this one. He nodded and she left the room.

Mikey, as always, was in R&D. Max went straight in. Professor Rapson was waiting by the door.

'Max . . . I saw Ellis and Miss North. It's bad news, isn't it?'

She swallowed and nodded.

He touched her arm very briefly. 'My dear . . . you are not alone.'

Lingoss was welding something in Mikey's usual corner. A couple of scruffy wooden tables were covered in what, to the uninitiated, looked like pre-Mikey junk. A small part of it was post-Mikey junk and therefore not actually junk at all. Nestled among all the clutter were several bits of kit that, should they ever see the light of day, would almost certainly change the world. Whether for better or worse would very much depend on your point of view.

Lingoss lifted her mask. 'Hey, Max.'

Today's hair was silver, tipped with black.

She looked from Max to Professor Rapson and then back to Max again, slipped off her mask and went to stand by the professor.

Max said hoarsely, 'Where's Mikey?'

Lingoss closed her eyes. 'It's not Adrian, is it? Is he hurt?'

'No.'

'She's next door in the lab.'

Max opened the door into the small room where Mikey and Lingoss carried out some of their more esoteric activities. Most of the room was taken up with a very large battered wooden table with some very serious scorch marks, one of which carried on across the old wooden floor and up the wall to terminate in a depression exactly the same size and dimension of a Civil War cannonball. Cracks radiated from the crater like a spider's web.

The remainder of the walls were covered in scribbles – many in Mikey's still childish handwriting. Sketches, diagrams, ideas, jokes, insults, cartoons, reminders, to-do lists and so forth. When the walls became too crowded, they would simply splash up another coat of whitewash and begin again. The room smelled of hot metal, engine oil, dubious chemicals and ants.

Mikey, bending over a cardboard box on the workbench, turned and smiled at Max.

As did Matthew.

The following ten minutes were very confused. R&D personnel milled around, all under the mistaken impression they were helping to clarify the situation. Obviously, there were a number of questions to be answered. Actually, there were an even greater number of questions to be asked. Max, however, seemed unable to get past, 'How? What? Who? Why?' And then back to 'How?' again.

Eventually, after a sip of something from Mr Swanson's Poisons Cabinet – the one with the skull and crossbones on the door – she was able to drag her hands across her face, sniff and say, very nearly normally, 'North and Ellis just told me you were dead.'

'Yeah,' said Matthew, shuffling his feet. 'Sorry about that.'

His mother, overcome with joy that one of the two most important people in her life was not only not dead but actually standing in front of her, thumped him hard on his arm.

'Ow. What was that for?'

'They told me you were dead. In fact, they're still telling

your father . . . Oh.' She got to her feet. 'I need to go and speak to Leon.'

Matthew stepped into her path. 'No. Mum. No.'

She turned in astonishment. 'Why ever not?'

'Well, that's just what we were talking about when you came in. I want to make sure I know what's happening first.' Matthew took a deep breath and drew himself up. 'And, for the avoidance of all doubt, can everyone please be aware I am very definitely wearing my Time Police hat.' He turned to Mikey, who had stiffened. 'I thought, some time ago, it was agreed you were to stop working on these.'

'We did,' said Mikey. 'And I have.'

'Then what's this?' He gestured at the box.

'I told you – they're not mine. I didn't make them.' She gestured at the box. 'I didn't make any of them.'

'For God's sake, Mikey . . . do you know the risks I'm taking by not arresting you on the spot?'

Mikey bristled. 'I told you . . .' and at the same time, Max said, 'No, you're fine. They think you're dead. Not to minimise the seriousness of the situation, but there's no risk. Just don't ever go back to TPHQ.'

Matthew thumped the table in frustration. 'Will you both shut up and listen to me. This is serious. I'm an officer of the Time Police. I'm chasing down someone who's murdered an entire street full of people just to send us a message to back off. I do not need to find that you and St Mary's are mixed up in it somehow.'

Now Mikey was angry as well. 'Well, you won't have to because I'm not.' She brandished a bracelet. 'This is not my work. I didn't do this. Yes, Adrian and I did the theory but that

266

was a long time ago and Chief Farrell told us to stop and we did. I haven't looked at this sort of thing for ages.'

'Well, someone must have got hold of your notes.'

'I didn't really make any notes. I scratched most of it in the sand. Chief Farrell took the little bit I had written down and burned it. You saw him do it. I'll tell you again, Matthew – it's not me – it's not my work. You're chasing the wrong person. Go and be a Time Police officer somewhere else.'

'So you're saying these are just a coincidence? That someone just happened to develop something exactly like what you'd been working on and they've done it quite independently?'

'Yes, I am. It's perfectly possible. Different people have the same ideas all the time. Look at Bell and whatshisname and the telephone. For heaven's sake, Matthew, stop being an arsehole for thirty seconds and look at this.' She thrust the bracelet under his nose. 'Really look at it. It's crude. It's clumsy. It's bigger than it needs to be and it's overpowered. The field generator's weak which makes it wildly unstable. Half the time it'll just blow your arm off. Look at this.' She flipped the control panel open to reveal some tangled internal workings. 'They've wired it wrong. You set your coordinates to, say, 1066, and the field's too weak to transport all of you, so your arm shoots off to 1066 all by itself – coincidentally taking the bracelet with it – and the rest of you is left behind, slowly bleeding to death. If the shock hasn't killed you first.'

Mikey banged the bracelet down on the worktable. Everyone else flinched and stepped back. 'Understand this, Mr Time Police officer – this is shoddy work that I'd be ashamed to show anyone. Now clear off out of my lab and let me get on.

If you still want to show off your Time Police qualities, then go off and look for some kittens to kick.'

Matthew said nothing, steadily holding her gaze.

She took a deep breath. 'I told you,' she said to him, more calmly. 'They're not mine. Or Adrian's.'

'And I'm telling you – the Time Police won't know that. Or care. It's the excuse they've been looking for. You and Adrian will be arrested faster than . . .' He stopped, unable to think of anything that could possibly be faster than the speed with which the Time Police would seize the opportunity to descend upon the perfidious Amelia and Adrian Meiklejohn.

There was a bit of a silence as Professor Rapson, Mr Swanson, Max, Mikey and Lingoss – none of whom had any conscience at all when it came to deceiving the Time Police – considered their next actions.

'I have to tell your dad you're alive,' said Max. 'And now. I can't delay that.'

'Bring him here,' said the professor. 'I'll go and put the kettle on.'

Max opened her com. 'Leon, could you come to R&D, please.'

'In a while, Max, I . . .'

'No. Now, please. Quick as you can.' She took a few deep breaths and when she turned back to Matthew, her face was nearly normal. 'Wait until your dad gets here and then tell us everything.'

'Is Hay here?'

'No. Just Ellis and North. What's this all about?'

'There's trouble coming. A lot of it.'

A few minutes later the door opened to reveal a grey-faced Leon standing on the threshold, staring at Matthew in disbelief.

There was a very long silence and then he said, 'I have to put up with this sort of thing from your mother. I didn't expect to get it from you as well.'

'Are you going to thump me too, because Mum's already had a go at me and my whole left arm has gone numb.'

Leon looked at Max. Slowly his colour began to return. 'Words fail me.'

Matthew put his hand on his father's arm. 'Dad . . .'

His father smiled at him. 'Good to see you, son.'

Matthew's chin trembled for one moment and then he smiled and nodded.

Everyone cleared their throat.

'Tea's ready,' said Professor Rapson, demonstrating that while all around might be descending into chaos, R&D would never let standards slip. 'I've made it in rather a hurry but I think it should be OK. If it tastes a bit salty, you should stop drinking it at once while Mr Swanson finds the antidote.'

Matthew was trying to peer through the grimy window. 'Have they gone?'

'They have,' said Dr Bairstow, appearing in the doorway. 'But I have not. While it is gratifying to see you are not dead, Officer Farrell, I believe we would all appreciate being brought up to speed on today's occurrences.'

Matthew took a large swig of tea. Saltiness was not apparent. 'There was an explosion in the 20th century,' he began. 'We'd paid what should have been a routine follow-up call to a known illegal and found he, his family and his entire street had been wiped out in a massive blast. Cause unknown. So we jumped back to before the explosion to ascertain what actually happened.'

'Dodgy,' said his mother. 'Anything could have gone wrong. And this is me saying that.'

'And it did go wrong,' said Matthew. 'I came across an unexpected pod. I was checking it out when the supposed owner – the illegal we were investigating – turned up. As did someone else and they shot him. Whether Henry was killed outright, I don't know – I was hiding behind a stack of crates at the time and couldn't see what was happening. I had only moments before the whole area went up so I reckoned it was safer to stay where I was. The pod jumped. With me still on board.'

Leon sighed and rolled his eyes. 'Was this Henry dead? Did you try to get help?'

'He wasn't there. I mean, there was no body when the pod landed. No bloodstains or anything. I assume he'd been shot and somehow fell *outside* the pod.'

'Wow,' said Max. 'Where did it jump to?'

'I don't know at the moment but I've got the coordinates.'

Leon held out his hand and Matthew passed over his recorder. Turning away, Leon opened his com. 'Dieter, can you check out some coordinates for me, please.' He rattled them off. 'Thank you.'

'So what happened next,' demanded Max, who never believed in letting anyone tell their story in their own way and in their own time. 'Where did it take you? What did you do? How did you get back here? And why not TPHQ?'

Her son regarded her in silence.

'Sorry. Carry on.'

Matthew sipped more of his tea. 'Well, that pod was rough, let me tell you.'

'Didn't you have any cheese?' asked Mikey.

'I did not.'

She grinned. 'You won't make that mistake again.'

'No.' He saw his mother open her mouth to speak and hastily continued. 'Anyway . . . I was worried they'd start unloading the contents of the pod immediately, which would be a bit of a problem for me because that was my hiding place, but the driver – whoever he or she was – opened the door and left as soon as they landed. I gave it about twenty seconds and then wriggled out from behind the crates to see what was going on.'

He paused to drink more tea.

'And?' demanded his mother.

'I couldn't see very much. The pod was very primitive and there was only one camera which was fixed so I couldn't toggle about. If I wanted to see what was going on, then I'd have to open the door.'

Max intervened again. 'Did you remember to . . .'

'Kneel on the floor below people's eyelines, yes.'

'I taught him that,' said his mother to the room at large.

Leon intervened. 'What did you see?'

'From that position, not a great deal. However, there was a wall not far away so I grabbed the top two boxes, exited the pod and went to stand by the wall, trying to look as if I really belonged there and was just searching for a place to stow them.'

'Neat,' said his mother, adding, 'Always try and have something in your hands. I taught him that as well.'

'I couldn't stay too long because I suspected they'd be along to unload the pod at any minute.'

He paused. His mother twitched but said nothing.

He closed his eyes, remembering.

'I was in a big warehouse. Bigger than here. Nearly as big as the Pod Bay at TPHQ.'

'Describe it,' said Dr Bairstow.

'It had an old-fashioned feel to it. Concrete floor with two lines of iron pillars holding up the roof, which appeared to be mainly massive iron girders. There were two rows of pod plinths, each set between the pillars, six on each side. Capacity for twelve pods, I think.'

'Twelve,' exclaimed his mother. 'That's more than we have here at St Mary's. Sorry. Carry on.'

Matthew closed his eyes again. 'There were four pods present, plus the one I'd stolen. The rest of the space was taken up with crates and boxes. The people were packing up. Working as a team, taking stuff off the metal shelves around the walls and packing it in boxes. Not in a rush. There was no panic – they weren't evacuating. The far end was done out like a loading bay, with big double doors. Wooden. On the opposite wall – to my right – they seemed to have thrown up some sort of partition with quite a modern-looking door. I suspected I was standing in a goods-in/goods-out area and – with no evidence at all – that the area behind the door might be a workshop. Or even a manufactory, perhaps. There were small metal windows around the top of three walls. Too high to see anything other than blue sky.

'Around ten to fifteen people – all men. No one wore smart overalls with a helpful logo. Most were in jeans and T-shirt. I blended right in. It was organised but nothing looked military.

'The hangar was noisy. I could hear generators running against the far wall. One was on its last legs and kicking out smoke everywhere. There was a lot of wiring looping between

272

the pillars. And a lot of jury-rigging and duct tape. Every pod had at least three umbilicals plugged into the wall. Parissa fittings. From where I was standing, I couldn't see inside any of the pods.'

'Shame,' said Leon. 'I would have liked a look.'

'There's one up in the woods,' said Matthew, casually. 'Looks a bit like a garden shed. You can take a peek any time you like.'

There was a short silence.

'Well, how did you think I got here?' he demanded.

'Shall we continue?' said Dr Bairstow, before a Farrell family fracas could engulf them all.

'There were people scurrying everywhere. I had to move before I started to stand out. I had no idea which, if any of them, could have been the driver of my pod. All I knew was that whoever it was had been out of the pod in a flash. He – or she – might even have gone outside through the loading bay or through the workshop and not been in the hangar at all. I had a bit of a think and decided to take a look around. No point in being there otherwise. So I took my boxes and went off to see what I could see.'

'What happened?' demanded his mother.

'Nothing happened. Nothing at all. No one shouted. No one took any notice of me. My recorder was in my pocket – where it was very definitely staying – so all this is from memory.

'There were two men I thought might be supervisors of some kind and another two, or possibly three, were security. I watched them for a while and came to the conclusion they were keeping people out rather than in. Which meant everyone was there more or less voluntarily. Interestingly, other than the security people, no one seemed to be armed. I had no idea where the place was – or when – and I thought if I wandered around listening, the language would give me a clue.'

'Risky,' said his father.

'Clever,' said his mother.

They scowled at each other.

'And what conclusions did you draw?' enquired Dr Bairstow.

'Mostly English, some Spanish, something East Asian, I think. And possibly something that sounded Eastern European. Again – no idea. Sorry.

'Anyway, I hefted the boxes up on to my shoulder – to conceal my face – and set off around the hangar. I exaggerated things a bit, supposedly watching where I put my feet because that gave me a good reason not to catch anyone's eye.'

He drank more tea. 'Now that I was moving, I could see two pods were open. I did my best to peer inside without rousing anyone's suspicions but they were both dark.

'I actually got all the way around the hangar. Shit security. No one took any notice of me. I was slightly miffed. You have to ask yourself if these people had ever watched a James Bond movie. I should have been seized, dragged in front of the evil mastermind who would immediately explain his plans to destroy the world, and then, instead of sensibly shooting me on the spot, he would fling me into a shark tank from which, inevitably, I would escape and save the day.'

'Some people just don't try,' said his mother, nodding.

'So, having made a complete circuit of the hangar, I checked a few of the shelves and there were several other boxes identical to this one here.' He indicated the box on the table. 'I couldn't start ripping them open without drawing attention to myself and

I really didn't know what to do next, so I stepped back inside the pod again to have another think.'

He drained his mug and set it down.

'Again,' said Dr Bairstow. 'Your conclusions?'

'Well, there were only two sets of doors and both were guarded, so I wasn't going to try and get out. Besides, where would I go? I had no idea when and where I was. And I couldn't keep walking around the hangar forever. And no one was taking any notice of me. I'm a Time Police officer, for heaven's sake – I'm supposed to be hated and feared wherever I go, not completely ignored.'

'Aw,' said his mother, patting his arm.

'So I put down my boxes. Because I'd had a Brilliant Idea.'

Someone groaned. Matthew's mother glared suspiciously at Matthew's father.

Dr Bairstow held up his hand. 'I wonder if I might interrupt for one brief moment?' He didn't wait for an answer. At St Mary's, it is always wise to hog the conversational ball while you still have it. 'Can I assume it was the contents of the boxes that caused you to return here rather than TPHQ, where, I should inform you, everyone is currently mourning what has been inaccurately described as your death. I find it surprising – though gratifying – to discover it is St Mary's to which you turn in a crisis, but I have to ask – why?'

Mikey stepped to one side, and gestured to the large table behind her, on which reposed a cardboard box lying on its side and tipping its contents across the table.

'Bracelets,' she said. 'Portable Time-travelling devices.'

Leon closed his eyes and sighed. 'Damn.'

**21**

Ellis and North, accompanied by a silent Evans, walked back across the grass towards their pod.

'Did you see that?' said Ellis quietly.

North had no need to ask him what he was talking about. 'Two people whose first instinct was to turn to each other for mutual comfort and support? Yes, I did.' She paused. 'Not something you often see at TPHQ. Or anywhere.'

'No.' Still staring straight ahead, he said, 'I'd like that.'

North nodded. 'So would I.'

They walked up the ramp and into their pod.

Evans stepped back out of range and a few seconds later, the pod blinked out of existence.

'They've gone,' reported Miss Lingoss, scrubbing a clean patch on the window and peering through.

Dr Bairstow nodded. 'To recap then. Officer Farrell has discovered a cache of Time-travelling bracelets similar, but not identical, to a design produced by Miss Meiklejohn some time ago. Before returning to TPHQ, he naturally wished to ascertain whether they had, in fact, been manufactured by Miss Meiklejohn.'

'To save time,' said Matthew. 'Otherwise, I suspect the Time Police would waste a great deal of it by focusing their attention on the wrong people.'

'Indeed. Having determined they are, in fact, nothing to do with Miss Meiklejohn or St Mary's, he now proposes to . . . ? Your plans, Officer Farrell?'

'To return to the hangar for further exploration,' announced Mikey before Matthew could speak. 'This time having the sense to take an expert with him to prevent any further jumping to wrong conclusions.' She glared at Matthew.

'Risky,' said Dr Bairstow.

'Not as risky as going without me,' said Mikey, stoutly.

Max beamed her approval at this can-do attitude.

Matthew drew himself up. 'A fact-finding jump only, sir. After which, having gleaned as much info as we can – and most importantly, proving none of it is anything to do with Mikey and St Mary's – I . . .'

'We,' said Mikey.

'We return to TPHQ to bring them up to speed and plan our next move.'

Dr Bairstow shook his head. 'I can see many things wrong with that plan, Officer Farrell, but since you are not a member of St Mary's, I can do nothing to prevent it. However, it is not just yourself you will be endangering.' He looked pointedly at Mikey.

Matthew shook his head. 'It will be just a brief visit, sir. From what I've seen so far, it's perfectly easy to get in and out of that hangar without anyone suspecting. Pods seemed to come and go all the time. I estimate we'll be about a quarter of an hour. Tops.'

Dr Bairstow looked at Chief Farrell. 'It would appear the next generation is carrying on the old traditions.'

Leon sighed. 'Welcome to my world.'

'Right,' said Mikey, who had donned battle gear, which in her case consisted of her battered flying jacket, Snoopy helmet and goggles. 'Shall we go?'

They set off towards the door.

Max went to follow on behind them.

'No,' said Leon, softly, putting his hand on her arm.

'But . . .'

'This is his job, Max. He's a Time Police officer. And he won't want his mum tagging along. Let him have an adventure with his girl. Like we used to.'

She stared at him for a moment then said sadly, 'Yes. I suppose so.'

He rubbed her arm. 'I'm certain you'll be involved in something dark and dirty before the end of the week. Just have patience.'

She grinned at him. 'True. Our own days of danger and disaster are not yet done.'

'Oh God, you're not making dinner again, are you?'

She laughed and walked away but, just for once – and astonishingly for St Mary's – she was right. Those days of danger and disaster were closer than she thought.

Matthew and Mikey touched down again in the stolen pod. Exactly the same spot as before, from which Matthew deduced each pod had its own designated plinth. A sensible precaution when pods were coming and going all the time.

They stayed quietly in the pod because even Matthew was

aware this second visit was pushing his luck. They waited as tense seconds ticked by but no one seemed to be paying them any attention.

'Pods must jump in and out all day long,' said Matthew, whispering for some reason. He ran his hands over the console, giving all his attention to the coordinates.

Mikey peered over his shoulder. 'What are you doing?'

'Setting up the return jump in case we have to get away in a hurry.'

Mikey nodded. 'Good plan. Shall we go?'

'Just a minute,' said Matthew.

She turned to face him. A blonde curl had escaped. Very gently, he tucked it back inside her Snoopy helmet. 'Is there any point asking you to stay behind in the pod?'

'As your mum would be the first to say, "I think we both know the answer to that one."'

'You could have the pod ready for a quick getaway. The few seconds saved could be vital.'

'Then how about I go and take a look around and you can stay inside the pod and save the seconds.'

'Oh, I think we both know the answer to that one, as well.'

She zipped up her flying jacket and grinned at him. 'Ready?'

'Just a minute.'

'What's the matter?'

'I want you to listen to me very carefully. This is a Time Police operation. I am a Time Police officer. I know you think that's quite funny but at this moment, that's what I am and it's important to me. If I was Mum or Dad, or Dr Bairstow, or anyone – you'd do as they told you without question. I'm asking you to accord me the same courtesy. Please.'

Opening her mouth to make an indignant response, she stopped, dimly aware this was an important moment in their relationship.

Matthew stood in front of her, ostensibly studying the console, but she knew he was watching her. Waiting for her reaction. Mikey remembered – a few years ago now – when he'd given her a small Christmas present he'd made himself and how he'd stood, twanging with tension, to see how she would take it. Whatever she said next might define their future – if they had one. And he was right – if it was anyone else . . . For the first time, she had an understanding of the problems with which he struggled. She was older than Matthew. Not by much, but enough to matter. She'd first known him when he was a small, traumatised boy – unable to speak, unable to relate to people. He'd made such enormous progress since those days that sometimes it was easy to forget how difficult things could still be for him. Had it been Major Ellis or the Grint gorilla or Mr Markham standing in front of her, then she would be doing as she was told. Probably. But it wasn't. It was Matthew Farrell – newly qualified Time Police officer and as unsure of himself now as he'd been on the day he gave her the cheese. Her lucky cheese. With a hole in it for a ribbon to tie around her neck. What must it be like to be him? Physically unimposing, awkward, inarticulate with those he didn't know, struggling to make his way in the world he had chosen for himself.

For a moment, she wanted to cry for him and then she managed a smile. 'You're right, Matthew. I'm a bit inexperienced in this sort of thing. It makes good sense for you to take the lead. How do you want to set about this?'

'We'll split up and take a quick look around first. Got your earpiece?'

She nodded.

'Radio silence except in an emergency.' He looked at her. 'Still not too late to change your mind.' He gestured around. 'You could stay here and tidy the pod. Knit something, perhaps.'

She grinned. As he had known she would. 'Pushing your luck, Officer Farrell.'

'I frequently do, Miss Meiklejohn. As you well know.'

Just a tiny moment between them, but in that second, they'd created a whole new world for themselves.

'Shall we go?' He handed her a few boxes. 'Disguise.'

He busied himself with boxes of his own, waiting for his heart rate to return to normal. The moment had blown up out of nowhere and he'd been completely unprepared for it. He still wasn't sure he'd handled it properly. It dawned on him again that Luke's father had been completely right when he'd said it was easier to hold on to old ways of thinking rather than address frightening new perspectives.

He turned to the door. 'Open.'

They stepped out into the warehouse. As far as he could see, nothing had changed in any way. Mikey stood beside him, partly obscured behind a pile of boxes.

'This is just a Pod Bay,' she said, quietly, looking at the activity around them. 'And a loading and distribution area.'

Matthew nodded. All around them men were loading, unloading and charging pods. Two men nearby were ticking off items on a clipboard. Two others were wheeling some sort of portable diagnostic device into a pod. This place was less sleek than TPHQ, but it was a working Pod Bay nevertheless.

'We should be looking for their workshop,' she whispered.

'Behind that door, I suspect,' said Matthew, nodding with his head at the single door in the partitioned wall.

Mikey nodded. 'Let's separate. You go clockwise – I'll go the other way. If one of us gets caught, the other one pushes off immediately. No heroics. No attempted rescues. That will be the time to go for help.' She caught herself just in time. 'Do you agree?'

He nodded. 'Agreed.'

Once again Matthew began to make his way around the hangar. Progress was still not easy. There were crates and equipment to dodge. Once, his way was blocked by one of the mobile diagnostic machines and he was forced to leave the shelter of the wall and venture further out into the main area of the warehouse.

Conspicuously, the Parrish logo was nowhere to be seen. Which could mean nothing, of course. Perhaps, for some reason, everything was repackaged into suitably anonymous crates for onward transmission elsewhere. That would make sense. This probably wasn't their only place of operations. And money had certainly been spent on this place. A lot of money. Probably beyond the means of any one private individual. But not an international corporation, perhaps.

For the first time he wondered if Luke's parental paranoia was, in fact, completely justified. Who but Raymond Parrish would have the facilities, the resources, the finances to put something like this together? Who had been clever enough to involve himself in the Site X investigation under the guise of assisting the Time Police with their enquiries? Matthew frowned and picked his way carefully, one eye on where he was putting his feet and the other eye on Mikey. Which turned out to be one eye too few on his feet, because he tripped over a pair of umbilicals and nearly fell.

By the time he'd got himself back together again and was able to look around, Mikey had vanished. Forcing himself to remain calm, he stood behind a rack of metal shelving and checked around the hangar. Mikey was nowhere to be seen. Breaking their agreed radio silence, he tapped his ear.

Nothing. No response. No sign of her anywhere.

The hair on the back of his neck began to lift. Very slowly and very carefully, he edged his way back around the shelving and along the wall. Was she perhaps back at the pod waiting for him? That seemed unlikely. They'd hardly had time even to begin to check out what was going on here. Where was she? How could anyone so completely disappear like that?

The thought exploded in his brain and hit him with the force of a thunderbolt. They'd got her. No mess. No fuss. Quick and quiet. No time for her even to call for help. And they could be coming for him any moment now!

Suddenly, the alarms went off. Men shouted and ran, grabbing weapons as they went.

Matthew stood very still. His instinct was to stay and look for Mikey. To search the hangar until he found her. His common sense sent him back to the pod. Tucking his boxes under one arm, he hugged the wall. Typically, at this moment, he was about as far from his pod/shed as it was possible to be, but the important thing was not to run. He was careful to move at the same pace as those around him, dodging people and boxes of equipment.

Suddenly – from nowhere – he found himself facing two

men. For a moment, everyone stared at everyone else. He watched a slow-dawning realisation spread over their faces. They didn't know who he was.

'Hey,' said one, shouting to make himself heard over the clanging bell. 'What . . . ?'

Matthew didn't wait. Time Police officers don't politely wait for other people to finish speaking. He threw both boxes at their heads and almost in the same moment, brought down a pile of wooden crates on top of them. Heads turned at the noise.

He didn't bother trying to hide.

'Over there,' he shouted, pointing to a corner well away from his pod. 'They ran over there.'

No one moved immediately. He could only hope their astonishment would buy him vital seconds, and began to dodge around the wrecked shelving.

His pod was tantalisingly close when a huge man in a sleeveless T-shirt stepped out from behind a stack of crates and swung an enormous wrench at his head.

Matthew ducked so fast and so violently that he almost lost his balance, only just saving himself from falling. He dodged between two generators. One of them was still kicking out blue smoke. The smell made him feel slightly sick.

A shout rang out behind him. 'Hold your fire. Don't damage the pods.' He'd heard that voice before but there was no time to think about that now.

There were more men between him and his pod. Matthew performed the sort of screeching U-turn of which any government would have been proud and headed for an open space.

And then . . . just a glimpse . . . was he going mad? It couldn't be him, surely? He dodged sideways for a better look.

Yes . . . it was. Bloody bollocking hell. Just vanishing through the other door. Matthew took two paces after him. He mustn't be allowed to get away.

He got no further. Completely unexpectedly, Major Callen appeared from nowhere, grabbed him by the scruff of his neck and dragged him roughly into a camouflaged pod. Matthew suddenly realised exactly whose voice he had heard.

Something impacted into the side of the pod. And again. The pod shuddered. Matthew realised they – whoever they were – were firing at him. Firing at them both.

He was sprawled on the floor, attempting to gather his scattered wits. He heard Callen shout for an emergency evac. Once again, Matthew's stomach slid south.

And once again he was without his cheese.

22

Jane and Luke had both been discharged from MedCen and were sitting in Jane's room because Team 236 – what was left of it – had been grounded until after the hearing into the events at Beaver Avenue. They'd given umpteen statements to umpteen people. They'd submitted their coms, their recorders and their weapons for inspection. Luke had folded his arms and looked mutinous until a tight-faced Ellis had informed him this was normal procedure on the death of an officer and he, Luke, knew that and was to get on with it.

Jane had a small dressing over her right eyebrow but otherwise both were unharmed. Neither had spoken for some time.

Eventually, Jane said, 'What will happen to us, do you think? Will we be split up and assigned to other teams?'

'Doubt it,' said Luke. 'Who would want us? Well – who would want me? I reckon Two-Three-Five would take you like a shot, Jane.'

'I wouldn't go without you,' said Jane, shaking her head.

He smiled. Or at least his face twisted in something resembling a smile. 'You may not have a choice, Jane. This is the Time Police. We're supposed to do as we're told.'

'That might apply to me,' said Jane. 'I don't think anyone here would expect it from you.'

Someone tapped on the door. Jane's first thought was that Major Ellis had returned from St Mary's or that there was some query with their statements. She climbed wearily to her feet to answer the door and found herself face to face with Commander Hay. Her initial reaction was relief that they were in her own always tidy room and not in Luke's personal-effects maelstrom next door.

Luke had had exactly the same thought. 'Well, thank God we're not in my room.'

'I think we're all grateful for that, Officer Parrish. May I come in?'

She was ushered into the nearest chair. The only chair, actually. Jane and Luke sat side by side on the bed.

Hay considered the remains of Team Weird. Jane, pale and anxious, was clearly still in shock – which would soon turn to disbelief and denial. Luke Parrish had skipped all the preliminary stages of grief and gone straight to anger. She could see it in his face. Both of them were experiencing very typical reactions which could be dealt with. Commander Hay had lost enough officers to have become a reluctant expert in this area.

'Major Ellis has gone to speak with Matthew's parents. Officer North has gone to support him and so you have me.'

'What happens now?' asked Jane, before Luke could say something rash and get them both into trouble again. Not that she really cared at the moment. She wondered if she would ever care for anything ever again.

'For a few days – nothing,' said Hay. 'There will be a

hearing, of course, to establish the facts and then, when things are a little calmer, we will discuss your future.'

'Not sure I have one,' said Luke. 'Not here in the Time Police, anyway. Or anywhere. People just drop like flies whenever I'm around. I'm sure you must have noticed.'

'No,' said Hay, calmly. 'I have not. No one has.'

'Suppose we want to leave?'

'You can do so, of course. I would never keep anyone who genuinely didn't want to be here. You would have to buy yourself out, and since you've only just qualified, it won't be cheap.'

'Not a problem for me. I can afford it,' said Luke. 'And I can buy Jane out too if she wants to.'

'I have nowhere to go,' said Jane, sadly, suddenly realising the fears that had beset her in Beaver Avenue were coming true.

Luke took her hand. 'Yes, you do. You're Luke Parrish's Female Friend Forty-Four – remember?'

Jane's lip trembled.

Hay clasped her hands in her lap. 'Officers, I do assure you, any decision you make will be honoured and I will do what I can to assist you in making that decision. But not now. Not today.'

She paused and considered them. 'You have both come a long way in the short time you have been here. Remember that. Now, Major Ellis will return soon. He will wish to see you as well. Please remember he has known Matthew for a very long time and his grief will reflect that. In fact, many here will have known Matthew for years. They will remember him – I remember him – as a very young child, rescued from an appalling life as a climbing boy. Brutalised, abused, almost unable to speak, damaged mentally and physically. And gifted.

Or weird – depending on your point of view. But, always, one of us. As are you both. You are not alone in your grief.'

Luke Parrish stood up abruptly. 'You mean I'm so selfish and self-centred I'm likely to forget Ellis has known Matthew far longer than we have? That he was his mentor for years? That he's extremely fond of him? Yes – I'm not likely to remember any of that, am I?'

There was a silence.

'Well?' said Luke, challenging her. 'Nothing to say?'

'I was just reflecting that Major Ellis's management skills are considerably more substantial than I had realised. Although not as substantial as his patience, obviously.'

'You've known Matthew as long as Ellis, haven't you, Commander?' said Jane, pulling at Luke's sleeve.

'I have. And on a less personal and more professional note – you made exactly the right decision, Officer Parrish. You saved two lives today. Remember that. And now, if you will excuse me . . .'

She closed the door behind her and headed back to her own office. Where more Team Weird-related trouble was waiting for her.

Barely had Hay seated herself at her desk than her adjutant laid an old-fashioned handwritten letter before her.

She regarded it with distaste. 'Oh God, Charlie – what's happened now?'

'Hardly anything, ma'am. In fact, if you were mulling over the future of Team Weird, the problem may be moot. This has just arrived.'

She closed her eyes. 'Tell me we haven't lost someone else.'

'Not in the way you are thinking, ma'am, but possibly, yes.

Officer Lockland's grandmother is ill and this is a request for us to release Lockland with immediate effect so she can discharge her social and familial duties.'

Hay sat back. 'In other words, return Lockland to the life of slavery from which she has escaped.'

'I believe social discharge to be the correct term, ma'am.'

Not being entirely comfortable with the word *compassionate*, the Time Police expression was *social* rather than *compassionate* discharge. As her grandmother's only living relative, this applied to Jane. Should the last remaining member of an officer's family require care and support, that officer was entitled to a discharge. Whatever the expression, however, one thing was clear – Jane's grandmother knew where she was and wanted her back. And was legally entitled to have her back. If Jane wished it.

Commander Hay frowned. 'I've not done many of these, but we have a procedure for releasing officers who have over-whelming social commitments, don't we?'

'We do, ma'am. Do you want me to set things in motion?'

'Can I somehow prevent this happening?'

'Not if Officer Lockland wishes to leave us, no.'

'And Matthew Farrell's dead. The team is breaking up. This couldn't have come at a worse time.'

'No, ma'am.'

'She'll do it, won't she? She won't want to, but she will.'

'She has a very strong sense of duty, ma'am.'

'Damn and blast it, Charlie.'

'Yes, ma'am.'

'What's the matter with her?'

'Nothing, ma'am. Lockland has always seemed perfectly pleasant to me.'

'I meant the grandmother.'

'A stroke, ma'am. Allegedly.'

'Is there some doubt?'

'Well . . . normally there would be a doctor's certificate or similar in support of this claim.'

Hay peered at the letter in front of her. 'Who wrote this? It reads as if the grandmother wrote it herself. Apparently,' she squinted, 'she raised Lockland as if she were her own flesh and blood – as her granddaughter, surely Lockland *is* her own flesh and blood – and now the time has come for Lockland to repay this considerable debt.'

'There's more but that is the gist of it, ma'am.'

'Hmm.' She turned her head to look out of the window. 'Did I actually receive this?'

There was a short silence and then Captain Farenden said, 'My apologies, ma'am, the letter appears to have been mis-routed. I shall obviously initiate an intensive search. I'm sure it will turn up again. In about twenty-four hours, perhaps.'

Hay turned back again. The letter had gone. 'What letter?'

'Indeed, ma'am.'

'I think this calls for special measures. When he returns, send Lt Grint to me, would you?'

He was startled. 'Grint?'

'Problem, Charlie?'

'None at all, ma'am, although my own recommendation would have been for someone a little more . . . socially adept in this sort of situation. Officer North, perhaps.'

'She shot four people at her briefing!'

'Well, strictly speaking, ma'am, they were only blanks. With Lt Grint, there is every possibility he'd be firing the real thing.

And he'll be tired and frustrated after his unsuccessful search for Matthew Farrell's body.'

Hay smiled grimly. 'Yes, you don't argue with Grint, do you? And he does have a bit of a vested interest in keeping Lockland with us.'

'Ah. Point taken, ma'am.' Farenden stood up to leave.

'Where are you going?'

'To make you a coffee, ma'am. Sadly, the only way in which I can express my appreciation of your genius. And to summon Lt Grint, of course.'

Lt Grint, returning dirty, weary and unsuccessful from the former Beaver Avenue, found himself being turned around almost immediately. He was briefed by Captain Farenden – who managed not to mention Lockland's name at all – and handed his travel docs.

Grint took them reluctantly. 'Don't we have a welfare section for this sort of thing?'

'Yes. And today it's you, Lieutenant.'

'I actually have to go and talk to this grandmother?'

'Your mission is to convince this elderly lady – without actually shooting her, please – to relinquish her claim upon her granddaughter, thus enabling Officer Lockland to continue her career within the Time Police.'

'Oh,' said Grint. He looked at Captain Farenden and said, 'Oh,' again.

'Exactly.'

Grint looked down at his grimy, dust-bedecked self. 'Should I . . .'

Captain Farenden contemplated the enormous, battle-hardened, gritty officer standing before him. As always, Grint was bristling with armaments and could probably have quelled a small city had he put his mind to it.

'I'm not sure that will be necessary, Lieutenant. First impressions are always important, don't you think?'

The penny did not so much drop as plummet. 'Oh. Right. Got you, sir.'

'Thank you, Lieutenant. Dismissed.'

As a member of the Time Police and on official duty, Lt Grint travelled for free, although given his size, his facial expression and the fact he was armed with not one but two blasters, it is possible that he would have travelled for free anyway, regardless of Time Police membership.

He took the old-fashioned Underground to catch the short-distance airship that served Jane's hometown. This antiquated system was used mainly by those not rich enough or able-bodied enough to use the walkways on the surface. But, it was fast – when it worked – and, in his case, free, and since he didn't mind the dark, the crowds, the smells, the rats and the occasional knife fight, it was ideal for his purposes.

On his arrival at Jane's hometown – a city permanently featured near the top of the nation's Least Favourite Place to Live list – he intended to disembark and walk to her grandmother's house.

His plans from this point were rather loose. Flexible, he told himself. The woman was a civilian and therefore bound to be guilty of something for which he could arrest her if all else failed.

The antiquated Underground train rattled into the station.

The crowd surged forwards. The doors jerked open. Grint shouldered his way through the crush. No one complained. He found himself a seat and followed the ancient ritual of completely ignoring his fellow passengers.

He was roused by something hitting his leg. An old lady, the only person standing, had stumbled against him as the train lurched around a bend. She apologised. He nodded and then looked casually around the carriage.

Everyone was sitting down except for the old lady, clutching her shopping with one hand and the rail with the other and swaying rather precariously. In some dim recess of his brain Grint was aware Jane would want him to do something. Something subtle. *Not* shooting the occupants of the carriage, for example. Turning his head, he poked the young man sitting next to him.

Who ignored him, jerking his head in time to the tinny music belting out of his headphones.

Grint tried again. Slightly less subtly this time. 'Oi.'

'Wha . . . ?' said the youth before he'd fully assimilated what and who was sitting next to him.

Grint cut his eyes to the old lady and raised his eyebrows.

Sadly, the young man seemed unable to understand.

Grint sighed. Subtle was for losers. And Jane would never know anything about it anyway.

He reached over his shoulder for his weapon. Time Police regulations require all weapons to be powered down in public and Lt Grint was a very conscientious officer. The whine of a charging blaster could clearly be heard over the clatter of the old train.

The young man, suddenly finding himself looking down

the barrel of something massive, leaped to his feet and headed rapidly for the other end of the carriage. Grint gestured to the empty seat and managed to produce what he fondly imagined was a smile. Not taking her eyes off him, the old lady edged carefully past him and sat down on the very edge of her seat.

Grint shut down and replaced his blaster, folded his arms and stretched out his legs. Jane would be pleased. He was a good person.

A brisk but enjoyable walk from the airship station brought Lt Grint to Jane's grandmother's house. Standing back, he surveyed the terrain. A normal person would see a tall, slightly shabby Regency-style house, one of many built around a square which contained well-maintained gardens behind iron railings. This was a perfect grandmother's house. Old-fashioned. Genteel, even. And in the best part of town. Jane's grandmother was obviously not short of a bob or two.

Grint, on the other hand, saw mature trees and shrubs that would provide adequate cover for a frontal assault. Unimpeded access to the front door. No secondary security systems visible. Front windows unprotected and vulnerable. Half a dozen stun grenades would sort out anyone unfortunate enough to be occupying the rooms at the time. There were two first-floor balconies, easily stormed. And a blind alleyway at the side. Yes – give him ten minutes and he could bring this house to its knees.

He contemplated his strategy for a moment or so, eventually deciding on a more conventional approach. Although all that could change soon enough if he didn't get what he wanted.

He plied the knocker with vigour and the front door was

opened by a frazzled-looking woman who was too tired to recoil at the sight of Grint on the doorstep.

Grint adopted a friendly attitude. 'Mrs Lockland? I'm here to speak to Mrs Lockland. Right now.'

The woman made a valiant but doomed effort. 'Mrs Lockland doesn't—'

Too late. Grint was already inside.

Another woman knelt on the stairs, dusting, and elsewhere Grint heard a door close, so there were at least three of them in the house.

'Mrs Lockland,' he said again, in the tones of one who wasn't going away.

The first woman appeared to be clutching a ladle. Grint performed a rapid risk assessment and decided she posed no threat. He could disarm her in no more than point seven of one second and with no injuries to himself. Some fractures to his opponent, possible internal organ damage but only minimal. Complete recovery possible in less than two months.

'Mrs Lockland is upstairs,' she began, 'but . . .'

Grint took the shallow stairs three at a time, rather pleased with himself for remembering to say, 'Excuse me,' to the dusting woman as he passed. Manners cost nothing, after all.

Another woman was on the first landing, wrestling with a large, old-fashioned, manual vacuum cleaner. One of the old models that needed a human being to push it around. He hadn't seen one of those for years. It was obviously extremely heavy.

He picked it up one-handed. 'Where do you want it?'

'Um. In there, please.'

He kicked open the door and lifted it into the room for her.

'Thank you,' she said faintly.

Grint nodded, conscious he was representing the Time Police at their best. He wasn't tremendously au fait with housework. He kept his room reasonably tidy – in that he could usually find the bed – and he remembered to change his sheets every couple of months. And his clothes, of course. Daily. Or nearly daily – especially when they were covered in bits of other people – but here was a whole new world of polishing and scrubbing and hoovering. He sniffed the air. And cooking. He remembered Jane had done all of this by herself.

Arriving at the top of the house, he was confronted by a headless seagull. *The* headless seagull, he presumed. The one Jane had told him about. The one whose inadvertent decapitation had led to her joining the Time Police. The one used to terrorise a young Jane.

Hmm . . .

Even without the head, it was an evil-looking creature and obviously constituted a major threat to the success of his mission. Pulling his sonic from his rip-grip patch, he aimed it at the glass case. With surprisingly little fuss the case crumbled into hundreds of tiny pieces. The seagull – rather more impressively – exploded in a shower of feathers and filler.

Grint replaced his weapon. Threat neutralised.

Ahead of him, opposite the top of the stairs, a wide door stood open. *All the better to spy on you with* . . . ran through his head.

A bell tinkled imperiously. 'What was that noise? What have you broken? Own up or I'll deduct it from everyone's wages. And who was that at the door?'

'Me,' said Grint, stepping into a room he realised too late was the old lady's bed/sitting room.

Mrs Lockland was equally taken by surprise, and both parties regarded each other in silence.

She saw a well-armed, black-clad giant standing in her bed-room doorway. He saw a skinny woman, not young, but not as old as he had expected, comfortably reclining on a daybed and wearing an expression of complete and utter malevolence.

She curled her lip at him. 'I can remember when my father wouldn't have let your sort into the house.'

Lt Grint was not a deep thinker. Or even a thinker at all, if you listened to Luke Parrish, but the thought flashed through his head that shooting her now, on her bed, right now ... was probably against Time Police regulations. Unless he could show just cause, of course. He waited hopefully for just cause to turn up.

'Who are you?'

'Time Police,' said Grint.

'What do you want?'

'You.'

'What for?'

It occurred to Grint that explaining that he'd come to talk her out of dragging her granddaughter back to a life of unpaid drudgery would not play well.

'Investigation,' he said, which was very nearly true.

'Why?'

Since he had no idea what to say to that, Grint began a slow tour of the room while he tried to think what to do next. Shooting her was still top of a very short list.

That the old lady was completely unimpressed by him was very obvious. Eyes narrowed, she watched his progress around the room like a hawk – as if she was expecting him to start stuffing his pockets with valuables. Which did not, in any way, endear her to Lt Grint, but that was the thing about old ladies – they didn't care. They said and did all sorts of horrible things and people would say, 'Oh, she's old. She didn't mean it.' Or, 'She didn't know what she was doing.' Or, 'Oh, you poor thing, let me help.' The main thing about old ladies, though, was that you weren't really supposed to shoot them. People didn't like it.

On the other hand, thought Grint, instinctively not standing with his back to the window, I am an officer in the Time Police and thereby authorised to shoot anyone I please. Almost anyone, he amended, Commander Hay's views on just opening fire willy-nilly and then dealing similarly with the survivors being well known.

He'd been silent a long time. Not through any carefully thought-out procedure but simply because he couldn't think what to say next. Lt Grint respected Commander Hay and her judgement but he rather thought she might have got this one wrong. Parrish and his sarcastic tongue might have been a better choice for this particular assignment.

Many people are not comfortable with long silences. Especially those who feel the need to dominate every situation. Jane's grandmother was one of these.

'Well? What do you want? Speak up. I'm an old woman.' She remembered her supposed frailty and assumed a tremulous voice. 'And sick. You can't just barge in here. Go away. Leave me in peace. The doctor says I need rest and care, not a great gorilla like you trampling all over everything. Go away.'

Grint paused. This old lady had written to the Time Police and a little while later an officer had called at her house. It must surely be obvious why he was here. Yes, all right, she might have expected someone a little more user-friendly. Someone with at least basic social skills who had come to talk to her about her granddaughter returning home to look after her old sick granny. Wasn't it obvious why he was here?

Grint fell back on Officer Varma's famously effective interrogation technique.

'You know why I'm here. What do you have to say for yourself?'

He fully expected her to launch into a speech about her declining health – her need for her granddaughter to minister to her and so forth – but it didn't happen. She narrowed her eyes and her face grew meaner.

'Oh, that's why you're here, is it? You've more than taken your time. I'd given up – tight bastards that you are.'

All at sea, Grint could think of nothing to say but, 'Watch your tongue.'

'You owe me.'

Even Grint knew better than to ask her what she was talking about. 'I don't think so.'

She narrowed her eyes. 'Yes, you do.'

Drawing himself up, he said, 'Make your case.'

'Information,' she said, shrilly. 'I gave you information. And don't tell me it wasn't useful. You – the Time Police – made arrests. You should have paid me. Where's my money?'

'All in good time,' said Grint, still none the wiser. He was struck by sudden inspiration. 'There was a counterclaim. You'll have to prove it was you who laid the information.'

'Of course it was me,' she snarled. 'No one was better placed than me to know what she was up to. Anyone who says otherwise is lying through their teeth. It was me. It's on record. I signed a statement. The Time Police thanked me for my cooperation. Why didn't I get my reward? Eh? Years I've been waiting. Years! Reward for information leading to an arrest, they said, and you got two of them. I should have got double and instead I got nothing. Lost the claim, did you?'

Grint said nothing. That was extremely likely. People had had more important things to do in those days. Or she'd annoyed someone at TPHQ and they'd just binned the claim. That was also extremely likely. Or it had simply been lost in the turmoil when Hay took command. That was most likely.

Grint took out his scratchpad. 'Names?'

'You know their names.'

'Verification.'

She gusted a sigh. 'I've told you all this. In my statement.'

Grint stared at her, wondering why she was so reluctant to give the names of those she informed against. Unless . . .

'Names,' he said shortly. 'Or you get nothing.'

She sighed again.

He put his scratchpad away. 'Information unverified. Claim denied.'

'Lockland,' she said quickly. 'Aaron and Helen Lockland.'

Grint retained his composure. 'Relationship?'

'Son. Daughter-in-law. But it was her. That trollop. *She* was the one. You weren't supposed to take him as well. He was just trying to protect his worthless wife and they were both shot. Stupid boy. I told him she was no good. He died at the scene. Outside in the gardens. She took a day or so. They thought she might live after all, but she didn't, I'm glad to say.' She squinted up at him. 'So – what am I entitled to? It should be more than agreed, what with me having had to wait all this time.'

301

Grint was thinking. He was certain Jane knew nothing of this. He certainly didn't. Before his time, perhaps. He could check it out on his return. In the meantime, there must be something he could get the old bat for. Or should he let sleeping dogs lie? This wasn't why he was here today, after all. Lt Grint was not a subtle man. His job did not require him to be.

Stifling his urge to implement Option A – shooting the old bag where she lay, and still his favourite – he perceived suddenly that this might be an occasion where the pen actually was mightier than the sword.

He pulled out a fragile-looking bedroom chair which creaked alarmingly, but held his weight. Sitting down, he began to type on his scratchpad.

She watched him suspiciously. 'What are you doing?'

He fixed her with his best Time Police stare. 'I know what you did.'

Grint had, on several occasions, been interviewed by Officer Varma – nothing serious, just minor infringements – but the lesson he'd taken away from all that was of the value of silence. Not on the part of the accused – that could easily be dealt with – but on the part of the interviewing officer. Make a statement, sit back and see what happens. Varma was very good at that sort of thing. Grint had actually had to struggle quite hard against an overwhelming impulse to confess to stealing a very small sum of money from his mother's purse when he was nine.

Her eyes narrowed. 'No, you don't.'

Grint waited, his attention still on his scratchpad in front of him. A man who could wait all day.

'I haven't done anything. I barely leave the house.'

Grint smiled slowly. 'I'm sorry . . .'

'So I should hope.'

'I'm sorry, I should have said, "I know what you did to Jane."'

She was suddenly watchful. 'What?'

He just smiled.

'I'm not telling you anything.'

He smiled again. Jane's grandmother was actually telling him a very great deal. He crossed his legs and waited, his scratchpad ostentatiously on the table beside him.

'I'm sick,' she said pitifully. 'I need my granddaughter to look after me.'

'You won't need her where you're going.'

'And where would that be?'

Inspiration sleeted down from wherever inspirations are born. He gave it a second or so and then said, 'I've seen Jane's feet.'

That brought her up short. She stared at him then said, 'Just like her mother – another lazy, ungrateful good-for-nothing. And a liar. Whatever she says, it's untrue. All those years she ate me out of house and home. Everyone said they didn't know how I put up with her for so long. Ungrateful little . . . She's always either lying or complaining. Gets it from her worthless mother.'

Grint, whose own mother had worked long hours and scrimped and saved to give him the very best she could afford and then quietly died just before he was awarded his commission, was really having to work quite hard not to shoot the old hag dead. Several times. He regarded her stonily.

'You can tell me now,' he said, picking up his scratchpad again. 'Or I can send for one of our specialist units. You'll have heard of those, I'm sure.' He looked around. 'I can't see it taking them long.'

Fortunately, it didn't occur to her to ask what might not take them long.

'You can't touch me. I'm old and sick.'

'I think you have become confused,' said Grint. 'Probably because you're old and sick. What you meant to say was, "You're a handsome man – and a Time Police officer, as well – you can do anything you want. Legally."' He smiled at her. 'When you're ready to begin, Mrs Lockland.'

'I'm saying nothing.'

'As you wish. Sign here.'

He rummaged in his pockets, found a piece of paper and placed it in front of her.

'What's this?'

'Your waiver.'

'And what am I waiving?'

'Your rights to claim your granddaughter's discharge.'

'You can't do that.'

'I'm an officer in the Time Police,' he said quietly. 'I can do anything I like. And I frequently do. I know what you did to Jane. There is no statute of limitations for abuse of a minor. Signing this document buys my silence. Sign.'

She made no move to sign, simply staring at him through narrowed eyes. Searching for a weakness to exploit. He sighed. He was going to have to shoot her after all. No great loss to the world, he decided. Jane would probably be upset but, on the other hand, Jane need never know.

The old lady signed. Angrily. Dashing her thick black signature all across the document without even looking at it. Which was just as well since closer examination would have revealed she'd just signed Grint's laundry docket.

He wasted no time, picking up it and his scratchpad and heading towards the door.

'No,' she said. 'Wait.'

He ignored her.

'Wait.'

He made his way down the stairs, her shrieks drifting after him.

One of the women – the one who'd been on the stairs – was waiting for him at the bottom. She beckoned mysteriously.

Grint brightened. Was there someone here he might legitimately be able to shoot after all?

He brightened even further when he smelled the coffee.

There were four of them around the kitchen table.

'Shh,' said one and reached under the table, pulling out a packet of biscuits.

'They're ours,' she said, 'but they'll be hers if she finds out about them. And if she finds out we're taking a break, we'll have no job.'

Grint reflected on the missed opportunities to shoot the old bag where she lay. Too late now. On the other hand . . . revenge is sweet. He let the silence gather so he had their full attention.

'She grassed up her daughter-in-law,' he said, munching on his biscuit. 'The daughter-in-law was arrested. Her son tried to save his wife and things got out of hand. Both of them died and left her granddaughter an orphan.' He raised his eyes to the ceiling. 'She's been trying to claim the reward.'

They gaped at him. Eyes and mouths wide open. 'You're kidding.'

'And now you're all out of a job,' he said, taking another biscuit from the plate offered him, 'because she wants her granddaughter back.' He gave them a moment to digest this. 'And her granddaughter will work for nothing.'

There was silence in the kitchen as they looked at each other.

One of them said, 'What are you cooking there, Liz?'

'Roast chicken for her dinner tonight.'

'Is it done?'

'All but the gravy.'

'You lay the table – I'll do the gravy.' She turned to Grint. 'You'll stay for a bite to eat?'

He hesitated. On the other hand, Jane would like him to be polite. 'I would be delighted. Thank you.'

They dined well – all of them. While above stairs, Mrs Lockland's bell rang and rang, and no one cared.

## 23

On his return to TPHQ, Lt Grint made his way directly to Commander Hay's office. 'I don't think we'll hear any more from her, ma'am.' He laid his laundry docket on her desk.

She blinked. 'What's this?'

'Mrs Lockland's waiver of her granddaughter's rights to a discharge.'

She blinked. 'Is there such a thing?'

Grint shrugged. Why was he expected to think of everything?

Commander Hay peered more closely. 'This appears to be your laundry docket.'

Lt Grint stared over her shoulder. 'I am reluctant to contradict you, ma'am, but I think not. Ma'am.'

She looked again. 'No, on closer inspection, I believe you are right, Lt Grint. It is definitely a waiver.' She stared up at him. 'How did you achieve this?'

'Blackmail, ma'am. Together with intimidation, misleading the witness, falsifying evidence, wanton destruction, and at least one bloody great gun.'

'Well . . . excellent work, Lieutenant.'

'Thank you, ma'am.'

'I'll talk to Lockland myself. Please don't mention anything about this unless she specifically asks you.'

'Understood, ma'am.'

Luke and Jane were in their suddenly much more spacious office. Matthew's chair was empty. Matthew's mug and personal effects still sat on the shelf. Matthew's poster of his beloved Time Map still hung on the wall. Matthew himself, however, was not there. They had been sitting in silence for quite some time.

Officer North stuck her head round the door. 'There you are. Hay wants to see you.'

'Oh God,' said Luke, wearily, getting to his feet. 'What have we done now?'

'Not you, Parrish – just Lockland.'

'Why?' said Jane, panicking. 'What have I done?'

'And what's the matter with me?' demanded Luke.

'I don't know what you've done, Lockland, and neither will you until you speak to Hay, and there are so many things the matter with you, Parrish, that I'm not going to waste the rest of my day listing them. Why are you still here, Lockland?'

Jane fled.

Commander Hay had thought long and hard about how much information to share with her officer. It would appear that Jane's grandmother had made plans to break up her son's marriage and earn herself a little – well, a great deal of – extra cash and these had backfired. Hay had no idea why the original reward hadn't been paid and nor did she care enough to pull the files. The results of Mrs Lockland's spite were that her son and his wife had died and she'd found herself saddled with the expense and effort of bringing up their child. Not that she appeared to have expended much of either on Jane, who had arrived at TPHQ borderline malnourished, exhausted and emotionally on the edge. If it hadn't been for the positive discrimination initiative at the time, she would certainly have been rejected. As it was, everyone had expected her to complete her gruntwork – if she lived long enough – and then slide into a quiet corner in Records out of everyone's way. That had not happened even a little bit. And Hay was extremely interested to see where Lockland's path would lead her.

Jane tapped on the door and entered, her face already glowing like a sunset.

'Sweetie, you have got to stop doing that,' said Bolshy Jane in exasperation.

Hay looked up. 'Lockland, sit down – I shan't keep you a moment. We've had a communication from your grandmother.'

She's found me, was Jane's first thought. She gripped her hands together in her lap.

'Your grandmother is, apparently, suffering from ill health and has claimed you as her sole surviving relative.'

'Claimed?' said Jane, all at sea.

'When social necessity can be proved, a relative can claim an officer, who then applies for a social discharge. It means that, should you choose to be claimed, you can leave the Time Police, without the necessity of buying yourself out.'

Jane sat, appalled. Was it her imagination or were the walls already beginning to close in? Was she to be sent back whence she came? Would these last months be the only bright spot in her life? How much bleaker would her life be, knowing there was something better out there and it had been taken away from her?

'However,' said Hay, 'the officer despatched to investigate this claim found no evidence of this supposed ill health. Nor has your grandmother's request been backed up with any medical paperwork or certificates. His conclusion was that this was a spurious claim and so I intend to deny her request. You have the right to object to my ruling and present your own case for a social discharge. Do you wish to do so?'

Jane shook her head vigorously. 'No. Not at all. No.'

Hay closed her file. 'Mrs Lockland will be formally notified that her claim has been rejected. I don't think it will come as a great surprise to her. The officer's opinion – and mine – is that she's unhappy with spending money on professional care and thought she'd have an unpaid granddaughter instead.'

Jane nodded. She was aware of how close she had come. Hay might simply have rubber-stamped the claim, and unless Jane had been prepared to repudiate her grandmother publicly and deal with the guilt afterwards, she would have been out. All this – her life, her career, her friends – everything she had painstakingly assembled would have been finished. Gone. Suddenly. Just like Matthew. Everything was happening a little too quickly for her these days.

She stood up on wobbly legs. 'Thank you, ma'am.'

'I always make every effort to retain good officers.'

Jane's flush, which had just begun to subside, started up again, but for good reasons this time. 'Thank you, ma'am.'

'That's all, Lockland. Dismissed.'

Left alone, Commander Hay pulled a piece of paper towards her and picked up her pen. She had a sad task before

310

her – composing Officer Farrell's eulogy. To be given by her at his memorial service being organised for next week. A difficult task that she found marginally easier if she wrote it out by hand. Nor would she delegate the task. Every deceased officer's family had either a visit or a personal handwritten letter from the officer commanding the Time Police. Every eulogy received her personal attention. She considered it her duty.

She stared out of the window for a while and then began to write. She sat in the silence of her office, her hand moving slowly across the paper. The world outside the window was full of sound and movement but in here there was only calm. The words began to flow. She knew what she wanted to say. She began to write faster.

Until the alarms went off. All of them. Sirens, bells, klaxons, hooters. The Time Police did not mess around when it came to informing its personnel that things were about to go tits up. For those who might have missed all the noise, fit-inducing red lights strobed overhead. The clamour was deafening. Popular opinion maintained it could wake the dead and, especially after a few drinks, officers did, occasionally, attempt to obtain a few dead people just to test this particular theory. Sadly, most were turned back at the front door with instructions to return the dead whence they came. The building shuddered as the blast doors thudded into position. Again.

Commander Hay hit her intercom, shouting to make herself heard. 'What the fire truck? Charlie . . . find out what's happening this time.'

He appeared in her doorway. 'Already on it, ma'am. Duty officer – report.'

He tilted his head, listening for a moment, his face completely blank. Then he closed his com and stared at his commanding officer.

'Well?' she said. 'Are we all about to be blown to kingdom come?'

'Um . . . no.' He raised his voice, competing with the din. 'Ma'am – I'm not sure how to tell you this. I'm afraid your eulogy – moving and inspirational though I'm sure it would have been – will not now be required.'

The alarms shut off quite suddenly. The absence of noise was equally deafening. Or would have been if Captain Farenden, slightly behind events due to ringing ears, had not bellowed into the silence, 'It would appear that Officer Farrell has returned.'

Hay recoiled.

'Sorry, ma'am.'

'For God's sake, don't tell me officers have started returning from the dead.'

'No, ma'am. He claims he was never dead in the first place.'

'What is it with Team Two-Three-Six? They don't even die conventionally.' She took a calming breath. 'To be perfectly clear – Matthew Farrell is still alive?'

'Very much so, ma'am, although he appears to be in a state of some considerable agitation. He is demanding your urgent attention. He won't speak to anyone else.'

'How did he get here?'

'The details are yet to be ascertained, ma'am, but it appears the alarms were activated because of an emergency landing.'

'Oh God, is he in a St Mary's pod? He hasn't brought his bloody mother with him, has he? Tell her I'm out. Or better yet – get Grint to shoot her. Tell him I'll sign the report saying it was an accident.'

'I shall endeavour to ascertain the exact circumstances, ma'am.'

He disappeared.

Meanwhile, down in the Pod Bay, Matthew had shot out of the pod faster than a hungry ferret up a pair of rabbit-smelling trousers, dodged past the Senior Mech who said, 'Hey, hang on a minute . . .' and dashed straight out of the door.

Arriving at the lift, he shouldered aside two other officers, one of whom said, 'You're supposed to be dead,' while the other demanded to know if this was the zombie apocalypse everyone was talking about.

Matthew had no time to reply. The lift doors slid open and he flung himself inside, stabbing repeatedly at the controls because everyone knows that always makes lifts function more quickly and efficiently.

Thoroughly confused by its conflicting instructions, the lift played safe by painstakingly stopping at every floor before finally arriving at the correct destination, pausing there for one brief microsecond before making a determined attempt to return all the way back down to the Pod Bay again. It was finally, and much against its will, forced to decant an agitated Officer Farrell at his requested destination.

Before Captain Farenden could update his commanding officer, the door to his outer office crashed open and bounced off the wall. Something shattered.

Farenden sighed. 'I suspect Officer Farrell might have arrived, ma'am.'

Hay shoved the now redundant draft eulogy into her top drawer. 'You'd better show him in, Charlie, before he brings the ceiling down.'

Captain Farenden wasn't granted that opportunity. Officer Farrell was already barrelling through the door.

'Ma'am. We've got it all wrong. Mr P is not Raymond Parrish. Or Eric Portman. Or any of the Portmans. Or even Pennyroyal.'

He dragged in a ragged breath.

'Mr P is Henry Plimpton.'

24

Mikey, meanwhile, was enveloped in darkness. Close, rank darkness. She suspected some kind of hood. They were hustling her somewhere. She was pushed along, disoriented and confused. Her head hurt. Her ear hurt where someone had wrenched off her Snoopy helmet and yanked out her earpiece. One moment she'd been crouched behind a stack of something, trying to make out what she was seeing – or rather what she wasn't seeing – because she was certain there was a camouflaged pod by that pillar. She was just squinting for a better look when someone had grabbed a handful of her flying jacket and dragged her backwards. Feet scrabbling for purchase, she'd been pulled along a cold, hard floor before someone had dropped something over her head. Her world instantly turned dark, hot and moist, and smelled of vomit. She wondered for a moment who had been the hood's previous occupant and what had happened to them.

She felt someone unzip her flying jacket. Presumably to check for concealed weapons, she told herself.

A man's voice said, 'Mr P says not to damage her.'

Not *don't hurt her* but *don't damage her*, which wasn't quite the same thing at all.

A second voice somewhere over her head enquired about the other one.

'If you catch him then you can kill him.'

In the distance, muffled by the hood, Mikey could hear a clanging alarm bell and then she was on the move again. Someone closed a door behind her, deadening the sound somewhat. She felt something hard on the back of her legs and was pushed into a cold metal chair. Before she could properly work out what was happening, the door opened again, briefly bringing in the noise from the hangar next door. A new voice, hesitant and softly spoken asked, 'The other one – is he dealt with?'

Someone reluctantly informed the new arrival that it would seem Matthew had got away. 'There was a pod here. We couldn't see it until it was too late. A door opened and someone yanked him in. We fired but he got away.' There was the sound of someone drawing breath. 'We think Time Police, probably.'

Mikey was conscious of a sudden surge of relief and hope. If Matthew had managed to get away somehow . . . but who was he with? Not to make a bad joke, but had he jumped from the frying pan into the fire?

There was a long silence which, somehow, was worse than prolonged cursing and threats.

'Did he indeed?' said the soft voice, eventually. 'That need not necessarily be a problem.'

'They could be here any moment.'

'Again, not necessarily a problem. I have a long reach and it is very possible our young friend will never have the opportunity to tell others what he's seen here. You all know what to do in the event of unexpected visitors. Go and do it.'

Footsteps faded to silence and the door closed. Inside her hood, Mikey tried hard to breathe quietly. To listen.

Still silence on this side of the wall. Total silence. Unnerving silence. The man with the soft voice hadn't gone away with the other footsteps. He was still here. Standing very close to her. Mikey could hear nothing but her own breathing. She tried very hard not to imagine a weapon being levelled at the back of her head. And what of Matthew? Why wouldn't he have the opportunity to report on what he'd seen here? Perhaps the wrath of the Time Police would not descend upon this place after all. Perhaps he was already dead and his body dumped somewhere it might never be found. And hers could be joining his at any moment. Mikey sat very, very still.

The voice spoke again, reassuringly far away.

'Miss Meiklejohn – welcome. Bless my soul, I could hardly believe my eyes when I saw you drifting around my warehouse. And did I catch sight of young Officer Farrell as well? A bit of a shock, let me tell you. So – good and bad happenings today. Good that we finally get to meet each other and bad that my deception appears to have been less successful than I had hoped.'

There was the sound of someone rubbing their hands together. 'Now then – before we waste each other's time in pointless denials, I should perhaps tell you that I know exactly who you are. I've followed your exploits – and those of your brother – with the greatest interest. I've always hoped our paths would cross one day. You all but disappeared yet now – suddenly – here you are. Exactly when and where I wanted you. You see, I need your talents, my dear.'

Mikey sat up straight. A show of defiance would be expected. 'Well, you won't get them.'

She could hear a slight smile in his voice. 'I want you to listen to me very carefully because this is the way things work in the real world. You will do as I command. You really have no other option. Refuse and I will kill you. With regret, but remember, your death will leave me no worse off. I shall simply have to find someone else to assist me. Your brother, perhaps.'

Mikey laughed. 'You've never met Adrian, have you?'

The man laughed too. 'You should pray I never have to.'

Delay him. Delay, delay, delay. Matthew had escaped. She had to believe that. He had escaped and the Time Police would come. They always came. She should know. When she and Adrian had been on the run, the Time Police had rarely been more than a couple of hours behind them. She remembered that mad period when she and Adrian had hopped all over the Time-line like demented rabbits. Always escaping by a combination of luck, optimism and the skin of their teeth. Right up until the day they hadn't. The buggers had appeared out of nowhere. Black shapes looming up out of the night. She remembered nothing after that because she'd been shot. Somehow Adrian had got her into the teapot – their pod – and back to St Mary's. Who had entered into the whole *let's deceive the Time Police* thing with massive enthusiasm.

Since then, she and Adrian had mostly been on the side of the angels but she still had memories of those times. The main one being that sooner or later the Time Police always turned up. She could only pray that today it would be sooner. Would they, just for once, manage to be in the right place at the right time? There was nothing she could do except slow things down and give them every chance to catch up.

Her first instinct was to get him to remove the hood so she could see where she was but her second told her to leave it in place. If she never saw his face, then there was the very faintest chance she would live. She would definitely die if she could identify him.

Delay . . .

Quaveringly, she said, 'I think you might have the wrong person. I've only just left college. Do you think you've confused me with someone else?'

She heard the sound of a file being flipped.

'Amelia Meiklejohn. Sister to Adrian Meiklejohn. Freelance troublemakers, the pair of you. According to this very helpful and very detailed file. My – you have been a naughty girl, haven't you? Oh look – there's even a photo.'

He had her Time Police file. Or a copy of it, anyway. How the hell had he managed that? No time to think about that. As Dr Maxwell herself was very fond of saying, 'Always deal with the now. If you do that, then quite often everything else looks after itself.'

Experience – and time spent at St Mary's – had taught her there was usually a way out. And if the way out wasn't immediately apparent, then it could always be manufactured.

Stage One consisted of bursting into tears.

'Really?' said the man, infuriatingly calm. 'Seriously?'

Mikey shook her head, bravely struggling for self-control.

He sighed. 'You have five seconds to stop that. Then I shoot you in the foot. Which will be very painful but will at least give you something to cry about. If that doesn't stop you, then

319

I shall shoot you in the knee. Same leg. And that, believe me, will be excruciating. You will never be free from pain again.'

Mikey stopped crying immediately, saying amiably, 'OK. Go on, then – what are your plans? What exactly is it you want me to do?'

'Well, I believe you and I, quite coincidentally, have been following the same line of research. You more successfully than I, it would seem.' She heard him snap the file shut. 'You see – I am a very reasonable man. I have no objection to being out-thought by a little girl.'

Oh yes, you do, thought Mikey, tucking that away for possible future use. If she lived that long.

She said, 'I'm engaged in a lot of research. You'll have to be more specific.'

'A wrist-mounted Time-travel device.'

'Oh, that,' said Mikey, dismissively. 'Don't bother. It doesn't work. It's almost impossible to get the field-generator-to-bracelet-size ratio correct. If you build something big enough to generate an adequate field, then the device is no longer portable. It's the size of a small table. If you keep the generator small, then the field size isn't large enough to transport a whole human. Only about one fifth arrives at the designated destination. The rest of it is left lying in a heap at the point of departure, slowly bleeding to death.'

'Well, I'm certain that a bright little thing like you will soon resolve the problem.'

'And then you'll shoot me. Great incentive.'

'No, I shall reward you. Handsomely. I am hoping this will be the beginning of a very profitable relationship for both of us. Don't tell me you don't miss the old days. The freedom to create whatever you like. The excitement of Time travel. And the jeopardy. Especially the jeopardy. Work with me and all that will be yours again. To say nothing of the financial rewards.'

Mikey shrugged. 'I don't really do money.'

'Then let me put it this way, you will have no choice. Not once the Time Police are informed – anonymously, of course – that you are enthusiastically working for me. You are one of the notorious Meiklejohn siblings. They will judge you to have reneged on the terms of your amnesty and hunt you down. And your brother. Unless you come to work for me, of course, and avail yourself of the protection I can offer.'

Stage Two. Time to give in gracefully. 'I don't appear to have a lot of choice, do I?'

'No, you don't. Shall we introduce ourselves properly?'

He pulled off her hood. Mikey regarded him. Short, plump, balding, benign expression, spectacles.

'I'm sorry, I don't have the faintest idea who you are.'

He bowed and smirked. 'My name is Henry Plimpton.'

'Oh yes,' said Mikey. 'You're the henpecked husband. Matthew told me all about you. That's disappointing. I was expecting a supervillain. With a cat. And a tank of piranha.'

For one moment, a very ugly expression passed across Henry Plimpton's mild-mannered countenance. She'd touched a nerve. Henry Plimpton was a very vain man. Perhaps it would be wise to back off – just a little.

She smiled. 'You don't have to threaten me, Henry. Make me an offer I can't refuse and I might be very interested, but I should warn you – if you're going to employ me, then you're going to have to keep me very, very safe. If I join you then the

321

Time Police will rip the Timeline apart to get to me. Are you sure I'm worth the risk?'

Benign Henry Plimpton was back. 'Absolutely certain. I think we can be of great benefit to each other, my dear. Welcome aboard.'

Mikey nodded. 'OK. I'll try to fix your bracelets for you.'

She stood up, stretched and looked around her with interest.

The first thing she noticed was the small pod standing in the back right-hand corner. The door was closed. She looked away casually, not wanting to show too much interest.

Behind her was the door presumably leading back into the hangar. The only door, she now saw. She could see no other way out. This room was about one third the size of the hangar outside and seemed to be the workroom she had been looking for. The brick walls were painted cream to maximise the light. The windows running around the top showed only a darkening sky. Four what looked like very large generators stood in a circle at the centre of the room. Mikey's eyes narrowed. They *looked* like generators but she wasn't entirely convinced.

Cables and wires were connected to banks of equipment piled high around the edges of the room or stacked neatly on workbenches. Whether the equipment fed the generators or vice versa she was unable to tell. Occasionally a light would blink or a list of readings would flash up on a display.

Lights hung from long cables, suspended from the iron girders overhead, and everything was very clean and neat. In perfect order.

'Nice workshop,' said Mikey, admiringly.

Henry beamed. 'Thank you, my dear.'

She strolled nonchalantly towards the generators. 'So what's going on here, then?'

'What's going on here is a demonstration of my power. This is the beginning of the end for the Time Police.'

Mikey looked round. 'Really? Tell me more.'

He smiled a little too widely. 'I don't want to spoil the surprise . . .'

Mikey remained silent because he was obviously itching to tell her.

'Well, all right then – with the equipment you see here, I am able . . .' he paused dramatically, 'to manipulate Time itself.'

She grinned at him. 'Can I make a guess?'

'Why not?'

'Are you manufacturing a Time-slip?'

Henry chuckled indulgently. This was obviously his Big Moment. 'No, Miss Meiklejohn, I am manufacturing a time-stop.'

Mikey's stomach turned over. She swallowed hard, and forced herself to look impressed.

'Really? Wow.' She peered at them. 'These are not electrical generators.'

'No. The real power source is external – it has to be.'

'You would need a lot of power for these babies.'

'I have a lot of power.'

Mikey looked around. 'When are we?'

'Paris, 1902.'

She frowned. 'Electrical power?'

He smiled. 'No.'

Mikey swallowed again.

'Nothing to say, Miss Meiklejohn?'

'Henry, I'm lost for words. How did you manage to . . . ?'

He smiled. 'I look forward to discussing the details when we have more time. I must say I'm very encouraged by your attitude. No "Oh my God, that is so dangerous. Are you out of your mind?" Or even "Are you mad? You could blow up the world."'

Now Mikey laughed. 'Not from me. I've gone far beyond sex, drugs and rock and roll. Obviously I don't want to boast, but I built a pod with no safety protocols. A pod in which you could go wherever you liked and do whatever you liked when you got there. Fancy one of those, Henry?'

He beamed, the light winking off his spectacles. 'I must say, Miss Meiklejohn – I do think you and I are going to get on splendidly.'

'Not going to shoot me in the foot after all?'

'Well, not today, certainly.'

She looked around again. 'I don't want to be rude, but I'm going to need better than this. I'll need tools. Decent lighting. And a proper workshop and . . .'

'And you shall have them. Everything you want. This is not my main place of residence. Consider this a kind of branch office.'

'Cool. Any chance of a hollowed-out volcano? I've always wanted to work in a hollowed-out volcano. Wherever it is, you'd better make it quick because the Time Police . . .'

She looked around as if expecting them at any moment.

'You don't need to worry about that, my dear. I have already taken steps to distract them.'

He looked up. Mikey followed his gaze. A ceiling-mounted laser was trained on the door.

'The Time Police are not noted for their subtle approach,' he said. 'They will find a great deal to keep them occupied in the warehouse next door. And as soon as the survivors – if there are any – burst through the door . . .'

He looked up again. 'However, your point about requiring better facilities is well, if a trifle impolitely, expressed. Shall we be going? This way.'

Delay.

'Where? Where are we going, Henry?'

In one rapid movement, he seized a handful of her hair and yanked her head backwards. The sudden pain made her eyes water. 'That's *Mr Plimpton* to you, my dear. It's *always* Mr Plimpton. Got it?'

Mikey's response was never uttered. An immense explosion on the other side of the door sent shafts of jagged white light flashing through the windows above them, distorting shapes and shadows. For one moment, Henry Plimpton appeared as a gross, misshapen, twisted being, looming over her like a thundercloud. The lights dimmed and went out. She could hear men shouting. It sounded as if an entire army was out there.

She tilted her head back and grinned at him.

'They're heeeeeeeeere . . .'

25

Matthew had arrived at Commander Hay's office alone, Major Callen having obviously been shed – or possibly trampled – along the way. He stood before Hay, his chest heaving, his hair in wild disarray, his clothing dishevelled and his eyes gleaming weirdly. In all her service career, Commander Hay had never seen anything look less like a Time Police officer.

Attempting to lower his emotional temperature, she said quietly, 'Henry Plimpton is dead. You informed us of that fact yourself. Killed in the explosion at Lower Spurting.'

Matthew was very nearly hopping from foot to foot with impatience. Words tumbled over each other. 'No, no, he isn't, ma'am. He's very much alive. I saw him. There. In the thing. Place. Hangar. The warehouse. Well, just his back view. But it was obviously him. He's making Time-travel bracelets. In the warehouse. He's got some sort of factory there. Tons of equipment inside it. About twelve pods. Between fifteen to twenty men. It's a big operation and now he's got Mikey and we have to get her out.'

Hay stared at him. The emotional temperature plummeted to around absolute zero.

'Sit down, Officer Farrell. A glass of water, please, Charlie. Now – report. Properly.'

Matthew took a deep breath and sorted through his thoughts. 'I wasn't killed in the explosion at Beaver Avenue.'

'I think we had gathered that.'

'Neither was Henry Plimpton. His garden shed was a pod. I mean his pod was disguised to look like a shed. Quite clever really. I was checking it out when he came in. Henry, I mean. I heard him doing some things. I don't know what – I couldn't see. Then someone knocked on the door. I don't know who – I never saw them and they didn't come in – and then they shot him. At least I thought they did. I thought it was Raymond Parrish. I don't mean in person, but I thought he'd sent someone to make sure Henry couldn't talk to us and to get the pod back. But that wasn't the case at all because he shot him. I mean Henry shot whoever it was. I think Henry set it all up. So people would think it was him who died. And we did. And then he just closed the door and jumped away. It was only seconds before the explosion.'

'Wait,' said Hay sharply. 'Are you saying that Plimpton himself was responsible for the explosion?'

Matthew nodded, his breathing coming more slowly now. 'It's possible, don't you think? To make us think he was dead, ma'am. To throw us off the scent.'

'Are you absolutely certain? That would mean the man's a cold-blooded bastard who murdered six people – including his own family.'

Matthew nodded again; the reality of what he was saying began to hit home. His legs began to shake. He remembered Mrs Plimpton, bringing in a tray full of cakes and scones. And Kylie and Dwayne, with their music. Even the bouncing dogs. All of them – gone forever because they'd been murdered by their own father . . . husband . . . whatever. Who would do that? Who *could* do that? And now that same person had Mikey. Thus reminded, he jumped to his feet again.

'Ma'am . . .' His need to convey the information quickly, his concern for Mikey, his shock at the implications . . . all combined to tie his tongue and make him stumble over his words again. 'I— We should— I mean—'

The logjam of words refused to budge. He clenched his fists, overwhelmed by his own frustration.

He was recalled by Commander Hay quietly instructing him to sit down again and continue. Which he should do. He was a Time Police officer, trained to observe and report. To impart the info as quickly as possible. Not stumble and stutter as he used to. He had to get things moving. There was no time to waste.

Matthew took a huge breath, sipped some water and started again. Slowly. 'Henry's pod jumped. With me hiding on board. It landed in a big hangar somewhere.' He patted his pocket. 'I have the coordinates on my recorder. It was really busy in there. There were people and pods everywhere. It was just the sort of place Parrish Industries would have. Like a warehouse. I went for a look round.'

He stopped and remembered to breathe.

'What did you see?'

'I saw someone I'm certain was Henry Plimpton. It was only a glimpse but it had to be, didn't it, since I'd been in his pod, I couldn't see any more because I was challenged. I tried to get back to the pod I'd arrived in but there were too many people and they were all looking at me. I tried to run and then someone grabbed me from behind and yanked me into a pod. Literally. My feet left the ground. I saw Major Callen very briefly, heard him shout for an emergency evacuation and then I was just trying not to be sick.'

If this information startled Commander Hay, her face showed nothing. Although to be fair, it rarely did.

Clasping her hands on her desk, she said, 'I am a little confused as to the appearance of Amelia Meiklejohn in all this. My understanding is that she was living under amnesty at St Mary's.'

Matthew swallowed. 'While I was hiding in the pod – before it jumped – I thought I'd take the opportunity to examine the boxes stacked up inside. The ones I hid behind. I opened one and it contained bracelets. Cuffs. Whatever you call them. You slide them on to your forearm and snap them shut. There's a mini touchpad and . . . all sorts of stuff I didn't get a chance to look at very closely . . .'

He tailed away. The room was very quiet as both Commander Hay and Captain Farenden waited for him to condemn himself.

With a sudden flash of insight, Matthew realised that Luke had been absolutely right. For him, there would always be this conflict between doing what he wanted to do and doing what was right. There should be no argument. He was a Time Police officer with all the rights that entailed but also with all the responsibilities. He'd been warned about his inability to sever his ties to St Mary's. Several times, actually. This would not be his first offence. Commander Hay had made her position completely clear. There had been no room for possible misinterpretation. No wriggle room at all. He swallowed.

Very quietly, Commander Hay said, 'Go on.'

Matthew swallowed again, choosing his words carefully. 'I

didn't have the technical knowledge to understand exactly how they work . . .' He tailed away.

Commander Hay regarded him. 'Correct me if I am wrong, but I'm guessing you knew someone who did.'

'Yes.'

'Someone not at TPHQ, perhaps? Someone not a member of the Time Police?'

There seemed nothing to say to that so he said nothing.

'I thought we had already discussed your potentially job-ending tendency to prioritise St Mary's above your current employers, Officer Farrell.'

'I haven't,' said Matthew, who actually had and was hoping to gloss over this part of his story. 'I mean I did, but I had a good reason. I wanted to show the bracelets to the one person who . . .' He stopped.

'Who *could* have manufactured them.'

Matthew lifted his chin. 'Yes. Although I didn't think she had. And I was right.'

'And you know this because . . . ?'

'She told me so.'

'Officer Farrell, did you actually do Module 33 in your training? The one where we teach trainees not to believe a word anyone says to them?'

Matthew dismissed Module 33 with a wave of his hand. 'And she was right. They were too crude. She reckons most of them were too unstable to use. And those that weren't – too unstable, I mean – couldn't possibly have been used more than once. Twice at the most. After that they'd have blown up and taken the user with them.'

'Could the bracelets have caused the explosion at Beaver Avenue?'

Matthew shook his head. 'No. They'd have blown out some windows and killed anyone standing nearby, but there's no way they could have caused the devastation we saw.'

Commander Hay glanced up at Captain Farenden, standing behind Matthew. Their eyes met.

'Charlie, could you ask Major Callen if he could spare me a moment, please.'

'He's already on his way here,' said Matthew, employing the time-honoured St Mary's method of blame dispersal by involving as many of their mates as possible. Not that Major Callen was a mate, but the principle was sound.

'How many other people did you pop off to visit before remembering your first priority is to the Time Police, Officer Farrell?'

'None. I mean just that one, but Major Callen's pod was already there. Camouflaged. Actually in the hangar.'

Commander Hay and Captain Farenden did not look at each other. 'In what capacity?' enquired Commander Hay.

'Don't know,' said Matthew, who had, until this moment, given Major Callen's unexpected appearance almost no consideration at all. 'He just pulled me into his pod – for which I was thankful because I had nowhere to go. Which gave away his own position, and Plimpton's men started firing at us and we made an emergency jump. Back here.'

'Really? You didn't feel the need to break your journey with a two-week break in the Seychelles, perhaps?'

Matthew, a past master at recognising sarcasm, wisely remained silent.

Hay shifted in her seat. 'Did Miss Meiklejohn think the bracelets were deliberately designed to be single-use?'

'No and yes. I mean, no, they weren't originally designed to be single-use but yes they were because the wiring was wrong. It looked as though Henry had tried to modify some of them. An attempt to rectify the problem, she said. Different wiring, adjusting the power levels in relation to the field generator and so on. She said she still didn't think they'd work properly. But the important thing is that now Henry Plimpton's got her and we have to get her back.'

'Because we don't want her knowledge falling into the wrong hands, obviously,' said Captain Farenden. His scratchpad bleeped and he glanced down. 'Major Callen will join us as soon as he is able.'

'Where is he?'

'In his section, collating relevant information to present to you, ma'am. He estimates a quarter of an hour. No more.'

Matthew went to speak, apparently thought better of it, took a deep breath, dropped his shoulders and said, 'Captain Farenden is right, ma'am. We mustn't let her knowledge fall into the wrong hands.'

'Well, it wouldn't have, would it, if you hadn't jumped to St Mary's first? For reasons I am still endeavouring to ascertain.'

'Because of the bracelets, ma'am.'

'You wanted to warn her.'

Matthew sat his ground. 'No – I wanted to discover whether she was the person who had made them. I didn't think she had and when I spoke to her, she confirmed that fact.'

'Well, she would, wouldn't she?'

'Thus saving the Time Police considerable time and effort pursuing the wrong . . .' He stopped.

'Offender? Suspect? Illegal?'

'Ma'am, the important information to take from this is that Amelia Meiklejohn did not manufacture those bracelets, but now we know who did.'

'And if she had? If she and her lunatic brother had reverted to their old ways – what would you have done then?'

Matthew hesitated and then stood up. As always, when he was overwhelmed with emotions and words, he spoke very slowly and carefully.

'I jumped to St Mary's as an officer of the Time Police. I interviewed Amelia Meiklejohn in the same capacity. I was investigating the origin of illegal Time-travel devices. As I am obliged to do. My duty was clear to me at all times. If I had been in any doubt, I would have sought advice from Dr Bairstow, who would, I am certain, have instructed me to return to TPHQ with all speed to update you on current events. As it happens, ma'am, thanks to my investigations, I am now in a position to say that Amelia Meiklejohn is not involved in their manufacture and we would be unwise to waste time pursuing that line of enquiry.'

He waited in the silence of Hay's office, small, scruffy and strangely impressive.

Commander Hay sat back. 'The discussion is slightly immaterial now that, thanks to you, Henry Plimpton has both Miss Meiklejohn and the bracelets.'

'Actually, ma'am – no. Our position is far stronger than it was half an hour ago. We now have valuable intel concerning a problem we didn't even know we had, together with some of the bracelets.'

'*Some* of the bracelets?'

'I stole a couple of boxes from the pod when . . .'

'When you and Miss Meiklejohn decided to take unilateral action. Illegal unilateral action. As soon as you were able to do so, you should have returned to TPHQ to report and sought instructions on how next to proceed.'

'Ma'am, with respect, yes, but if I had done so we would still be thinking Henry Plimpton had been killed in the explosion. We would have no idea that he was Mr P and possibly wasted a considerable amount of time concentrating on the wrong suspect. As it is, we now know who we're looking for and where and when he is.'

'I don't think he's going to sit around and wait for us to come crashing through the door. You have, as usual, precipitated events, Officer Farrell, and once again we have to scramble to catch up.'

'Ma'am, again, with respect. Thirty minutes ago, you didn't even know there were any events to precipitate. You – we – the Time Police – would have closed the file on Henry Plimpton and he would have been free to operate with impunity. It's unfortunate he has Amelia Meiklejohn and we have to get her back and . . .'

Captain Farenden appeared in the doorway, which was a surprise to Matthew who hadn't noticed he'd left. 'Ma'am. Your urgent attention is required.'

She slapped the table in frustration. 'Seriously, Captain?'

'I'm afraid so, ma'am. Mrs Farnborough is here and would like a word.'

'Do we know why?'

He shook his head. 'For your ears only, ma'am.'

'Ask her to come in, please. Officer Farrell, you are dismissed.'

His mouth dropped open. 'But what about Mikey? What about Henry Plimpton? What about . . . ?'

'You have the coordinates?'

'Yes, in my recorder.'

She nodded. 'Hand it to Captain Farenden. You will not return to St Mary's. In fact, you will not leave TPHQ. We will resume this discussion later.' She took a deep breath. 'In the meantime, Officer Farrell, welcome home. Go and see your team.'

Suddenly conscious that his legs were trembling and he was exhausted, Matthew left the room.

**26**

It is possible Commander Hay might have appreciated at least a few moments' breathing space. She was not to be granted them. The Right Honourable Patricia Farnborough strode commandingly into the room. To be fair, this was nothing unusual. The Right Honourable Mrs Farnborough strode commandingly everywhere.

As always, she was dressed in her trademark tweed suit, white blouse and sensible shoes and would have looked more at home with a shotgun on the moors hunting peasants. Or *constituents*, as she was forced to refer to them these days. If she was still mourning her daughter, then she was doing so in private.

'I am here officially,' she announced. 'I have no objection to our meeting being minuted, but I think, when you have heard what I have to say, you will agree to my request for complete secrecy.'

Matthew was ushered out through Captain Farenden's office and into the corridor. The door closed behind him and he had no opportunity to hear any more.

Mrs Farnborough swept on. 'I regret to inform you, Commander, that a new and serious threat has materialised. We appear to be looking at our first case of Temporal Terrorism.'

'Well,' said Hay. 'It was only a matter of time, I suppose. May I have the details, please.'

'I think this speaks for itself.' Mrs Farnborough held out a data stick.

'This was sent to you personally?'

'The message was sent to my office. The security services have people trying to trace its origin but I'm certain they won't find anything. This is a copy.'

'Why was the message sent to you?'

She hesitated for only a moment. 'I suspect my – Imogen's – connection to the Time Police is well known in certain circles.'

'This sounds serious.'

'It is very serious. I would be grateful if you could watch this and let me have your thoughts.'

Hay held up the data stick and raised the eyebrow that still worked.

'Perfectly safe,' said Mrs Farnborough. 'Standard departmental-issue data stick and the download has been mega-checked for viruses, Trojans and the like.'

Captain Farenden plugged in the data stick and activated the big screen. For a moment it remained blank and then was filled with an image that was both familiar and unfamiliar.

'You are looking at the Acropolis,' announced an unseen voice, metallic and heavily distorted by voice-altering equipment. 'A monument to the triumph of Athens. A World Heritage site. An iconic image. A symbol of democracy and freedom known the world over. It is about to be destroyed and there is nothing the Time Police can do about it.'

Both women stared at the screen. At the half-constructed buildings encased in a cat's cradle of wooden scaffolding.

337

'Do we know when this is?' enquired Hay.

'Not the exact date, no. Obviously during the time of its construction.' She paused. 'There has been a great deal of discussion as to why the terrorists have chosen to do this in the past and not the present day.'

'To challenge us,' said Hay, immediately. 'To demonstrate their ability to move through Time. To show they have access to at least one pod. If they blew up the Acropolis today, then it would be just terrorism. They want to make the point that this is *Temporal* Terrorism. Destroying the Acropolis before it's completed will profoundly affect the course of history. If it was destroyed today, then yes, there would be a world outcry of grief and outrage, but after a while the world would just shrug its shoulders and carry on. Governments would pompously declare they don't do deals with terrorist organisations, thus enabling them to claim the moral high ground while justifying their refusal to pay the ransom and . . .'

'That's just it. There is no ransom demand, Commander. Please watch.'

The point of view narrowed to focus on a small, square, apparently wooden shack parked at the foot of a flight of steps that seemed to lead to some kind of open-air altar. Despite the heavy rain slanting down, slightly obscuring the image, there was no mistaking a pod. The camera panned back out again and the voice continued.

'This is not a ransom demand. You have nothing we want. This is a demonstration of our power. We will destroy this site at a time of our choosing. There is nothing you can do to prevent this. Any attempt to remove or tamper with the pod will result in a premature explosion, the consequences of which will be felt across all time. While you contemplate your failure, a second demonstration will follow – the effects of which will be considerably more severe. After which you will disband the Time Police.'

The screen went blank.

Commander Hay sat very still for one moment and then enquired whether Major Callen had yet arrived.

'Waiting in my office, ma'am.'

'Send for Major Ellis as well, please. Immediately. And Officer North, I think. Get on to the Senior Mech. I want a full download from Major Callen's pod – cameras, coordinates, everything. Cross-reference against Farrell's recorder. When you've done that, get someone to organise a roll call. How many people can we muster? What are our resources at this moment? How many can we recall safely from their current assignments and how long to do so?'

Captain Farenden disappeared.

'Mrs Farnborough, we were discussing another matter before your arrival. A different threat, but equally serious in its own way. We have, for some time, been pursuing the manufacturers of highly unstable Time-travelling equipment. Simultaneously, we have been monitoring the activities of a supposedly minor illegal who has suddenly revealed himself to be not quite as minor as we thought. I now have reason to believe the two are connected.' She gestured at the screen. 'I don't believe this is a coincidence, either. How long have you had this and do you know whence it originated?'

'Its origin is untraceable but it was transmitted to a public access com device in my department approximately two hours ago. The Greek government is very keen for this to be dealt with quickly and quietly. As are we.'

There were voices in the outer office.

Captain Farenden appeared. 'Majors Ellis and Callen and Officer North are here, ma'am.'

'Bring them all up to speed, Charlie, and then wheel them in.'

Hay turned back to Mrs Farnborough. 'This is a very public challenge to which we have no choice but to respond. With deadly force. They are making a statement and so must we. Do you have any thoughts on who could have made this threat? Is this politically motivated? They may say there is no ransom to be paid but I find it hard to believe no demands have or will be made.'

The door opened. 'Come in, please. I'm assuming you've all heard about Officer Farrell?'

Ellis and North nodded. 'Although I haven't heard the details yet,' said Ellis.

'That will be for later,' said Hay. 'We have something more important to discuss at the moment. Officer North, I'd like you to take a look at this.'

The clip played again. At the end there was silence.

'From what we have just seen, are you able to identify the date? Even approximately.'

North seated herself at the table and pulled out her scratchpad. 'May I see it again, please.'

The clip played again. North stared at the screen.

'Your thoughts, Officer North.'

'This is, I think, around the time of Pericles. The Golden Age of Athens. The Persians have been defeated after the Battle of Salamis but not before they torched Athens, destroying the old Temple of Athena. I would hazard a guess that this is after the Persian Wars but before the Athenians begin to lose

340

the war with Sparta. Ma'am, I should tell you this is not my speciality. I can go off and research this – attempt to identify the actual date as far as I am able – but it will take time and we both know someone who can probably pinpoint almost the exact moment this is taking place. It's 4th or 5th century BC, I'm certain, but exactly when . . .'

Major Callen interrupted. 'I can see where you are going with this, officer, but we ourselves have access to people who can advise us. Commander, it surely isn't necessary to involve St Mary's.'

'I don't want even a hint of this getting out. To anyone. St Mary's is the quickest and easiest way to verify the target on the quiet. If she gives us any trouble, Major, you may shoot her yourself.'

Callen smiled grimly. 'I find myself suddenly reconciled to your actions, Commander.'

Hay turned to North. 'Get her here. My compliments to Dr Bairstow but no arguments. Sonic her if necessary. Sonic the whole bloody lot of them if you have to. Just get her here. We'll apologise to the survivors afterwards.'

'Yes, ma'am.' North left at a trot.

Commander Hay turned to Mrs Farnborough. 'I've just sent for an expert who, hopefully, can identify exactly when these events are occurring. We don't have time to do this ourselves. We have to get this exactly right and so I'm consulting a . . . specialist. She's undisciplined and irritating, but she knows her stuff. *Our* time, I think, will be best spent discussing possible plans of attack. Major Callen – your thoughts.'

'My first thought, Commander, is that we have all been guilty of grossly underestimating Henry Plimpton. Not only

341

is he nowhere near as dead as we thought, but also a considerably greater threat than realised. It's not a top priority at the moment, but the Beaver Avenue explosion certainly warrants closer examination.' He looked around. 'Does anyone else think this is all rather too much of a coincidence? Henry Plimpton dead then not dead? He's discovered and then this happens?' He gestured at the screen.

'Yes,' said Ellis. 'If I was Henry Plimpton, this is exactly the sort of thing I would do to distract you while I made my no doubt well-planned getaway. Although his getaway from what?'

'From whatever he was up to in that hangar,' said Hay. 'Which was, no doubt, what Major Callen was investigating, under cover so deep that even I didn't know of it.'

'You surely mean when I was so fortunately in the right place and Time to rescue Officer Farrell and return us both to TPHQ to make our report, Commander.'

She held his gaze for a moment and then continued. 'I've asked the Senior Mech to download the information from your pod.'

'An excellent idea. Let us hope you find something relevant and useful.'

'There will, I am sure, be something we can cross-reference against anything Dr Maxwell might suggest.'

'Again, Commander, can I place on record my misgivings over involving anyone from St Mary's, and Dr Maxwell in particular? Which I feel sure you will ignore.'

'You may and I shall. Let us move on.' She gestured at the screen. 'Your thoughts, please.'

'Well,' said Callen, 'in this case, I recommend the traditional, unsubtle approach. We pre-empt any action they might take and

342

destroy that pod ourselves. Everything else will probably go up with it – the entire Acropolis, the rock on which it stands, and possibly a good part of Athens itself – all gone forever. Yes, we'd be doing the terrorists' work for them, but our point would be more than made. We *must* demonstrate to the world that history is not our weakness. That we don't care about ancient ruins. Notre Dame, Stonehenge, Angkor Wat, Uluru – they're not important to us. Our message should always be: commit a Time Crime and the Time Police will take you out. No messing. We can always apologise afterwards. Sorry about your religious site, but we don't tolerate Temporal Terrorism in any form. Mess with Time and you will die.'

'That is an option,' said Hay, 'but the final option, I think.'

'So I should bloody well hope,' said Mrs Farnborough, visibly shaken. As people often were at a close-up glimpse of Time Police methods.

'An EMP to disable the pod?' said Ellis. 'Although that's so obvious I'm sure there will be some kind of shielding.'

'Do we know if this pod is manned?' asked Callen, gesturing at the screen.

'We do not,' replied Mrs Farnborough. 'You know what we know. However, since this is not a ransom situation and since there is no hope of negotiation, I think it makes sense to assume the pod is not manned.'

'So somewhere there will be a remote device to detonate the pod,' said Ellis.

'Or it's on a timer,' said Callen. 'Although that can have problems. Yes, a timer precludes any human action, but it means the time and date is fixed; it's less flexible. Unless there is a manual override, of course,' he added thoughtfully.

Hay drummed her fingers on the table.

'Another matter, Major, which you might find interesting. Officer Farrell has acquired a quantity of what appear to be Time-travelling bracelets. These have been subject to a cursory examination by . . . an expert . . . and her initial comment was that in the majority of cases they would be so unreliable and dangerous that using them would almost always result in catastrophic damage to the user. Does this ring any bells?'

'It does indeed,' said Callen slowly. 'I would very much like a word with this expert although I strongly suspect I may have just personally witnessed her unexpectedly falling into unfriendly hands. Which is unfortunate.'

'Very.'

At that moment, Mrs Farnborough's com bleeped. She turned away. 'Yes?'

She listened in silence for a while and then closed it without speaking.

'What?' said Hay.

'There has been another communication. It's being flashed to you now. Watch your screen.'

The same picture. The same scaffolding-encased buildings. This time with a message scrolling across the screen.

**TIME POLICE UNABLE TO PREVENT
WIDESPREAD DESTRUCTION OF WORLD'S
MOST IMPORTANT HISTORICAL SITE.**

Hay compressed her lips. 'To whom was this sent?'

'Everyone,' said Mrs Farnborough, suddenly looking very tired. 'All the major news feeds, social media networks,

344

international broadcasts – even people's personal coms. Everyone everywhere. The world now knows. Calls are flooding in. The pressure is on.'

As soon as he was clear of Commander Hay's office, Matthew broke into a run. He wanted to see his team. Unable to wait for the traditionally slow lift – with whom he was not on the best terms anyway – he trotted down two flights of stairs and came face to face with both Jane and Luke as he rounded a corner.

There was a moment's stunned silence as they all looked at each other and then Jane flung herself at him.

'Oh, my God.'

'No,' said Matthew, shakily. 'Just me, Matthew.'

He patted her shoulder and murmured soothingly until finally she stepped back. Tears rolled down her cheeks.

'Blow your nose, sweetie,' said Luke, strolling forwards. 'Has no one ever told you that as a girl, it's your duty always to look dainty and appealing so that boys will like you?'

'Kill him now,' said Wimpy Jane, outraged.

'Hang on, sweetie,' said Bolshy Jane. 'He might have a point there. Not your best look.'

Jane turned aside to blow her nose.

Luke and Matthew looked at each other.

'Well . . . good,' said Luke, eventually.

'Yes,' said Matthew.

'Fancy a drink?'

'No time,' said Matthew, hoarsely. 'They've got Mikey.'

'Who has?'

'Henry Plimpton. We got everything wrong and now he's got Mikey and we have to do something.'

'Henry Plimpton?' said Jane in amazement. 'Our Henry Plimpton? But he's dead . . .'

'No, he's not, but that's not important at the moment. We . . .'

'. . . obviously have a lot to talk about,' said Luke, swiftly. 'But not here. Go and get the coffee on. I'll be along in a minute.'

Matthew and Jane set off for their office, Jane holding on to Matthew as if she feared to lose him again.

Luke turned away, blew his nose, took a deep breath and then followed on.

27

'Just when you think it's safe to come back into the office,' growled Grint, colliding with Dr Maxwell as she emerged from the pod with Officer North.

'Lovely to see you too,' said Max, beaming at him. 'In touch with your feelings yet or are you still the same lump of inanimate matter you've always been?'

To her astonishment Grint turned scarlet – or as scarlet as he was able – and walked away.

Turning to North, Max raised her eyebrows. 'What was that about?'

'Girlfriend,' said North briefly.

'Really? Was the poor girl sentenced to six months' hard labour and mistakenly thought Grint would be the softer option? Dare I ask who?'

'Lockland.'

Max blinked. 'You do surprise me. I thought young Parrish was rather keen.'

North shook her head. 'Neither of them has yet worked that out.'

Max regarded the speedily departing Grint. 'She does like a

347

challenge, doesn't she, young Jane?' She turned back to North. 'Lead on, Macduff.'

'Actually, it's "Lay on . . ."'

'Now you sound like Markham.'

'How is he, by the way?'

'Fine.'

'Where is he?'

'China.'

There was a pause. 'Intentionally?'

'Mostly.'

They made their way to Commander Hay's office.

Farenden was reporting. 'Our people are mustering, ma'am. We need only a specific destination.'

Hay looked up as Max and North entered the room. 'Well, with luck, Dr Maxwell will be able to help us there.'

'Dragged back to TPHQ again,' said Max, looking around. 'Brings back so many happy memories.'

Ellis looked up. 'Max, you do know that Matthew isn't . . . ?'

'Dead? Yes, I do, thanks.'

Hay gestured. 'Mrs Farnborough. This is the expert I mentioned earlier. Dr Maxwell.'

'Dr Maxwell,' said Callen with a sigh. 'Please believe I say this with genuine regret – not dead yet?'

'Never mind,' said Max. 'If your looks don't kill, I'm sure you can arrange for me to fall victim to friendly fire.'

Hay intervened. 'Polite greetings and catch-ups can follow later.' She brought up a static image showing the pod and as much of its surroundings as possible. 'Dr Maxwell. Is it possible for you to pinpoint the exact time, date and place, please? And quickly.'

Max seated herself and stared intently at the screen. 'I am assuming this pod isn't one of yours.'

'That is correct.'

'And you want me to identify, if possible, where and when this is?'

'Where, we know. When is not so easy.'

'It's a little bit murky. That's some heavy rain going on there. The site's deserted because they can't work in this. Winter storm, perhaps.' She sat back. 'Well, I can tell you immediately that this is sometime between 460 and 409BC.'

'Can you narrow it down any further?'

'Yes. You can see the giant bronze statue of Athena Promachos is finished, so some time after 448BC.'

There was a dissatisfied silence from her audience. More was obviously required.

'OK. They've started the Propylaea – that's the building you can just see a small part of – so this is after 437BC. We know the internal colonnades were almost finished by 432BC and here they are, look.' She pointed. 'We can't see all of them but they look finished to me. So, let's say after 432BC.'

Now she squinted. 'We only have a limited view and it's nearly dark and the visibility's poor, but I think those must be the foundations of the Temple of Athena Nike – also begun in 432BC. We know – well, I know – it was finished between 421 and 409BC and if we look here . . .' she gestured, 'it's definitely not finished. Nowhere near. Nor is anything else, so definitely between 432 and 421.

'They started building the Erechtheion in 421BC and there it is – barely got its foundations down and scaffolding everywhere. Piles of dressed stones all ready to go, and that looks

349

very much like some sort of heavy-lifting device there . . . So, given that and all the other stuff – at a rough guess, we're looking at 421BC.'

'Can you narrow it down any further?'

She frowned. 'Can someone enhance that area there? The small olive grove alongside the Erechtheion . . . Yes, there. Can you enlarge? Any more?'

Captain Farenden shook his head. 'Not without losing resolution. The rain is very heavy.'

Max leaned forwards, rummaging in her pocket for her spectacles. 'Olives ripen in midwinter. These trees are bare.'

'Could be spring or summer and they haven't ripened yet,' said Hay.

'No. These trees have been picked. Look – you can see what could be broken twigs and leaves lying on the ground where they've shaken the trees to make the fruit fall. And yes, they do pick green olives, but if you look closely, I think you can see a few on the ground that they've missed and they're black. Or it's too dark, I'm completely wrong and they're goat droppings, of course.'

'Can you narrow it down any further, Dr Maxwell? I can assure you this is important.'

She frowned again. 'The women hold a winter festival in the month of Poseidon. The Haloa. The festival is in honour of Demeter and Dionysus, but I suspect there would still be offerings at the foot of Athena Promachos as well, which there aren't, so I'm saying . . . olives picked – no festival yet – say the last two weeks in December.'

'Can you narrow it down any further?'

'Of course I can.' She pointed to the screen. 'I'll just home in on that calendar pinned to the wall by the Temple of Athena Nike over there. Or the newspaper fluttering in the wind, shall I? And before anyone curses useless historians, can I just point out that in less than ten minutes, I've narrowed it down from the typical clueless Time Police "some time that isn't now" to possibly the last two weeks in December 421BC.'

'Disappointing,' said Callen. 'But unsurprising. Typical St Mary's.'

Commander Hay intervened. 'Dr Maxwell, I don't think you realise quite how critical this situation is.'

'Hardly surprising,' said Max. 'You just swooped in and grabbed me. No apology – far less an explanation. Typical Time Police.'

Major Callen scowled. 'The Time Police have better things to do than enjoy the dubious pleasure of St Mary's company and I feel it should have been obvious to even the meanest intelligence – i.e. yours – that you are not here for frivolous reasons. This is a serious matter.'

'A bit of an overreaction, surely? He didn't mean any harm.'

Callen blinked. 'What are you talking about?'

'I think,' said Commander Hay, hastily, 'that we are talking at cross purposes here. Dr Maxwell, this has nothing to do with your son's recent unauthorised visit to St Mary's.' She paused. Honesty compelled her to add, 'Not a great deal, anyway. Show her the full clip.'

'Commander . . .'

'If you would, please, Major Callen.'

Sighing, he replayed the clip and they all watched in silence, enjoying, for a few brief seconds, the unusual sight of an historian struggling for words. But only for a few brief seconds.

Max wheeled on Hay. 'Are you kidding me? What are you doing about this? You can't let this happen.'

She paused the image. 'We don't intend to – which is why you are here, Dr Maxwell. Can you do any better than the last two weeks in December?'

Max placed two fingers to each temple and appeared to concentrate hard. 'Yes . . . yes . . . I'm getting it. 17th December 421BC. Around four in the afternoon. Phew. St Mary's saves the day yet again. Good job I was here.'

'You might be in the minority with that point of view,' said Major Callen, drily.

She beamed at him. 'You're welcome.'

'If you could stop messing about for one moment . . .'

'I'm not messing about.'

'If you haven't already realised, Dr Maxwell, this is no time for St Mary's particular brand of juvenile humour.'

'You say that every time St Mary's saves the day. You could try a quick *thank you* occasionally.'

Hay smiled slightly. 'Dr Maxwell, we know Officer Farrell visited St Mary's in a stolen pod. If St Mary's hasn't illegally downloaded and checked its coordinates, then you're not the people I take you for. Officer Farrell appears, unknowingly, to have done us all a favour, so please hold nothing back. I think you will agree that this is far more important than him sneaking back to St Mary's.'

Max nodded at the screen. 'In that case, Matthew's stolen pod has visited the Acropolis on several occasions, the last being late afternoon, 17th December 421BC. I believe the saying is, "And you can take that to the bank."'

She paused. 'If someone asks me to speculate – which they

352

haven't, but I don't care anyway – I'd say there were two pods – that one there . . .' she pointed to the screen, 'and the one Matthew stole. I suspect its purpose was to escort Pod Number One,' she nodded at the screen again, 'and then to record these images to prove whatever's going on there is genuine. You know – like the kidnap victim holding up today's newspaper. It's a filthy day, which is probably why they chose it – there's no one working. No one in their right minds is out in this weather, so events can proceed more or less unhindered. And then, having taken their images, Pod Two – Matthew's pod – then departs and that one stays behind. Silent and sinister as night closes in.'

'They won't explode it in the dark, surely,' said Ellis.

'No, probably not,' agreed Hay. 'Dawn perhaps. Much more powerful image. What else did St Mary's discover?'

'Well, the pod was very basic and only the last six sets of coordinates were held in the memory, but the very excellent Chief Farrell was able to recover them all. Three sets are relevant to this particular situation.'

'Anything else?' enquired Callen, sharply.

'Yes. The return coordinates were the same for every jump. Their base, I suppose we could assume. So what's this all about, then?'

Callen stood up. 'I don't think it's necessary to involve St Mary's any further.'

'Too late, sunshine. Already involved. Did you miss my first-class historical analysis?'

Mrs Farnborough, who had hitherto remained silent, leaned forwards. 'Pardon me – I appreciate that I am a layman, but the Acropolis still exists today so surely whatever they're threatening to do to it in 421BC never happens. Happened. Does it? Did it?'

It was Max who responded. 'Well, that's the problem. We wouldn't know, would we?'

'I don't understand.'

'Well – Stonehenge.'

Mrs Farnborough visibly paled. 'Oh my God – what about Stonehenge?'

'It's a ruin.'

'Yes?'

'Well, suppose that up until last month it had survived the millennia in perfect condition. Then suppose that last month a temporal villain jumped back a couple of thousand years and planted a spot of C4 – or something – demanded a ransom – which wasn't paid – then detonated his explosives and most of Stonehenge came tumbling down, leaving it as it is today. We wouldn't know any different, would we? Because to us it has always been like that. To us it's never been any other way.'

Mrs Farnborough groaned and put a hand over her eyes. A fine example of someone on the receiving end of an historian explanation of complex temporal issues.

Max turned to Commander Hay. 'When do we jump?'

'We do. You don't. Officer Farrell had no right to involve St Mary's in this. I shall be discussing that decision with him at a later date.'

'Righto,' said Max, cheerfully. 'Will that be before or after you discuss *your* decision to involve *me*.'

'The decision to consult an expert was forced on me by circumstances.'

'I believe Officer Farrell will be adopting the same defence.

354

Now – shall we stop arsing around. You have an expert in your midst. I'm the one person who can tell you – at a glance – whether you're in the right time or not. I'm familiar with the layout. I can distinguish between guards, priests, masons, labourers and the general public. Normally I'd happily leave you to bimble around getting everything wrong, but the future of the Acropolis and Athens is at stake, so far too important to leave to the Time Police, don't you think?'

Hay frowned. 'Are you able to give us the precise location of this pod?'

'To within twenty feet or so, yes. Behind the Propylaea but in front of Athena Promachos. Temple of Erechtheion diagonally to your left.' She pointed to a spot on the plan of the Acropolis lying open on Hay's briefing table. 'Exactly . . . there. Depending on how many pods you take – I recommend no more than three – your best hiding places are there – the Chalcotheke; there – behind the Erechtheion; and there – inside the Propylaea.' She pointed. 'We'll be out of their pod's direct lines of sight and each location will give us plenty of cover in which to advance. Although as soon as we break cover, we will be seen – with who knows what consequences. And we'll need to clear the site of any con-temporaries, of course. I suspect the labourers have already pushed off due to the weather but there will still be guards. Possibly even a few priests, temple servants and so on living on site. We don't want anyone caught in the crossfire in case they're an ancestor.'

'Sonic Scream,' said Ellis briefly. 'We can have contempor-aries neutralised in seconds.'

Commander Hay broke the silence. 'It would appear I have

three major emergencies on my hands. I would welcome suggestions as to how we should prioritise.'

'Three?' said Mrs Farnborough.

'Yes. Henry Plimpton's base will need to be neutralised as soon as possible. Along with Henry Plimpton himself. Then there's this threat to the Acropolis. And finally, today, we lost sight of someone we really should have neutralised years ago. Along with her wretched brother.'

Max started. 'You've lost Mikey? How? Does Matthew know?'

'She and Farrell became separated. She disappeared. We're certain Plimpton has her. Steps must be taken to ensure her recovery.'

Max's lip curled. 'Dead or alive?'

'Whichever is most expedient.'

'So,' said Mrs Farnborough, slowly. 'Three problems, but only one source.'

'Henry Plimpton,' said Ellis, nodding. 'Clever. He's been discovered but he recovers brilliantly. Tracked back to his base – or one of them – he retaliates by seizing Mikey. Knowing that the Time Police will be descending upon him at any moment, he seeks to distract us by sending a pod packed with explosives to one of the most famous sites in the world. He thinks we'll prioritise the Acropolis, giving him the opportunity to escape safely with equipment, Meiklejohn, everything, and continue somewhere else.'

Hay stirred. 'I agree. Whether Meiklejohn is Plimpton's prisoner, willing accomplice or hostage is not clear at the moment, but I shall have to send people I cannot easily spare to sort out that situation.'

'A rescue team?'

'A clean-up crew.'

There was silence and then Ellis said, 'To be clear – we take her out?'

'We take them all out,' said Callen. 'These are not circumstances in which we can afford anything other than a strong response.'

Max stirred. 'Dear God – how stupid are you people? And the question is not rhetorical.'

Commander Hay twisted in her seat. 'Ah, Dr Maxwell. I shall arrange for your immediate return to St Mary's. Thank you for your assistance.' She turned back again.

Sadly, St Mary's, rather like an STD, is not shifted so easily. 'Seriously – do I have to bail out you idiots yet again? Listen to me very carefully, everyone. Firstly, stop punishing people for innovative thinking. There will always be people out there pushing the boundaries and as today's events have clearly shown, you need to get ahead of them otherwise you'll spend all your time trying to play catch-up and failing. Miserably. Stop and think for a moment. You need a poacher turned gamekeeper. You need Amelia Meiklejohn on your side. Bring her back here where you can keep an eye on her. Set up a department. Make her the head of it. Give her a Batcave to work in. You probably won't even have to pay her that much because she's not interested in money, but *get her on your side.*'

Max paused to draw breath. 'Secondly – so you might not have sufficient manpower. Boohoo. Use what you've got. Send in a team to grab Mikey because that's what you do. But leave the Acropolis to St Mary's. Because that's what we do. We have the expertise. We'll handle it.'

Callen's head jerked up. 'Don't be ridiculous. Out of the question.'

'Fine – attempt to do it all yourself and you'll fail across the board. Worse – you'll fail publicly. The world will see the Time Police crash and burn. You won't have to disband – it will be done for you. For God's sake, this is a major crisis and you need to use every tool you can lay your hands on.'

Callen shook his head. 'From what I can remember, St Mary's is not riddled with bomb disposal experts.'

'No – our talents actually lie in the opposite direction, so you'll have to lend us one. Or two, possibly.'

Hay was thoughtful, drumming her fingers on the table.

Callen shook his head. 'Henry Plimpton and his base are the most serious threats at the moment and cannot be ignored. He and his organisation must be shut down with all speed before they can do any more damage. My recommendation is that we concentrate our forces there. We need to go in fast and hard with everything we can muster. We need to send a powerful message. Mess with Time and the Time Police will crush you. Protecting Time should always be our priority. The Acropolis incident is serious but not life-threatening.'

'I disagree,' said Ellis. 'The Acropolis incident does threaten Time but in a different way. If the Acropolis is destroyed, the Golden Age of Athens will not take place. Their experiments in democracy will not occur. The world will become a very different place. Paradoxes will abound. We cannot run that risk. Two very different threats but equally serious.'

Hay looked up. 'Do we have the results of our muster, Charlie?'

Captain Farenden was consulting his scratchpad. 'We do,

ma'am. We can muster seven pods excluding medical facilities. Four more are undergoing routine maintenance but could be ready within six hours. There are thirty-five officers on the premises now. If we wait to pull people off their current assignments, we can muster another twenty-four but it will cost us valuable time. If we include secondary staff – clerks, medics, civilians and so on – we can muster another possible twenty. However, ma'am, remembering what happened the last time we emptied the building – do we actually want to do that? How vulnerable would we be?'

'Very,' said Callen. 'Commander, I recommend all secondary staff remain on site to defend the building. And that we leave a minimum of two teams to reinforce and lead them. The last thing we need is a threat on a fourth front.'

Hay stared out of the window. Long seconds passed as she considered the circumstances and weighed the arguments. No one else moved or spoke.

Farenden's com bleeped. He listened briefly and then shut it down. 'Ma'am – they have the location and date from Farrell's recorder and Major Callen's pod. They confirm each other . . .'

'Obviously,' said Callen.

'. . . 29th December 1902. Paris.'

Hay blinked. 'Is there any significance to that particular date?'

Maxwell shook her head. 'Nothing that I know of.'

Farenden and North had been consulting their scratchpads. They shook their heads. 'Nothing known, Commander.'

Hay rose to her feet. 'Two pods and two teams to the Acropolis. I suspect stealth and guile will be more important than numbers. Major Ellis to command. Dr Maxwell will accompany you in a purely advisory category. Dr Maxwell, please be aware that all officers will be authorised to shoot you for even the smallest infringement of our rules. And indeed, will be delighted to do so.'

Max grinned. 'They'll have to catch me first.'

'Major Callen, given your concerns over TPHQ security, you will remain here.'

His head jerked up. 'Commander? If you are thinking my principles will prevent me arguing with you in public, then you are mistaken.'

'You will remain here, Major, and take control of our defence. I want you to put the building on lockdown immediately. Secure all exits. No one in – no one out. We don't want any inadvertent tipping-off, do we?'

'Commander, I must protest. I should be the one leading the assault on the hangar. As you yourself know, I've been pursuing this line of enquiry for some time. I admit I had no idea about Henry Plimpton's involvement, but neither did anyone else. I'm the one who discovered the hangar, I've been there already. I have an idea of the layout – and not to put too fine a point on it – I command the Hunter Division.'

'No, Major, you will remain here.'

Callen opened his mouth but Hay swept on. 'You and one of the two teams will be on standby, should reinforcements be required either in Paris or at the Acropolis. I think the key to this situation is flexibility.'

'Asking rather a lot of me, aren't you, Commander?'

'I'm sure you'll prove equal to the challenges.' Hay paused and frowned. 'I want Fanboten and his expertise to go with you, Major Ellis. Chigozie can lead your second team. I shall

360

give control of the Paris jump to Lt Grint. He can take two pods and three teams to Henry Plimpton's hangar. Tell him to liaise with Officer Farrell and get a detailed layout. Their objective will be to secure the hangar and all materiel therein, after which they can look for anything that could give us an idea of what he's been up to recently. Should they still be on site, I want Plimpton and Meiklejohn alive enough to talk to me afterwards. Whatever's going on in that hangar, I want to know all about it. If that isn't possible, then I want them too dead to talk to anyone else. Take a clean-up crew just in case things go wrong. Everyone else here on high alert.'

'From what would you be defending yourselves?' asked Mrs Farnborough.

'From anything else that might arise to try us,' said Hay, grimly.

'Such as, Commander?'

'We're being tested, Mrs Farnborough. Someone is piling on the pressure to see if we break.' She looked around the room. 'Time to show the world what we are made of, I think. Are there any questions?'

'Yes,' said Max. 'This Plimpton bloke. The one who isn't dead after all. The one behind all this?' She pointed to the screen still showing the frozen image of the Acropolis, blurred in the driving rain. 'Promise me something truly terrible will happen to him.'

Commander Hay's tone was frigid. 'We are the Time Police, Dr Maxwell.'

Max grinned. 'Good enough for me.'

There was a major row once Matthew discovered he was not to be included in the Paris assault.

'But . . .' he protested, trotting alongside Ellis as he strode down the corridor.

'No.'

'But . . .'

'For the last time – no. One more *but* from you and I'll feed you alive to Lt Filbert and you can spend the next three days in a cell contemplating the folly of arguing with senior officers. Got it?' He strode on.

Beneath his hair, Matthew scowled. Filbert was known to be a bit of a bastard, even by Time Police standards.

'I can hear you scowling,' said Ellis. He turned. 'Look – you're too personally involved. The most helpful thing you can do is stay out of everyone's way.'

Matthew stood his ground and prepared to argue. Ellis, who had known his mother for years, struggled with a sense of déjà vu.

'They should include me. Mikey knows me. She trusts me. There's no way she'll go quietly with you lot. Not after the last time when you shot her.'

'*We* shot her,' said Ellis, gently. 'The Time Police. Of whom you are a member.'

Matthew ignored this. 'I can persuade her to come quietly. Otherwise, she'll probably bring the roof down on you. The objective is to pull her out alive so she can be of future value. You need me for that.'

Ellis stood still, taking a moment to think. Eventually he sighed. 'If Lt Grint will take you, then all right, but be aware there are any number of officers who would give a week's pay to shoot Mikey at the first opportunity and would probably consider it a happy bonus if they could include you too.'

Matthew nodded and shot off to find Lt Grint and his team.


The Acropolis briefing was held in Briefing Room 3. Present were Major Ellis, Officer North, Dr Maxwell and two other teams under the command of Lieutenants Fanboten and Chigozie.

'Right,' said Ellis. 'Listen up, everyone. You all know why you're here. This is Dr Maxwell – yes, a member of St Mary's – who, however, is not to be shot unless as a very last resort.'

Max grinned, not endearing herself in any way to her future teammates.

'If you could brief us on what we can expect to find, Dr Maxwell.'

With North bringing up a number of 3D images and plans of the Acropolis, Max began to point out the location of the unknown pod and the major landmarks surrounding it.

'Be aware it's a massive building site. In addition to scaffolding and half-completed buildings, there will be piles of sand, stone, wood and so on – all of which will offer cover but interfere with your sight lines. Plus, it's December. You'll be exposed on a giant rock high above the city of Athens and the rain is hurling down. Visibility will be poor.

'My advice is that your two pods land here . . .' she pointed to the Temple of Erechtheion, 'which will put you slightly behind and to the right of the unknown pod, and here . . .' she pointed to the back of the Propylaea, 'which will place you in front of the pod, but the building itself should offer you plenty of cover. Be aware this is a large site. Should you find yourself disoriented in the rain and the dark, just head for the thirty-foot-high bronze statue. The illegal pod is close by.'

'That covers *where*,' said Ellis. 'Let's talk about what we do when we get there. It will be dark and no one's likely to be about in this weather, but on landing, both pods will activate their Sonic Screams. It's unlikely there will still be workmen present but watch out for guards and priests. It's vital we get everyone neutralised asap. Makes it much easier for us. And them too, because once that's done, we can assume anyone we see after that is an illegal and deal with them accordingly. Be aware, Commander Hay wants any illegals as alive as possible. They don't have to be in perfect health but they do have to be capable of telling us what we want to know.'

Someone raised a hand. 'Will the illegal pod already be there when we land?'

'Yes,' said Ellis. 'And possibly a second pod acting as escort as well.'

They nodded, typing busily on their scratchpads. Ellis deliberately waited until they'd finished. One by one, as the silence lengthened, they lifted their heads.

Ellis spoke quietly because that always makes people listen.

'I want everyone to pay attention. If a second pod is present, we can do nothing until it leaves. We do not even make our presence known. The second pod *must* be free to return whence it came. I know you think I'm tying your hands, but in simple terms, that pod has a part to play elsewhere, and if it can't do that then we'll be looking at all sorts of trouble, so be aware. Whatever happens – we wait until the other pod jumps away. Is everyone clear on that?'

There was a chorus of *Yes, sir*s.

An officer gestured to the pod on the screen. 'How do we deal with that one?'

'After the Sonic Scream and when the area is secure, we'll hit them with a couple of strategically placed EMPs.'

'They'll be shielded, surely,' said someone.

'Almost certainly,' said Ellis. 'Too basic a precaution to be overlooked.'

'What then?' asked someone.

'You may regret asking me that. Regard.'

He upended Matthew's small box on to the table. Five metallic cuffs scattered across the table.

Chairs scraped back out of the way.

'I've heard about these,' said someone. 'Don't they blow your arms off?'

'Not every time,' said Ellis, soothingly, 'but we don't have anything else. We can't gain access to the pod and any attempt to do so will certainly set it off. Nor, for the same reason, can we carry out a controlled explosion. So we intend to lay these in a circle around it. The thinking is that they will form the same sort of temporal field generated by the pods themselves. We initiate simultaneous activation and poof – no more pod.'

'Or,' said someone, 'poof – massive explosion as they all go off and an even more massive explosion as that sets the pod off, followed by complete annihilation of the Acropolis, most of Athens, widespread damage to a large part of the Greek mainland and possible tsunamis hitting the coastline for hundreds of miles around.'

'Won't do us any good, either,' said someone else, gloomily.

'Yes, well, looking on the bright side, we're hoping that won't happen,' said Ellis. 'I'll remain behind to oversee the detonation. All non-essential personnel – which is everyone who isn't me – will have retreated back to the pods and jumped to a safe distance. Go and get yourselves kitted out. Draw whatever you need from the armoury. Don't forget your wet-weather gear. Any questions?'

There were none.

Ellis accompanied Max to the armoury. To show her the way, he said, and not in any way to prevent her inadvertently arming herself with something that, in the hands of an idiot, could wipe out the western hemisphere.

She grinned. 'You know you're not doing this right, don't you?'

He sighed. 'Enlighten me.'

'Shouldn't there be a montage of scenes – us applying camouflage make-up – suiting up – seizing massive weapons off the wall in well-coordinated movements – and striding boldly down the corridor with a bass-enhanced version of "Swords of a Thousand Men" thudding in the background?'

He looked down at her. 'No.'

As Ellis said afterwards – when it was all over – it began so well.

A white-faced North nodded her agreement. 'How's Matthew holding up?'

'Surprisingly calm at the moment although that won't last.'

'Not your fault, sir. She knew the risks.'

'Even so.'

'It wasn't your fault, Matthew.'

## 29

The two Time Police pods landed exactly where they should. Pod One, led by Major Ellis, settled itself in the narrow space between the north side of the Erechtheion and the outer Acropolis wall, while the smaller Pod Two, led by Lt Chigozie, put down in the back portico of the Propylaea.

Ellis turned to Lt Fanboten who was scanning the console. 'Any evidence of pod activity? Other than ours, that is?'

Fanboten, his eyes fixed on his instruments, nodded. 'Yes, sir. Two signatures. Varying strengths. Going by what we know, that might be the illegals popping in and out, but there's definitely been pod activity in the last twenty-four hours.'

'Good. We're in the right place.'

Around the pod, officers were climbing to their feet and checking their weapons.

'Anything from Lt Chigozie?'

'Yes, sir. He'd like a word.'

Ellis opened his com. 'Ellis here.'

'Chigozie reporting, sir. Safe landing. The illegal's pod is already on site. We have eyes on. No info on a second pod and nothing on our instruments. We are assuming it's been and gone. Standing by and awaiting your instructions.'

'Right, everyone,' said Ellis, addressing both pods. 'Listen up. Both pods will saturate the area with the Sonic Scream. Dial it up, please. Harsh, I know, but we need to neutralise contemporaries as quickly as possible. Safer for them in the long run. Ready in five, four, three, two, one . . .'

Watching the screen over Fanboten's shoulder, Max could see almost nothing. One camera showed only the rain-dampened stones of the Acropolis wall. The others showed gusts of rain sleeting across the cameras under a darkening sky.

They gave the area a good thirty-second burst, just to be on the safe side. From the safety of their pods, no one felt anything, but a dog erupted out of the darkness, yelping, and scuttled away with its tail between its legs. From somewhere, giant flocks of what looked like starlings erupted into the air, twittering in agitation, soaring and swooping, forming fantastic shapes on the screen, before, moving as one, they left the Acropolis to make for an alternative roost somewhere else.

After that, all was silent and still.

'All done, sir,' reported Fanboten.

Ellis nodded. 'All right, everyone. Be aware it's a filthy day out there, and very soon to become a filthy night. You all know what to do. Scour the area for contemporaries. A soft immobilisation, if you don't mind. Recovery positions and *gentle* restraints. We want them to survive the night.'

'Never mind them – I want to survive the night,' muttered someone behind Max.

'It's that awkward moment between day and night, so engage night visors as conditions dictate. And stay out of sight,' ordered Ellis as officers began to disappear into the rain and the gathering darkness.

Max was struggling into her wet-weather gear. 'What is this weird stuff? I knew it. You're all some kind of fetishists, aren't you? I bet at least half of you have a dead chicken stuffed down the front of your underpants.'

Several officers eyed their weapons yearningly.

'Wet-weather gear,' said Fanboten. 'Keeps you dry. Although, ironically, you'll sweat like a pig.'

Ellis turned from the console. 'And where do you think you're going?'

Max blinked. 'To take a look around, of course.'

'No, you wait here where it's safe.'

'Not a good idea. I can tell you if anything's out of place or just plain wrong. I can identify anyone who doesn't look as if they should be here. I'm here as a resource. Use me.'

There was a bit of a silence. Ellis sighed and signalled to the last two officers squeezing through the door. 'Curtis, Rockmeyer, go with Dr Maxwell. Stay out of trouble. We don't yet know the status of that pod.'

Two officers shouldered their weapons and nodded at Max. 'Stay behind us.'

'Why?'

'Makes it more of a challenge to shoot you accidentally.'

The rain was still sleeting down. The sort of rain that soaks a body in seconds. The sky overhead was dark and threatening. Streaks of cream, grey, dark red and purple showed above the horizon. Night was almost upon them. The rain lashed down, splattering off the hard surfaces and making it difficult to hear properly. Little rivers of water swirled past their boots.

'That way,' whispered Max. 'And be careful. The pod will

be almost directly in front of us. About sixty to seventy yards and slightly to our left.'

The two officers nodded and they began to work their way around piles of neatly stacked timber and stone. Curtis pointed downwards. 'Watch where you put your feet. Trip hazards everywhere.'

They edged their way around the corner of the Erechtheion and stopped dead.

Even the most ungracious officer could acknowledge that Dr Maxwell had been spot on in her assessment of the pod position. Could have but didn't. It never paid to encourage St Mary's. The pod crouched, dark and silent, in the rain.

'Wow,' said Curtis, looking up. 'She's a big girl.'

Thirty feet above them, Athena Promachos emerged from the darkness.

'Ah, yes,' said Max, tilting her head back to take her in. 'The very large lady looming in front of us is Athena of the Front Line. A very warlike lady. Note the giant spear. Ditto the shield. Do *not* go upsetting Athena. Not in front of her own statue in her own city. Greek gods are neither slow nor squeamish when it comes to avenging perceived disrespect.'

'I thought everything would be less, well, cluttered,' said Curtis, looking around. 'And all nicely paved and regular. Like you see in the pictures.'

Max shook her head. 'No, this is a building site.' She gestured at the piles of timber, stone, metalworks, barrels of water, equipment, stores and so on. 'See those chunks of marble over there? Pillar drums. When they assemble them, the middle ones are fatter and then they narrow again towards the top. I know the Acropolis looks beautifully geometric, but there isn't actually a straight line in the place. It's all carefully designed to deceive the eye. The other thing you never see in pictures are all these olive groves and little vegetable gardens. When the sun comes up, there will be builders, masons, labourers, priests, acolytes, the general public, dogs, cats, chickens, even the occasional donkey or goat.'

'There's rubble everywhere,' said Rockmeyer, critically.

'Yes. Watch where you're going because there will be pits, puddles and potholes as well.'

They were joined by Ellis and North. Ellis squinted through the driving rain. 'What are these patches of turned earth?'

'Little vegetable patches probably,' said Max, making one of the greatest mistakes of her life. 'To supplement the diet of the priests and temple servants.'

The wind whipped around their legs. There were no lights showing on this windswept plateau. The wind and rain would long ago have extinguished any torches left burning. The workmen had departed for the night – and possibly the next day, too, if this weather didn't let up – but they'd left everything secured. In the distance, Max could hear the corner of a canvas flapping in the wind. Below them, on the plain, tiny lights had sprung up in the town. They could make out the faint smell of woodsmoke and cooking.

Curtis stood on a pile of timber and peered over the wall. 'Is the city on fire?'

Max shook her head. 'Every house will have at least one fire going. On a calm night, a vast smoky haze hangs over the city. Especially if there's no wind. Lots of bad chests down there.'

'Doesn't sound very healthy,' said Curtis.

'Try London in the late 19th century if you want to hear what a really good cough sounds like,' said North, drily. 'Some of those Londoners could bring up their own lungs.'

Around the site, officers were reporting buildings cleared and contemporaries secured and settled comfortably. No fatalities among the contemporaries.

'Good,' said Ellis, drawing back into the minimal shelter offered by the Erechtheion's stunted walls. 'Fanboten, I want EMPs set up on the highest points we can manage. Narrow focus – we don't want to take out our own pods. Two-man teams. No one goes anywhere alone tonight. Everyone else, find yourselves a secure position out of the way. And remember to stay out of sight.'

The rain was lessening to a gentle drizzle. Above their heads, the clouds began to break up, driven by the wind. Water splashed somewhere, but the EMPs were deployed in complete silence.

They waited.

Fanboten spoke. 'EMPs deployed, sir. My equipment shows no visible effects on the pod.'

Ellis sighed. 'No, that would have been too easy, wouldn't it? All right, people. Time for the personal approach.'

Far away, down in the city, a dog barked and another answered. Up here there was just the sound of the wind. The night was getting colder all the time. Max blew gently on her hands and stuffed them into her armpits to keep them warm. And Fanboten had been right about the wet-weather gear. It did make you sweat like a pig.

Chigozie's voice sounded in her ear. 'Sir, we're moving out from the Propylaea. No signs of life from the pod and I'm not detecting electronic signals of any kind. It's just sitting there.'

'Any clues as to whether it's manned?'

'None.'

'Well, we can't hang around. It could go off at any moment.'

'I'm not so sure,' said Max, easing herself back around the corner. 'Hay said they'd wait until daylight for more impact and I think she was right. We've probably got hours yet.'

Ellis straightened up and shook his head. 'We can't bank on that. Let's go. Everyone – stay in your teams. And remember – just because we can't see any life out here doesn't mean there isn't any.'

Fanning out, the teams began to move forwards, gliding silently from one area of cover to another. Over their heads the moon was lighting up the shredded clouds dancing across its face. Shadows came and went. The wind moaned through the half-built pillars. This was a cold and lonely place. A dark time in a darker world. When gods walked and talked with mortals and the massive Athena Promachos watched over her city. Anything further from the sun-soaked buildings with which modern people were familiar could not be imagined. Every shadow could hold a vengeful deity – not that there was any other type – who was probably slightly pissed off at the blasphemy in this sacred site.

'Place gives me the creeps,' said someone.

Ellis inched his way around what looked like a random heap of broken stone. They were using their night visors but the ground underfoot was rough and treacherous. Silently, and from all directions, they began to close in on the dark pod. One step at a time. Weapons ready. Invisible in the dark. Still no sign from the pod. Ellis began to entertain hopes this might be easier than they'd thought.

Suddenly, out of the darkness, off to his right, he heard Max shout. 'Everyone stop. Don't move. Everyone stand very still.'

Ellis cursed under his breath. Bloody St Mary's. If the pod *was* occupied and by some chance they hadn't known of the Time Police presence before – they did now.

He flipped up his visor. 'Stop making such a row. What's happened?'

'Tell everyone to stand still. Something just moved and clicked under my foot.' He heard her take a breath. 'I think . . . I think I might be standing on some sort of landmine.'

Ellis caught his breath. Suddenly it all made sense. *This* was what the illegals had been doing during their previous visits. Laying booby traps. Not only as defence against the Time Police, but should an officer activate one, there was a very good chance it would set off the pod. The Time Police would cause the very catastrophe they had come to prevent.

It was a miracle no contemporary had inadvertently set one off. But, of course, clearly no one had worked today because of the dreadful weather. Clever. Henry Plimpton had planned this meticulously. Thought through every eventuality. Ellis sighed. There was no approaching the pod now. And a stranded historian to rescue. Somehow.

Ellis raised his voice. Secrecy had blown away on the wind. 'Everyone stand still. Now. Who's still in our pods?'

Grayling's voice sounded in his ear. 'Grayling, sir. In Pod One.'

'Chigozie in Pod Two, sir.'

'Right, everyone – listen very carefully. Wherever you are – back to the nearest pod. Torches on. Watch where you're putting your feet. This area may be booby-trapped. Retrace your steps exactly. Then let's get some sort of lighting grid set up. I want to see exactly what's going on here. Sod the need for discretion.

Make sure you check the ground under your feet every step of the way. Stay on rock where possible. Avoid soft soil. Don't worry, Max. We'll get you out.'

'*That's* what the turned earth is,' said Fanboten. 'They've seeded the place.'

Ellis was puzzled. 'We did scan for anti-personnel devices; why didn't we pick them up?'

'They're plastic, perhaps. Or ceramic. Difficult to detect. Inert until pressure is applied – I'll investigate later. But I think this means we can assume the illegal pod is empty. I suspect these were laid by its crew when they left. Arm the pod, out of the door, arm the IEDs, into the second pod and away. Job done and go.'

'Good,' said Ellis. 'One less thing to worry about.'

Rockmeyer reported everyone was back at the pods and that the area was clear.

'So that's just you then, Max,' said Ellis, cheerfully.

'Phew,' said Max, her voice not quite steady. 'What a relief. Now what?'

'We get you out. And all in one piece.'

'Jolly good,' said Max, faintly.

Lt Fanboten spoke in her ear. 'You must stand completely still, Dr Maxwell. Don't even shift your weight. We don't know how sensitive these things are. Or even how stable. Try to relax. Find something on which to focus and breathe slowly. Don't pant. Don't faint.'

'Gotcha. No panting. No fainting. Relax.'

Powerful lights came on, bathing the whole area in a brilliant white light. From the corner of his eye, Ellis could see the enormous bronze sandalled feet of Athena Promachos exposed in the harsh glare. Max stood, frozen, about twenty feet from the illegal pod, which was still dark and silent. Ellis was more convinced than ever that it was empty. Fanboten was right. The illegals had exited the pod, set the traps and buggered off.

'Chigozie, take a couple of people and guard the Propylaea in case anyone climbs up here to investigate the lights. For their own good, don't let anyone in. Silent but not deadly, please.'

'Yes, sir.'

Ellis turned back. 'Well now, Max. What are we going to do with you?'

'Buy me a bloody great drink afterwards.'

'The Time Police hospitality budget will probably stretch to one small, cheap lemonade.' He could see her face, eyes screwed up in the white glare of the lights. 'Do *not* fall over.'

'As if,' she said.

'You forget, I've seen you in action.'

She swallowed. 'Listen, this doesn't change anything. I think you're just going to have to work around me. I'm not the priority here.'

'No, we can't leave you there . . .'

'Aw, that's so sweet.'

'. . . in case your exploding mine sets the pod off as well.'

'OK – less sweet.'

'So – tonight's order of business: we get you out and then deal with the pod. Not to worry – we've probably got all night.'

Ellis turned away and closed his eyes for a moment.

Fanboten appeared. He'd disconnected his com and signed for Ellis to do the same. 'Sir, we can't save her. I think it might be a belly-buster. They're the worst. Rigged to blow at belly height as soon as she eases off the pressure plate.'

377

Ellis struggled to breathe calmly. 'If it does blow – what's the likely damage?'

'To her? Both legs gone. Guts everywhere. Torso shredded. Blood loss. Shock. Death in seconds. If she's lucky. Definitely not survivable. And she's too close to the pod. It's very possible that will set the pod off too, in which case no one up here will survive, and possibly there will be significant damage and loss of life down in the town as well.'

Ellis compressed his lips and stared over Fanboten's shoulder. 'What happens if we shoot her? Quick and clean.'

'It won't help, sir. I suspect it's rigged to blow when she lifts her foot. Or even if she so much as shifts her weight. She has to stand stock-still.'

'Right, damage limitation. Emergency evac. You and Chigozie sort it out between you.'

Another voice spoke behind him. 'Sir?'

'North? Get yourself back into the nearest pod.'

'Sir, I have an idea.'

# 30

Major Ellis had known Dr Maxwell for a long time. She'd saved him at Pompeii. And again when a wall was about to collapse on him during the 1204 Sack of Constantinople, when murderous Crusaders were putting everyone to the sword. He'd been present at the birth of her son. Not entirely voluntarily, but he'd been there nevertheless. They went back a long way. They'd worked together – more or less amicably – on the Mary Tudor mission when they'd struggled to get Jane Grey off the throne and he and Max had been trapped in a contracting bubble universe. He'd helped raise her son. He wasn't going to let her go without a fight.

'Please tell me this isn't a St Mary's idea.'

North shook her head. 'No. Although it isn't without some risk.'

'We're about to be bombed out of existence, Celia. Define risk.'

'We brought five bracelets.'

'We did.'

'We use four on the pod and the fifth on Max.'

'Four won't be enough to shift the pod,' said Fanboten. 'I'm convinced of it. Five might have done it but four definitely won't.'

'Getting the pod out of here won't solve Max's problem,' said North.

'If we . . .' Fanboten stopped, looking uncertain.

'. . . waste,' supplied North. 'You were going to say, *If we waste a bracelet on Maxwell . . .*'

Fanboten drew himself up. 'I was. I'm sorry, North, but if we adopt your plan and try to jump them both, then we run the risk of achieving nothing and Maxwell dies anyway. Our objective is to remove the pod. That's where our focus should lie.'

'He's right, North,' said Ellis, quietly.

'She's too close,' argued North. 'Whichever explodes first – bracelet or landmine – is almost certain to set off the pod. We have to deal with everything simultaneously. I think I can make this work.'

'How?'

She drew a breath. 'Meiklejohn.'

'She's fallen into enemy hands.'

'Not her – the other one. There are two of them, remember?'

There was a short silence as everyone conjured up images of the tall, skinny, but above all, *chatty* Adrian Meiklejohn.

Having reduced her opponents to stunned silence, North pressed home her advantage. 'Next to Mikey – and their inventor, of course – Adrian probably knows more about these bracelets than anyone. Five minutes to get him, sir. That's all it will take me.'

'It will take you longer than that,' said Ellis. 'Pod protocols won't permit you to land back here any sooner than thirty minutes from now and we don't have thirty minutes. Sooner or later Max is going to twitch.'

'Sir, I did say I'd have Adrian Meiklejohn on board. For him, pod protocols are something that happen to other people.'

'Oh God.' Fanboten closed his eyes.

Ellis looked at her. 'Even if you *can* get a bracelet to

Maxwell, the IED will still blow as soon as she jumps away. And that will set off the pod. We can't take that risk.'

'Sir. Five bracelets. One for Maxwell. Four for the pod. One for each corner. Coordinates synchronised and preset. We get Maxwell *and* pod out of here simultaneously.'

'It could blow her arm off. There's a very good chance the bracelet will kill her as quickly as the IED.'

'How is death by bracelet any worse than death by IED? Or, if she lives long enough, death by pod?'

'She's got a point, you know,' called Maxwell.

Ellis turned to her. 'Shut up, Max. You're not supposed to be listening.'

'Sorry, I'll just wander out of range, shall I? Bloody Time Police idiots.'

'We're trying to save your life,' shouted Fanboten. 'Tell me again why you're worth it?'

'How long have you got?'

Ellis turned back to North. 'We don't know what the field is on those things, Celia. If we spare one for Maxwell, that only leaves four for the pod and Fanboten says that won't be enough.'

She spoke with quiet determination. 'Sir, this is a stalemate situation. We can't save one without setting off the other. We have to save them both. We rig them all to jump simultaneously and, as everyone keeps saying, poof – no pod.'

'And possibly no Acropolis either.'

'Or Maxwell,' called a plaintive voice from the darkness.

'No worse than the situation we're in at the moment, sir.'

Ellis stared at her. 'Jesus, Celia . . .' He stood for a moment . . . thinking . . . weighing up the risks . . . conscious of Time ticking on . . . Surely someone had noticed what was going on up here by now . . . all these lights . . . What if they turned out the city guard? The longer they waited, the more likely that was to happen. If he was to make a decision, it had to be now.

He sucked in a deep breath. 'All right. Practical issues – how do we get these bracelets close enough to the pod now we know there's a minefield out there?'

'Throw them,' shouted Max.

'Shut up, Max. This is nothing to do with you.'

'Fine – take a peaceful stroll through the possible minefield and gently place them all in a pretty pattern. When did the Time Police get to be such wusses?'

'Or we could just shoot you where you stand and go home saying there was nothing we could do and sorry about Athens. Shut up and let us think.'

North was surveying the ground. 'I don't think we have too much to worry about. It's mostly rock. Very little soil. Max was just unlucky.'

'How easy are they to programme?'

'Well, that's just it, sir. We'll need to send Max in one direction and the pod in another but both at exactly the same time.'

'Conflicting fields.'

'Yes, sir.'

'Equally devastating if we get it wrong. We could still be looking at the destruction of the Acropolis. Only this time we'll be the ones responsible.'

Ellis stared at his feet, thinking. 'Fanboten?'

'Sir?'

'Hold Pod One back. Everyone else evacuates in Two.'

'Yes, sir. With your permission, sir, I'll remain behind as well. You might need my expertise.'

'Thank you, Lieutenant. Get everyone else out of here. We're about to do something amazingly stupid.'

'Sounds like fun, sir. I was getting bored.'

'Officer North, you take Pod One. Jump to St Mary's and grab that irritating little bugger, Meiklejohn. Do whatever it takes. Sonic anyone you have to. Just get him here. If I live long enough, I'll apologise afterwards.' He sighed. 'Perhaps a miracle will occur while you're gone and we can all go down the pub instead.'

She grinned. 'St Mary's thinking, sir. I like it.'

Ellis watched North splash her way back around the Erechtheion, sighed and then turned back to Fanboten. 'Right, despite what she said, we have a minimum of thirty minutes before North can get back here with Meiklejohn so let's use the Time to . . .'

North and Adrian appeared from behind the Erechtheion.

Adrian was dressed for dramatic effect in his swirling leather coat. Equally unsurprisingly, he was talking.

'And seventhly,' he was saying to North, who was wearing the expression of one whose ears weren't yet bleeding but it was only a matter of time, 'presetting coordinates in a linear matrix imposes certain restrictions that can only be overcome if— oh, hey, Max.'

Her voice floated across to them. 'Hey, Adrian. How's things?'

'Fine, fine. Chief Farrell wants to know if you'll be much longer.'

There was a bit of a pause. 'Oh, probably not long now.'

'Well, you should get a move on. It's fish and chips and a holo night tonight. Wouldn't want to miss that.'

'No, indeed.'

Ellis recovered the power of speech. 'How the hell . . . how did you manage that?'

North gazed innocently up at him. 'I'm sorry, sir, were you not aware I had Adrian Meiklejohn with me?'

He spoke softly. 'You will pay for that remark later tonight.'

'I was very much hoping I would. How are we doing for time?'

'I'm not thinking about that now. I'm just concentrating on our current crisis. Get yourself back into Pod One and await instructions, North. No arguments.'

'I'm not going to argue, sir. I'm simply going to point out you can set the coordinates considerably more quickly if you have more than one person.'

'That's very true,' said Adrian, amiably. 'Chuck one of those bracelets over. Let's have a look.'

'No chucking,' said Ellis sternly. 'These are unstable, volatile, unreliable, and many other words that apply equally to St Mary's.'

Adrian had stopped listening. His head was bent over a bracelet as he made a series of ambiguous noises to himself.

Ellis gazed about him. The clouds were breaking up. One or two stars had appeared. The rain had now stopped entirely but the night was turning very cold.

'You all right over there, Max?'

'Bloody freezing. I can't feel my feet. Are we going to be much longer?'

'No. Just concentrate on standing still. Don't even shiver.' He turned back to Adrian. 'Your thoughts?'

'I think we can do this,' said Adrian. 'Four won't be quite enough but . . .' He paused for a moment, thinking. 'You were right about one in each corner. If we programme them to jump in fractionally different directions . . .'

'Are you mad?' said Fanboten, shocked. 'That could tear the pod apart. It will definitely explode.'

'Exactly, but it might reduce the force of the detonation and most importantly, it won't explode here.'

'Where then?'

Adrian shrugged. 'A safe destination.'

'And what about Max?' said North.

'She goes in a completely different direction.'

'We'll send her back to TPHQ,' said Ellis. 'I'll do that one.' He looked at Adrian. 'Is it difficult to do?'

'No,' said Adrian. 'But I can do it.'

Ellis frowned. 'We don't want everyone knowing our co-ordinates.'

'Oh, mate,' said Adrian, shaking his head. 'You live in one of the most easily identifiable national landmarks in the country. Everyone knows your coordinates.'

'No, they don't.'

'I do,' said Adrian. 'And so does Mikey.'

'And me,' shouted a voice from over by the pod.

'Adrian and I will do the ones for the pod,' said North, quickly. 'Any suggestion for an appropriate destination?'

'Sometime back in the past.'

'Not here,' called Max. 'We can't risk damaging this rock. The whole history of Athens revolves around it.'

'Out to sea, then,' suggested Adrian. 'Prehistory. Way back.'

'No,' called Max, again. 'This part of the world has always been populated.'

'Siberia,' said North. 'A long time ago. Deep in the Ice Age. No one lived there then.'

385

'I don't know . . .' said Max.

Fanboten shifted impatiently. 'We need to get a move on.'

'Siberia,' said Ellis decisively.

'OK.' Adrian slid aside a small panel to reveal the controls and began to mutter to himself again. 'Small pod – about ten by ten – if a person's about two feet wide . . .' he looked over at Max, still standing stock-still in the merciless glare of the searchlights, 'or slightly more – then one in each corner . . . The pod will certainly break up, which could very possibly reduce the force of the detonation.'

'Or precipitate the explosion.'

'Or that,' he said, cheerfully.

'How will it reduce the detonation?' enquired North.

'Well, if the pod breaks up then it'll spread the force of the explosion. Or, if we're really lucky, it might not explode at all if the detonator goes in one direction and everything else in another.'

Ellis looked at Adrian. 'Is there really no other way?'

'I'm sure there is, but do we have the time?'

Ellis frowned at the bracelet in his hand.

Adrian waited. 'What do you want me to do?'

Ellis took a breath. 'Do it.'

'OK.' He bent over his work. 'You align this with this. Select the coordinates here. Press and hold. See? Easy.' He paused. 'How are we going to get Max's to her?'

'I'll take them all,' said North. 'I'll walk in her footsteps, give her this one and then walk around her to the pod. If I avoid soft earth and stay on solid rock as much as I can, I'll be fine.'

'Yes,' said Ellis, his head bent over the bracelet as he worked. 'You will be fine, because as soon as these bracelets are programmed, then you, Adrian and Lt Fanboten will go back to the pod and depart and I'll deliver them.'

North, holding the bracelets as Adrian finished with them, glanced up at him. 'I'm not leaving you.'

'Yes, you are, Celia. Common sense. If this works, then it doesn't matter whether I'm here or not and I can be retrieved later. If it doesn't work, then it matters very much to me that you're not here.'

'Matthew . . .'

'Finished,' said Adrian.

Ellis frowned. 'How will we know when they're about to . . . ?'

Adrian shrugged. 'Some sort of signal. A flashing light, perhaps, or beeping. I'd go with beeping if it was me. 'I've programmed all of them for Siberia in the Ice Age. Have you finished yours, Major Ellis? And have you decided how to deliver them?'

Max's voice drifted across. 'I told you – throw them.'

'No,' said Adrian, shaking his head. 'That could be dangerous. And this is me saying that. They need to be set with precision. And the major himself said no chucking, remember?'

'I'll set them,' said North, getting to her feet.

'I think it should be me,' said Adrian. 'I'm faster and lighter than both of you.' He gestured at the wet-weather gear covering their body armour.

'I don't think . . .' began North.

'Yes, yes,' said Max, impatiently. 'You're all very brave. Can we get a move on? I'm getting pins and needles here.'

'Go,' said Ellis to North. 'And at this moment I speak as Major Ellis. Return to the pod, Officer North.'

'But . . .'

'Go, Celia. Make me happy.'

She took a step away and then turned back. 'Get this done, Matthew. You can't allow the Acropolis to be destroyed.'

She leaned forwards, briefly kissed him and walked quickly back to the pod with a grinning Adrian. 'One word from you and I'll kill you deader than all those bracelets combined.'

'Got it,' said Adrian, not ceasing to grin.

Ellis watched them walk away. 'You too, Fanboten.'

'Relax, sir. I'm not going to kiss you.'

'For that, Fanboten, you are duty officer every night for the rest of your life. Now go.'

'Sir . . .'

'An order, Lieutenant.'

'Yes, sir. Good luck.'

Fanboten disappeared after North and Adrian, leaving Ellis and Max alone and exposed in the harsh glare of the lights. If he succeeded in this, then the Time Police could return and collect their equipment and clear the site properly. If he didn't – well, it wouldn't matter, would it?

He dropped his shoulders and lifted his chin. 'All right, Max – let's do this, shall we?'

'So soon?'

'Shut up.' He scanned the ground. 'I can see where you walked. Thank goodness you have a weight problem.'

'Did you know women with a supposed weight problem live longer than men who mention it?'

'Ready?'

'Yeah.'

'Close your eyes.'

'How does that help?'

'It helps me.'

Progress was faster and easier than he thought it would be. There was some soft, wet soil but that meant he could see where Max had walked. He began to place his feet very slowly and carefully in her footprints, willing himself to be eleven and a half stone lighter, but to be on the safe side, sticking to rocky ground wherever possible.

He was drawing closer, but now he had to change direction slightly – the strong lights were directly behind him, causing his black shadow to run before him, making it more difficult to follow Max's footsteps exactly.

He lifted his head, squinting. 'Don't try and look behind you, Max. I'm getting close. Just concentrate on standing still.'

'OK.'

'I'm only a few yards away.'

'OK.'

'Nearly there.'

'OK.'

'I'm behind you.'

'Lovely. Because that's not unsettling at all, is it?'

'Can you hold out your right arm without falling over?'

'What? Of course I can. Why would you even ask that?'

'Well – you know – St Mary's.'

'You are so dead.'

'That could still happen to both of us.'

She managed a tired smile. 'No, it won't, Matthew. Everything's going to be absolutely fine.'

'I'm as close to you as is probably safe. Without shifting your weight in any way, bend your arm at the elbow and hold up your forearm.'

'Like this?'

'Perfect.'

He snapped on her cuff. 'Can you see the controls?'

She held her arm out into the light. 'Yes. I can.'

'OK. It's all preset. You have only to touch the square panel at the bottom.'

'Got it. Now what?'

'Now I work my way to the pod.'

'Don't stand on any freshly turned earth.'

'Thank you for reminding me. It had completely slipped my mind.'

'No problem. Always happy to assist the Time Police. Listen, I've had a Brilliant Idea.'

'Oh, God . . .'

'No, listen. You were going to walk around the pod and place a bracelet at each corner of the pod, weren't you?'

'Yes.'

'Too risky. You should stay off the ground as much as possible. Climb up and put them on the roof. One in each corner. About eighteen inches in.'

Ellis paused. 'That's actually a very good idea.'

'Well, yes, obviously.'

She watched him – still walking like a haemorrhoidal bear with a too full bladder – make his way slowly towards the pod.

'Do you have any idea how much longer we have before it detonates?'

'I was trying not to think about that, but as you said, the general – and completely uninformed – consensus is that the pod will explode after the sun comes up.'

'Any idea how long that will be?'

'I'm trying not to think about that, either.'

'Sorry.' She paused. 'Bit chilly for the time of year, don't you think?'

'Just shut up, Max.'

Reaching the pod, he unhooked the bag from his shoulder and, as gently as he could, tossed it up on to the roof.

It landed with a metallic chink. Max tried very hard not to flinch.

'Good job you're tall, isn't it?' she said, cheerfully.

'We in the Time Police do not employ short people. We believe in getting a lot of person for our money. I'm amazed we even let you through the door.'

Careful not to move his feet, he bent his knees and jumped, hooking the tips of his fingers over the edge of the roof. Kicking and scrabbling with his feet, he pulled himself up.

'Neat,' called Max. 'Not sure I could have done that.'

'Of course you bloody couldn't. Now shut up and let me get on.'

Ellis picked up the bag, carefully pulled out a bracelet, checked it over and very gently placed it near one corner of the pod. Working his way around the roof, he placed one in every corner. When he'd finished, he took a moment to look around him. At the shadowy outlines of the half-built struc-tures, the cats' cradles of scaffolding, the piles of stone and timber, and the clouds scudding across the sky. Faint stars showed and the temperature was still dropping. This place was already old. How many thousands of feet had trodden these stones before today? He could only hope it survived long enough for thousands more to do the same. If he'd got any part of this wrong, then he might be the last person in the world ever to see the Acropolis rock. Although not for very long.

Max, meanwhile, had been examining her bracelet. 'Matthew, what should I expect?'

He returned to the present. 'Adrian says there will probably be beeping. When that happens, it's very important that you—'

The night air was rent with electronic beeping. Red lights flashed from every corner of the pod. And from down below, too.

'What?' shouted Ellis. 'No! Too soon! What did you do?'

'Nothing,' shouted Max. 'You need to get out of here. Go. Now. Just jump and run.'

Ellis slithered down the side of the pod.

'Find your footprints. Run.'

He paused. 'Max . . .'

'The Time Police are rubbish. I want that on my headstone.'

There wouldn't be enough of her left even for a grave, let alone a headstone.

'Tell Leon . . .' She stopped.

'I will,' he said. 'Oh God, Max . . . I'm so sorry.'

'For fire truck's sake, Matthew – move.'

He edged carefully past her and began to run, heading for a substantial pile of cut timber that would provide absolutely no protection at all.

Max stared at her bleeping, flashing arm and then up at the uncaring stars. 'Did anyone catch what he said I had to do when it started to bleep?'

The bleeping stopped. For one long moment there was utter silence.

And then the explosion lit up the night sky.

31

A couple of thousand years later and yet at exactly the same time, Lt Grint had assembled his teams in Briefing Room 4. Present were Varma's security team, standing behind the four members of Clean-up Crew 29 who were blinking in all this unaccustomed light. Clean-up crews are bad news. They do exactly what it says on the tin. No one was particularly keen to bring themselves to their attention.

Also present were Grint's own team of Scrape, Hansen, Kohl and Rossi, together with the temporarily seconded Jane and Luke and the reluctantly included Matthew, and all of them reinforced by a security contingent led by Officer Varma.

'Settle down, everyone,' said Grint, and silence fell around the briefing room. 'Right, we'll be taking two pods. The biggest, Pod One, will land outside the hangar – Hangar A as it's been designated in your briefing material.'

He paused. There was no other hangar involved, but Time Police protocols are very rigid and it is clearly stated that for each mission, buildings be designated unambiguously and alphabetically, pods the same but numerically, and who was he to argue.

'This pod will contain Clean-up Crew 29 and the security

contingent under the command of Officer Varma. Their priority will be to throw a cordon around the hangar. It is very important that no one gets in or out. We don't know who's there voluntarily and who isn't, so treat everyone as suspicious. Be aware, Commander Hay wants all of them alive. *All of them.* That bastard Plimpton, the Meikeljohn girl, minions, everyone. We want to know what they know. Who they work for or whether they're an independent outfit. Team leaders, make sure that is clearly understood by everyone.

'The second pod, Pod Two, containing Teams Two-Three-Five and Two-Three-Six, will land directly *inside* Hangar A. Our objective will be to secure the hangar, arrest everyone on site, impound all pods and equipment, and extract Amelia Meiklejohn who, you will not be surprised to hear, has managed to fall into the wrong hands.'

There was a certain amount of murmuring. 'Yes,' said Grint. '*That* Amelia Meiklejohn. Anyone got a problem with that particular part of the mission?' He looked challengingly around the room. Everyone suddenly became very busy with their scratchpads. 'So – we go in, secure the area, locate and extract Plimpton and Meiklejohn.' He glanced at Matthew. 'Alive.'

'Conscious?' asked Hansen, hopefully.

'Not mandatory. Use your own judgement.'

'Remember, she doesn't love us,' said Matthew. 'That's why I'm going along. To reassure her and to prevent trouble.'

'So we can legitimately shoot both of you?' said Kohl.

Several faces brightened.

'Steady on,' said Luke, turning around. 'He's only just risen from the dead. We don't want him sinking back down into the underworld again, do we? You know – like Persephone.'

People stared blankly. Luke sighed and turned to Matthew. 'Just don't eat any pomegranate seeds and you should be fine.'

Grint cleared his throat. 'Crew 29.'

Their heads lifted simultaneously. Jane could see Luke gearing himself up to ask if they were all on the same piece of string and nudged him warningly. Clean-up crews have no sense of humour. No sense of anything, really, according to Luke Parrish, most of them being little more than uniform-clad lumps of inanimate matter. 'You will take your instructions from Officer Varma. Stay outside the hangar unless specifically instructed otherwise. It is vital no one escapes. And remember what I said – we want these people alive.'

Faces drooped.

'But that doesn't mean unharmed. As long as they're still able to tell us what we want to know, I'm not inclined to be fussy.'

Faces perked up again. Done properly, a good sonicking could be considerably more painful than a simple bullet. Jane tried hard to be outraged, remembered the devastated Beaver Avenue and all the people who had died there, and decided she couldn't be bothered.

'You should be ashamed,' said Wimpy Jane, primly.

'Well done, sweetie,' said Bolshy Jane. 'Slowly acquiring more balls than Wimbledon.'

Jane was finding herself more and more inclined to listen to Bolshy Jane these days and occasionally wondered what this said about her. At this rate, another six months in the Time Police and she'd be mowing people down without a care in the world.

Wimpy Jane tutted.

Actual Jane dragged her concentration back to Grint.

'Using intel provided by Officer Farrell, Teams Two-Three-Five and Two-Three-Six will land in the centre of the hangar. We'll take a dual-ramp pod and we come out shooting. The chances are they'll be waiting for us, so we hit them with everything we've got. Hard and fast. We don't give them a chance. Thanks to Officer Farrell, we've all had the description and layout of the hangar flashed to our scratchpads so we know what we're jumping into.

'On successful completion, Officer Varma's team will return to TPHQ with all the prisoners and any wounded. My teams will secure the hangar while we wait for the mechs and IT specialists to turn up. Any questions?'

'What's Meiklejohn wearing? We don't want to hit her by mistake.'

Grint gestured to Matthew who stood up. 'Flying jacket, Snoopy helmet and goggles – but she's probably the only female there. And she's not stupid. She'll either find shelter until it's all over or blow them up herself. They'll be distracted by everything else going on and she'll spot an opportunity. You know she's good at this sort of thing. She and her brother have avoided capture for years.'

'True,' said Grint. 'A young madam if ever I saw one. However . . .' he looked around, 'our mission is to secure the hangar, Plimpton *and* Meiklejohn. This is not an either/or situation.'

'And,' said Matthew, 'it might be an idea *not* to blow everything out of existence. Henry Plimpton is a bit of an inventor himself. There might be all sorts of treasures there.'

The clean-up crew shifted uneasily. These were deep ethical and intellectual waters in which they preferred not to paddle.

Recognising this, Grint moved swiftly on. 'Are there any questions?'

There were none.

'OK, everyone. Get yourselves kitted out. Full body armour and as many weapons as you can carry. Let's go.'

Team 236 assembled in the Pod Bay with the others.

Most officers have their own individual rituals to be employed before combat. Tiny, unaccountable, but incredibly important routines, the completion of which was to ensure they would always return safely from whatever they were about to face.

Even the relatively inexperienced Team 236 had quite unconsciously developed little rituals of their own before going into action. Luke would obsessively check over his weapons and carefully replace them around his person. Five minutes later he would do it all again.

For reasons she could not have explained, Jane always left her helmet off until the very last moment.

Matthew would stamp his boots, tighten his belt, flex his shoulders and jump up and down on the spot to see if anything jangled.

Their rituals completed, they waited in silence until the order came to board the pods.

'What date are we aiming for specifically?' enquired Grint on entering the pod.

Hansen peered at the coordinates. 'Paris. 29th December 1902.'

Grint blinked and looked around. 'Date mean anything to anyone?'

People shook their heads.

'All right, people. You know what to do. We go as soon as we touch down. No time for them to know what's hit them. Scrape, take Two-Three-Five down the front ramp. I'll lead Two-Three-Six down the back. Hansen, you'll be i/c the pod. Leave the door open in case anyone's wounded and needs to get back inside in a hurry. Have the medkits ready. We go on three. Everyone set?'

A number of voices said yes.

'Commence jump procedures.'

The world flickered like a bad film, followed by a slight jolt.

They landed to complete darkness and silence.

Matthew could hear his own breathing inside his helmet. He tightened his grip on his blaster. His palms felt sticky. Would the illegals have fled already? Or were the Time Police walking into a carefully prepared ambush? He pushed that thought from his head. Concentrate on the job in hand. It was the only way to get through this.

Grint's voice sounded in his ears. 'One. Two. Three. Go go go.'

The two teams went, piling down both front and rear ramps simultaneously, firing as they came, breaking alternately right and left and heading for the nearest cover. The hangar echoed to the sound of their gunfire.

Matthew, last one out, raced down the ramp after Luke, feeling it bounce slightly under his feet. He caught only the briefest glimpse of a hazy green world before his eyes nearly exploded with hard, white light. A second later he was completely blind. No, that wasn't quite right – his vision was filled with jagged streaks of after-colours – green, purple and blue.

His eyes were on fire. He was barely out through the door and already he was crippled and helpless.

Night visors are very effective in the dark. They're invaluable – until someone switches on the lights. Or, in this case, sets off a fizzer. Night visors massively magnify the effect, and temporary blindness was not unknown. Matthew groped for his visor controls. Grint was shouting at everyone to disengage their night vision.

Matthew collided with the corner of something substantial, identified it as some sort of metal box, rolled behind it and flipped up his visor to wipe his streaming eyes. They'd covered this in training. It would pass. He should close his eyes and stay safe. Easier said than done. He could hear gunfire all around him, together with the whining roar of discharging blasters. He was completely disoriented. And vulnerable. He had no idea where he was or where his teammates were. No idea of who was firing at whom, but he was surrounded by bangs and explosions. He could feel debris raining down upon him.

He scrunched himself up even smaller. There was no way to tell from which direction he was being attacked. He could smell pepper. Someone had deployed gas canisters. He flipped his visor back down again. His helmet had a built-in filter that would deal with that. All around was noise and utter chaos. Sound and fury. Typical Time Police. He could hear Socko shouting to Rossi, and Grint roaring above everyone. Matthew dared not fire. He had no idea where he was in relation to everyone else and he didn't want to take out anyone from his own side. Time Police officers do not look kindly on being shot by their own colleagues.

He had no idea for how long he was pinned down. It seemed

forever. His eyes streamed. His nose ran. His worst fear had been realised. They'd walked into an ambush. And where was Mikey in all this? Finding herself a safe refuge, he hoped.

More fizzers went up. Bright, blinding lights exploded all around him, illuminating the hangar but compounding the pain in his eyes. If he was blind, then so must everyone else be. There was nothing to stop the illegals strolling around the hangar, picking off stricken officers at their leisure.

Inside his helmet, his eyes and nose were streaming. The green and purple streaks were fading. They weren't real. The increasingly brilliant red and orange flashes of discharging weapons, however, were.

Matthew blinked and blinked, feeling his wet eyelashes on his cheeks. His eyes began to feel a little less like boiled jelly. He switched his light filter to maximum which helped a little, tightened his grip on his weapon and risked a quick look around.

He seemed to be concealed behind a small pile of anonymous metal boxes, right in the centre of the hangar and horribly vulnerable. He needed to find a more secure position. And as soon as possible. A savage gunfight was raging around him. Bullets ricocheted off the hangar's walls. He could hear the roar of blasters. The air was growing hot and thick. He could see a very blurry and equally exposed Luke over to his right. Luke gave him a thumbs up, clenched his fist and began to beat a rhythm. One . . . two . . . three . . .

You always go on three.

They went.

Matthew pulled himself up on to his knees and laid down a hail of covering fire. Luke moved forwards, found himself somewhere safe-ish behind a pillar and then, in turn, covered Matthew's advance. They worked their way forwards, guns swinging back and forth, covering each other. Sending out short, sharp blasts of flame ahead of them. Others were doing the same.

Finally gaining the comparative safety of a wall, they both dropped to their knees, facing in different directions, watching over each other's shoulders while they pulled themselves together after the initial shock.

'Heads down. Heads down,' roared Grint from somewhere. 'Grenades.'

His team were lobbing percussion grenades that would take out everyone not benefitting from the protection of their helmets.

Matthew and Luke ducked and closed their eyes. Five or six flat cracks echoed around the hangar. Matthew felt the shock deep within his chest. Like a kick from a horse. Without giving the illegals time to recover, the Time Police deployed more gas canisters and then followed that through with sweeping blasts of low-charge blaster fire at knee height because that sort of thing always tends to sort the men from the boys. For a few colourful moments, the inside of the hangar was lit up like Bonfire Night and then they waited, teeth clenched, to see from which direction any returning fire would come.

There was no returning fire. Not that Matthew expected there would be after that little lot. He waggled his jaw to unblock his ears, sniffed mightily to reverse the flow of snot and prepared himself for the next push.

There was no need. Slowly, all gunfire dwindled and died away. A kind of throbbing silence fell. Now that he was no longer in imminent danger of death, Matthew pushed back his visor to have a look around.

The hangar was wrecked. Fanlike scorch marks imprinted the walls. Most of the wall shelving had collapsed. Boxes, crates, whatever, were no longer stacked in neat piles but scattered across the floor. Several were on fire and crackled merrily. Most of them seemed to have been empty. Matthew was surprised to see there were no bodies. Other than the crackling flames, there was silence in the hangar.

Gradually, officers began to emerge from whatever shelter they'd managed to find, still unsure of the situation in which they found themselves, weapons ready, jumpy, covering every inch of what they were now beginning to suspect was an empty hangar. Matthew saw Jane about ten feet away, tending to Scrape who was sprawled in a heap.

The smoke and gas were clearing away. Someone – Rossi, perhaps – was having a massive sneezing fit. That would be the remains of the gas. Matthew could feel the tickle in his own eyes and nose but the effects were bearable. His eyesight was watery but more or less restored. All the better with which to see the horrible truth. They were alone. The hangar was full of Time Police officers and no one else. No illegals. No Henry Plimpton. And no Mikey. Their birds had flown. They were too late.

Grint pushed up his visor. 'Casualties?'

Officers looked down at themselves and each other.

Jane's voice was raised. 'Scrape, sir.'

Ignoring Jane's protest, Scrape yanked some sort of flechette from his armour and flung it across the hangar. Matthew could hear it skittering across the floor. 'It's nothing, sir. Barely penetrated my armour.'

'Anyone else?'

Astonishingly, given the number of weapons discharged in such a small area – no. Although all of them were red-eyed and snotty.

'Well,' said Luke. 'Isn't this embarrassing?'

No one replied.

'So who fired the fizzers?' said Rossi, looking around. 'And who shot Scrape?'

'Booby traps,' said Socko, in disgust. 'Triggered by us as we disembarked. They probably hoped we'd all kill each other and save them the bother.'

'It's a bloody miracle we didn't,' said Luke.

Grint grunted and pushed past him. 'That will be because not one of you useless jugheads could hit a barn door even if you tried. Book yourself some sessions on the range when we get back. Bloody rubbish, all of you. Right, don't just stand around wondering what to do next – search this hangar. Watch out for more booby traps, mines, whatever. When we've cleared this area, we'll move on to the other room.'

Matthew never knew what made him look down. Not twelve inches away, a tiny shiny wire stretched between two wooden crates. At shin height.

'Stand still,' he shouted – very much in the same way his mother was, at that very moment and several thousand years ago, shouting at her colleagues to do the same. 'Tripwire. Trip-wire. Tripwire.'

All around him, officers stood frozen. Like statues. And as silent.

'Don't move, lad,' said Grint – as if Matthew was likely to start dancing a jig. He pulled out his com. 'Varma?'

She responded immediately. 'You all right in there? Do you want us to come in and hold your hands?'

'There's no one here.'

They could hear the grin in her voice. 'Then what was all the shooting?'

Grint scowled and remained silent.

Varma didn't seem able to let it go. 'You weren't shooting at each other, were you?'

'No,' said Grint defensively. And probably inaccurately. 'They've booby-trapped the place to attack us. Anti-personnel devices.'

'They may be planning to return, sir. To mop up the survivors. Watch your backs.'

'Copy that. There's at least one device left active. Stay outside until I give the all-clear.'

'Yes, sir.'

He closed his com. 'Night visors on, lads. Makes it easier to see the wires. Hold your current position and take a good long look around. Don't move your feet. Full sweep.'

Silence followed as every officer checked his – or her – personal space.

'Anyone else found anything?'

No, that seemed to be it.

'So just you then, Farrell.'

Matthew nodded. Just him. That figured.

'Can you see where it's wired to?' enquired Grint.

'Yes,' said Matthew. 'I can see the whole set-up. Tiny device duct-taped to this crate on my left. Wire stretched across to another crate . . .' he pointed, 'two feet away. End hooked over a nail. What happens if I just gently unhook it?'

'Don't know,' said Grint, appearing beside him. 'But I do know what happens if you do this.'

He aimed and fired his blaster at the device. Which flared briefly and then melted.

'Bloody hell,' said Luke, straightening up and trying to look as if he hadn't been on the point of flinging himself behind a pile of packing cases. 'I can't imagine the circumstances under which you discovered that.'

'Thank you, sir,' said Matthew, swallowing hard. 'How did you know it wouldn't explode?'

'I didn't,' said Grint. 'But I had my fingers crossed, if that helps. Everyone else report.'

A number of voices shouted, 'Clear.'

'All right,' said Grint. 'We'll work our way towards the far end of the hangar. Everyone watch where you put your feet. Not just wires – there could be pressure plates as well. Commander Hay wants this entire hangar intact and I'm not going to be the one telling her a bunch of clumsy oiks inadvertently blew up the best lead we've had in months and themselves along with it. Got it?'

He clapped Matthew on the shoulder, causing him to stagger slightly. 'Off you go, lad. Varma, we've cleared the device and are moving on to the secondary area at the far end.'

'Copy that, sir.'

Easing their way very slowly and very cautiously through the clutter of discarded equipment, scorched crates and stuff that hadn't survived their recent incursion, they gathered round the door at the far end. The one that led to the concealed part of the hangar.

No one touched the door. Grint approached and peered closely while the others stood back.

'Everyone ready?'

Matthew, Jane and Luke crouched to the left of the door – Rossi, Hansen and Socko to the right.

'I can't see anything.' Grint ran a reader around the door. 'Looks OK. I'm going in.'

Scrape stepped up behind him. 'Got your back, sir.'

'OK,' said Grint. 'Let's do this.'

He took a deep breath, reached out, very, very slowly took hold of the handle and pushed open the door.

A tiny red dot danced between his eyes.

## 32

Even with a solid wall between them and the hangar outside, Mikey and Henry Plimpton were rocked by the immense explosion that greeted the arrival of the Time Police. The lights dimmed, flickered and then recovered. Mikey could hear shouting. It sounded as if an entire army was on the other side of the door.

She grinned mockingly. 'They're heeeeeeeeere . . .'

The whole building shuddered under the impact of another series of explosions. Dust and dirt dropped down on them from the high ceiling. There was the roar of blaster fire. Then more explosions. Mikey could hear Time Police officers shouting to people to get down on the ground. A minute at the most and they'd be through the door.

Plimpton was still too far away from her. She needed him to come closer. Much closer. Perhaps this might be a good time to scream. She opened her mouth to do so.

'A complete waste of time,' said Henry, raising his voice over the Time Police-generated racket. 'Even if they could hear you – which they can't – they've got rather a lot on at the moment.'

'I'm in here,' shouted Mikey, who always enjoyed pandering

to other people's ideas of how women should behave. 'Save me. Oh, save me.' She turned towards the door as if about to make a run for it.

Henry Plimpton took two long steps forwards, hooked one arm around her throat and yanked her backwards. 'Oh no, you don't. I've got you.'

'Um . . . no, actually,' said Mikey, breathlessly, because his grip was surprisingly strong. 'I've got you. Look.'

She pushed back her sleeve and held up her arm. Beneath her flying jacket and her long-sleeved T-shirt she was wearing a bracelet. It was only inches from both their faces. While he stared at it, she twisted one leg around his and grabbed for the arm across her throat with her free hand. 'Shall I blow both our heads off, Henry?'

She felt him shake his head. 'You won't use that. We'd both die. You won't risk it.'

'Not much of a risk for me, Henry. You were going to shoot me, remember? Big risk for you though. What do you want to do?'

'You can't hold on to me forever.'

'Don't have to. Only until the Time Police get themselves in here.'

'I would not hold my breath if I were you. If my people haven't taken the opportunity to put together a few welcoming surprises out there, then I shall be rather unhappy with them when we next meet and they've been learning recently – quite painfully in some cases – not to make me unhappy.'

Plimpton paused, listening. At some point the sounds of conflict next door had died away. There was now complete silence outside in the hangar. Apparently satisfied, he continued in a cajoling tone of voice, 'Why won't you join me, Miss Meiklejohn? We could do great things together.'

Mikey was conscious her leg – the one twisted around Henry Plimpton's – was beginning to cramp. The grip on her throat was making her head pound. Fainting now would not be a good idea, but all she had to do was hold on until someone came through the door. 'I'm already doing great things, Henry.'

'Not as great as the ventures I currently have in hand, I'm betting.'

Play for time. 'Really? Tell me what you have in hand.'

'You don't want me to spoil the surprise, surely.' He tightened his grip again. Mikey could feel the blood pounding behind her eyes. Her face felt hot and swollen.

'Last chance, Miss Meiklejohn.'

She sucked in air and managed to say, 'For me or for you?'

'For us both. What do you say?'

'You threatened to maim me for life, Henry. I don't take kindly to that sort of thing, you know.'

'I wanted you to work for me and I didn't think flowers would do the trick. Is your arm beginning to ache? Vision blurred? Leg going numb yet?'

Still silence from next door. Mikey wasn't sure she could hold on much longer. What the hell were they doing out there?

'They're all dead, you know,' said Henry Plimpton, chattily. 'No one's coming to your rescue. Take off the bracelet, join me and I'll give you whatever you want in the way of facilities.'

Her pulse was pounding inside her head. 'Generous. How long would I live to enjoy them, I wonder?'

Her straining ears caught a slight sound on the other side of the door. As did Henry Plimpton apparently.

409

'Looks like they're not all dead after all, Henry.'

'So it would seem,' he said calmly. 'Would you like me to declaim dramatically that you'll never take me alive?'

'By all means.'

'You'll never take me alive,' he cried. 'How was that?'

Mikey made one last effort. 'Bloody rubbish.'

'Try this instead. Open.'

Wrenching his leg free, he began to drag her backwards towards the open pod doorway. She struggled but he was stronger than he looked. Another second or two . . . Conscious that if she allowed him to pull her inside this pod she might well be lost forever, Mikey curled her fingers around the door jamb and hung on for dear life. Henry could use his last few seconds struggling with her or let her go and save himself. Sensibly, he decided to go with the latter. Pushing her away from him, he slammed the door.

She would have fallen face down but something jerked her to a halt. Part of her jacket was caught in the door which now couldn't close properly. She could hear him trying to get the door shut, panting and cursing. No pod can jump with an open door. Ask Commander Hay. The obvious solution was for him to whip the door back open again, shoot her, slam the door shut again and jump.

She struggled to extricate herself from her jacket, wriggling frantically to get her arms free. She tugged so hard she lost her balance completely and fell heavily to the floor, but her weight dragged her jacket loose. Behind her, the door clicked shut.

Mikey struggled to roll away. Out of range. She was too close. Far too close. The forces would drag her along with the pod. Or rip her to pieces.

A warm, strong wind ruffled her hair. She could feel the pull. In desperation, she actually clawed at the concrete floor. As if that would do any good. She was going to die . . . She'd finally run out of the famous Meiklejohn luck. She closed her eyes.

Her final thought – shit, no cheese – was lost in a kaleidoscope of bright lights, vertigo, seeming weightlessness and nausea.

# 33

Either a few seconds later – or possibly an entire lifetime – Mikey opened her eyes, quite surprised to find herself lying on the ground. No – the floor. The cold, hard concrete floor. The *familiar* cold, hard concrete floor. She hadn't jumped. She was still here. Intact. Not pulled apart. She'd been very, very lucky.

She sat up slowly. The sensations were subsiding but she still felt weak. Drained, almost. The world seemed indistinct. As if she had some kind of film over her eyes. She blinked hard and rubbed her eyes to clear them. That had been rough – even by the standards of one who, not so long ago, had been leaping around the Timeline in a giant teapot. She patted her jeans' pockets hopefully, just on the off-chance . . . Nope, no cheese. Typical. Blinking and shaking her head did not help. The world seemed . . . not blurred, not hazy, not fuzzy, but paler. Somehow less substantial.

There was a sound in the doorway. Memories came crashing back. The Time Police had arrived. They were no friends of hers.

An enormous officer with 'Grint' emblazoned on his helmet crouched in the doorway, pointing his gun directly at her. A small red dot danced across his face and down to his breast-plate.

'No,' she shouted, making sure he could see her hands. No one knew better than Mikey that the Time Police almost invariably shot first and didn't bother asking questions afterwards. 'Never mind me. Look up. Laser gun. Ceiling. I'm unarmed.'

The words tumbled over themselves in her desperation to warn him.

Another officer appeared behind the first, shouting, 'Look out, sir,' just as a ruler-straight red line sliced through the smoky atmosphere to kiss the dancing red dot on Grint's breastplate. Grint was shouldered aside just one second too late. The laser blast caught him full in the chest.

He staggered to his right. She caught just the briefest glimpse of Matthew, and possibly another officer, before Grint smashed into them, knocking them both off their feet.

Mikey watched, horrified, as the second officer's momentum carried him onwards, in through the door. Once again, the same red beam lanced across the room, slicing him across the middle of his body. He screamed and jerked, seemingly unable to move. Two officers, both with the same thought, rolled into the doorway, sweeping the ceiling with their blasters. The ceiling-mounted laser cannon exploded into a hundred pieces and then the mangled remains of the officer's smoking body hit the floor.

Mikey still sprawled on the concrete, hands in the air, open-mouthed with shock.

Matthew was struggling to get out from beneath a fallen Grint, who lay still, his eyes empty.

Scrape lay in a silent, smoking heap that no one wanted to look at too closely.

Jane was on her knees covering Matthew, Luke and Grint, shouting, 'Men down. Men down.'

Rossi crawled to where Scrape lay. Socko covered them, his gun jerking around as he tried to cover all angles at once.

'Don't touch them,' shouted Hansen from the pod. 'You'll do more harm than good. I'm on my way.'

'Possibility of second attack,' shouted Rossi into his com. 'Possible hostiles still in the unsecured area.'

'The room's empty,' said Matthew, sadly, risking a look through the door. 'They've gone. We've lost them both.'

'No, you haven't,' called Mikey, scrambling to her feet. 'It's OK. I'm still here. Don't come in, whatever you do. I'll come to you.'

She took a couple of paces towards him. He didn't even look at her.

She stopped uncertainly. Something wasn't right. 'Matthew?'

He went to step in through the doorway.

'Stay where you are, Matthew,' said Luke, holding him back. 'There could be more booby traps. No one else goes in until the area's cleared.'

'Matthew?' called Mikey again. 'Hello? Anyone? Can anyone hear me?'

She knew the answer to that question before she even asked it. Her world was changed. There was no colour. No depth. She looked about her. She looked at the officers, tending to their wounded. They couldn't see her. She could see them but they couldn't see her. Why? What had just happened? Was this a Time-slip, perhaps? Had Henry Plimpton, in attempting to manufacture a time-stop, accidentally managed to generate a small, localised Time-slip instead?

She thought not. The symptoms were similar but everyone else was going about their business – tending the wounded and securing the area. It was just her. And yet everything had been perfectly normal – right up until . . . right up until the moment Henry jumped.

Mikey bent over to pick up her flying jacket lying on the ground only a few paces away.

Well . . . bugger. Just . . . bugger.

Her beloved jacket. They'd been through a lot together. She and her jacket had danced from crisis to catastrophe and back again. Now half of it was gone. Completely. It wasn't burned or melted away – it was just gone. As cleanly as a surgical cut. Mikey swallowed. That could have been her. She shivered.

She'd been too close. Safety lines are there for a reason. How many times had she heard Mr Dieter saying that back at St Mary's? And Chief Farrell. Even Dr Maxwell had been known to adhere to that particular rule. Because get too close . . . get caught in the slipstream . . . she looked down at the remains of her jacket again . . . and this was what happened. She'd more or less fallen out of it and that had saved her life. She'd been just far enough away to escape . . . she looked at the remains of her flying jacket again . . . that particular fate.

But she hadn't escaped completely, had she?

OK. Stop and think. She was here. They were here. She could see them. They couldn't see her. Why? Had she been too close after all? Was this what happened when . . . ?

Panic galloped through her. She looked down at herself. No, she looked fine. Arms. Legs. Everything was here. Everything was intact and working. Nothing had changed.

Except . . .

She held up her right arm and pushed back her T-shirt sleeve. The one with the cuff. Even as she stared at it, a small red light flashed. Every thirty seconds or so.

Again – bugger.

Stop. Stop and think. Don't panic. Think your way out of this one, Mikey. The bracelet was active. Why? She hadn't done anything. Yes, the cuffs were unstable but they weren't supposed to be able to switch themselves on and off. That was just asking for trouble. And even if it had – which it shouldn't have done, but if it had – why was she still here? Why hadn't it whipped her off to . . . wherever and whenever it was set for? Or, given these bracelets' catastrophic performance to date – why hadn't it whipped half of her away while leaving the other half bleeding to death on the ground?

Instinctively, she went to take it off before it did something stupid to both of them. And then she paused.

Something had activated the bracelet. It wasn't anything she'd done and the only other candidate was Henry. Or no, no, not Henry himself, but his pod. Had she been too close after all and the field generated by the pod had been strong enough to activate her bracelet? It shouldn't have – she had no idea how that could have happened; an interesting conundrum for the future – but happen it had.

And with the bracelet activated . . . it would be generating a field. Not strong enough to jump but strong enough to . . . what? Strong enough to render her invisible? Like a ghost, perhaps? Could she touch anything?

Yes, she'd patted herself down. Several times, actually. So she could touch herself. She could touch the bracelet. And her jacket. Because the jacket had also been caught in the field. She

416

reached out to touch the nearest generator. It felt cold under her hand and strangely . . . not solid. Which couldn't be. The generator was solid – she wasn't. That must be why they couldn't see or hear her. She wasn't quite here. The field was too weak to send her off anywhere else but she wasn't quite here.

Again . . . bugger.

More panic galloped through her. Unpleasant images of the possible consequences burned their way into her mind. None of them were good. Fear clutched at her. Terror waited its turn.

Mikey did as she always did. Panic, horror, despair at the situation in which she found herself – everything was allowed free reign for thirty seconds. This was her safety valve – her way to work things through. At the end of thirty seconds, having had their little party, panic was sent packing, horror and despair were booted out of the door, and she would begin to think again.

She spent a very unenjoyable half minute imagining the worst and then drew herself up, took three long deep breaths, and started to take stock of the situation.

There were several possibilities. The bracelet, lacking any further instructions, could quietly shut itself down and everything would return to normal. Her preferred outcome, obviously. In which case, should she leave the bracelet on her wrist? If it shut itself down and she wasn't wearing it, could she be like this forever?

Or, the bracelet, still in its half-activated state, could decide it had messed around long enough and lacking any further instructions to the contrary, could jump. To where and whenever. Possibly taking all of her with it or possibly not. How much notice would it give? It seemed too much to hope that a neat little light would flash green. Or start a countdown. Or anything . . .

Or the bracelet could remain permanently frozen. She could stay like this forever. Half in and half out of this world. A ghost in her own lifetime.

That could be it. She was dead – her physical body destroyed when Henry's pod jumped – but her spirit would remain here. Forever.

Or the field generated by the bracelet had actually protected her from being torn apart as the pod jumped. That was equally possible. Perhaps she should be grateful.

More deep breaths, Mikey. The first rule was always switch it off, then switch it back on again. But what would happen if she did? Would that make things better or worse? Another of Dieter's famous sayings – *if in doubt, do nowt*. Always spoken in an interesting combination of Austrian Yorkshire. No – do nothing for the time being. Give the situation time to develop and then choose a course of action. And besides, she wasn't the only one with problems.

Back at the door, Rossi was bending over Scrape who lay in a pool of his own agony, his eyes half closed, his breath coming in hoarse, sharp pants of pain.

'Hey, mate, how are you doing?' he said softly, raising Scrape's visor.

Scrape's eyes flickered. Shock, pain and blood loss were claiming him. 'Not . . . my best day. But not . . . my . . . worst.'

Having no idea whether his team leader was still alive or not, Rossi leaned in close. 'You saved Grint's life. He says thank you.'

418

For a long moment, Scrape hovered. Going . . . but not quite gone. Then he exhaled a long sigh and closed his eyes.

Rossi cursed mightily and turned away.

Mikey halted about six feet away. Very quietly, she said, 'Can anyone . . . ?'

Luke spoke across her. 'Jane – what's happening with Grint?'

Jane was bending over him. 'His armour seems to have borne the brunt of the blast but he's not good. There's a big hole in his breastplate. I'm not even going to try to get it off him.' Her voice trembled. 'It seems . . . glued to him.'

And indeed, part of Grint's breastplate did appear to have melted in the blast. Mikey could see raw flesh, seared and burned, but very little blood. Grint was barely conscious, his half-closed eyes staring blankly at nothing.

'They'll have stuff to get it off him in MedCen,' said Jane. 'We just have to keep him alive until we can get him back there.'

Luke opened his com. 'Varma – Scrape's dead and Grint is down. Keep your people outside. This place is lethal. Plimpton and Meiklejohn have escaped . . .'

'No, I haven't, dumbass,' said Mikey, angry and frightened. 'I'm still here.' She looked down at herself again, terrified she might find she'd faded some more. 'I think.'

Luke continued. 'They must have had a pod in there. One or both of them might try to come back. Be aware.'

'Copy that. Do you require assistance?'

'Not at the moment.'

Hansen had appeared and was unfastening one of his med-kits. 'Anyone see how this happened?'

'There was a flash and a bang,' said Luke, never big on

419

technical detail. 'Some sort of laser cannon up there . . .' He pointed up to the smoking hole in the ceiling. 'Scrape pushed Grint out of the way and took the main blast. If Grint survives, then Scrape will have saved his life. All our lives, perhaps.'

Mikey edged past Scrape, carefully not looking at him, to stand by Matthew. 'I'm here,' she whispered, trying to pull at his arm. He felt spongey but she could feel him. Why couldn't he feel her?

Delicately, and without touching his breastplate, Hansen was examining Grint's wound. The smell was unpleasant.

'That's not me, is it?' said Grint, faintly, opening his eyes.

'You or your socks, sir,' said Hansen, spraying him liberally with medical plastic that would cool and protect his burned flesh. 'Hold still now – this is for the pain.'

There was the hiss of a hypo. Grint's eyes closed. 'It's not . . . working.'

'Give it time,' said Hansen, but another hypo hissed anyway.

Jane stood with her back to them, weapon raised. I'm securing the hangar, she told herself. Never mind what's happening behind me. I'm securing the hangar. I'm securing the hangar.

Luke took Hansen aside. 'Is it OK to move him?'

'Yes,' said Hansen, beginning to pack away his equipment.

Grint opened his eyes again. Bets were later placed on how many hypos it would actually take to knock him out. 'No,' he said, between gritted teeth. 'Job to do.'

Luke bent beside him. 'Lt Grint, you are unable to continue. I am reluctantly relieving you of your duties. Sir.'

Grint blinked, teeth clenched against the pain. 'Did you just call me "sir"?'

'Don't forget to mention it to Ellis –' Luke paused meaningfully – 'on your return to TPHQ. Hansen, Socko – soon as you can – get him out of here. Rossi, Matthew – give them a hand to get him back to the pod.'

Socko wasn't happy. Frowning, he demanded to know who had put Luke in charge.

'I did,' said Luke. 'Obviously.'

'I have seniority. We graduated long before you.'

'I have more medals than you.'

'I have more fingers.'

'For God's sake,' shouted Mikey, greatly regretting she was unable to bang their stupid heads together.

'Rock paper scissors?' suggested Rossi.

There was a brief pause as everyone opened their mouths to say don't be so bloody silly.

Luke stirred impatiently. 'We'll vote. Socko and Hansen are to return with Grint to TPHQ.'

Matthew nodded.

'Off you go,' said Luke.

'We're the fire-trucking Time Police,' shouted Socko in exasperation. 'Not a bloody knitting circle. I've got seniority here – you go.'

'For fire truck's sake, get in the pod or I'll shoot you all,' said Jane, lifting her blaster and secretly rather enjoying the moment.

Rossi looked at her mournfully. 'What happened to you, Jane?'

'Oh, well done, sweetie,' cried Bolshy Jane.

Rossi looked down. 'What about Scrape?'

'We'll find something to cover him and leave him here for

421

the time being,' said Luke, gently. 'He won't mind. Hansen –
when you get back to TPHQ, can you organise us whatever
you can in the way of reinforcements, please. I think most of
this is well above our pay grade.'

Hansen looked around and nodded. 'Agreed.'

'And Socko – back as soon as you can, please.'

It took the four of them to get Grint into the pod. They did
their best but they hurt him. Mikey watched silently from the
doorway to the generator room. Luke and Jane went ahead,
checking every inch of the way. I'm checking it's safe, Jane
told herself. I'm checking everything is safe. And it did seem
the hangar had no more surprises for them. Rossi stepped back
out of range and they watched as the pod jumped away.

'And then there were four,' said Luke brightly.

'Five,' said Mikey angrily, because no one was listening
and she was frightened, had no idea what to do next, and was
feeling very, very alone. The pod would come back for them,
but suppose the Time Police decided the job was done and they
all climbed inside and jumped away to safety, leaving her here.
Alone, unseen, unheard – forever.

'Three, actually,' said Jane. 'Because Matthew's just gone
into that room.' She nodded towards the rear of the hangar.

Rossi tutted. 'You really need to put a bell around his neck.
Like a cat.'

'He's so irritating,' said Luke. 'There could be more booby
traps and God knows what in there. *I'm* supposed to be the stupid
one around here. Stay alert, Jane. Rossi, watch our backs.'

He and Jane lowered their visors, brought up their weapons
and edged their way towards the door into the back of the
hangar.

This was the first chance they'd had to have a proper look through the door. Most of the space was taken up by what looked like four massive generators arranged in a rough circle and bolted to the floor. Various associated pieces of equipment were ranged around the walls. Cables ran everywhere. There was a smell of hot electrics. The whole set-up rather reminded Matthew of St Mary's.

Pausing in the doorway and without any hope that he would listen, Luke called to Matthew. 'Come out of there. You don't know what other traps have been set.'

'No,' said Mikey, sadly. 'It's safe. Henry wouldn't want anything happening to this little lot. Matthew, Henry got away but I'm still here. Look at me.'

Matthew was pacing out the dimensions. 'Just give me a minute.'

Luke was exasperated. 'It's not bloody safe in there.'

'Oh, I think it is. Remember that Henry Plimpton and Mikey . . .' He stopped for a moment because he mustn't think about Mikey – not even for a second – and then continued, 'were both in here and there are no bodies, so no harm came to them.'

'Yes, it bloody did,' shouted Mikey. 'Lots of harm came to me. Will you, for God's sake, stop and think. Henry dis-appeared. He jumped. He had a pod. I'm still here. You have to realise that. Matthew . . . please . . .' She tried to shake his arm. 'Look at me. Please look at me.'

She broke off, choking, feeling herself lose control. Fighting the urge to shout, scream, throw something – to do something – anything – that would show them she was still here . . . Yes. Could she perhaps . . . ? She stepped back from Matthew and tried to find something small and light that would make a noise if dropped. There was a pair of long-nosed pliers. It wasn't easy. Trying to pick them up was like trying to pick up jelly. Eventually she just gave it up and, using her forearm, nudged them along the workbench. Further . . . just a little further . . .

At exactly that moment, Matthew called out, 'Luke,' and no one heard them clatter to the floor.

She could have cried.

'Luke, these things are huge. That's a lot of power. And there are four of them. And they're linked in a circle. And then there's all these cables leading to all this other stuff built around them. I haven't a clue what any of it's for. I can't even see if these generator things power the equipment or vice versa.'

'Electrical generators?' shouted Luke.

'Are they on?' asked Jane, betraying her ignorance of all things generator.

'Not sure,' said Luke, betraying his.

Matthew seemed puzzled. He was walking around each one. Pausing, he rested a hand on one of them. It was quite cold and still.

'Not a lot of electricity about in 1902, surely,' said Luke.

'Actually,' said Matthew very slowly, because his brain was racing. 'There were massive generators at the Paris Exhibition in 1900. They were particularly remarked upon.' He tailed away again, staring up at the brooding giants.

Mikey waved her arms. 'Yes, yes. Come on – electricity. Time. Put the two together. While you still can. If this lot switches itself on, then we're all in dead trouble.'

'You're not saying these are them, are you?' demanded Luke. He frowned. 'Do I mean they are those? These are they?'

424

'I don't know,' said Matthew, answering all his questions. 'Shouldn't think so. These are massive pieces of kit, but what do they do? What are these things actually for?' He resumed his vague wandering, running his hand over the nearest generator.

Mikey resisted the urge to hit him with one of them. 'Matthew, will you stop looking at that bloody generator and look at me.'

Matthew sighed. 'I let her down. I was supposed to rescue her.'

Mikey tried to laugh. 'Were you? Bloody useless Time Police. Can't do anything right, can you?'

'And Plimpton,' said Luke. 'We were supposed to arrest him as well and we didn't.'

Mikey sighed. 'Well, at least you are consistent in your failures.'

Matthew bent and tried to see underneath the nearest generator.

Luke frowned. 'What on earth are you looking for?'

'The on-switch.'

Luke stiffened. 'Matthew, I forbid you to touch *anything*.'

'Mm . . .'

'No, I mean it. You're not at St Mary's now. Absolutely no *I wonder what happens if I press this*. Got it?'

'It's all quite safe,' said Matthew. 'Completely inert.' Apparently losing interest in his colleagues, he continued his vague perambulations.

Mikey waved her arms in frustration. 'They are *not* safe. MATTHEW – LOOK AT ME.'

Matthew looked around. 'Did you hear something?'

Mikey froze. 'Did you hear me? Was it me you heard? MATTHEW?'

'They must have jumped away together,' said Jane, still striving to put pictures of a burned and blackened Grint out of her mind. He was tough. He'd survive. She should concentrate. They weren't safe yet. 'Plimpton, I mean. And Mikey.' She waved her reader around. 'I'm picking up a reading. Over there. Not long ago. Quite recent perhaps and . . .'

She became aware she was beginning to gabble. Luke touched her shoulder, saying softly, 'Hey.'

'Sorry. I'm just . . .'

'You need to hang in there, Jane. You're the brains of the outfit and we need you.'

'Yes. OK.' She took a breath. 'There must have been a pod in here and they used it to escape.'

Matthew shook his head. 'Not necessarily. She had one of those bracelets on under her clothes. I expect she thought I wouldn't notice.'

'Well, yes,' said Mikey, surprised and guilty in equal measure. 'But let's not talk about that now.'

Once again, she considered wrestling open the control panel on her bracelet, and once again, she changed her mind. Perhaps it couldn't be opened if active. Like a washing machine door. The red light still flashed.

She shook her arm. 'You've frozen, haven't you? I should switch you off and on again. Except I don't dare. Are we going to stay like this forever? What happens when your power pack dies? Will we both just fade away?'

She pulled herself up. Don't think about that.

Jane was still talking. 'Why didn't you say something to her, Matthew? About the bracelet, I mean?'

For one reason or another, Matthew Farrell had always

walked softly through life. He'd learned the hard way never to draw attention to himself. This, coupled with a placid nature that calmly accepted whatever the world was throwing at him at the time, meant he very rarely lost his temper. Or needed to. Or even raised his voice in anger.

He didn't mean to now, but the last forty-eight hours had been rough. Something snapped within him. He rounded on Jane, anger and hurt and resentment bleeding into his voice.

'Because I don't have that sort of authority over her. Because I'm younger than her. Because she doesn't know how I feel. Because I don't have the words. Because I'm little. Because everyone thinks I'm stupid. And weird. Choose any or all of those.'

About to say even more, he pulled himself up. He'd never, ever shouted at Jane before. Her eyes had filled with tears. That was all he needed. Why was everyone so . . . ?

And then he took a deep breath. 'Jane . . . Jane, I'm sorry. I didn't mean . . .'

He stopped and scowled ferociously at the floor.

Mikey stared, open-mouthed.

There was a somewhat sticky silence. Jane and Luke looked at each other, then Jane reached out and gently rubbed Matthew's arm. 'It's all right, Matthew.'

'No,' he said, not meeting her eyes. 'It's not. I shouldn't have . . . Sorry, everyone.'

Luke said, 'Mate . . .' and left it at that.

Rossi cleared his throat. 'Can we please concentrate on the matter in hand?' He shook his head. 'I genuinely do not know how you people are still alive.' He paused. 'Don't take this the wrong way, anyone, but do you think they were in it together? Plimpton and Meiklejohn, I mean.'

'No,' said Matthew immediately.

Jane sighed. 'I wonder where they are now?'

'Here,' shouted Mikey. 'Right here. Bloody hell, how many more times?'

Luke interrupted. 'I don't know where they are now, but I bet I know where Henry Plimpton will be soon.'

'And where's that?'

Luke gestured around the generator room and the hangar outside. 'Back here. This – all of this – represents possibly years of work and colossal expense. He's not going to abandon it. Sooner or later – he'll be back. With reinforcements, probably.'

'Not necessarily,' said Matthew. 'It might all be set up to operate automatically and all he has to do is activate it. He might not even have to be physically here to do that.' He paused. 'He might not *want* to be physically here when it all kicks off. In which case, neither should we.'

'Should we evacuate?' said Rossi, glancing around.

Matthew shook his head. 'I don't think we should leave this lot unguarded. But what's it all for?'

'I don't know,' said Luke, worried. 'Let's hope Hansen brings back someone who does.'

## 34

Lt Grint, almost unconscious from the pain but still managing to protest at being removed from where all the action was taking place, had to be forcibly dragged off to MedCen by two burly medtecs who knew him of old. Hansen was commanded to accompany them. His protests joined with those of his team leader as they disappeared through the door to MedCen. Socko remained behind to report to the Senior Mech.

'Sir, I can't hang around here. Lt Varma has thrown a perimeter around the hangar but only Rossi and Two-Three-Six are still inside. Hansen has orders to report and liaise over the personnel and equipment necessary to deal with the situation. I've been ordered to return as soon as possible.'

The Senior Mech frowned. 'Who ordered this? Grint's out of action.'

'Parrish, sir.'

'Are you saying *Parrish* ordered you to . . .'

'Yes, sir. Now, if you don't mind . . .' He stepped back into the pod.

Thirty minutes later, Commander Hay was arming herself and issuing last-minute instructions to Captain Farenden.

'I'm taking Callen with me, so secure the building, Charlie. I won't have us caught out for a second time.'

'Ma'am . . .'

'Yes, I know what you're going to say but I really want to see what's going on in that hangar and I'm not going to be able to do that from here, am I?'

She hefted a medium-sized blaster over her shoulder and attached two sonics to her rip-grip patches.

'Ma'am . . .'

'Your protests are duly noted, Captain. If I don't return, you can make them in full at my memorial service.'

He sighed. 'Not protests, ma'am. Just a recommendation.'

'And what is that?'

'That you stay well behind Major Callen, ma'am. You could be entering a theatre of war. How easy would it be to engineer some sort of unfortunate accident?'

'I'm not going to inadvertently shoot Major Callen, if that's what you mean.'

'No, it wasn't, as you well know.'

She grinned at him, suddenly looking ten years younger. 'Don't worry about me, Charlie. I fought in the Time Wars.'

'So did he, ma'am.'

She started towards the door. 'This time I want the people who are running the show. I want to know what they know. Where the money comes from. How does this fit in with Site X and Shoreditch? I want intel. What I don't want are any unfortunate accidents occurring before I get the opportunity to speak to them.'

'Unfortunate accidents occurring to whom, ma'am?'

Hay checked her utility belt for string. 'Mind the shop while I'm gone.'

Captain Farenden sighed. 'Yes, ma'am.'

'Any update on Ellis and events at the Acropolis?'

'The situation is uncertain, ma'am. All personnel have evacuated. Those who can, anyway. But both Dr Maxwell and Major Ellis remain unaccounted for. Lt Chigozie is mustering rescue teams at this moment, ma'am.'

'Stay on top of that one while I'm gone, Charlie.'

'Yes, ma'am. Good luck.'

'I shall be back before you know it, when I shall expect a stiff drink as I regale you with tales of my exploits and derring-do.'

'Something for me to look forward to, ma'am.'

She strode swiftly from the room and the door closed behind her.

Sighing, Captain Farenden turned to Mrs Farnborough – still somewhat stunned, as many often were after an insight into the intimate workings of the Time Police. 'Can I organise you any refreshments, ma'am?'

Back at the hangar, Rossi was still covering the door while Luke worked his way clockwise around the generator room and Jane anti-clockwise. Neither of them had any idea what they were looking for so it was no surprise when they didn't find it. Watching him from the corner of her eye, Jane was convinced Luke was looking for evidence of Parrish Industries involvement. Matthew was still pottering around the generators.

Mikey was slumped on her chair, trying to think. The discarded hood lay at her feet nearby.

'Well,' said Luke as he and Jane met in the middle of the room. 'Henry Plimpton is Mr P. Who'd have thought? I certainly didn't.'

'Nor me.'

'Do you feel as stupid as I do?'

She sighed. 'More so, I think. I felt so sorry for him.'

'Made complete arses of ourselves over that one, didn't we?'

Jane nodded, gloomily.

Mikey lifted her head. 'Not exactly covering yourselves in glory now, are you?'

Luke forged on. 'Last time I play Mr Nice Guy, let me tell you. In fact, for me, the whole Time Police *shoot everyone on sight, raze the place to the ground, and then arrest their relatives unto the fourth and fifth generation* is beginning to have great appeal. How many people would still be alive if we'd just gunned down Henry Plimpton as soon as we clapped eyes on him and then gone home?'

'A very good question,' said Mikey, nodding. 'I think it's only fair to tell you I'm holding the three of you entirely to blame for this.'

Jane was struggling with new perspectives. 'So who blew up Beaver Avenue?'

'Henry,' said Luke. 'Got to be.'

'So what was in the delivery?'

Matthew shrugged. 'Could have been anything. As far as I could tell, he didn't bring anything with him into the pod. Could have been a box of explosives – could have been an innocent package.'

'He blew up his own house?'

'Why not? The whole house might have been riddled with explosives already wired and ready to detonate at a moment's notice. He didn't need his family –' he paused, thoughtfully, 'if indeed they were his family – any longer. He needed to cover his tracks, so he destroyed his previous life – completely – and has embarked upon a new one.'

They watched Matthew for a while and then Jane turned to Luke. 'That's just it, Luke – that's what's puzzling me. We arrested him. We took him back to TPHQ. Why would he let himself be arrested?'

Luke had resumed his inspection of the generator room again. Jane was unsure whether actually finding his dad's logo would make him more or less happy. He turned to look at her. 'What?'

'Well – why bring himself to our attention? He was nicely hidden in the 20th century – we hadn't a clue he even existed – and yet he did that stupid thing with the lottery ticket and suddenly we're all over him. Why would he do that?'

Luke stopped scanning the walls and stood still. Because that was a very good point. Matthew's footsteps sounded loud as he prowled around the generators. Jane stared at the floor, thinking. Everything Henry Plimpton did had been designed to mislead them. He wasn't a helpless henpecked husband. He wasn't a little man, harmlessly tinkering away in his garden shed. No, he wasn't, was he . . . ?

'It was deliberate,' she said, suddenly.

Luke looked up in surprise. 'How do you work that out?'

Jane turned to him. 'Ellis told us the Time Police had a tip-off from the public. Remember? Well, suppose *he* did it. Suppose he informed on himself. Or arranged it, anyway.'

Luke frowned. 'Why would he do that? He was lucky to escape imprisonment. We normally chuck away the key for that sort of thing. He could have spent the rest of his life banged up in one of our quality establishments.'

'But he didn't, did he, Luke? Because the Time Police thought he had more value as an informer. So we let him go.'

'But he couldn't know we'd do that. He could have gone to prison for years.' He paused and then said, 'We might even have had him executed.'

'It was a gamble – he took it and it paid off.'

'What – mild-mannered Henry?' said Luke. 'The brains behind Site X? And Shoreditch?' He gestured to the giant generators behind them. 'And all this?'

'Not so mild-mannered, Luke. He destroyed Beaver Avenue to cover his tracks. We thought he was dead, remember?'

Luke frowned. 'There's a question no one has asked yet.'

'What's that?'

'Who was shot?'

'What?'

'Well, if Henry's still alive, then who was shot? And by whom?'

Jane shrugged. 'Well, Henry, presumably.'

'But why?'

'To provide a fourth body, perhaps. Henry must have set it up. Mr Fernley said they found four bodies. Well, not four complete bodies, but bits from four different bodies.'

She was talking to herself now, pacing about to help herself think.

'The Time Police can't have taken the original tip-off seriously. Otherwise, they wouldn't have sent *us*. I should imagine Henry Plimpton had the three of us summed up the moment we walked through his door.'

'Wish we could return the compliment,' said Matthew,

bending to pick up a pair of pliers off the floor. 'He really played us, didn't he?'

Luke nodded reluctantly. 'I'm beginning to think he did. Soft-hearted Jane . . .' He gestured to Soft-hearted Jane, presumably to dispel any possible confusion as to whom he was referring. 'His sob story about wanting to provide for his family was just what would appeal to Jane. And then he thought the idea of easy money would appeal to me – did appeal to me, actually,' he added, remembering his foiled attempt to steal Henry's winning lottery ticket.

'What about me?' said Matthew.

'No one knows how *your* brain works,' said Luke, scathingly. 'Or even whether it works at all.'

Matthew scowled at him. 'This *oh my God, Matthew, you're alive, how wonderful* didn't last very long, did it?'

Luke grinned. 'Long enough.'

'I think I'm right,' said Jane. 'He must have grassed himself up to the Time Police.'

'All very well,' said Luke. 'But why? He could have continued to operate in perfect safety. Why would he bring himself to our attention like that?'

The enthusiastic discussion dwindled into thoughtful silence.

'Come on, idiots,' cried Mikey. 'Think it through.'

'Yes,' said Jane, thoughtfully. 'You'd have thought he'd want to avoid the Time Police like the plague, wouldn't you, and yet he deliberately engineered . . .' She tailed away. Team 236 collectively frowned.

'Because he wanted to be at TPHQ, obviously,' shouted Rossi from the door. 'Thickos.'

435

Mikey nodded, finding herself in unexpected agreement with a member of the Time Police.

Luke frowned. 'But why?'

The answer occurred to everyone at the same time. Everyone looked at everyone else, unwilling to put it into words.

'Someone at TPHQ is . . .'

'He's got someone . . .'

'He wanted to make contact with someone specific,' said Jane.

Luke nodded. 'Yes. Either to receive or pass on instructions.'

There was more silence.

It was Luke who said the unthinkable. 'Someone at TPHQ is working with or for Henry Plimpton. Mr P. Who?'

'I think we can assume none of us,' said Jane. 'We're just the pasties.'

'Patsies, sweetie,' said Bolshy Jane. 'But we know what you mean.'

Jane looked at Luke. 'Who could it be?'

'Well, not North. Nor Ellis.'

'Nor Hay,' said Matthew. 'Nor Farenden. Probably not Grint.'

'Not anyone in Two-Three-Five,' said Rossi, still in the doorway, memories of former teammate Alek Anders never that far away.

'Hang on,' said Luke. 'Hang on. We can't just go naming people we like. Anyway, it's probably someone we don't know. We don't know a lot of people in the Time Police. If it's anyone, it'll be one of them. Bound to be.'

They stood in silence.

'But what a risk to take,' said Jane. 'Suppose it hadn't been our team sent after him. Suppose it had been Sawney and his team.'

'Well,' said Luke thoughtfully. 'I expect they'd have roughed him up a bit – and his family as well – but presumably he was prepared to put up with all that to get back to TPHQ. To instruct or be instructed by his associate. Which brings us back to who that could be.'

'It could be anyone,' said Jane. 'Anyone who was on the premises at the time.'

'True,' said Luke, 'but so is the converse. How did he know the person he wanted wouldn't be out on a mission? That would have been a bit of a bugger, wouldn't it? He'd have gone through all that for nothing.'

'All right, who do we know was at TPHQ at the time?'

Luke began to count on his fingers. 'As the arresting officers, all of Two-Three-Six. Including North and Ellis. That's five.'

'The doctor who examined him,' said Jane. 'To make sure he was fit enough to withstand interrogation.'

'Six.'

'Varma – who conducted the preliminary interviews.'

'Seven.'

'Me,' said Rossi. 'In fact, all my team.'

Luke, already digitally challenged, ran out of fingers again.

'Farenden and Hay – obviously.'

'Clean-up Crew 29,' said Luke. 'Who were part of the mission with us.'

Their voices tailed away.

Luke frowned. 'No, no. Too many. Stop and think. The only thing of which he could be certain was that whoever arrested him, he'd be interviewed by someone from security. Whoever else's hands he passed through, he was always going to end up there.'

'Varma?' said Jane, incredulously. She lowered her voice, even though Varma was at least a hundred yards and two walls away. 'I don't believe it.'

Luke grinned at her. 'Still putting the sisterhood first, Jane?'

'Shut up. It's not Varma.'

'She interviewed him.'

Jane fell silent. That was true.

'No, she didn't,' said Matthew, dragging his attention away from the generators again to rejoin Planet Earth. 'I mean she did, but then she didn't.'

Luke sighed. 'Should I recommend you resit Module 21? Concise and accurate reporting?'

Matthew ignored him. 'Varma was the initial interviewing officer and then, when it was apparent Henry had some interesting things to say – he was transferred to Filbert.'

They contemplated that in silence.

'I'll tell you who it wasn't,' said Jane. 'Callen. Remember he was up north with his team. Recruiting.'

Still covering the doorway, Rossi spoke again.

'So all we need to do is consult the tapes and see who he spoke to alone.'

Luke shook his head. 'I suspect those tapes will have long since disappeared, but we'll try anyway. But if it's true, then at least we probably now know how Klein and Nuñez were betrayed.'

Jane shivered. 'The two agents we replaced?'

'Yeah. Hay's instincts were sound when she kept quiet about us, Jane. Otherwise we'd have gone the same way.'

Jane shivered. 'They were murdered.'

'They were still alive when they were tossed into the river,' said Luke grimly.

'Who would do something like that?' said Jane, almost to herself.

'Well, our Henry's just killed a street, so I think he's proved he has a ruthless streak bigger than he is.'

'No, I mean, who would betray their fellow officers? And Klein and Nuñez were tortured first. They were only grunts, just like us. That would be like me grassing up you two knowing you'd be killed.'

'Never mind all that,' shouted Mikey in frustration. 'None of it means anything if you can't shut all this down.' She tried to shake Matthew's arm and failed.

Luke was watching Matthew wander around the generator room. 'Henry Plimpton is a very clever man. A massively underestimated, clever man.'

Matthew looked at the giant machinery around them. 'I wonder . . .'

'Yes,' said Mikey, excited. 'What do you wonder, Matthew? Come on. Work it out.'

'Incoming,' shouted Rossi as two big pods materialised inside the hangar.

Team 236 sought cover and raised their weapons with a speed and efficiency that would have made Major Ellis quietly proud. And probably equally quietly astonished. Luke and Jane covered the door. Matthew hunkered down behind a generator.

'They're ours,' said Luke. 'Stand down, everyone.'

Two ramps crashed down, raising all the dust which had just begun to settle. Time Police officers roared into the hangar like the wrath of God. The wrath of several gods, actually, bristling with weapons and attitude, shouting instructions, ready to annihilate whatever was waiting for them.

'Impressive,' said Luke. 'Shame it's only us. Stand very still, everyone. A bit of a bugger if we were shot now. And by our own people.'

Officers now covered every point of the hangar.

'Good afternoon,' said Luke, strolling forwards. 'Welcome to the Plimpton House of Fun.'

Callen strode down the ramp with Commander Hay two paces behind him. Half a dozen mechs and IT personnel followed her out, obviously itching to get to grips with the contents of this hangar.

Callen halted. 'Report.'

Mikey inserted herself between Luke and Callen, nearly frantic with the need to make herself understood. 'Someone listen to me. I think you need to find the power supply and shut it down.'

Luke stepped up. 'Both the hangar and generator room are secure. They've been checked for IEDs and no more have been found, but we don't have any specialist equipment so that doesn't mean there aren't any.

'Present on site are Team Two-Three-Six and Officer Rossi from Two-Three-Five. Officer Scrape's body has been covered and moved to a quiet corner. The place seems to be powered by portable generators over there, which are, at present, not working.

'There are any number of unexamined boxes and crates, and four enormous what appear to be generators of some kind on the other side of that partition. Purpose as yet unknown. They appear to be inert. Officer Varma reports the external perimeter is secure. Awaiting instructions.'

'Good work, Parrish,' said Callen. 'Good work, all of you. Dal, Filbert – take a team and check out those doors, will you?' He stared over Luke's shoulder and his gaze sharpened. 'Who's that in there?'

'Farrell. Checking out the generators and speculating on their purpose.'

'Well, for God's sake, don't let him touch anything.'

The Senior Mech halted at the door into the generator room, acknowledging Matthew's presence with a nod. 'Any thoughts?'

'It's a lot of power,' said Matthew vaguely.

The Senior Mech nodded. 'It is, isn't it?'

'Yes, it bloody is,' shouted Mikey. 'Think about it. Why would he need so much power? Bloody Time Police – you're about as much use as a 2020 events planner. Think!'

Officers swarmed everywhere in the hangar. Matthew recognised one of Lt Fanboten's teams from IT, running diagnostics inside one of the pods – he must remember to ask how things had gone at the Acropolis. Partly to get out of the way, Jane and Luke joined him back in the generator room.

Looking around, it crossed Matthew's mind there must be the best part of thirty officers on site at the moment, all swarming over the hangar . . . doing their jobs . . . here . . . now . . .

Suppose . . .

If anything happened . . . if this hangar were to explode, for instance – then they'd have lost the commander of the Time Police, her second in command, and several of her most senior officers. And a good number of others as well, including vital

441

specialist staff. And probably the teams outside. Thirty officers in one go.

He stopped. Did Plimpton know Hay would turn up? Was this his plan? Cut off the head and watch the body writhe and die? Or was there a more sinister purpose to all this equipment?

It might be either. Or both. Or neither. He opened his mouth to utter a warning but that was the moment when they all ran out of Time.

Behind him, on the wall, something clunked. A giant hidden switch perhaps. The room was suddenly filled with a rising whine that hurt his ears. A big red light began to flash. Another flashed a response. And then another. As if they were talking to each other. There was a sound of giant machinery starting up . . .

Every officer froze on the spot and then—

'Back to your pods,' roared Callen. 'Dal – get everyone into their pods. Varma – something's switched itself on in here. Be ready to pull out in a hurry.'

Dal pointed. 'Sir – Commander Hay.'

Callen looked back to see Hay draw her gun and run, shouting, towards the generator room. Towards trouble. Because that's what Time Police officers do.

Callen swore beneath his breath. 'Leave this to me, Lieutenant. Get everyone else into the pods until we know what we're dealing with,' and set off after Hay, pushing his way through the last few officers racing towards the pods.

The whining roar increased to an uncomfortable pitch. The air around the generators began to ripple.

With all officers heading in the other direction, Major Callen came to a halt behind one of the metal pillars, adjusted the

442

settings on his blaster to the tightest beam possible, steadied his breathing, took careful aim, breathed out, and fired.

It was not an easy shot. The angle was all wrong, but he had no time. A narrow, white-hot stream of light seared past Hay's cheek. She fell across the threshold and the beam from Callen's weapon went on to impact the control panel on the first generator. Such was the intensity of the stream that within a very short space of time, a small square of metal began to glow red, spreading outwards, then orange, then white and then a whole panel began to bubble. Something shorted out.

Lights flashed wildly and for some reason, the lights on their long chains began to swing to and fro. Like pendulums, but every single one swung in a different direction.

The room was filled with the very nasty smell of burning chlorine. Sparks flew, crackling as they collided with each other. Over by the wall, a bank of equipment flashed umpteen red warning lights and then, with a bang, shorted itself out. Whining, the stricken generator began to emit black smoke. The other three, possibly in an effort to take up the slack, tried to increase their rate. Their noise rose to a shriek. Clouds of pungent smoke drifted across the generating room. A huge shower of bluey-purple sparks erupted vertically. Yellowish white droplets of burning metal dripped to the floor.

The Senior Mech bolted from the room. 'Team Two-Three-Six are in there. We need to get them out.'

Weapon raised, Callen started to move towards Commander Hay.

'Sir.'

He turned to find Lt Dal at his elbow. 'What?'

Dal was shouting over the noise. 'Sir, the mechs say the

room is kicking out some sort of invisible field. Our instruments are going haywire.'

Callen frowned. 'Smoke. Bring smoke.'

Dal disappeared.

As a younger boy, Matthew Farrell had spent a great deal of time in R&D at St Mary's. He was more than familiar with the smell of electricity going wrong. That burned-chlorine smell, sharp and bitter that irritated the throat, was a sure sign something hadn't gone quite according to plan. Rising over that came the pungent smell of fish, signifying the insulators had probably melted.

He could feel the static in the air. His hair stood out around his head, crackling. Lightning was arcing from one piece of equipment to another in an unbroken circle. There was a succession of small explosions. Something blew across the room and clattered across the floor. And then, with a crack that hurt his ears, some sort of shock wave radiated outwards, hitting him in the chest. He felt the vibration of it through his entire body. His teeth rattled in his head.

Imperceptibly, Time began to slow.

35

It should not be possible to stop Time. Not without involving the speed of light in some way. Time can be manipulated or bent, but to stop Time is a physical impossibility. Silence would fall. Forever. The earth would stop turning. There would be no cold, no heat, no light, no wind, no rain, no gravity – nothing. Forever. Time could never be restarted because who would be around to do it? Everything – the universe – would be frozen for eternity in this one moment. Except there would be no moment. And no eternity.

For Matthew – closest to the generators – this was a hundred, a thousand times worse than the Time-slip he'd experienced at Versailles. The world slowed even further. The dirty smoke ceased to swirl. He was in such pain. He couldn't move. His sight darkened. His thoughts fell apart. Time was slowing. He was dying . . . The world was ending . . .

Slowly, inexorably, the shock wave spread outwards. One tiny, invisible inch at a time, enveloping everything in its path.

Dal screeched to a halt in the doorway, his arms full of smoke canisters. Callen seized two, pulled the rings and tossed them into the generator room where the bright red smoke began to behave very oddly, swirling around an almost invisible disc of . . . something nearly, but not quite, solid spreading outwards from the generators.

Dal peered. 'What *is* that? Is it a Time-slip?'

The Senior Mech appeared at his elbow.

'Sir, this is much more than a Time-slip. We need to destroy this room and everything in it. Now. Before it's too late. While we still have a "now".'

Callen nodded, shouting. 'Varma?'

'Sir?'

'Situation critical. Cancel the evac. Get your people around the back of the hangar. Every weapon you've got. Take out the back wall and destroy whatever you find inside. Take it all out. We'll do the same from this side.'

She hesitated. 'Our people?'

He stood still for a moment, saying quietly, 'None of us are likely to get out of this alive, Varma. Our duty is to contain whatever is happening here. Everything else is unimportant. I'm sorry.'

There was a pause and then she said, 'Deploying my team now, sir,' and shut down her com.

He turned his head. 'Dal. Leave one person to mind the pod. Everyone else to me.'

He became aware of Hay struggling to get up. He pulled her to her feet. She leaned against the pillar, suddenly aware her face felt as if it were on fire.

'Get that seen to,' said Callen.

She blinked to try to clear her vision. 'Major? *You shot me.*'

'You were in my way.'

'And long may I continue to be so. Where are our people?'

'Most are safe. Some are still in there.'

446

She pushed herself off the pillar. 'Then we should . . .'

He caught her arm. 'It will make no difference, Marietta. We have to destroy this room before the field spreads beyond this building. I doubt any of us will survive. It might be kinder to leave them where they are. Beyond fear. Or pain.'

They both looked through the door.

It was like a scene from hell. Jane and Luke were not ten feet away, facing the door, frozen in the act of running. Caught in the moment forever. And then he could just make out – Luke's arm was moving. Reaching out towards them. Acrid red smoke eddied around them, rendering their lower bodies invisible, but they were still just on the very edge of the field. Saveable, perhaps.

The noise from the generators was increasing every second. Reaching the point of pain. Even though they were standing next to each other, Callen and Hay had to shout to make themselves heard.

'What's happening?' shouted Hay.

Callen was standing in the doorway, measuring distances and angles. 'We have to get them out.'

'Major?'

'I can assure you I haven't suddenly developed a compassionate streak, Commander. They're in our way. They're right in our line of fire and we, literally, don't have a second to waste.'

She frowned and then, apparently struck with an idea, she flicked open her baton. 'This will give us extra reach.'

'Excellent thought, Commander.'

Grasping the other end of her baton, he stepped into the generator room.

Catching hold of the jamb with one hand, Hay leaned into the room, arm and baton extended. Callen took a firm hold of her baton and extended his other arm out towards Luke.

'Some luck at last, Commander. Parrish has hold of Lockland. If I can move him, I might be able to move them both.'

He caught hold of Parrish's wrist as he spoke. It felt cool to his touch but firm enough. Tightening his grip, he began to pull. It was like trying to move a heavy weight under water. He strained harder. If he could just get them moving . . . work up some momentum. Every inch he could pull Parrish towards him would lessen the drag. They were both still wreathed in red smoke. Not yet within the disc itself. He pulled again, feeling his grasp slip on Hay's baton. She was leaning into the room. One side of her face was red and ridged – her eye almost completely closed. She must have been in considerable pain.

At her side, Dal was also reaching into the room. The Senior Mech was hanging on to his belt. If they all pulled together, they might get Parrish moving. They heaved. Battling Time itself as it rolled relentlessly towards them.

'Push,' shouted the Senior Mech. 'Push then pull. Jerk them free of their inertia. On three.'

With a sudden jolt – as if he'd just been pulled from quicksand – Luke emerged from the red smoke.

Dal reached past him for Lockland, now within his grasp. They heaved again. It would probably have been easier to pull half a dozen stubborn elephants backwards out of the mud. And then, suddenly, about eighteen inches away from them, Time finally let go and Lockland, Parrish, Hay, Callen, Grayling and the Senior Mech fell backwards into the safety – for the time being – of the hangar.

'No time to lie around,' shouted Callen. 'The field is still expanding. All officers to me. Destroy this room and everything in it.'

Varma's voice came over his com. 'Sir, Farrell is still inside.'

'That is a very great shame,' said Callen quietly, 'but carry out your orders, please.' He turned to the officers clustering around the door. 'Start with the generators in the middle. Tight beam. Shut them down. Two rows. Simultaneous fire. Execute.'

Two rows of four officers each knelt or stood in the doorway and opened fire. A crash and the sound of falling masonry in the distance indicated that Varma's team had successfully dealt with the back wall. He could hear her shouting to hold their fire.

'Varma – what's going on?'

'Sir, I can see Farrell. He's close enough for me to reach. We're going in now.'

'Get him out if you can, but your priority is to destroy this place. Link arms or use your batons. No one goes in alone. The field is expanding. One attempt only, Varma. Make it count.'

Matthew was floating in the cold and the dark. There was no pain. Nothing moved. Nothing worked. Everything was just nothing.

Taking care to avoid the field, Mikey was screaming at him to get up. 'Matthew, come on. You have to move.'

Grasping his arm, she tried to move him but he was a dead weight. She moved to his other end and scrabbled at his boot. For some reason this was easier. Further from the centre of the field perhaps.

Matthew Farrell was famed for being small and light. But not today.

449

She began to pull. Straining every muscle. Screaming through clenched teeth, 'Come on, damn you. Move.'

Matthew's foot moved perhaps a fraction of an inch.

A security officer nudged Varma. 'Did you see that?'

'Never mind that now. Can we reach him?'

'Nearly.'

Mikey strained again. 'Aaaagggh. Shit bugger bollocks, Matthew. Will you move?'

Clean-up Crew 29 perceived that their moment had come. Effortlessly heaving everyone aside, they organised them-selves – two at the front, each grasping a foot – two at the back to pull.

Grunting and straining, inch by inch, they pulled him to safety. That this involved dragging him, visor up, face down, over a pile of smoking rubble was simply unfortunate. They'd been instructed to pull him out and that was what they'd done. No one had said anything about gently. Someone winced. 'That's going to sting in the morning.'

Varma opened her com. 'We've got Farrell. Opening fire on the generators now.'

'Watch you don't hit us.'

'And the same to you, too, sir. Ready, team. On my mark. Fire.'

Streams of white-hot blaster fire converged on the centre of the room. Pyrotechnically speaking, it was a spectacular sight. There were multi-coloured flashes of light. More sparks. Green this time, so there was copper in there somewhere. Lighting arced. Small fires sprang up.

The lights, their bulbs long since extinguished, were still swinging erratically. Some in one direction, some in another.

Which surely should be impossible. One was rotating – anti-clockwise, Callen noted.

'Bugger,' shouted a security officer, ducking to avoid a spitting plume of plasma. 'I think I've just crossed the streams.'

Lt Dal shoved up his visor. 'Sir, it's not working. We can't touch them. There's no time for the beams to reach the generators – if that makes sense.'

Callen shouted to cease fire.

Mikey was kneeling beside Matthew, shouting and waving her arms. 'It's not enough to destroy the generators. You have to find the source of the power and shut it down. It's external, obviously, otherwise it would have stopped working by now. Why can't you bloody hear me? Bloody useless Time Police fire truck-wits . . . you never lift a finger until . . .'

She stopped suddenly. Just because they were a bit dim, there was no need for her to be as well. There were other forms of communication besides shouting.

The area was thick with dust. Could she . . . ? She tried to drag a finger through the dust. A few grains moved – as in a gentle breeze – but it wasn't enough. It would take too long. Her finger wasn't enough.

Struck by a sudden idea, she groped for Matthew's wrist. She could still touch him. She hadn't been able to drag him out but she could . . . she could lift a finger.

She lifted his hand. Not far – just an inch or so.

Around her, all shooting had ceased. Hot, sweating officers were taking a moment to catch their breath. It was very obvious none of their weapons were powerful enough to penetrate the Time Field. Varma glanced down at Matthew, stared for a moment and then groped for her com.

451

'Sir. Wait. Wait one.'

'What's happening, Varma?'

'I think Farrell's trying to tell us something.'

'He can speak?'

'No, sir.'

'Then how?'

'Sir, something's happening. Just give us a moment.'

Matthew's hand had lifted itself a couple of inches into the air. Somehow his forefinger extended itself.

'What the . . . ?' said someone, stepping back and losing his footing on the rubble.

'That's not spooky at all,' said someone else. 'I always said he was weird.'

Matthew's finger was pushing its way through the dirt and dust.

'Is he trying to write something?'

'No . . . no, he's drawing. It looks like . . . the letter A.'

Infinitely slowly, Matthew's finger pushed another shape into the dirt.

Heads bent. 'No, it's a triangle.'

'Wait. There's another. What is it? A propeller?'

'For God's sake,' shouted Mikey. 'Have you any idea what bloody hard work this is? Find someone with a brain cell, will you?'

Callen was losing patience. 'What the fire truck's going on there, Varma? Report.'

'Sir . . . a bit weird . . . Farrell's out cold but his hand is moving itself.'

'It's Farrell, Varma – that hardly rates on his scale of weirdness. What's he doing?'

'Drawing in the dust, sir. A triangle, I think, with . . .' she twisted her head, 'triangles inside it. Meeting in the middle. I don't understand. Is it a foreign language? Cuneiform?'

'Flash it to my scratchpad.'

A second later, his scratchpad lit up and there was Matthew's finger, wobbling away as Mikey struggled to achieve the third inner triangle.

Officer Rossi found himself shoved sideways. The Senior Mech grabbed the scratchpad out of Callen's hand. 'I know what this is.' He showed it to one of his team. 'What do you see?'

The officer squinted. 'If I didn't know better, sir, I'd say it was the symbol for a radhaz threat alert.'

'Shit. An external nuclear power source,' whispered the Senior Mech. Callen turned to him. 'You heard – get out there and find it.'

Dal stared at him. 'Nuclear power? In 1902?'

'That's why it should be easy to find. If we can shut that down, then surely all this should go away. Shouldn't it?'

The Senior Mech said nothing in a very particular way.

'Just do what you can.'

'Yes, sir. Open the pod bay doors, Dal. This way, lads.'

The Senior Mech and his team departed through the loading bay doors. There was the very briefest glimpse of the nearly completed Sacré-Cœur Basilica high above the city on the Butte Montmartre, dramatically silhouetted against the moonlit clouds, and then the doors slammed shut again. Callen stared into the generator room. Red smoke swirled through the door, pushed outwards by the ever-expanding field. So far, the field was contained within the hangar, but for how much longer?

Callen sighed. 'All right, we all know what we have to do. Two rows – as before. We have to rupture that field. Everyone aim at the same spot. Keep firing until either it's dead or we are. Stay out of the field. Be prepared to keep moving backwards. On my mark.'

He turned to Commander Hay. 'Commander, you should return to the pod. No arguments.'

She scrambled clumsily to her feet. 'And no compliance, Major. I shan't be making my way back to the pod.'

He looked at her sharply. 'Are you badly hurt?'

'No, but unfortunately, I do seem to be almost completely blind.'

## 36

If Major Callen felt guilt or regret, nothing showed in his face. Guilt and regret never featured regularly in the Time Police emotional spectrum. Not on the outside, anyway.

'Then stay out of the way, Commander. Things are about to get rough.'

'You should get the pods out of here, Major. If that lot next door goes up, they could be caught in the blast – which won't do Paris any good – and if we don't manage to destroy the power source and they're caught in the field, then we'll have even more problems.'

'Agreed, Commander, but I need everyone here. Destroying the generator room is our first priority, which is why I want to send you back to safety with Lockland and Parrish.'

'You're not sending me anywhere, Major. Just point me in the right direction.'

The Senior Mech's voice came over the com. 'Sir, we've found it.'

Callen paused. 'That was quick.'

The Senior Mech replied in the tone of voice he kept for the technically uninitiated. Which, in his opinion, was ninety-eight per cent of the world's population and one hundred per cent of officers who weren't actually in his department. 'Locating a nuclear reactor in 1902 is not hard, sir.'

'Can you shut it down?'

The mech allowed an edge to creep into his voice. 'I probably could, given the right facilities, tools and personnel, but at this precise moment . . .' His voice tailed away.

'Can it be moved?'

'It's one of the old SSTAR types – small, sealed, transportable, autonomous reactors – God knows where Plimpton got it from. It's about thirty feet by six, so theoretically, yes.'

'Practically?'

'No.'

Callen swore.

'They're deliberately designed to be tamper-proof – to prevent naughty people stealing the plutonium, sir. Moving it will be a specialist job.'

'Suggestions?'

'I take my team and we try to shut it down.'

'Can you?'

'I don't think so, Major, but I'm out of options and so are you.'

'If we destroy the field in here – what will happen to the reactor?'

'In a perfect world, the fail-safe will cut in and it *should* shut itself down automatically.

'Will it?'

'God knows, sir. If anyone has any bright ideas, I'm very open to suggestions.'

'We have no choice, Senior. A nuclear explosion could be the least of Paris's problems. Do it. That's an order. We'll deal with things here. You deal with things there.'

'Yes, sir.'

Callen turned his attention back to the problems at his end. 'Varma – do you copy?'

'Yes.'

'We're going to hit the field with everything we've got. You do the same from your side. If you've got grenades, then use them. Keep at it until either it's destroyed or we are. Keep your com open.'

He could hear her instructing her team. Turning to Hay, he said, 'Commander, I'm holding you in reserve. Along with Lockland and Parrish. If we fail, you should get back to TPHQ and . . .' He stopped.

Jane and Luke, as white and gasping as landed fish, sprawled against a couple of shattered crates.

Callen bent over them. 'Situation critical. You have your instructions. Do you copy?'

Luke made a series of uncoordinated movements. 'Red sliver functioning problem that have women right hesitate,' he croaked, maintaining to the end of his days that he'd actually said, 'We'll wait for Matthew. We've lost him once this week. Don't want to do that again.'

'Get me up, Major, and point me at the problem.'

'Commander . . .'

'That's an order, Major.'

He propped her against a pillar.

'Just aim at the glow, Commander. All right. Let's get this done.'

As before, two rows of officers stood and knelt in the doorway.

Callen issued his instructions. 'Don't stop. That field must be

457

destroyed. When it gets too close, retreat in an orderly fashion, regroup and resume. Pick your target. Ready? Fire.'

They poured their firepower into the room.

Such equipment not protected by the field exploded instantly. Two of the generators were running red hot. The heat was intense. The air danced and rippled around them. Sparks flew in all directions. At the other end of the building, Varma and her team were rolling in grenades and all the time, inch by inch, the field was expanding. Every moment decreased their chances of destroying it.

'Pull back. Everyone pull back.'

A kneeling officer fell forwards.

'Leave him,' yelled Callen. 'Back two paces.' They shuffled backwards.

The generator room was a spectacular sound and light show. Flashes of eye-searing light coupled with the whine of deeply unhappy equipment.

Another officer went down.

Varma, shouting to her team to pull back, was suddenly cut off mid-word. They could only assume she and her team had been overwhelmed.

'Back,' shouted Callen. 'Back two paces. Keep firing.'

On the end of the front row, Socko crumpled to the ground. A second later, Rossi followed suit.

Callen was shouting to Varma. There was no response.

And then something kicked him in the chest. For a moment, he swayed. The heat and noise receded . . .

Hay shouldered her smoking weapon and turned to Luke and Jane. 'On your feet, officers. We're up.'

She doubted they heard her over the screaming generators,

458

far less understood her. Groping, she hauled Parrish to his feet, put a gun in his hand and prayed that such instincts as he'd managed to absorb during his time in the Time Police would take over.

Jane struggled to her feet, not entirely comprehending what was happening, but everyone else was getting up and who was she to argue. Around them, the building was vibrating. Dust rained down from the ceiling. The iron girders groaned with the strain. She found Luke standing alongside her, although whether he was aware of the fact was unknown. Jane was careful to ensure both their guns were pointing into the red haze of the generator room. Half the floor seemed to have melted away but still the generators thundered on.

'Fire at the field,' shouted Hay. 'Bring it down.'

Squinting, Jane raised her gun. Not too difficult. Just aim at the glowing red metallic heart.

She heard Luke open fire, dropped her visor and followed suit. They would keep firing until their weapons were completely discharged. And then what would they do? Throw rocks?

Streams of white light crossed in all directions. Everyone was past caring.

The heat was intense. How much longer could they last?

They all heard it at the same time. The Senior Mech's voice in their ears. 'Reactor down. I say again – reactor down. Keep firing.'

There was an ear-splitting crack and bang. Without warning, the strange disc expanded so rapidly there was no chance to avoid it. The leading edge of the blast wave, pushing pressure ahead of it, knocked those few officers still on their feet to the floor.

459

Jane felt the second and the third waves pass. Her ears popped painfully. Nausea overwhelmed her. She curled into a ball, clutching her chest. The pressure waves passed through the warehouse, spreading outwards as they went. On their way to encompass all of Paris. And then they were gone.

Bereft of power, the generators' roar dropped to a whine. Then a drone. Then a clank. Then silence. The flames were dying. Blown out by the blast wave, perhaps. People lay like felled trees. Walls had fallen down, giving them glimpses of the outside world. At some point, and completely unnoticed, darkness had fallen.

Silence lay heavy. Apart from the incessant tink-tink of hugely overheated metal.

For a moment the only thing moving was the slowly swirling smoke. Long, long seconds passed. And then, slowly, warily, Rossi lifted his head. Then Dal. Then another. Someone groaned. Someone else was throwing up. Slowly, stiffly, officers began to pick themselves up. All were unsteady on their feet.

The hangar was wrecked. Two walls of the former generator room were barely standing. A tangled mass of glowing metal at the bottom of a shallow crater was all that remained.

Officer Varma and her team had been thrown backwards. They lay among the rubble. Groaning, a member of Clean-up Crew 29 lifted his head, pushed a piece of burning wood off his chest and stood up. Shaking his head, he began to pull his colleagues to their feet.

Callen lay face downwards, half hidden by the rubble.

Commander Hay sat up. Her hands shaking, she holstered her gun and opened her com. 'Varma – report.'

Varma coughed dust and spat, slurring her response. 'Shaken but not stirred, ma'am.'

'Soon as you can, start picking up the wounded. Senior – we need you back here for a safety check.'

'Copy that, ma'am.'

'How did you shut down the reactor?'

'We didn't.'

She blinked and struggled to comprehend. 'Then how . . . ?'

'We shot at it. The fail-safe is designed to prevent exactly that sort of thing. Realising it was under attack, it cut in and performed an emergency stop. We shouldn't leave it too long, though. We need to get some specialists here asap.'

Callen groaned, stirred and rolled over, shedding bricks and rubble. Coughing, he sat up and then used a pillar to pull himself to his feet and look around. Henry Plimpton's hangar was wrecked. Dust. Smoke. Debris. Small fires. Wreckage everywhere. The traditional smoking crater.

He nodded in satisfaction.

Jane opened her eyes and gazed around her. She was in a pod. How had that happened? What was going on? She lifted her hand and stared at it, giddy and disoriented. Her thoughts felt sluggish. The last thing she remembered was talking about . . . about . . . no – it was gone. She could see Hay opposite, propped against a wall with a wound dressing across half her face. Luke lay beside her. Someone had put him in the recovery position. They were bringing in Matthew. His face was a mess. What could be seen of it through the dirt and blood was very pale. Surely he couldn't be dead again.

The doctor bent over her. 'Went always too pies,' she said, gesturing at Matthew. 'Distracted lives the not hands?'

He grinned at her. She stared back, completely confused.

461

He turned to Callen, sitting nearby. 'I've told everyone not to try and speak,' he said. 'You've all been exposed to some kind of Time Field. You're recovering but we won't move you just yet. Like equalising pressures for a diver.'

'Rat tiles on half tree perimeter the,' said Callen, who knew this hadn't happened to him and that he was making perfect sense.

The doctor patted him gently on the shoulder and moved on to tend the other wounded.

Callen looked at Jane. 'John attempt whole are discovers?'

Thoroughly disoriented but desperate not to seem rude, Jane turned her head and vomited all over him.

At exactly the same time, over two thousand years ago, Major Ellis lay curled in a tight ball, genuinely expecting each second to be his last.

It seemed to take a very long time for the echoes of the explosion to die away. Clods of mud, splinters of wood and small rocks were plummeting all around the Acropolis. Ellis lay waiting for the much bigger explosion that would end his life. The one that would rip the sky apart – and possibly Athens itself.

After a while, it dawned on him that he'd had rather a lot of last seconds. Very slowly, he uncurled himself, rolled on to his back and looked up at the sky. All he could see was an ocean of darkness and several smudgy yellow blurs he rather thought might be stars. Or they were small fires and for some reason he was upside down. Which, given how he felt, was perfectly possible.

The repeated staccato noise he could hear resolved itself into several hundred dogs all barking their heads off in the city below.

Slowly, achingly, he lifted his head. It wasn't the first explosion he'd been involved in – it certainly wouldn't be his last, either – but they never got any easier. Or perhaps he was just too old for this sort of thing. He should retire and grow something. Something that didn't grow very quickly or require a lot of effort. Grapes, for instance. He could sit in the sun and watch them ripen and then he could sit in the shade and drink them. With Celia, perhaps. Yes – a good plan. He'd get on it immediately. Just as soon as his body reported for duty again.

Rather astonishingly, Ellis found both his arms. And they were still attached. And, as far as he could tell, he still had both legs, too. This was going well. He could see – admittedly not brilliantly, but he could see. And hear. Although ditto with the not very well. He lifted what he thought might be his right arm and waved it vaguely in front of his eyes. Yes, that definitely looked like one of his.

All at once, his fingers were seized and a voice that was, at one and the same time, both very close and a long way off, said, 'Matthew? Sir? Major Ellis?'

'I think that's me,' he said vaguely.

The voice spoke urgently. 'Can you sit up, sir? We have to leave now. They've turned out the city guard. There are a lot of people on their way. We really have to get out of here *now*.'

Other arms seized him and hauled him to his feet. He staggered a little, blinking to clear his eyes. He'd obviously been thrown some distance. Which might have saved his life.

He shook his head to clear it. He'd been very lucky. Amazingly lucky. The detonation had obviously set off all the other concealed devices and every single one of them had failed to kill him. A number of small craters had been carved out of the ground and smoke and dirt still hung in the air.

Of the pod there was no sign, but the Acropolis seemed

464

intact. Big lumps of building still stood dark against the sky, surrounded by tangles of wooden scaffolding. Certainly not much worse than when they'd arrived. Of Dr Maxwell there was also no sign.

He tried to pull his thoughts together. 'Did she get away?'

No one answered.

'We should search the area.'

'No time,' said a shape that resolved itself into Officer North. 'I can see lights approaching. Get the major into the pod.'

'Max?'

'I'm sorry, Matthew. I don't think she made it.'

'She must have,' he said, desperately. 'If the IED had got her, then there would at least be something left. She'll be back at TPHQ. Where we programmed the . . . the . . . thing to take her.' He shook his head, unable to remember the word for bracelet.

The silence spoke volumes.

'Isn't she there?'

'Not that we are aware of, sir, and it's been several hours.'

'She must be.'

Silence again.

'Well, it's Maxwell,' he said, wondering who he was trying to convince. 'She'll turn up.'

'Sir, there's been no sign of her.' He heard her swallow before continuing. 'We're forced to conclude that the IED killed her and the explosion caused the bracelet to malfunction and take her body off somewhere else. Or that the bracelet activated itself and killed her, again taking the body elsewhere. Or that she was caught in the pod slipstream and was killed when it jumped. I'm sorry, sir, but there is no scenario in which she survived. She's gone.'

Lights were showing among the colonnades in the Propylaea. North spoke to the two officers holding Ellis up. 'Back to the pod. We need to leave now.'

They landed back in the Pod Bay, which was almost deserted.

'Where is everyone?' demanded North.

A harassed-looking mech stepped out from behind another pod. 'The Senior Mech and all available people have gone with Commander Hay and Major Callen.'

'Team Two-Three-Six?' slurred Ellis.

'No knowledge, sir. They're not back yet.' He paused. 'There have been casualties. Scrape didn't make it and Lt Grint's badly injured.'

'Who's in charge there?'

'Parrish – until Hay takes over.'

Well, that settled it. He'd been blown into an alternative universe. These things happen. Ellis tried to inform Officer North of this fact and found, to his surprise, that he was in MedCen. Without passing Go or collecting two hundred pounds. How had that happened? *When* had that happened?

'Impressive work,' he said to North, who, on closer inspection, turned out to be a grinning medtech.

Deciding that the world had suddenly become far too complex for him to deal with at the moment, he closed his eyes.

38

MedCen was packed. Every officer who had been in Paris required medical treatment, together with Major Ellis from the Acropolis assignment. Every single cubicle was full. Despite their successes, the mood at TPHQ was subdued.

In the separate room to which her rank entitled her, Commander Hay was reclining on her pillows in the manner approved for patients everywhere, but with her arms folded and the sort of expression that conveyed very clearly that this state of affairs could not be expected to last much longer.

The doctor was reading through his notes and saying nothing.

She cleared her throat. 'Well, doctor?'

'Lt Grint has suffered burns to his chest but will recover. Those affected by the Time Field are recovering well. Everything else is minor.'

'Good. When can I expect to be discharged?'

'Subject to satisfactory test results, ma'am, this afternoon, probably. I just want to check your eyes again.'

He pulled out his penlight and began to examine the eye on the damaged side of her face. 'Look at the light, please. Now up. Now down. And again. Thank you.'

He flicked the light away and then back again. 'To the left. And to the right. Thank you.'

He switched off his penlight and stuffed it away in a pocket.

'My eye isn't getting any better, is it?'

'No, ma'am, but we didn't expect it to, did we? And the damage from the blaster fire hasn't helped at all. Your sight – in that one eye – has been failing for some time.'

'So, what's the treatment now?'

He rummaged in his pocket and pulled out a pair of spectacles.

Commander Hay regarded them with a distinct lack of enthusiasm. 'No.'

'Ma'am, we've done what we can with laser treatment. These will help for a little while.'

'But it's not a permanent solution, is it?'

'Probably not, no. Try them on.'

She put on the spectacles and looked about her.

'Better?' enquired the doctor.

Commander Hay said grudgingly, 'A little. Why can't I have lenses?'

'Your eyes are not suitable. Well, one isn't, and that's the one causing the problems, so no lenses.'

'No one here wears glasses.'

'Then once again, ma'am, you are leading the way. As we have all come to expect of you.'

He held out his hand for the glasses. 'These are not your prescription, of course. I'll need to give you a full eye test and so forth. Fortunately, there's nothing wrong with your other eye but wearing spectacles will lessen its burden.'

'For a while.'

'For a while, yes.'

'And then what?'

'And then we think of something else. In the meantime, I have a very good friend at Moorfields Ocular Technology Research Centre to whom I shall refer you. The whole thing can be dealt with away from TPHQ, and although it pains me to lessen my own prestige – she's better at eyes than me. I'm always more comfortable with the traditional gushing blood and missing limbs.'

There was a short pause.

'Thank you, doctor.'

'Thank you, ma'am.'

He left.

His place was taken by Captain Farenden who sat down next to Hay's bed. 'I know the tradition is for me to be injured and you to hang threateningly over my sickbed making non-veiled threats to encourage my recovery, ma'am, but on this occasion, the boot seems to be on the other foot.'

'I'm fine, Charlie.'

'Yes, ma'am.'

'I promise you, I'm fine.'

'In that case, ma'am, with my worst fears allayed, I shall depart.'

'Not before you've updated me on what's happening.'

'There are countless minor injuries, ma'am, but Officer Scrape was the only fatality.'

'And Max, of course.'

'Yes, I'm sorry. And Dr Maxwell.'

'I shall have to speak to Officer Farrell.'

Farenden shook his head. 'He really hasn't had a good week, has he?'

'No. And I'm going to have to face his father, as well.' She sighed. 'Right. What else? What's the damage to Paris?'

'Well, fortunately we already had a clean-up crew on site. It was the middle of a very cold night. All sensible citizens were in bed, so Paris was able to gain a pile of smoking rubble with a mild radiation signature without knowing anything about it.'

He paused.

'You're wearing your bad news face, Charlie. Go on.'

'The temporal shock waves, ma'am.'

'One of the after-effects of the explosion?'

'Yes. There was nothing we could do about them.'

'I'm not holding anyone to blame, Charlie. I think we all got off quite lightly.'

'Not so the citizens of Paris, ma'am.'

She sighed. 'What is it about Paris? Is there something in the area that renders them particularly prone to Time-slips and the like? Or do they suffer more than their fair share of unbalanced nutters trying to manipulate Time or save Marie Antoinette or whatever? Do you remember that lunatic who thought he could change the outcome of the St Bartholomew's Day Massacre?'

'Vividly, ma'am, but we were successful on that occasion. This time, sadly, slightly less so.'

She sighed. 'We're the Time Police, Charlie, but even we can't change the laws of physics.'

'No. Unfortunately. Although something to work on in the future, perhaps?'

Hay nodded thoughtfully. 'I have had some thoughts in that area, but carry on.'

'Well – it would appear the effects of the shock wave had

470

an unfortunate effect on nearly all the pendulum clocks in the city. Every one of them stopped at 0102.'

'Every single one?'

'Including one that runs on the Earth's gravitational rotation, ma'am.'

'Good God – whatever did we do?'

'No one's quite sure. But the effects were temporary – they're all working again. Unfortunately, many people woke the next morning feeling extremely unwell, but no one died. So good news there.'

'And no sign of Henry himself? Or the wretched Meiklejohn girl?'

'None at all. They could be anywhere. I can, if you wish, organise a search . . .'

'No. Waste of time. Plimpton will surface soon enough and we'll have him then. And pass this down, Charlie – I know I usually bang on about taking illegals alive and the value of intel, but somehow, in the case of Henry Plimpton, I find myself less enthusiastic. Let's embrace the old ways just for once. Shoot the bastard on sight, Charlie. I'll sign the order.'

'Yes, ma'am.' Farenden stood up. 'I'll go and do the paperwork now and allow you to continue your recovery. And you have another visitor.'

Hay looked around and silently groaned. Major Callen was approaching.

'I shall leave you now, ma'am. Please try not to kill him.'

'I make no promises.'

Captain Farenden departed. Major Callen arrived. 'Commander.'

'Major.'

'You've been in the wars again.'

'*You shot me.*'

'I regret to be obliged to correct my commanding officer, but I did not. I shot at the control panel.'

'Hitting me in the process.'

'That is a very narrow view of events, Commander. I was able to damage one of the generators . . .'

'Which set them all off . . .'

'Which weakened them sufficiently to enable us to avert major temporal catastrophe. To hit the generator and miss you completely required a level of skill I do not feel is being adequately recognised.'

'You didn't miss me.'

'My apologies, Commander. You may be certain I will do better next time.'

'Let us hope that next time the circumstances are not reversed. It is very possible, since I am not nearly as good a shot as you, Major, that I would not miss at all.'

'Do not reproach yourself, Commander. No one is as good a shot as I.' He regarded her face with its shiny medical-plastic coating. 'Your face again.'

'Yes, I think my face is rather fed up with me. I've not treated it well.'

There was a very long pause and then he cleared his throat. 'Actually, Marietta, I think your face is beautiful. I cannot think of anything that gives me such joy. To see your face once every day is all I ever ask.'

Between shock, surprise, her natural lack of expression and the restrictive properties of medical plastic, Commander Hay's face remained impassive.

472

Callen smiled slightly. 'Having robbed you of speech – much as your lovely face does to me every time I see it – I shall take myself away. Before the delightfully loyal Charlie Farenden comes back and does me an injury. Get well soon, Marietta.'

He touched her hand very briefly and then departed.

The next day, and in another part of MedCen, a slightly wobbly Jane was visiting Lt Grint to enquire after his injuries. Expecting the worst, she had tiptoed into his cubicle, only to find him sitting up in bed, wearing a hefty body bandage and steadily working his way through a very large and unhealthy breakfast.

Surprise and relief led to her bursting into tears. Much to the consternation of both of them.

Collapsing into the visitor's chair, she buried her head in his bedcovers and Grint stopped eating to regard her with helpless dismay.

The doctor, sticking his head into the cubicle to ascertain the source of all the noise, gave Grint to understand – in surprisingly articulate gestures – that this was his responsibility to deal with and to be quick about it.

Staring down at the back of her sobbing head, Grint made a massive effort.

'Um . . .' He gritted his teeth. '. . . Jane . . .'

He'd used her name and the sky had not fallen. Encouraged, he tentatively patted the nearest shoulder.

Nothing happened. Greater effort was obviously required. The Time Police do *not* have a procedure for this sort of thing. Time to improvise. He ran swiftly through the resources at his disposal and made a tactical decision.

'Um . . . Jane . . . would you like some bacon?'

The doctor rolled his eyes in a *seriously?* gesture and withdrew, possibly in search of less hopeless patients.

From her extensive reading, Jane was aware that heroines spurned food at every opportunity, wafting waiflike through the pages of their improbable adventures, but as Luke frequently reminded her, Jane was not heroine material. Besides, this was Grint and it was very possible that offering up a portion of his breakfast constituted a major step forward in their relationship.

She sniffed, wiped her nose on her sleeve, smiled at him and tentatively accepted a crisply grilled rasher of bacon.

Alas, from this promising beginning, neither of them was quite sure what to do next. But, decided Grint, resuming his interrupted meal, they would at least be facing the future on full stomachs.

Downstairs in the atrium, Raymond Parrish was demanding to see Officer Parrish. The duty officer stared at him expressionlessly and then stepped aside to open his com.

'Major Callen, sir. Raymond Parrish is here requesting an interview with Officer Parrish.'

On his way back to his office, Callen slowed and frowned. 'Permission granted.'

He pushed his way through the doors and set off across the atrium, ostensibly heading for the lift, just as Raymond Parrish was turning aside to await his son. For a moment their eyes met and then Raymond Parrish's gaze drifted casually across the atrium and Major Callen continued on his way.

Three minutes later, Luke appeared.

'Dad?'

'Luke. I wonder if I might have a few minutes of your time.'

474

'I expect so.' He turned to the officer in charge. 'Is there an interview room free?'

'Number 6.'

'Thank you. This way.'

Number 6 was small and featureless – the whole point being not to distract members of the public from whatever damaging admissions they could be persuaded to make.

This one was painted in the bog-standard grey. The more exciting interview rooms were done out in beige – the thinking being that this additional visual impact would stimulate wrong-doers to an immediate confession. The jury was still out on the effectiveness of this brave new idea in the world of Time Police interior design.

In short, these were the rooms where members of the public – public-spirited members of the . . . er . . . public – came to grass up their nearest and dearest and claim the reward.

The subsequently arrested nearest and dearest, however, would find themselves being entertained in a completely different suite of rooms in a completely different part of the building where none of the walls – nor the floors or ceilings – benefitted from the traditional Time Police grey or beige. In fact, they weren't painted at all. It was rumoured no paint in the world could cover those stains and so no one bothered.

'I'm sorry it's not as opulent as your place,' said Luke, waving his father to the seat opposite.

'It is of no matter,' said Raymond Parrish, making himself comfortable. 'I have some news and a confession to make.'

Luke regarded his father warily. 'Should I call for an additional officer?'

'That is your decision.'

475

'I should inform you this interview is being recorded.'

'I have no objection.'

'And you are making this confession of your own free will?'

'I am.'

'Then proceed.'

'I have news. Eric Portman was found dead in his apartment this morning. You should be aware he has, apparently, taken his own life. I have no knowledge of how this news has been received by the Portmans but it seems safe to assume they will not be happy.'

There was a long pause and then Luke said very carefully, 'Are you confessing to killing him?'

'No. I am confessing to a course of action of which you may not approve.'

Luke felt his blood turn cold. 'Which was?'

'I will come to that. First things first. For over a year now, I have suspected that I and my company were being set up. Used as a shield. Lately I have become convinced of it and so I began my own investigations.'

'Did you inform the Time Police of these investigations?'

'No.'

'Why not?'

'Because I wanted a free hand. Because – and I suspect you might already have some suspicions in this area – your organisation is not as secure as it might be. So I embarked upon a little private enterprise.'

'And did this enterprise yield fruit?'

'Initially no, so without troubling the Time Police, I went on to employ people who possessed skills I do not and instructed them to investigate further.'

'And then, of course, you had your spot of bother at Site X, and as part of my cooperation with the Time Police, I searched our records – well, I commanded our records to be searched – and nowhere could I find a single order relating to Site X or the facility at Shoreditch that seemed anything other than innocent, so I asked my specialists to investigate further.

'It would appear that orders were channelled through five apparently minor companies over a period of about eighteen months. My people investigated the companies and at least three of them have been traced back to an organisation not unconnected to Portman and Webber. My theory – take it or leave it – is that there has been a deliberate attempt to frame Parrish Industries. I really should send them my compliments. It very nearly worked. Even my own son believed I was implicated in some very unsavoury activities.'

Luke ignored this. 'So who did kill Eric Portman?'

'Well, I haven't completely closed the door on the Portmans themselves, but that might be wishful thinking on my part. Honestly compels me to admit that at the moment, I have no idea.'

'Then why are you here?'

'I told you. I have a confession to make.'

'Wasn't that it?'

'No.'

Luke swallowed. 'Go on.'

'You came to my house – our house – looking for news of Birgitte von Essendorf.'

'You've found her?'

'I never lost her. I had Ms von Essendorf and her wife removed from their place of residence not two hours after your visit to Glasgow earlier this year.'

Luke stiffened in his seat. 'What?'

Raymond Parrish waved a hand. 'They are, at this very moment, cruising through the Suez Canal on their way to India. And before you leap to your feet in alarm and condemnation, it was for their own safety. You were asking awkward questions and not being particularly discreet about it and they were living outside my sphere of protection. And again, before you indulge in overhasty comments on my high-handedness, I should perhaps inform you there was a small electrical fire at their home some twelve hours after their unobtrusive departure. Thanks to prompt action by someone whose timely appearance on the scene was not a coincidence, the damage was minimal. For your peace of mind, but not for public consumption, Ms von Essendorf and her wife are enjoying an all-expenses-paid trip through the Mediterranean and then, ultimately, on to Hong Kong where they will spend a month or so as the guests of Sally Yang and Parrish Industries.'

He smiled slightly at Luke's speechlessness. 'Voluntarily, I assure you.'

Luke continued with the speechlessness theme.

His father smiled. 'Shall I give you a moment to adjust your mindset?'

Luke swallowed. 'When Jane and I were at Site X, we heard someone say they took their instructions from Mr P. With that and your stupid logo everywhere, I really thought that was you. Everyone did.'

'As they were supposed to, Luke.'

'And now it's turned out to be a bloke called Henry Plimpton.'

His father nodded. 'So I had heard.'

'We don't know where he is. He might be dead. And now you tell me Eric Portman's dead, as well. One moment we're swamped in Mr Ps and now it would seem there's only you left.'

'I have frequently found that I am the last man standing, Luke.'

'You might be the last member of an endangered species.'

'As you say.'

'Well,' said Luke, getting to his feet. 'In that case you'd better take care.'

Raymond Parrish stood up. 'I always do. It's the reason I have lasted this long. In a completely unrelated matter, I was wondering if you would care to join me for dinner sometime next month. And Officers Lockland and Farrell as well. Two intelligent and resourceful young people who have, nevertheless, decided that you are their friend.'

Luke hesitated. 'Matthew has recently suffered a bereavement.'

'That is unfortunate but if he feels able to join us, I shall be delighted to renew my acquaintanceship with him.'

Luke grinned at his father. 'You mean I am only socially acceptable if I bring Jane and Matthew with me.'

'Well, obviously, I was trying very hard not to say so, but since you mention it – yes.'

Luke paused for a moment and then, with the air of one stepping into the unknown, said, 'Next month then.'

Raymond Parrish held out his hand. 'I shall look forward to it.'

Matthew's facial injuries were not severe. The bruising and swelling would subside. The burns would heal. His helmet had protected him from most of it. He was told to take things easy for forty-eight hours and discharged.

Commander Hay visited him in his room to brief him on events at the Acropolis. Matthew listened to her impassively, his eyes fixed on his feet. Mikey stood by the window, crying quietly. For Matthew, for Max, for herself, for the situation in which she found herself.

At the end, Hay said, 'Sadly, I have to confirm that after an exhaustive search of the area, there is no trace anywhere of Dr Maxwell. Since she has not reappeared here – the designated destination – we are forced to conclude that either she and her bracelet perished in the explosion, or that the bracelet malfunctioned somehow. I want to assure you that the Map Master and all her teams are searching the Time Map for any anomalies that might . . . enable us to locate her. She has asked me to tell you that should you wish to join their efforts, they will welcome your assistance.'

Matthew nodded but said nothing.

After a while, Hay said, 'Have you understood what I've said to you, Officer Farrell?'

He nodded.

'Major Ellis is not quite recovered from recent events but he will be available to answer your questions very soon.'

Matthew nodded.

'And St Mary's has been advised. I'm sure Chief Farrell will . . .'

He nodded.

'Your face looks very painful. Are you sure you are completely recovered?'

He nodded.

'I regret to say that as yet, we've found no trace of Amelia Meiklejohn either, but be assured the Paris hangar is secured and all officers are looking for clues as to where she and Henry Plimpton could have gone.'

He nodded.

She got up to leave. 'I'm so sorry, Matthew.'

He nodded and she gave it up. The doctor had warned her he might react in this way, advising her to give him some space. 'He's an intense lad. It all stays inside him. He just needs time to process everything.'

After Commander Hay had left, Matthew sat on his bed, staring at the wall. Mikey carefully sat herself down next to him.

'Oh, Matthew . . .'

His thoughts were sluggish and slow. Struggling to catch up. A large part of his life had gone forever. Here was yet another new world for him to adjust to. A new world without people he loved. He didn't love many people and now there were even fewer.

There would be conversations to have, decisions to be made. Things he should get to grips with. His mind skidded away.

Words – always a problem for him – buzzed around inside his head, refusing to coalesce into coherent phrases. Words he could have . . . *should* have spoken and hadn't, and now two of the most important people in his life would never hear them. Because it was too late. The words beat inside his brain. *Too late*. Too late to save Mikey. Worse – it was all his fault. If he'd never gone to St Mary's with the bracelets, then Mikey would still be alive. He remembered her bending over her workbench . . . scribbling an equation on the wall . . . frowning

481

over a blueprint . . . her hair catching the sun . . . always totally absorbed in everything she did. He'd never see that again.

And what of Max. His quietly loved mother. Dying alone on a Greek rock. How afraid would she have been at the end? Did her heart race? Did her brain scream? Were her last thoughts of her family? Of him? Would she have cried? Tears running down her face like rain?

What had happened to her? Had she ended her days lost somewhere in Time? Her body shattered. Watching her life-blood flow into the dirt. Without the comfort of dying among those who knew her. How much had it hurt? Would she have known anything about it?

He clenched his fists. Why had she done it? She shouldn't have gone. She wasn't supposed to be doing this sort of thing any longer. She'd agreed. How could she have gone off and left them like this? What was he to do now?

Beside him, Mikey tried to take his hand, whispering, 'It's not your fault. You shouldn't blame yourself,' and struggled with the futility of her words. Just as well he couldn't hear her.

'Life's a shit sandwich,' Matthew suddenly said aloud, start-ling them both. 'All that pain and crap at the beginning, then the thin layer of good things in the middle – just enough to trick you into thinking they could last forever – and then – wham – straight back into the crap again. With the knowledge that every time there's a little bit of good, the crap will come boomeranging back to get you. Every time.'

His voice was hoarse with disuse. The last time he'd spoken had been in the hangar in Paris as the darkness closed in around him. And even then, his last thought had been of Mikey. Where was she? Was she alive? Was she dead? Was she hurt some-where, lying in pain and fear and trusting him to come and rescue her? Dying by inches as he failed her?

He closed his eyes and a single, solitary tear trickled down his cheek.

Mikey's heart ached with the knowledge there was nothing she could do for him. Nothing at all. Matthew didn't even know she was there. He thought she was dead. And perhaps she was.

And then Matthew turned his head. 'Mikey . . .'

Her heart leaped. Oh my God. Finally. He could see her. She touched him gently. Something she didn't do very often. He didn't always like to be touched. 'Matthew, I'm here.'

'I wish you were here.'

Her heart plummeted with disappointment. She felt her eyes fill up. 'I am here, Matthew. I'm right here. Right now. I'm so sorry about Max and . . .'

'I've been living in some sort of fool's paradise, haven't I? Whatever made me think this would work? Me here – you there. We weren't even in the same Time, were we? And Mum's gone. I never told her, either, and I don't know what to do. What do I say to Dad? I don't know where I want to be. I wish you were here so I could ask you, but if you were here then I wouldn't have to.'

His voice broke. 'You coloured my world. You made it sharp and bright and happy and I was too stupid, too scared, too useless, to tell you how much you meant to me and now it's too late. You'll never know how much I wish I'd told you.'

Mikey wiped her nose on her sleeve. 'Matthew – please try to hear me. I wasn't dragged along with Henry Plimpton's pod. I wasn't torn to pieces in the Time-Stream. I'm not dying

483

in agony at the hands of Henry Plimpton or any of the things you're torturing yourself with. I'm here now. With you.'

He stood up abruptly to stare out of the window. 'Everyone always thinks there will be plenty of time and there never is.'

'It's not your fault, Matthew. I could have told you how I felt and I didn't. I wish I had. I wish you had. It would be something to take with me. To hold on to in this nothing world. Because I'm frightened and I don't know what's going to happen to me. Will I stay like this forever? Or will I just fade away to nothing, shouting in the darkness. Hay told you Max went quickly. I don't think I'll be that lucky. Do you mind if I sit and hold your hand while I still can?'

She rested her head on his shoulder and tears ran down her cheeks.

Matthew Farrell never cried. In his experience, crying only made things worse. Now a deep sob forced its way to the surface. 'We could have had a life together. I don't know where or when, but we would. We might have had a little house somewhere.'

That made her laugh. 'More likely we would have been on the run and in fear for our lives.'

'With children, perhaps.'

'Oh – yuk.'

'And a puppy.'

'More likely half a dozen arrest warrants and a wonky pod.' Mikey sighed. 'It would have been such fun.'

Matthew dragged his sleeve across his eyes.

She sighed again. 'What are we going to do, Matthew? Whatever are we going to do?'

484

39

Commander Hay was back at her desk dealing with the aftermath.

'Not one of my favourite words, Charlie.'

'Worse even than harbinger, ma'am?'

'At the moment, yes.'

'Well, I shall do my best, ma'am, obviously, but I think it only fair to warn you that my update is conspicuously lacking the words pink, fluffy, delightful, heart-warming . . .'

'Never mind that, does it include the word success?'

'Partially, ma'am.'

'So just succ?'

'I feel that may be somewhat understating our succ. We achieved most of our objectives.'

'Very well, Charlie, upgrade to succe.'

'As you command, ma'am. Time Police intervention saved the Acropolis. Mrs Farnborough has forwarded a message of congratulations from the PM and indicated that now might be a good time to ask for an increase in our pocket money.'

'Excellent. Draft something up for me, will you, Charlie.'

He pushed a folder across her desk. 'Already done, ma'am.'

'No one likes a smart arse, Captain.'

'So I am frequently told, ma'am.'

'What's the damage to the Acropolis?'

'Superficial. Light damage to the Temple of Erechtheion – nothing that can't be repaired – and a number of small craters. The area has been cleared of any unexploded devices. All contemporaries have been revived and released. They're bleary but safe. A very large quantity of empty wineskins has been left nearby.'

'Subtle,' remarked Hay.

'Thank you, ma'am. I was quite proud of that little touch.'

'Did they establish whether the cause of the primary explosion was the pod, the IED, or Dr Maxwell's bracelet?'

'The IED, ma'am. Which was the best we could hope for. Damage from the pod or bracelet would probably have been considerably more extensive.'

She sighed. 'Yes. I have spoken to young Farrell. He's not good.'

'No.'

'Max died saving the Acropolis. I don't think she'd find that too shabby a way to go.'

'No, ma'am. Although I think Officer Farrell would have preferred she didn't go at all.'

'No. We'll honour her, of course. We can do no less. When's the service?'

'The day after tomorrow. Dr Bairstow has indicated there will be a considerable contingent from St Mary's.'

'I want everyone on their best behaviour, Charlie. Make that clear.'

'Again, ma'am. Already done.'

Hay sighed. 'I don't really need to come in at all, do I? I

486

could just lounge around in my room all day and let you get on with it. Update me on the Paris end of things.'

'The portable nuclear reactor was successfully removed, ma'am, and is now enjoying the attentions of the Nuclear Regulatory Board. As I mentioned, the former premises and everything in them are now just a heap of smoking rubble. All officers affected have recovered.' He sat back to look at her. 'We were lucky, ma'am. The potential for damaging Time was enormous. A very large area of Paris was affected, albeit mildly, but it could have been an utter catastrophe.'

'Well, not to toot our own trumpet, Charlie, but thanks to us, it wasn't.'

'No, ma'am.'

'Neither did we manage to preside over the destruction of one of the most romantic and historical cities in Europe.'

'Astonishingly, ma'am – no. Although the Time Field did have a definite impact on the city.'

'All information is to be suppressed. I don't want a word of this getting out anywhere. Put Records on it . . .' She stopped. 'You already have, haven't you?'

'I'm rather embarrassed to admit it, ma'am, but yes. And I instructed them the job was top priority and to draft in any resources they might need.'

'Spare no expense, Charlie.'

'Absolutely, ma'am. I threw the entire budget at it.'

'The *entire* admin budget?'

'The entire *everyone's* budget, ma'am. We now cannot afford to buy so much as a new pencil until the year after next.'

'Oh,' said Commander Hay, faintly. 'Just as well we're flavour of the month with the government.'

'Indeed, ma'am. However, you will be pleased to hear our efforts have been largely successful. There is almost no record of events in Paris on the 29th December 1902 anywhere.'

'Almost?'

'I believe there was once a TV programme put out by a streaming service . . .'

'A what?'

'A streaming service, ma'am. They were very popular at one time and this one had quite a large following. They reported it – somewhat dramatically – as the Paris Time-Stop of 1902, when all the clocks stopped and the inhabitants woke up feeling nauseous and disoriented. Which was perfectly true – they did, poor buggers. And we couldn't do anything about the clocks, of course. I thought we'd be best served by just letting it go, ma'am. We don't want to draw attention, do we?'

He paused. 'Our other little spot of bother, however . . . removing the illegal pod from the Acropolis to explode elsewhere . . .' He stopped, grimacing.

Hay groaned. 'Just tell me, Charlie.'

'Well, the good news is that we successfully managed to jump it away from the Acropolis, and that it did explode in Siberia. As intended.' He drew a breath. 'However . . .' He paused.

She closed her eyes. 'Go on.'

'While the location was successful, the date . . . was not.'

Her eyes flew open and she sat forwards suddenly. 'Oh God – why do I know what you're going to say?'

'Well, thank you, ma'am. I must admit I wasn't looking forward to breaking this one to you.'

'Break it anyway, Charlie. Why should I suffer alone?'

488

He sighed. 'The pod exploded in Siberia, ma'am, but not in the Ice Age.'

'When?'

'Well, ma'am . . .'

'Yes?'

'Well, ma'am . . .'

'Just say it, Charlie.'

'30th June 1908, ma'am.'

She stared at him. 'Oh my God, Charlie – are you telling me *we* were the Tunguska event?'

'We were indeed, ma'am.'

'It's nothing to be proud of.'

'No, ma'am.'

'Hundreds and hundreds of square miles of forest devastated?'

'Some trees fell down, yes.'

'Massive devastation . . . dead reindeer . . . That was all us?'

'I'm afraid so. On the bright side . . .'

'Will you *stop* finding bright sides.'

'My apologies, ma'am, but you might take comfort in the knowledge that even St Mary's has never achieved devastation on that sort of scale.'

'I thought the official report had decided it was an air burst. An asteroid breaking up in mid-air.'

'I'm quite proud of that little touch as well, ma'am.'

She regarded him. 'Your skill set is beginning to cause me some concern.'

He beamed. 'Thank you, ma'am.'

Hay covered her still shiny face with her hands and groaned. 'Shitting bloody bollocking fire-trucking hell.'

'Indeed, ma'am. But it could have been worse.'

She took her hands away. 'How?'

'Fifty years later and we could have triggered the Cold War.'

'One of the few events for which the Time Police are not responsible.'

He grinned. 'Not yet, ma'am.'

At the same time, a very wobbly Major Ellis was lunching with Officer North. They had chosen a quiet table in the corner. The room was crowded. They'd been lucky to get it. Now they had to hang on to it.

A team from IT, spotting empty seats at their table, headed towards them, caught sight of Officer North's expression, simultaneously remembered her propensity for shooting people just to make a point, and veered off elsewhere.

With his back to the room, Major Ellis refused to look round. 'I felt a disturbance in the Force. What did you just do?'

'Hardly anything.'

He sighed. 'If I don't turn around, then I won't see, and if I don't see, then I don't have to take any action, and I'd prefer to finish my rather excellent steak and kidney pudding.'

She smiled. 'My advice to you is suddenly to become enthralled by my scintillating conversation.'

'Your conversation is always scintillating and enthralling, Celia.'

'You don't know what I'm going to say.'

'No matter. What's important is who's saying it.'

'I do actually have something important to say but I'm just wondering . . .'

'Go ahead. Say it.'

'Well – since you insist – since you're convalescing . . .' She broke off to frown at a group of rowdy officers heading their way. They spontaneously changed their minds. '. . . and since you certainly won't get any peace here, my mother was wondering whether you would care to spend a few days with us. And because our last visit was cut short.'

Ellis put down his knife and fork. An action that would have had him expelled from St Mary's on the spot.

'Your mother?'

'Yes.'

'Lady Blackbourne?'

'Yes.'

'To spend a few days?'

'Yes.'

'With you?'

'I will certainly be there – yes.'

'With your family?'

'Not all of them, I hope. Aunt Harriet and Cousin Felix have been certified under the Act and Uncles John and St John are currently enjoying separate spells at His Majesty's pleasure. Cousin Helen is, at this moment, halfway across the world because she's been crossed in love and is taking it out on the Andes for some reason. Cousin Annabel is about to figure prominently in the tabloids along with a well-known member of the government, a number of esoteric kitchen implements and an unbelievable amount of body glitter. And Papa's dead, of course – so not all of them.'

Across the room, an argument was developing nicely. Surrounding tables were taking sides. Boisterousness was in the air.

Ellis looked at North. 'Can you really take me away from all this?'

'I can certainly try.'

He smiled and picked up his cutlery again. 'Then – all right – yes.'

# Epilogue

The atrium was packed. Serving officers lined up in militarily precise rows along the left-hand side while a large party from St Mary's defiantly formed a more informal clump on the right.

The two contingents eyed each other with some hostility, but their instructions to behave themselves had been precise, specific and not in any way disobeyable.

Neatly solving the problem of with which organisation he was to stand, Matthew Farrell stood midpoint between the two groups. Mikey, hoarse and exhausted from alternately shouting and crying, stood at Matthew's shoulder, trying to take comfort from his nearness.

Even Luke was surprised at the turnout. It had crossed his mind that many officers had probably turned up for the sole purpose of confirming Dr Maxwell was actually dead, but after one killer look from Jane, who knew exactly what he was thinking, he refrained from comment.

As a mark of respect, Time Police flags flew at half mast. A black-draped podium stood ready. The silence was absolute.

On the stroke of eleven, Commander Hay took her place under the giant clock, symbol of Time Police power and authority. Taking a pair of spectacles from her pocket, she arranged her notes in front of her and began.

'We are gathered here today to pay tribute to someone who has, on many occasions, been involved in Time Police affairs. Indeed, rather more often than the Time Police themselves have been comfortable with.'

There was a small rumble of laughter.

'Many of us, over the years, have, for better or worse, encountered Dr Maxwell in the course of our duties. I don't for one moment think she would object to being described as a little bit of a misguided missile. In fact, I suspect she would be rather pleased. However, no one could fault her passion or her dedication to her job – even if it was, from the Time Police point of view, sometimes a little misplaced. I remember on one occasion . . .'

Alas, Commander Hay's recollection was destined to go unrecounted.

Above their heads, the air cracked like a whip. There was a brief blast of blinding white light and heat, followed by the smell of rain. A considerable amount of mud, loose rubble and splintered wood materialised at head height, hung for one improbably gravity-free moment – rather like a cartoon, Jane thought later – and then, having gained everyone's attention, dropped heavily on to the immaculately tiled floor.

Closely followed by a heap of wet-weather gear that managed, at one and the same time, to be both smouldering and soaking wet. The clothing splatted to the tiles and lay motionless. For a long second nothing happened. Everyone stood stunned, staring at the bloody bundle of clothing. Which groaned and stirred slightly, struggling to pull its hair out of its eyes.

'*It's alive*,' murmured Luke and received a swift, accurate, but above all, painful kick to one ankle from Jane.

In one beautifully synchronised movement, every Time

494

Police officer present drew their weapon to focus on the muddy, bloody heap on the floor. The sound of charging blasters drowned even the massive tick of the Time clock.

Without thinking, Mikey ran forwards, waving her arms. 'No. No. Stop. Don't shoot.'

Matthew Farrell turned his head to look at her.

Major Callen strode forwards, gun raised.

Moaning, the bedraggled figure thrashed wildly, fighting to extricate itself from the tangle of clothing and debris. Using language that would be considered inappropriate even in a dockside brothel, it struggled to its feet, swaying dramatically.

Callen lowered his weapon and sighed. 'Dr Maxwell – and believe me, I say this with genuine regret – still not dead.'

The sodden figure regarded him silently for one moment and then convulsed horribly. The universe held its breath. With a dreadful sound that caused any number of stomachs to heave in sympathy, a massive stream of vomit arced improbably across the atrium and found its target.

Major Callen leaped back, but too late. Far, far too late. It would be fair to say he dripped.

Commander Hay became extraordinarily busy putting her notes away and taking off her spectacles.

It is possible that every other officer in the building involuntarily glanced upwards towards the security cameras and made plans for a new screensaver.

It is equally possible that every IT officer reviewed their understanding of the laws of copyright and anticipated untold wealth coming their way.

Max held up her arm and squinted at her bracelet. A green light blinked for one moment and then went out. The bracelet clicked open and clattered to the floor. She kicked it away from her. It skidded towards the unseen Mikey, coming to rest at her feet.

At exactly that moment, Mikey's own bracelet flashed green. Without stopping to think, she scrabbled frantically at her wrist. A moment later, that one was also spinning across the floor as Amelia Meiklejohn stood, exposed and alone in the very heart of TPHQ.

In another beautifully synchronised movement, all weapons were turned in Mikey's direction, wavered for one moment and then swung back to their original target, as many officers experienced what would later be designated as target overload. As one officer said afterwards, it was as if all his dreams had come true at once.

Ignoring everyone, Mikey bent over the two bracelets. 'Oh, that's interesting.' Hands on hips, she stirred one with her foot and addressed the atrium at large. 'The field from the pod set it off and the field from the other bracelet knocked it off again. I never thought of that. I wonder . . .'

A security contingent approached, but very, very cautiously.

A medical contingent approached, even more cautiously.

Max wiped her mouth and rested her hands on her knees.

'Bloody bollocking hell, that hurt. Where the hell am I?'

Receiving no response, she straightened up, taking in the flags at half mast, her family, her boss, the otherwise occupied Mikey, the phenomenal range and number of weapons pointed at them both, the nearby vomit-covered officer, the black armbands . . .

'Just a random guess, but this isn't fish and chips night, is it?'

THE END

PROTECTING THE PAST
TO ENSURE YOUR FUTURE
TP

# Acknowledgements

Thanks to Steve and Sharon who allowed me to explore the lethal potential of their kitchen when writing Jane's Battle of the Kitchen. Thanks especially to Steve, who actually went to stand in the garden to check whether he could hear me screaming in the kitchen. I told him it was to check a plot point but actually it was just to get him into trouble with his neighbours.

Thanks as always to Phil – my go-to guy for advice on how to break the law convincingly.

Thanks to Hazel whose ideas for destroying the power source in Paris consisted of:

1. Floating a fire ship up the Seine for the sole purpose of being able to do half a dozen In-Seine jokes. No one has any idea how I suffer.

2. That the power source itself should be steam-driven, which enabled me to spend a happy half hour envisaging some sort of steam-punk scenario. All carefully stored away for the future.

Massive thanks, as always, to all the people at Headline who work so hard on my behalf.

Frankie Edwards – editor in chief.

Bea Grabowska – editorial assistant, right-hand woman for the production side of the book and many other things besides.

Jo Liddiard and Shadé Owomoyela – Marketing.

Antonia Whitton – Publicity.

Hannah Cause – Audio.

Sharona Selby – Copy Editor.

And everyone in the Sales, Rights, Art and Production teams.